THE MAN ON TOP
OF THE WORLD

Visit us at www.boldstrokesbooks.com

THE MAN ON TOP OF THE WORLD

by

Vanessa Clark

A Division of Bold Strokes Books

2016

THE MAN ON TOP OF THE WORLD

ISBN 13: 978-1-62639-699-9

This Trade Paperback Original Is Published By
Bold Strokes Books, Inc.
P.O. Box 249
Valley Falls, NY 12185

First Edition: August 2016e

CREDITS
EDITOR: JERRY L. WHEELER
PRODUCTION DESIGN: STACIA SEAMAN
COVER DESIGN BY MELODY POND

Acknowledgments

I never thought I'd write a novel. I always thought that I'd only write short stories, which was how *The Man on Top of the World* began. Somehow, a beautiful accident happened. I had a novel. I'm humbled that this is my first one. Two years was spent on me disciplining this project entirely by myself. No beta readers. Nobody other than my own eyes oh so carefully and critically looking over the manuscript from its rough stages to its diamond promises. Constantly rereading, rewriting, re-plotting, and re-self-editing this book over and over again until everything was just right. Just me getting to know Jonathan, Izzy, and Roxanne, fleshing them out deeper and deeper with each rewrite that I've lost count on, until I felt that it was time to send them and their story to a home. It was a lot of work doing this by my lonesome, but with all the fun, the growth, and the development that went with it, I'd do it all over again in a heartbeat.

I may have been a person alone, but it truly takes a team of hardworking, passionate, and devoted people to journey a book home from acceptance to publication. Those people are the lovely folks at Bold Strokes Books. A major thank you to my editor extraordinaire, Jerry L. Wheeler, for taking the chance on this project and for being an uplifting encourager from the very start of our editorial relationship. Thank you for letting me rework this manuscript again, one last time, by myself before it was your turn to polish it in such a way that I couldn't have done on my own, not without your expertise. Your kindness, warmth, and professionalism made the entire editing process so positive, fun, and amazing! Working with you was an honor. And much love and respect to BSB greats Len Barot/Radclyffe, Sandy Lowe, Connie Ward, Cindy Cresap, and Ruth Sternglantz.

To them and to everyone on the BSB team—thank you all for everything, for believing in this.

Humongous gratitude to all of my followers on Twitter, my blog, and my Facebook author page for continuously being the supportive, intelligent, funny, and open-minded community that you are. I'll never stop appreciating you. To those who have been eagerly waiting and are so excited for this book—you know who you are. At last, your patience is rewarded!

Anyone who's a believer, a dreamer, a lover, a fighter, a survivor, a hero, essentially, a rock 'n' roller—this book's for you.

CHAPTER ONE

Nothing in the world was more exciting than being backstage with Izzy Rich before his show began. The unbearable anticipation. The unimaginable tension. The mystifying transformation. Unpredictable. No way of knowing when it would come and when it would end, not that it mattered to him either way. He lived for the moment and would die for it all: the rock and roll, the glitter, the makeup, the flamboyant clothes, the drugs, the booze, the debauchery, and the androgyny. Who would dare join him on the ride? I did as many others before and after me.

He was overloaded with so much anticipation, adrenaline, and tension that it welled up in his crotch. Everyone backstage could not stop looking at it. Izzy's beloved groupies could not stop touching it. Every single one of them titillated him, hoping they would be the lucky one chosen to set the angry beast in Izzy's loins free before he would embark on the concert stage and perform in front of thousands.

Thirty minutes. Only thirty minutes to apply his lipstick, mascara, eye shadow, eye liner, and face powder. He was the master multitasker, so he managed to do that and before the show. He earned a reputation for being a last-minute man, but he could deliver a mind-blowing concert as rehearsed without a single misstep.

Even when it came to a quickie, sex with Izzy was absolute perfection, a performance for the ages. He made it seem so easy. Because, for him, it was. Izzy's dressing room was usually wide open like a book. What went on inside was unabashedly displayed for peeping toms like me who couldn't help but watch and stare. How could I not? Izzy's desperate, star-craved groupies were gorgeous with their sequined high heel shoes, body glitter, sparkly eye shadow, gloss-heavy lips, gaudy earrings, and colorful skin-tight pants, booty-shorts, and skimpy tops. They were too physically phenomenal for words.

He'd have as many as ten in his dressing room, where they'd all sniff a line of cocaine and drink a couple shots of whiskey with him. He'd make all of them laugh with his crass jokes. He could drive them all crazy with the way he'd caress their hairspray-drenched tresses, fondle their cheeks with the tip of his polished fingernails, and whisper naughty nothings into their ears with his hand on a breast or two. Or up a skirt, cupping a crotch. Or two. Not a single one of these glitter groupies was left untouched. He shared his focus and attention with all of them at once, and how he did it was as mysterious as space and time. When the "thirty minutes" call came from management, he had no choice but to make all the groupies leave his dressing room.

Except for one.

The one that stayed behind would be the luckiest bitch on Earth. I never thought it would be me, his own drummer. It started out as a joke, a tease. Neither of us ever thought it would become something more.

"Fresh out of pussy tonight?" I asked Izzy as I stepped into his dressing room. We were performing at London's Hammersmith Odeon that night. "It's a ghost town in here."

He was sitting down, organizing his makeup appliances on the countertop. To my astonishment, not a single woman paraded around the room, sniffing out his boner like a ravenous dog. "I wanted to see if I can perform without needing some assistance beforehand." He winked.

"Oh, this I'd like to see!" I laughed, sitting beside him. "Did you lose a bet or something?"

"Yes, you guessed it! Fucking bets."

"With who?"

"William James."

He was Izzy's manager from Trident Studios. "Dare I ask what the bet was?"

"A blasted drinking game, that's all. If I lost, I would go one show without having a groupie give me a 'helping hand' or 'jump-start,' as he calls it. So, here I am!"

"The loser."

"Yeah, yeah, don't rub it in."

"How are you taking it so far?" I snickered, kicking back in the chair.

"Not very well. I'm just dying for a blowjob!"

"Poor baby." I snorted. "Want me to suck it for you?"

"If you suck cock as well as you play the drums, I might consider it."

Though I perceived the hint of sarcasm in his voice, his enticing, bright blue eyes told me he was serious. He stared at me with an intoxicating mixture of gentle feminine innocence and strong manly lust.

"You ever sucked cock before?" he asked as he eyed the mirror, brushing his fox-red bob and giving it a shimmering sparkle with hairspray.

"No." I bit my lower lip.

"Bollocks!"

"How the bloody hell would you know if I was bluffing or not? I've only ever told you stories about my past relationships and sexcapades with women."

"And one trans-woman."

Odette, my ex-girlfriend. "And?"

"You liked her cock, didn't you, Johnny?" he stated as fact.

I nodded slowly. "Yes, I did."

"You wanted to touch it, hold it, kiss it, and suck on it, but she wouldn't let you. You pretended you didn't care, but I could tell how badly you wanted her dick."

Everything he said was the absolute truth. But I'd be damned before I gave him the satisfaction of knowing it. "So what makes you think that I've sucked cock since she and I broke up?" I continued to interrogate him. "Have you ever seen me go down on a bloke?"

He shook his head, placing his brush on the countertop. "But I've seen the way you flirt with men and work your charm on them, the same as you do with women. If you can charm the knickers off women, then, you've charmed the boxers off men, too. Have you not, Mr. Maxwell?"

"I sure have, Mr. Rich," I proudly admitted.

"You like sucking cock?" he asked bluntly.

I swallowed my shyness, feeling more at ease. "It's one of my favorite hobbies."

"I've never had a bloke suck on my cock before a show."

He gave me that look again. I snapped my head toward the mirror, looking myself over. Disheveled dirty blond hair partially obscured my light blue eyes, my lids painted with shimmery green eye shadow.

The eyeshadow almost matched my dazzling green coat, and the pink sequined tie atop my frilly white blouse was the perfect complement to my salmon-painted lips.

But as hard as I tried, I couldn't keep my eyes off his crotch. He wore shiny, bright red vinyl pants that hugged his erection. They outlined the shaft and mushroom-like head so clearly I couldn't ignore it. It was thicker than I had ever seen. He noticed my staring. I swore I saw his cock twitch for me. I couldn't tear my eyes of him, and I didn't know what to say. We were mute. All we could hear was the screaming, the chants, the cheering of his fans. It was all so far off, and yet so close within our reach. Their anticipation was like our own. Desperate. Needy for release. Now.

"You want to be the first man to go down on Izzy Rich before we go on?"

He had read my mind.

"I'd be honored, but—" I turned my head, looking at the door. "What if we get caught?"

"Lock the door."

Without saying a word in response, I walked over and locked it.

My heart was beating fast and loud. I thought I could almost hear his as well, louder than the cheers of his glitter-faced fangirls and red-lipped, sparkly-haired fanboys. What a strange, unnerving sensation it was. Maybe it was the unknown…the forbidden. He was my boss. We were bandmates. More than that, we were best friends. No, closer than that. We were like brothers. Yet I had been drawn to Izzy Rich sexually from the moment I auditioned to be part of his band, The Diamonds. That was three years ago in 1970, at the dawn of *Rich Girl*, his famous, critically acclaimed glitter rock opera.

The first time I laid my eyes on him in person, I thought he was a woman. He had me and every drummer at the auditions gawking. His slender, shapely body sat on the most voluptuous, womanly ass, thighs, and hips I'd ever seen. His fox-red bob framed his high cheekbones in a feminine curl, and he walked in his sapphire blue five-inch fuck-me pumps like a goddess. He easily pulled off the androgynous alter-ego he had been perfecting since the day he was born. His alter-ego was himself. Izzy Rich was the epitome of androgyny at its most natural and striking best, more divine than most men and women will ever come across in their lifetime.

"Ready?" he murmured, his voice deep, daring.

Izzy stood tall, cupping his cock in the palm of his hand, tempting me. As I walked toward him, he yanked down the zipper of his pants. My mouth instantly watered the moment I saw it. His dick was long and impressively thick. The veins were full and prominent, and the head wonderfully plump and glistening with pre-come. Izzy had one of the finest cocks I had come across. Sure, it wasn't the first time I'd seen it, but I'd never looked at it like this.

Izzy gripped the base of his dick and gave it a playful wave. "You sure you can handle all this?"

I swallowed hard. "I can handle it just fine."

"That's the spirit." He sat down in his chair again and kicked his head back with a sigh.

I went to my knees in front of him and rested my hands on top of his glittering, five-inch platforms. He trembled as I pressed my lips to his smooth, hairless scrotum. I slapped and teased it with my long, wet tongue. I glanced up, looked at him over the arch of his cock, and drank in the sight of him. He clenched his eyes shut and smiled. As I sucked on his huge sac, he let out a high-pitched whine.

"Hot damn," he cooed as he ran his fingers through my hair. I sucked on his balls as he went to work sculpting his face into a god/goddess of glam. I saw Izzy pick up the cherry-red lipstick and slide it over his thick, pouty lips before I closed my eyes to concentrate on how good Izzy's dick felt in my mouth.

I circled the head of his cock playfully with my tongue. Izzy acted composed and focused on applying his makeup, but I could feel his legs tremble under my hands. He bucked and forced half of his cock into my mouth, then he began thrusting into my mouth as if some barrier had broken between us. The more I sucked at him, the thicker I thought his cock became. I didn't know if it was wishful thinking or my excitement, but I didn't care. I wanted to give the best head he'd ever had.

I could still hear the cheers and cries of Izzy's fans, but they were slowly being drowned out by the wet sound of my mouth on his cock. Izzy gasped, and the slap of his balls against my chin seemed deafening. I opened my eyes again in time to see him gliding the thin, wet eyeliner brush along his glittering golden eyelids. He stood up slowly, his legs trembling, but I didn't let go of his cock. I clutched at his bare ass cheeks, my fingernails biting into the soft flesh. I rode his cock with my mouth, faster and harder, as I clung to him. His moaning grew louder, and I pulled back enough to catch my breath and gaze up at the genderfuck masterpiece that was his face. His makeup was perfect, unbelievably beautiful.

Izzy grinned down at me, and he licked his pearly white teeth. He caressed my hair once more as he pressed his cock against the side of my mouth and grazed his smooth, soft fingers along my cheek to fondle his cockhead through my skin. He pressed his palm against my cheek as I continued to suck and pump him. His eyes rolled back, and his grip on my face tightened as he took control of the blowjob. His thrusts were determined, controlled, and I knew why. He was so close to coming, I could feel it. He was right on the edge. I felt that tell-tale swelling of him in my mouth, until—

Someone knocked at the door.

We froze. Benson, our guitarist, shouted through the door. "We are on in ten minutes!"

"Okay!" Izzy replied, only a slight shake in his voice. He waited to see if Benson was going to try and open the door, but he didn't. We heard the muffled sound of his feet as he walked away.

The moment we were alone again, Izzy grabbed a handful of my hair, yanked hard, and forced his entire cock down my throat in a merciless move that had me flailing to remain upright. He pushed my face firmly against him. I couldn't breathe with my nose crushed against his body. He started to fuck my mouth, thrusting furiously. My head spun and my eyes watered as I fought against my gag reflex. I could feel mascara run down my rouge-colored cheeks as he roared. His come flooded my mouth. He pulled his cock back before pushing it down my throat again, making quick thrusts to prolong his pleasure. I licked the underside of his cock as I swallowed around him. After I drank down those first thick and hot spurts, I sucked hard, gulping loudly.

"Fuck!" he shouted. "John, where the bloody hell did you learn to suck cock like that?"

My answer was simply to not stop sucking.

"You lied to me. You don't like sucking cock. You fucking *love* it."

Well, he couldn't be more right about that. I loved cock, and if he could see it, then all the better.

I drew harder on his cock until my jaw ached, trying to show him how much I loved sucking *his* cock. He cried out, twisting his hands in my hair, and I felt his dick pulse in my mouth. I looked back up at him, and he gave me a breathless, toothy grin. I was flying high, and when his cock was drained, I gave one last, long suck before letting him slip from my mouth. I placed a lingering kiss on the wet, silky-smooth tip of him.

Izzy panted, the smile on his face smugly satisfied. "Now that's what I call a blowjob."

I couldn't help the rush of pride I felt as I got to my feet, wiping at my lips, chin, and cheeks. "Did I live up to your standards, Mr. Rich?" I asked, heart racing to hear his answer.

"You gave better head than any woman who's gone down on me before a show."

"You can't be serious."

He tucked his impressive cock back into his pants, and then zipped himself up again. "You were phenomenal, baby," he cooed with a wink.

That was the first time he ever called me baby, and it wouldn't be the last. I looked into the mirror to see how badly the blowjob had ruined my makeup. Unlike Izzy, I was a fucking mess.

Time was ticking. I grabbed a tissue and wiped away the smears of lipstick, and then I quickly reapplied it. Rivulets of gray and glitter ran down my cheeks, dried remnants of the mascara my tears had run. I caught sight of Izzy in the mirror. He hung golden chandelier earrings on his ears and he slipped into a short-sleeved golden shirt with a long V-neck that revealed his hairless chest. He topped that off with a flowing red vinyl jacket that fell down to his buttocks and matched his pants. He looked at me in the mirror as he wrapped a black and red feather boa around his neck. His transformation from eccentric pretty boy to glam rock royalty was almost complete.

He posed, showing off every inch of his body to its best. "How do I look?"

"Like Izzy Rich. How do I look?"

"Like a whore."

My cheeks burned at the plain statement. "Classy," I muttered. I focused on my reflection again and snatched up a tissue. "Thanks to you, I have to do my makeup all over again, dammit."

"No, you don't." He leaped toward me and joined me at the mirror. "I like this."

"You do?"

He grinned. "It's kinky. It'll remind me of how I fucked your throat so good, it made you cry." He smacked my ass, and I thought he was implying that my throat wouldn't be the only place he'd fuck me to tears.

The final prop to his transformation was his electric guitar. Once the strap was over his shoulder and the guitar in his arms, he plucked the strings. In that moment, he was a man on top of the world. And I knew from the instant he'd step out onto that stage, he was ready to fall from it.

CHAPTER TWO

The heels of my platforms clopped loudly in the wings. Panting, I caught my breath, and smiled when I saw Benson, Phil, Tim, and Larry standing single file near the stage sideline, as glammed up as I was. I stood behind Larry.

"Where the bloody hell were you, man?" Phil asked me, smoothing down his shiny piano key tie.

"Last-minute piss. Sorry."

Larry snorted, cradling his purple bass guitar. "Took you long enough."

Benson raised his brow at me. "You okay? What's with the mascara tears?"

"Too much mascara. Made me all teary. Didn't have time to fix it."

Tim's eyes lit up as he embraced his shiny bronze saxophone. "*Finally*, the man is here."

I looked over my shoulder and saw Izzy sashaying toward us. His fans couldn't have seen him, yet they roared as if they knew he was back there.

"It's show time!" Izzy said joyfully, a proud mama-papa bliss in those baby blues.

He pointed two fingers at his eyes, then he shaped his fingers, four of them, into a heart. After he spun on his heels, as graceful as a ballerina he stopped and pointed one finger at us. Quickly and in unison, I and the gang reenacted the same *I love you* signal back at him.

"You're on, Diamonds!" someone from management shouted.

I shook the last-minute tension out of my hands, taking one last breath. Benson stepped to the stage first. The crowd's roar boomed, spiking higher when Phil, Tim, and Larry went. Then it was my turn. The gold, purple, and pink stage lights weighed down on me. The sauna-warm smoke in the air surrounded me. As I drew toward my drum set, *The Diamonds* in rhinestone-studded words on the center base drums, flickered before me. My glossy bronze cymbals, wind chimes, toms, snares, and many microphones all waited for me. I set my left foot on the bass pedal and looked out to the sea of faces. In that moment, the stage was as much ours as it was Izzy's. I picked up my drumsticks and raised my arms high, tapping them. The light glared down on us. The fans screamed louder, feeding off us like we were feeding off them. We were eaten alive by love. Their love. But their love wasn't for us. The Diamonds were nothing. Izzy was their love, the man they paid to see, the rock star they were waiting for.

And their wait, at last, was over.

The lights dimmed. The adrenaline rush made me so hot that hell seemed like a sauna, yet it soothed me and made me shiver from head to toe. With my foot tapping into the bass pedal, the beater knocking on the base, I banged lightly on the toms and snares, nodding my head to the upbeat rhythm of Benson and Larry's guitars, Phil's piano, and Tim's saxophone.

As we played, a single fuchsia stage light centered on a microphone. Izzy, standing in the wings, cooed into the mic, "Love." The howling turned into maddened screaming. My ears popped, and I whipped my head back, pounding the bass pedal with my foot, my cymbals rippling song.

Still obscured from view, Izzy sang with moxie in his voice. "There's always time to make it, can't fake it, baby. *My* love. There's never a wrong or a right when you can just *take it*."

The fuchsia lighting crept to the wings and froze on that spot, teasing the audience, keeping them waiting. And then Izzy sashayed out from the dark. The floor trembled beneath my feet as Izzy yanked the microphone off from the stand and sang menacingly, "*Take me!*" The lights shone on him, strobing as I banged my toms, snares, and cymbals like a madman. As I played, plumes of rainbow smoke enveloped Izzy. The rock-star aura wasn't that or the lights.

It was *him.*

The moment he strummed that first wicked chord, leaped into the air, and opened his vermillion lips, the goose bumps broke out on my arms. The energy he possessed burst forth like a powder keg and affected everyone around him: the audience, the band, the backstage crew. He moved his hips, slid his hand down his body, and sang as if he were fucking the very beat and groove of his own music. Or, better yet, fucking a woman and his ego at the same time. When Izzy lay on his back and belted into a mic, he was pretty much jacking off. Only Izzy could pull that off without looking like a sleaze. It was crazy, hyper, and such a goddamn turn-on. I wonder that half the audience didn't come when Izzy hit a high note. As Izzy's voice rose above the screams of the women jostling to be closer to the stage, my heart raced.

That voice. His voice. I knew what the critics said. I knew what the fans thought. But for me, it was everything and more. High and low. Male and female. It slithered through me, heated me from the inside out, and left me panting. How could one man be gifted with such a bluesy, soulful voice? The heartache and triumph in those notes made my mouth dry. I now knew he uttered some of those intimate sounds in the throes of passion. I thought about that blowjob as Izzy writhed and crooned at the edge of the stage. In the midst of the music was the answer to why the ladies—and the men—would trample their way to get a foot closer to the stage. It was sex. Pure, unadulterated sex. It screamed into their minds and shook their bodies to the core. Every song was a chance for them to be fucked by that voice.

With four albums to pull material from, Izzy strung them along, tiptoeing them through his world, a place without labels, without shame, and no apologies, only dripping with need. And, God, did it make them need...make *me* need. The heat from my body was trapped in my clothes and even in my platforms, drowning me. My arms were tired, beat down from the music, but the concert was only beginning.

As we played, the fans reached out to Izzy, desperate for a glance or a touch, and Izzy never disappointed them. They'd stretch to brush his platforms, or he'd deign to bend over and allow their fingers to tease his wrist or palm. It was all a show for Izzy, a power trip full of glitter, throbbing beats, and swooning fans, and I wanted a piece of him. Not the fame, but him, a glitterotica fantasy, *mine*. I caught my breath, my focus hard on the rhythm, harder on him. Why him? Damn him. Why did he make me feel like this for doing nothing more than being himself? With every chameleon-like transformation of his— eight costume *and* makeup changes—I wanted to scream, for I was Izzy Rich's number one fan. Who was kidding?

As Izzy was singing, "Don't use me to define your laws," he stopped, and then drew his microphone toward the fans. They sang, "Because even diamonds have flaws!" back at him. Izzy stood, smiling, nodding to them singing the rest of the chorus. *All* his fans were number one, and yet I foolishly felt I was the only one. But then again, what fan didn't believe the same? The men screamed, but it was the women, the glitter rock queens, dominating the glitter rock kings. I took a deep breath and mouthed, "Whoa!" My drumsticks on my lap, I breathed in the heat, licked the beads of sweat from the corner of my mouth, tasting lipstick. Izzy had exited the stage, but his fans screamed as if he were still there.

When he returned, they went wild. Deep inside, so did I.

Izzy wore a shimmering gold, pink, blue, and teal colored cat suit that hugged his body. His pumps matched the color-blend in glitter. Izzy's hips swayed seductively as he caressed the mic stand from top to bottom. Izzy turned his back to the audience, stretching his arms behind his back as he grooved his body against the microphone stand, shaking his ass. He turned around, shimmying his chest, kicking his leg up, flashing his thigh. He jumped and landed on his knees, his legs spread, his groin bulging. His shoulders swung back to the floor, and his back arched as he played a catchy, rolling guitar riff.

It was the sex-charged melody to "Dirty Dancer." Izzy let out a manic, orgasmic howl, shaking his head, his guitar solo dominating him, dominating me until he stopped cold. All I could do was ogle him as the lights dimmed until only one light was shining on him. He curled his fingers around the mic stand and bobbed his hand on it in slow jerks.

"Nobody likes to dance alone," he crooned with a most menacing smile of lust. "Oh, no," he cooed, his head shaking with a tinge of innocence. "Not even a *dirty dancer* like me."

The band and I softly played the harmony of the song.

Izzy crept across the stage to his left, belly dancing. He crept to the right side, leaning back as he strutted, swaying his ass slowly, scooting deeper in his groove. Center stage, Izzy stood sideways and bent over. The audience roared as he caressed his body from legs to shoulders. The band and I stopped.

"Ladies at the Hammersmith Odeon tonight…" he purred into the microphone. They screamed deliriously. "Who wants to rule the world with me on this stage? Make it ours."

Thousands of hands reached out to him as he sashayed to his right, walking the length of the stage, his silhouette a most beautiful shadow. He walked the length of the left side and stopped at the center stage. He struck a pose, bent over, and swayed his hips like the hot tramp that he was. The audience threw knickers on the stage. Izzy had an armful of them. He sniffed them. He tossed them in the air. As they were falling, he was shoulder-rolling and hip-shaking, strumming on his guitar madly. His bodyguards stepped out from the sidelines.

He stopped. The audience screamed louder as Izzy pointed at one woman. I wondered who he'd bring up on the stage this time. She was a gorgeous, short-statured, wide-eyed Latina bombshell with long-flowing coily dark hair, glowing light brown skin, red lips, and sparkling eye shadow. The bodyguards took her close to Izzy and stepped aside.

A gap divided her and Izzy. He curled his finger to her in a come-hither motion. She broke out in a scream as if he was making love to her. I breathed slowly as he shimmied toward her. He stooped down to her height, wrapped his arms around her, and lifted her up from the ground. He whispered questions the audience couldn't possibly hear. But I knew exactly what he'd ask, every time.

"May I have permission to touch your body? Your ass, your thighs, and your breasts?"

The woman nodded her head excitedly. "Yes!"

He stopped whispering to her and said into the mic, "You don't have to dance if you don't want to. I only want you to feel me..." He caressed her cheek. "Like I'm feeling you."

He strummed on his guitar.

"You don't need to know how to dance for me, honey," he sang. I picked up my drumsticks, banging on my toms and snares, my foot on the pedal, the band playing as Izzy crooned to her, "As long as you're dirty, let's show the world how freaky-deaky you and I can be!"

I whipped my hair to my hyper, galloping drumming, to Izzy's androgynous, otherworldly voice. Oh, how he danced in circles around the girl. Still screaming like a maniac, she gawked as he'd stop to stroke her thighs and pat her bottom as he sang. As the music grew hotter, I drummed with my hip thrust, turned on by the woman, a slave to him, and to Izzy. My cock throbbed as he bumped his crotch against her ass, caressing her thighs, belly, and breasts while singing the last verse. Her pleasure was my envy, taking me over. The air was hot, and it wasn't because of the lights. Sweat bullets were dripping down to my neck.

"Man or woman," he sang to her in a shout. "Dance with me!" he howled and dared. "Be the man and the woman that you see, baby, outside and within the dirty dancer inside of me." Caressing her cheek with one hand, strumming on his guitar with the other, he sang "Or..." He lowered his knees and inched his face closer to hers as he crooned, "Or you can just..."

Izzy's guitar was silent. So was I and the band.

Instead of singing *kiss me*, Izzy pressed his lips to hers. The woman held on to him as they snogged. Passionately, deeply. The audience screamed. My heart beat so fast my drums couldn't compare. That most supreme onstage kiss seemed to last forever, but in reality, it didn't. In my head, I counted the seconds, the only numbers that mattered. *Five, four, three, two...*

When my head counted to *one*, Izzy broke the kiss. His bodyguards rushed up and took the woman by her arms. She screamed, "Izzy, I'll never let go! I love you!" as they pulled her away. Izzy bowed and blew her a kiss as his bodyguards escorted her back to the front row.

"Kiss me till our lips hurt..." Izzy sang helplessly. "Kiss me till we can't dance dirty anymore."

As the audience roared, I sighed, wishing that he'd kiss me until our lips hurt. Oh, if only... The lights darkened. Izzy dashed to the wings for his Delilah Starr drag.

I took a deep breath as I drummed to the pounding beats. Our music went on for three minutes, and then it segued into the theatrical melody of the *Rich Girl* theme. The harmony washed over me—the lively, dramatic piano and the soaring, sweeping romantic guitars. The aching saxophone was bleeding a tragedy, my heroic drums lifting it into heaven. The lights dimmed; the stage was dark again. And then a sparkling diamond-like light nearly blinded me, but it wasn't the lights. It was Delilah Starr.

She was statuesque in her diamond-studded five-inch pumps. Her off-the-shoulder ruby red furs waved as her diamonds sparkled around her neck, in her ears, on her wrists, and over the bodice of her body-hugging, sequined white dress. Her diamond-studded art-deco headdress brought a touch of elegance to her bob. Her face was porcelain perfection with long lashes, her lids painted with shimmery black eyeshadow. Her cinched waist complemented her hourglass figure and her big, round breasts, but they were only an illusion. That ass was not. It was natural. Perfect. Like her.

As I sounded the wind chimes, she struck a pose, holding her head high like a queen, stroking her diamonds and furs. When she caressed her bare shoulders and hugged herself, rocking slow, I was breathless. She was untouchable. A diva. A dark twisted fantasy. A beauty. A dream. A nightmare.

We pulled five songs from the *Rich Girl* album, sung in a medley. Every passionate beat from my drums was for her as she belted her songs. Even the way she'd strut, those breasts bouncing, those hands to her hips, her ass shaking, was a revelation. She jumped off the piano, landing on her heels. She twirled toward center stage and froze in the spotlight.

"I'm not a boy. Not even a poor boy." She stepped back, the light following her. "I may have been that once, but now…" She pressed a balled hand to her chest. "A girl is what I am, and what I was always meant to be. Not just any girl." Her head cocked up high, she belted triumphantly, "I'm Delilah Starr, a *rich girl*! Yes, world, that's me. This is me. A rich girl is all that fame—my fame—is seeing." She looked out to the audience, embracing herself as she wailed, "But will my man love me for who I really am? A human being!"

As she sang the last verse, she unembraced herself, her arms open. "If I could pray, I'd pray to be his wife."

Surrounded by darkness, only one light shined on her. She sat on her knees, her hands in prayer. The audience was eerily quiet as she closed her eyes, and, after seconds of silence, she belted, "God. I'm praying that my love won't take my life!"

Delilah stood. My drumming rolled. And then—

"Baby?" Delilah cooed ecstatically in her weak voice, reaching her hands out to her love. "Can't you see?" She stepped closer, touching her heart as she crooned, "*I love you* like I love…me."

The audience shrieked when the sound of a gunshot cracked the air.

Delilah's scream was heart-piercing. Liquid red bled through the dress and dripped from Delilah's chest to her stomach. Another shot went off. She crashed to the ground in a loud thud. The light shined on her, her headdress glittering. A chorus line of men appeared with cameras, snapping pictures. Placing my drumsticks on my snares, I stood. The band and I together drew toward her slowly and somberly, shooing the paparazzi away. They were gone, and we were alone. I covered Delilah's wide-open eyes with my palm. When I moved it away, they were closed. I placed my hands underneath her headdress. Benson stood to her right, Phil to her left, their hands beneath her body. Larry had her by the ankles. Roadies pushed out a diamond-bedazzled stretcher for Delilah. We carried her away and set her on the ground backstage. She seemed lifeless, even when only playing dead.

Crouched on my knees, I said into Izzy's ear, "Wake up. You aren't dead yet."

He didn't flinch, blink, or move. I patted his cheek. He still didn't budge, not even a little. I felt panic on my face and saw it on everyone's faces, too. My hands shook, my mind blown, dizzy, racing. As I was about to check for Izzy's pulse, he popped his eyes open.

"Boo!" he declared in his voice, not Delilah's.

My heart dropped. "*Wanker!*" I growled after he jumped back on his heels, cackling.

He grabbed my wrists, and he laughed louder as I was about to wring his neck, our foreheads almost touching. "I had you fooled, Johnny, ha!" He let go of my wrists and pointed his finger at everyone. "I had all of you fooled!"

Larry, Tim, Benson, and Phil gave him the middle finger, and crew members slapped his ass with their clipboards, many on his team pelting him with paper balls.

"Sorry, everyone. I had to do that. I'm such a baddy!" Izzy cackled, smearing the fake blood from the plunging neckline of his dress to his chest, sucking the red stuff off his fingertips.

"All right, Izzy, your show's not over yet," someone from management said. "Twenty minutes."

I watched as Izzy's assistants helped him remove his gear as fast as possible, storing his headdress, furs, shoes, and diamonds in a safe. Izzy dashed to the hall. After a quick water break, I headed back to where he went off to, to the only place where I wanted to be.

Izzy's bodyguard, Rick, barked at the men and women crowding the halls as I pushed my way through. Rick stepped aside when he saw me, then he stood behind me and blocked the door. I knocked three times. Paused. Knocked on it three more times.

"Come in, Johnny!" I heard Izzy shout.

The groupies behind us howled and screamed, chanting Izzy's name.

I rushed into the room, slamming my back against the door and locking it quickly. I looked ahead, crossing my arms and shaking my head. I wrinkled my nose at the smell of marijuana. "Well…somebody's having a party."

Izzy stretched out in his chair, wearing only red panties and a bra stuffed with fake titties. He was smoking a fat blunt.

"Any time is the right time to party," he said with a wink.

I laughed. "You got to get dressed. We have—"

He removed the silicone breast form from his bra, squeezed it, and tossed it at me. It flew over my head, hitting the wall. That cracked me up. "Ha! You missed!"

He tossed the second one across the room at me, but I ducked.

"Missed again!" I laughed.

The blunt in his mouth, he leaned forward and unlatched the hook from his bra, revealing his perky, dark pink nipples. He threw the bra at me.

"Ooh." I shook my head and tsked. "Close, oh so bloody close."

"But this is no cigar." He waved the reefer at me. "Want some?"

I looked at the clock. "We only got—"

"Fifteen minutes is *plenty* of time." He puffed the blunt, holding in the smoke and coughing harshly. "Here. Take it."

When I swiped it from him, he crossed his legs, flashing me his nude thigh. I looked for only a split second and then I leaned against the wall, pressing the hot bud against my mouth, sucking in the skunky aroma. I closed my eyes and coughed when I felt that tickling, burning itch in my throat.

"Good stuff, huh?"

I nodded. "I needed this."

"I bet you did."

When I opened my eyes, he uncrossed his legs, spreading them.

"There's a lot more if you want it," he said, caressing his bob.

Flaccid, it was still an exquisite beast, stealing my breath. My mouth watered, my throat craving it. I turned my back toward Izzy, sucking the blunt, already feeling a heady buzz sabotaging my brain.

I heard him snort. "Damn, you really needed it bad, didn't you?"

"Needed what?"

"The reefer. What did you think I was talking about?"

I cleared my throat, unsure what to say. I took two more hits and turned around. Izzy had his back to me, standing before a rack of stunning, outrageous frocks. "Can't decide what to wear?"

He looked over his shoulder. "I waited for you. Pick one for me, Johnny Angel."

I smiled at him calling me by that nickname. "My pleasure, captain."

Standing beside him, I pressed my hand to my chin, rubbing it. "Hmm…" My eyes lit up. "Ooh!" I took out a sky blue, baby pink, and white striped three-piece ensemble of a butch blazer, a femme mini-top, and a slutty skirt. "This is going to look *hot*. Put it on."

He looked at the rack. "What about—"

"You're going to wear it, Izzy!" I barked. "We don't have all bloody night."

Izzy's eyes widened, and he smiled smugly. He shivered, but I wasn't sure if that was an act or if he was submitting to me. "Well, then." His voice changed to a woman's. "As you wish, sir."

I'd never heard him use that warm, sweet voice before. Izzy looked at me with those seductive eyes and naughty smirk as if he knew that my cock twitched with that *as you wish, sir.*

I sat in Izzy's chair, smoking the blunt as I watched him fit into the outfit. The mini-top was cut at the midriff, so his toned abs were proudly bare, shiny with sweat. The skirt hugged his ass, showing off his legs. The blazer made him look militant, a kick-ass woman. He shook his rump, turned around, and faced me with a grin. "Brilliant choice, Johnny," he said as he slipped his feet into a pair of glossy white pumps.

"And you almost doubted me, didn't you?"

"Like I'd ever do that." He posed in front of the mirror, checking himself out.

"Want more of this?" I waved the blunt at him.

"Snub it out. I'll save it for after the show."

I got off the chair and drew to the ashtray on the table, doing as told. "What about this?" I asked about the two lines of cocaine on the table. "Is it for later?"

"It's for now. For us."

"Aw, you were thinking about me."

"Always."

I returned back to his chair. "Such a doll you are. Sometimes."

After he inserted the pearl earrings in his ears, he went toward me. Not seeing it coming at all, I gasped when Izzy jumped in my lap. I flailed back a little as he straddled me, his arms slumped over my shoulders. How tempting it was to ride my hand up Izzy's skirt to squeeze his beautiful ass. I jumped nervously again when he reached into my pocket and removed my lipstick. Exposing the slender, smooth tip, he looked at my lips with a serious expression as he glided the salmon-pink hue over them.

"Smack them."

"What?"

"Your lips. Smack them."

I pressed my lips together, spreading the smooth and luscious lipstick evenly from upper to lower lip, and then smacking them, flashing Izzy a smile. He slipped the applicator back in my pocket.

He looked into my eyes and at my lips. "Now *you* look like a doll."

"Instead of a whore?"

"You're a pretty mess, and I wouldn't know what to do without you." He cupped my face, and my eyes widened when he licked the dimple of my chin.

"You're so bloody stoned!"

"No, I'm not."

He licked me again. I could hardly keep a straight face. I snorted. "Ah, you and your dimpled-chin fetish."

"Shut up."

He ran his tongue from my left cheek to my lower eyelid, and I had to hold back my moan. "Bloody hell, Izzy." I chuckled. "What are you doing?"

"Licking off your sweat," he said breathily. "And your mascara lines."

I didn't bother asking why. It wasn't as if I wasn't enjoying it. I let him do it to my other cheek. The way his long tongue danced along my skin was strangely exciting. He licked my cheeks not once, but twice. It was hard not to love the smooth texture of his tongue. The warmth of his breath. The plump softness of his lips brushing along my flesh as he licked me. My legs trembled when he started to *suck* my skin. I squirmed, and then I squeaked. My moan wasn't all that broke free.

Izzy looked down at my boner.

"Bloody hell. This is embarrassing."

"Why? What's the big deal?"

"It's not…um…big."

"Average and fat is sexy, too, you know," he said, gazing deeply into my eyes. "Addictive."

"Huh?"

"You know what I'm talking about." He nodded at my hard-on.

My cheeks burned hotly as my cock throbbed. "How would you know that?"

"I've watched the groupies go down on you many times," Izzy said, caressing the back of my neck. "How they ride you. They can't seem to get enough of your cock."

"Um…"

"Um, um, um," he laughed. "Hell, for someone who's as much a freak as me, you sometimes act like such a virginal schoolboy."

"Since when?"

"Since I've known you." He pinched my cheek. I chuckled. "What's funny?" he asked.

I smacked his wrist as he tried to pinch me again. "I never knew you were a peeping tom." I bit my lower lip. "I thought it was only me peeping on you."

I gasped when Izzy unbuttoned my pants, and I snickered when he yanked down my zipper. "Funny, Izzy. You can stop now."

"You want me to stop?"

"No! I mean—" He pulled my pants down lower, exposing my pubic hair. "Bloody hell, Iz." I breathed slowly, in disbelief of what was happening. "You are serious."

"You sucked off my cock. So, I'll wank off yours."

"That's…" I gulped, nervous and excited. "Fair…"

He put his hand down my pants, our eyes meeting as he squeezed my fat, average-length cock. When he wrapped his fingers around my big cockhead, a bud of pre-come formed instantly.

I trembled when he squeezed me hard. "Izzy…"

He relaxed his grip on my cock. "John, if you don't want me to do this, I'll let you wank it, okay?"

"No, no, I want you to do it," I squeaked, my voice shaking. "It's…the time…"

"We have plenty of that."

I looked at the clock from across the room. "We got only t-ten minutes…"

My cock throbbed more than ever when Izzy squeezed me harder. "I can do this in two."

He yanked my pants down to my knees. The rings on his fingers were cool, making me shiver. I swiveled my hips when Izzy slowly wanked my cock. I closed my eyes and bucked slowly into the hole of his grip. When my eyes fluttered, I saw him spit a thick saliva wad into that hole. So warm, so wet. He squeezed me, wanking me faster. I whimpered when Izzy thrust his tongue into my ear. When he sucked me there, my sweet spot, my body melted. I panted as he fucked my ear with his tongue, wanking me at the same time. My toes curled in my platforms when he gently tugged my diamond stud with his sucking. My hands shook when he wanked faster. He sucked my ear harder, the tip of his tongue teasing the backing of my earring. I writhed as he panted with me. I opened my eyes, wanting to squeal, to beg, cry for more, but I thought about Izzy's bodyguards and the fans hearing me through the door, and I bit my lower lip hard.

His fingers felt like a cock ring around the base of my big sack. Except better. My balls bulged when he tightened his fingers around me. He wanked me so feverishly that my eyes rolled to the back of my head. And then I looked down, marveling at Izzy's right hand. I bucked, I let out a pained gasp. Izzy moaned desperately, my ear in his mouth, as I was coming. I gasped at how sticky his hand was, more from my come than his spit, as he was still wanking me. My teeth gritted from the overwhelming pleasure. My cock was soft, but he kept going.

"That's enough!" I ordered, my voice shaky.

"Yes, sir!" Izzy squeaked. He clearly sounded submissive that time. Not a tease, not being sarcastic. It was the real deal. He let go of my cock and took his tongue out of my ear. His eyes lit up when he looked at his hand. Even his diamonds were glazed with my come. "Damn, Johnny."

"Sorry." I blushed, reaching out for a tissue.

He got off my lap. As I reached out for a clean towel instead, I froze, watching him remove his rings. He sucked my jizz off them, one by one. Setting them on the counter, he held his hand up and licked from his wrists to his fingertips, lapping up more of my come. I leaned back in the chair, pulled up my pants, zipped, and buttoned myself as he swallowed. I breathed slowly. What to say, what to think? I looked down, shaking my head. What happened was surreal, and yet as ordinary as breathing.

"Towel," he ordered. I tossed it at him. He caught it, drying his hands and fingers.

I looked at the clock. "Bloody hell. You were quick."

He slipped his rings back on. "Told you so."

Standing on his knees before the table, Izzy looked over his shoulder at me.

I grinned, sitting on my knees beside him. With our tightly rolled piece of paper in hand, our noses raced from the beginning to the end of the line. My nose burned and tingled. Izzy rubbed his nose, and he smiled goofily.

He giggled. "Feeling it, baby?"

The rush of euphoria made me giddy, too. "I can feel *everything*."

He draped his arm over my shoulder, letting out a bubbly, obnoxious giggle. He took my hand, and we stood looking at each other. Unsure if it was because of the reefer and coke, suddenly, all I could think about was kissing the man. I dared myself. *Go ahead. Kiss Izzy.* I closed my eyes, drawing my lips toward his. As I did it, I could've sworn this lips were drawing closer to mine, too, until—

He cackled.

I opened my eyes, blinking.

Izzy raised his brow. "What are you doing?"

"What did you think I was doing?"

"I'm asking *you*, silly. You tell me!"

"God, we are stoned. That's what it is."

"That's what I love about you," he slurred. "Us mucking about like this. I bloody love it."

"I love..." I stopped. "I love that, too, Izzy."

He hugged me, and I hugged him. He held me closer, rocking me. I smiled warmly, and then gently let go of him. "Okay, okay. Seriously, Iz. We need to *go*."

He turned his back to me and unlocked the door, but before he opened it, I touched his shoulder. "Wait. Iz..."

He looked over his shoulder at me. "Yeah?"

"Everything we did here tonight was...fun."

Izzy nodded.

"But was it, like, only for laughs, I guess? Like, does it change anything between us?"

He blinked. He grinned. And then, he burst out in laughter.

I rolled my eyes. "Izzy, c'mon. I'm serious!"

"I don't bloody know! All I know is that..." He cackled. "You're something else tonight!"

He laughed harder, he made me laugh harder. I forgot what I asked.

He opened the door. There were no groupies; only his bodyguards. Hand in hand, we ran down the hall, the clopping of our heels echoing. He let go of my hand and left my side as soon as we were surrounded by the entourage. I rushed to Phil, standing behind him, rubbing my nose. The Diamonds were on for the encore.

They chanted Izzy's name when The Diamonds returned to the stage. The air was hotter, the smoke more colorful, and the lights heavier than ever. I looked out at the audience as I struck my cymbals, toms, and snares, pumping my feet madly on the bass pedal. I bobbed my head to the melody of Izzy's song. The darkness to me intensified the audience's screaming that was as hard as my drumming, numbing my hearing. A bright, loud purple light crept to the wings. Izzy danced backward toward the mic, rolling his shoulders and shaking his ass. He spun on his heels and stopped to show off his ensemble. I smiled proudly. His fans were cheering about *my* choice. Izzy turned around again with a hip wiggle and a pelvic thrust.

He blew kisses, giving a bow and a curtsy. "Everyone have a bloody good time tonight?" He giggled boyishly when the audience roared. He put the stand between his legs and wanked it fast, immediately taking me back to the dressing room. I grinned, my cock throbbing as Izzy squatted and bobbed his ass above the floor, pressing his lips to the center of the stand. He slowly licked the silver head of the mic, sealing his sweet affection with his kiss. Izzy rolled his shoulders and cooed in the most wicked voice, "Who wants some more?"

His fans screamed so loud I almost couldn't hear my drums.

Putting his hand up to his ear, Izzy purred, "Ladies! Let me hear you. Do you want some more?" Their horny screams grew as I and the band jammed light and low. He stopped and cooed, "Boys! Now it's *your* turn." They were screaming and hollering before Izzy said, "Do you want some more?" He giggled as they shouted at the top of their lungs. I smiled when Izzy declared, "You got it, ladies and gents and those who identify in-between or nowhere at all." He spread his arms. "You'll have all of me, tonight and forever!"

The purple light followed him as he crossed to his guitar. The crowd went wild when he put the strap over his shoulder. He cradled the guitar in his arms and rocked his hips as the audience roared. He made it screech and howl pure sex and rock and roll, but then he suddenly stopped playing, pointing at us. "But first, I must introduce…"

The band and I played in the same tempo, my cymbals chiming, my snares and toms knocking.

"My band," Izzy said, sounding breathless. "These old and young dudes up here, they're the extension of me."

The audience howled, "The Diamonds!"

Izzy giggled. "That's right, riches. I *love* my boys. They're my divas, especially…" He raced to the piano and howled, "This is my lovely piano man, Phil Weintraub!"

The audience cheered as Phil rocked it out on his piano, his soulful keys dark, playful, and romantic. No matter how many times I heard him play, I was in awe of his major brilliance.

"Ooh," Izzy moaned. "He's bloody *amazing* with his fingers."

After Phil's solo, he danced toward Tim. "And this man here, he sure can *blow*. This is my sax man, Tim Murphy. Give him a hand, my glitter rock and rollers."

They cheered as Tim blew his horn louder. Izzy bobbed his head, rolling his shoulders to his soulful, bluesy solo. Then Izzy shimmied over to Benson and Larry, standing between them as the two were grooving on their guitars.

"And these two, Benson Campbell and Larry Dorsey, they sure know how to *party!*"

Benson had his solo, then Larry had his. As the two played together, Izzy went down on his knees before them. Then Izzy, Benson and Larry faced each other. The three jammed, their unique guitar stylings electrifying. The three did the pelvic thrust, crotches touching. Izzy, strumming on his guitar, grooved toward me.

"And here's the best for last, the man who loves to *bang* as much as I do, my drummer boy…" He stopped playing his guitar, and he howled, "Jonathan Maxwell!"

A radiant glow warmed my face as the audience applauded. Standing behind me, Izzy grabbed two canisters from the floor. He popped them open, and as I did a few rolls on my drums, he dusted glitter over our heads. We head banged, and glitter from our hair rained down, sprinkling the drums. He gave me my thirty-second solo. I banged wildly as Izzy shouted and danced. Then everyone jammed as Izzy scooted center stage, his hips jerking and head rolling as he started singing. Throughout the entire three-song encore, I was reminded yet again that a boundless number of women and men wanted him as much as I did. When the encore was over, Izzy jumped, landed on his pumps, and surrendered, dropping to his knees.

The band stopped and stood behind him. Izzy let go of the microphone and covered his eyes with his arm. I saw sweat, mascara, and glittered tears rolling down his cheeks. Moving his arm away, he grabbed the microphone and sat on his knees.

His voice quivered. "Thank you. All of you. You're *wonderful*. Fucking beautiful." He rubbed his eyes, smearing his tears. "See what a *wreck* you make out of me? I live and die for *you*."

He pointed at his fans, looking tired and out of air, but his smile was strong. He shook his head, and a stage crew member tossed a towel to him. He stood, wiping his face. With a hair flip, he held his arm high, waving the towel like a flag. His face was nude, free from the makeup, glitter, and glam. Proudly *au naturel*, Izzy's god/goddess face was now exposed for his fans to worship. And how they did. Izzy stood still, looking out to them. He tossed the towel to them. Many hands jostled to catch it. It was a young man. When he screamed—

I thought it was me.

I and the band clapped for Izzy. He took one giant breath of the hot, smoky, glittery air and gave the audience one last spellbinding grin. We backed away. Izzy was center stage, alone. The purple, pink, and gold lights shone on him. He cupped his face in the palms of his hands. "This is me." He smiled, opening his arms. "And I am you." He blew the last kiss. He turned to his band, and we embraced one another, all joined hands. We bowed to the fans up to the count of three. "Good night, Hammersmith Odeon. Good night, my darling riches." Izzy waved. "God bless you all." He did the heart sign to his chest. "I *love* you."

We waved good night as Izzy exited the stage. One by one, we exited, too. Those final cries, shouts, and screams that rang in my ear may have harkened the end to another spectacular Izzy Rich concert, but it was only the beginning to what was yet to come. A new dawn, a new day, a new adventure in the world of Izzy's tour, a day in the life of his rock and roll. Another concert, as new as the first. A new sensual daydream. A new hopeless fantasy. A new heady trip into the realm of my unreality, of my undying wish that one day Izzy Rich would be mine.

CHAPTER THREE

Even with shades over my eyes, I could already see the many flashing lights. I could hear the groupies from outside the exit door of the venue. When Izzy's bodyguards opened the door, hundreds must have been waiting for him. They screamed, chanting Izzy's name. I ran behind Tim as the five of us dashed to the limousine. As soon as we were inside and the door closed, I kicked back in the plush seating, removing my shades and wiping sweat from my brow. We were waiting for Izzy.

Benson patted his afro, doing the same. "A drink, anyone?"

Phil slicked back his short brown hair. "Ale, please, B."

"The baby bottle of rum for me," Tim ordered, his Welsh accent coarse.

I crossed my legs. "Cider, B-man. Make it snappy!"

"Why not ask for the moon, all of you?" Benson chuckled as he went into the fridge crowded with booze. He handed us our poisons of choice. "What about you, Larry?"

He leaned back, running his fingers through his long salt-and-pepper hair. "Nah, I'll pass."

After I twisted the cap off my bottle, the sound of mayhem shook the limousine walls. Izzy's name was all I could hear. I watched him through the dark glass of the limo as I sipped my bubbly. He strolled down the red carpet like a supermodel, showing off his frock and newly dolled-up face. He stopped to hold, kiss, and shake as many hands as possible, sign as much merchandise as he could grasp, and autograph his name on skin—on the breasts and asses of oh so many sexy women and on the chests and stomachs of very pretty men. As the guys and I were laughing and talking, from time to time, I'd look out the window again, seeing Izzy still giving love and appreciation to his fans. I nursed my cider as Tim kicked back a third drink, and Benson and Phil were on their fourth.

Someone from management shouted, "Izzy, we've *got* to go!"

Izzy rushed to the limo with his four guards in tow. We could still hear the fans screaming and chanting his name as he got in and the limo moved off. Izzy wiggled himself between Larry and me.

"Everyone's doing all right?" he asked like a concerned parent.

"Splendid." Phil smiled.

"Tad bit tipsy," Benson slurred, reaching out to straighten Izzy's tie clumsily.

"Oh dear, some feathers are missing," Tim said, caressing Izzy's boa. Larry playfully stroked the bald parts.

"Shh," Izzy whispered to the boa, petting it. "No one can harm you now."

We chuckled.

"How are *you* feeling, Iz?" I asked him.

"Bloody *fantastic!*" Izzy howled, his arm flirtatiously over my shoulder. "What a show tonight. I'd say that was one of the *best* performances we had at the Hammersmith. All of you *killed* it."

I took a swig from my bottle. The cider was almost flat. "No, *you* did."

"It's a wonder that you aren't knocked out cold right now," said Larry.

Izzy jumped in the seat. "I have so much energy now, I don't know what to do with myself!"

Benson laughed. "I'm sure you can think of *something* to do."

Tim snorted. "Or *someone* who can do something to you. Maybe tire you out."

Izzy grinned and nodded. "I'll tell you what, boys, the after-party tonight is going to be jamming. I invited *a lot* of supermodels. My date tonight will be with Yasmin Ahmed."

Our jaws dropped. I nearly panted at the thought of her striking dark brown skin, regal face, thick lips, seductive brown eyes, petite body, and long, breathtaking legs.

"You lucky dog." Phil smirked.

Izzy beamed. "We've been keeping in touch since we bumped into each other at one of my *Vogue* shoots," he said hyperly. "We never had time to meet face-to-face again until now. I asked her out on a date and invited her to the party this morning."

"Wow, this morning?" Phil asked, sounding surprised.

"She flew straight from Somalia to London just to see me," Izzy squeaked giddily.

"Lucky bastard," I said. "You know she's one of my favorite African models."

"Speaking of African models, Gobey Elmi will be at the party, too. Another favorite of yours."

My eyes lit up. "Damn. Who else did you invite?"

"A few lesser known models that I've had my eye on."

"So basically," Tim said, "a lot of the world's most beautiful people are coming to the party."

"Everyone, except for *Izzy*," I said, laughing. Everyone else laughed, too, even Izzy.

"Maybe I'll come. Maybe I won't. It's up to Yasmin. So, anyway. What's everyone's plans for tomorrow?"

"What's tomorrow?" Tim asked.

"Whatever you want to make of it."

"That's right. We actually have a day off tomorrow."

"You deserve it, boys."

"Well, I know exactly what I'm doing," Larry said. "Sleeping in."

Tim and Phil nodded to that.

"Oh dear, that sounds dreadfully boring," Izzy scoffed with a playful snicker at them.

"Of course you'd say that." Tim chuckled. "You hardly ever sleep."

"I don't need sleep. Music and sex keeps me up."

"Literally." Larry laughed, looking at Izzy's groin.

"Geezer." Izzy caressed the wrinkles on Larry's face. "I'm surprised you can still keep *yours* up."

Larry cackled. "All on its own! Only the wifey gets to jump this bone."

"I don't get how you can *still* stay committed on tour," Benson said. "I can't stand one day without fucking a hot lady. Or two. Or three."

Tim, Phil, Benson, and I toasted and drank to that.

"That's what my right hand is for. I look, but don't touch. Except myself."

"That's a good husband," Izzy said. "How's ol' Nancy?"

"She's doing well. And the little ones miss me like crazy, I hear."

Izzy crossed his arms with a pout. "I wish I was in your shoes," he mumbled.

Larry smirked. "I know, love. But you got plenty of time. Don't rush a thing like that."

"Not too much time left. I want to be a family man by the time I'm thirty."

"That only gives you nine months, Iz," I said.

"Don't remind me." He sighed and looked at me. "What are your plans tomorrow?"

"Visiting the folks."

He beamed. "Send them my love, especially to baby Zachary. How old is he now?"

"Three. Growing like a weed, I hear, and taking after his uncle Johnny when I was his age. Being such a brat already, but I bloody adore him for that, I do. Takes so much after Emma, too."

"I still remember when she was pregnant, as big as a house when I met her."

"I know! Jeez, time flies when we're having way too much fun."

"Especially *you*, baby John, you party animal," Phil teased.

Izzy looked at me. "I've heard through the grapevine that at my parties, you get *a lot* of tail."

My eyes widened. "Who told you that?"

"*You*. You were drunk."

"What did I say?"

"That you have sex six times a day."

"Yeah, right. And you have sex like, what, eight times a day?"

"And more." He winked.

"I must have been bluffing. I'm lucky if I make it to three."

"How many times today?" he asked, that question catching me by surprise.

My cheeks blushed warmly. I wasn't thinking of what happened before the concert but what Izzy and I did. "I lost count."

"That's what I like to hear." He stroked my shoulder. "My boys having a bloody good time."

"I'm having a bloody good time all right." I grinned. "And I'm only getting started."

❖

A rock star is always a rock star. Day in, day out. From sunrise to sunset. In life and in death. Izzy was living proof of that. No matter where he went, who he was with, or what he was doing, he was Izzy

Rich, the Prince of Glam Rock. He lived in a world of excess very few people in the universe were lucky enough to be in. I was one of those few lucky ones to eat, drink, live, breathe, and *be* it, letting it take a life of its own in me, with him. As his bandmate, as his close friend. I could only wish he was my lover.

Alone in my hotel room suite, after taking a long shower, I sat at the edge of my bed with the phone on my lap. I dialed the number to my parents' place. After three rings, our family butler, Nolan, answered. As usual, his voice was a ray of sunshine.

Twirling the phone cord around my finger, I said, "I know it's late. I was going to call you this morning to let everyone know that I'll still be making it to brunch tomorrow, but—"

"No need to explain. We know how busy you are." Nolan chuckled.

"Just got back from the Hammersmith. Izzy said it was one of our best shows there."

"Still the perfectionist, is he?"

"You kidding me? He works us like mad, but he's so worth it."

"How is Mr. Rich?" Nolan asked, sounding eager to know.

"Nolan, is that baby John?" I heard Emma's voice in the background before I could respond.

"At Mum and Papa's place already?" I snickered when she took over the phone.

"They couldn't wait to see the baby. You know how they are with him."

"Jared is the worst. How's my brother-in-law?"

"Overseas in India on business."

"Damn, I was hoping I'd see him tomorrow. Who else is coming?"

"*Maybe* Leo."

I scoffed at the mention of our older brother. "He can kiss my bisexual ass."

Emma sighed. "I thought you'd moved on."

"He's the one who hasn't moved on! The way he bloody looks at me always brings me back to when he said that Izzy's a..." I gritted my teeth and growled. "A freak, a faggot like me."

"John, calm down, please. It's not as if he said it to his face."

"Oh, if he did, I would've punched him, seriously I would have!" I fumed.

"I wanted to slap him, too. Always a bully."

"He's disgusting. And in front of *family* on Boxing Day of all days." Emma was about to speak, but I continued, "*And* he never apologized, the bastard. Anyway, I'm going to Izzy's party soon." I told Emma about Yasmin Ahmed. She was thrilled and jealous.

"If those two ever got together and made babies..."

"The world would explode. I hope I'll meet her tonight, if Izzy actually comes to the party."

"How is Izzy?"

"He's still wonderful."

"You still *love* him," Emma said teasingly. "I can hear it in your voice."

"Nolan's out of the room, right?"

"Of course."

I lay down in the bed. "You'd think after three years, I'd get over this silly...I guess it's puppy love. Whatever it is, I can't help how I feel, Emma. Is that foolish of me?"

"Well, he is Izzy Rich."

"Don't I know it. And I love everything about him, Emma."

"Ask him out, already."

I let out a laugh so hard it almost made me choke. "You're crazy. I'm in no rush to date again, honestly. Nothing serious, anyway."

"You'd date Izzy in a heartbeat, wouldn't you?"

"Yes, but that wouldn't happen. Besides, I've been extra careful since Odette."

Emma broke the sudden silence between us. "I hate that bitch."

"Hey, watch it." I sat up. "I was going to ask that bitch to marry me."

"That was a long time ago, John."

My lips trembled. "Not long enough for me to forget her."

"I wish you would."

I rubbed my temples, shaking my head, unsure of what to say to that. I looked at the time. "Oh, got to go! Yasmin is waiting for me downstairs."

"Really?"

"I wish! Anyway, I can't wait to see you tomorrow. I'll be there half past noon."

"I'll tell Nolan and Mom and Dad."

After we hung up, I got dressed in silver and purple striped pants and a matching-colored vest with no shirt. In the bathroom, I smeared dark purple on my lips, and applied mascara, blue eye shadow, and face powder. With silver platforms on my feet, I stepped out of the hotel and made my way to the club by myself. Without any drugs in my system, I could feel everything.

❖

Lights flashed everywhere, but it was the glitter instead of the paparazzi. In the club, all around me, women and men were dressed in glitter. Glitter in their hair. Glitter on their shoes. Glitter on their clothing. Glitter on their faces. Hell, even glitter in their eyes.

I could hardly taste the ecstasy in my mouth, but I felt it to the core of my marrow. I was floating in my mind. The weed was to blame for that, but it was also the atmosphere that skyrocketed me to the moon, around the world, and back in the speed of a zillion miles. Then again, both ecstasy and weed had nothing on this reality.

Booze was everywhere. Ecstasy, cocaine, and LSD were piled high in bowls and lined on silver platters, passed around like candy. Far more addicting were the beautiful people in attendance. Hardly a face in the club hadn't been on the cover of a magazine. The male supermodels were dressed as drop-dead gorgeous women. The female supermodels, debonair men. Those lady-men kissing their fellow lady-man. Those sir-women kissing their fellow sir-woman. In twos, in threes, in fours, and more. My head was spinning, trying to keep up with the orgies. But who was counting the fucks, the kissing, groping, fingering, tonguing, S&M, and buggering. My lips were sore, my tongue was numb, my fingers were sticky, my palms were red, my asshole was gapped, and my cock was throbbing.

And the after-party was only beginning.

On a couch behind the curtain of the lounge room, I couldn't believe it. Gobey Elmi was giving me the rim-job from heaven. I had no idea that he was gay until now. I gasped at the way his long tongue split my asshole in two. He wrapped his toned arms around my thighs and pushed my legs up high, tongue-fucking me deeper, harder. I moaned, looking down at him from between my legs, caressing his cheeks, smudging his pink glitter.

"You got one sweet ass," he cooed, his Nigerian accent so bloody deep and sexy.

I shivered, caressing his bald head. "Bottom bitch."

He nodded, licking the crack of my ass.

My cock twitched as he kissed my asshole. "You've been greedy enough." He whimpered when I gently pushed his head away from my bottom, blowing him kisses. I pulled my pants back up, zipping and buttoning myself as he blew a kiss back and left. I closed my eyes, grinding my teeth while grinning. The darkness, music, and drugs took over. The high was my life. I hugged myself, in my own world, until a most adorable lisp cooed into my ear.

"Johnny…"

Silky-soft hands caressed my face. I opened my eyes, lying sideways and smiling goofily at Andrea Biggins, London's one of few plus-sized models. She wasn't a top model, but she was my star, topless, wearing only her knickers. Her shoulder-length brown hair sparkled with glitter, framing her gorgeous fair-skinned face. Her red lipstick was smeared, and her eye shadow was fucked, too. Oh how her smile, and her gapped teeth, made me shiver.

"Why, hello again, sexy. Missed me?"

Andrea straddled my lap. I wrapped my arms around her body, smacking her big ass, her soft, warm flesh rippling beneath my palms. As I sucked on her tongue, I rolled her hard nipples with my fingers, pinching them, making her squeal. When I pulled her nipples toward me, she moaned my name, louder when I smacked those jugs until her flesh warmed beneath my hands. I caressed her pussy, feeling a thick wet patch.

"Oh, Andrea, darling." I slapped her muff, and she swiveled. "You're so wet."

She gyrated harder with a growl, looking down at me. "Fuck me!"

"Haven't I fucked you open enough times already, you naughty minx?"

She let out an orgasmic laugh when I grabbed her tits, biting down on her left nipple.

Running her fingers through my hair, she trembled as I sucked, spinning my tongue around her velvety-soft areola. I stopped and let the nip slip from my mouth, sucking as much of her other tit in my mouth as I could. With my free hand, I cupped her other breast, rolling a throbbing, wet nip between my fingers. Andrea moaned, writhing. I opened my eyes, suckling on her harder as she pulled my hair with trembling fingers. As I greedily sucked some more, I moaned, slapping her nipple around with my ruthless tongue. I nursed on her nip as Andrea cried for more. I let go with a loud wet sound, smacking her tits.

"Why did you stop?" She pouted.

I panted. "Water."

She was about to raise her hand to call a waiter, but I grabbed her wrist and growled. "No." Tightening my grip around her wrist, I leaned and hissed into her ear, "I want *you* to get it."

I let go of her wrist. "Why should I?" she sassed.

I batted my lashes. "I *love* your walk." I licked my lips. "Makes me want to fuck your ass silly again."

She grinned, caressing my face. "Slut."

"You've seen nothing yet, sweetie."

She shivered when I licked her ear. She was practically melting on top of me.

"C'mon." I pushed her off me and smacked her ass. "Get what I asked for, baby. Please."

Her dopey smile made me chuckle. She made only a step and was about to fall to the floor.

"Whoops!" I got up from the couch quick, holding her up. "What happened?"

"It's your fault! You do this to me."

I pinched her butt, smacking it again as she walked toward the bar adjacent to the lounge room. Stepping out of the lounge, I eyed Andrea, my cock throbbing as her ass jiggled. My cock also twitched at the sex shows going on—so many dildos, butt plugs, sex swings, bondage toys, and floggers being put to use by all the drunkards, druggies, dykes, faggots, and bisexuals. The party was a Garden of Eden. Who needed the apples when all of us were the forbidden fruit?

I felt Izzy's presence like light in the room as he entered, glammed and dressed in clothes nearly identical to mine. He commanded the room as much as he did a stage, camera, recording studio, or photo shoot. Ruling by his side was Yasmin Ahmed, elegance in human form. I forgot how to breathe. She was even more otherworldly than in the magazines and on the runways. People turned their heads to gawk at the two, but nobody did or said anything. Everyone minded their fuckery. After wiping my mouth, I returned to the lounge, lying on the couch. I turned my head when the curtain opened and Andrea came back with my water.

"I saw Izzy Rich!" she squealed, jumping, those tits bouncing fast.

"Shh!" I put a finger over my mouth, shaking my head. "Don't behave like that."

"It's really him," she said fast three times. I snatched the bottle from her hand as she said, "I knew he'd look *gorgeous* in person, but bloody hell, he's not of this planet."

"Silly girl. You're a model. You see beautiful men like him every day."

"None like *him*, though." She sat on my lap. "Izzy Rich is the supermodel's supermodel."

"Well, I can't argue with you about that."

"I'm curious, Johnny." She smiled naughtily. "What's Izzy really like?"

I drank the water slowly, squeezing the bottle like a cock. "Izzy's all sorts of things."

"I mean, like, is he really as…confusing as he seems?"

I took another sip of water. "Izzy is confusing, but not confused." I set the bottle on the table.

She got off my lap, rushing to the curtain. "Fuck," she said when she opened it.

I rolled my eyes. "What now?"

She looked at me, and I saw excitement and fright on her face. "He's coming here."

"Is Yasmin still with him?"

She nodded. "Johnny, I'm getting nervous. What do I do? What do I say?"

"Come back here." I patted my lap.

She straddled me and my boner. "I want to scream. This is so overwhelming!"

I growled, covering her mouth. "What did I bloody say?" I whispered hotly into her ear.

I let go of her mouth. "I don't remember…" she replied.

Covering her mouth again, I whispered, "Notice how nobody's freaking out like you are?"

She nodded slowly.

"There's only *one* rule at Izzy's parties, one only." I stared deeply into her eyes. "Be a freak, but don't freak over him. Treat him like any other guest here and you won't be escorted out. You want to make a fool of yourself and get banned from here and from all his parties?"

She shook her head.

"You will act *normal* around him, understand?"

All I could hear her say was "Yes, sir" against my palm.

I let go of her mouth and licked her ear as I murmured, "Good, because I'm not done with you yet." I stroked her thigh and her back. "You'll be a really good girl for me?"

She cooed breathily, "I promise."

"Keep calm, as you are now." I yanked down my zipper. "And blow me."

Her eyes lit up, and straight away she pulled down my pants, her head between my legs. I licked my lips when she engulfed my cock with her mouth. Her cheeks hollowed as she sucked and pumped.

"That's a good girl." I swiveled my hips to the motion of her bobbing, twisting my fingers in her hair. "Mmm. Filthy."

"Did somebody say *filthy*? Why, that's my middle name! Izzy *Filthy* Rich."

Izzy made me smile, but Yasmin's playful and snotty giggle made my cock twitch in Andrea's mouth. I looked over my shoulder, even more in awe at Yasmin's striking presence. Her dark brown afro was boyish, yet had a femme-sophistication. The gold hoop earrings in her ears, the gold hue of her eyelids, and the zebra-striped red and gold body-hugging dress brought out the rich glow of her skin. She and Izzy were arm in arm. Together, they were more than a star-power couple. They were more perfect than sin.

"See, I knew that was Johnny," Izzy said to Yasmin. "I know his voice anywhere."

I arched my back, looking down at Andrea.

She stopped. I saw embarrassment and arousal. She was about to pull up, but I kept my hand to the back of her head, being in control of her cock-sucking. I flashed a smile at Yasmin.

Her eyes lit up, and she graced me the most seductive grin. "So you're Jonathan Maxwell?" she said, her thick Somalian accent alluring and sexy.

I slowly pushed Andrea's head away from my cock. I got up from the couch, pulled up my pants, zipped myself, and approached her. "Enchanté, Ms. Ahmed." I took her hand, giving it a kiss.

Yasmin batted her lashes at me with a most stunning red-lipped pout.

Izzy's eyes lit up when he saw Andrea. He pointed a finger at her. "Ah, I know who *you* are."

Andrea's jaw dropped. "Y-you do?"

"The Body Beautiful. Ms. Andrea Biggins. I'm a fan of your body...of work, I mean."

She froze, gawking at Izzy, her mouth open.

Yasmin smirked. Izzy said, "Ms. Biggins?"

I glared at her. That didn't work. I sat down beside her and snapped my fingers at her eyes and ears.

She blinked and blushed, biting her lower lip. "I'm so bloody sorry, Mr. Rich."

"Darling, please, call me Izzy." He winked at her. I caught him eyeing her breasts.

"Izzy, I'm very flattered that you know me."

"What can I say? I have an eye for young and refreshing talent like yourself." Izzy took Yasmin's hand, drawing toward Andrea and me. Izzy sat next to me, Yasmin sat beside him.

Andrea gawked at Izzy again, as dumb and mute as ever. She snapped out of it again this time when I nibbled on her shoulder. "Stop it!" She chuckled loudly when I did it harder.

I let go and grinned. "Now are you done being starstruck?"

"As if you aren't." She looked at Yasmin. "John's a big fan of yours."

"I know. Izzy told me."

I grabbed my water, taking a sip to distract from my infatuation and my surprise.

"You're even cuter in person than how he described you."

I nearly choked on the water as I swallowed. "You don't say?"

Izzy cleared his throat and put his arm around Yasmin's waist, scooting her closer to him and making her sit on his lap. When she crossed her legs, she flashed her thigh. Izzy stroked it.

"What else has he said?"

"That you're the youngest son of Charles Maxwell. Maxwell Diamonds are my favorite."

"I'll definitely let my old man know. He'll be flattered to know that."

Andrea slapped my shoulder. "Hey, why didn't you tell me you're the son of a millionaire?"

I smirked. "I'm too humble, I suppose."

"If my family was that stinking rich, I'd tell the whole bloody world about it."

"I like my privacy, and I'm grateful my parents let me and my siblings grow up away from the spotlight."

"They did a fantastic job, let me tell you." Izzy looked at Andrea and Yasmin. "I had no bloody clue who John was when he auditioned for my band. The eeriest thing was, before the auditions, the first company I had in mind for Delilah's headdress and shoes was Maxwell Diamonds."

Andrea and Yasmin looked *stunned.*

"Unfortunately, the collaboration never happened because—"

"No, no, let me tell them!" I laughed. "First of all, my parents never took me being a drummer seriously. They thought it was a phase. And they thought Izzy was odd, like, *really* bloody odd." Izzy snickered as I continued, "They thought he was a woman, and they nearly had a heart attack when I told them he's a man. Oh, their reaction! They didn't understand how he could be a boy-girl, girl-boy, and why he'd wear makeup, women's clothes, and be such a shouter and screamer. They were petrified!"

"They must've freaked out when you were hired to be in Izzy's band," Andrea said.

"They practically wanted me committed when I told them that I was auditioning."

Yasmin asked Izzy, "When you met the Maxwells, did you mention wanting to work with them?"

Izzy winced. "It wasn't appropriate. I was almost going to call Mr. Maxwell and pitch the idea to him after we'd meet, but Johnny changed my mind. He was like..." He imitated my voice when he mocked, "'It would be too bloody weird, having two Maxwells working for you.' Ah, well. At least Jonathan's family likes me now."

"Like you? They *adore* you, Iz."

"I noticed something," Andrea said. "You two are dressed alike. Was that on purpose?"

We both chuckled. "No," we said and shook our heads at the same time.

"It doesn't surprise me at all that you two have the same taste in fashion." Yasmin smiled.

"And in women," Izzy purred, kissing Yasmin's cheek.

I cleared my throat, looking at Yasmin. "Has Izzy been behaving with you, love?"

Izzy sucked the side of her neck, making me gulp at how much skin he was sucking in. Yasmin closed her eyes and moaned, her lips quivering, nodding. She moaned louder when Izzy cupped her little breasts in his palms, circling her nipples with his thumbs. He kissed each hard nip back and forth. She caressed his bob as he sucked her nips through the fabric of her dress. My cock twitched, and Andrea was turned on, too.

"You naughty devil!" Yasmin laughed when Izzy crept his hand up her dress.

"My secret's out!" Izzy winked at Andrea, touching her knee. She squeaked.

"Ooh, look at that, Iz." I snorted. "You hit her G-spot."

"Johnny!" She covered her face and fanned herself. "Bloody hell. Mr. Rich, I'm—"

"Nuh-uh…" Izzy leaned over to Andrea's ear. "Am I making you forgetful?"

"No, sir. I mean…"

"Sir will do, too," Izzy slurred, circling Andrea's nipple. "Or you can call me Mistress, if that gets you off. You don't need to be nervous around me. It's not like I bite. Much."

Andrea gasped. "Fuck. Am I dreaming?" She closed her eyes and whimpered when Izzy nibbled the side of her neck, rolling her nipple between his thumb and forefinger. In unison, he groped Yasmin's breasts, teasing her nips, making her moan, making the two moan together.

With a snicker, I pinched Andrea's ass.

"Ouch! Johnny!" she yelped.

Izzy let go of Andrea's skin between his teeth. "What did he do?"

"He pinched me!"

"You see? You aren't dreaming."

She looked at me and then at Izzy. "I feel like I'm Alice and have fallen down the rabbit hole."

"And here I am, the Queen of Hearts! And bad boy Johnny here is the Cheshire Cat." Izzy reached out to caress my cheeks, poking my tiny dimples. "See how he grins."

"See how he's blushing! He hasn't glowed like this until you came," Andrea said.

I sucked her bottom lip in my mouth to shut her up, giving it a pull and tug.

"Izzy…" I heard Yasmin sigh. "Johnny's even *hotter* than how you described him."

I gasped in Andrea's mouth as we snogged, my hard-on intensifying. I panted, looking at Yasmin and then at Izzy.

He whistled at the scantily clad glam-boi waiter. "Shots. Brandy."

Izzy grinned when the boi returned with the brandy, placing the shots on the table. I reached out for mine as did Izzy, Yasmin, and Andrea. "Cheers," Izzy said. We clinked our drinks together.

"Wait," I said before anyone chugged their brandy, looking at Andrea with a sly smirk. "Remember what you did for me earlier, baby? Show Izzy and Yasmin."

She faced her back to us. Izzy and Yasmin watched as she put her arm behind her back, sticking her butt out. Slowly, she set her shot glass on her ass. It stayed, and not a drop of liquor was spilled.

Izzy whistled and clapped.

Yasmin slowly placed her shot glass on Andrea's ass. "It can hold *two* glasses!"

"Now *that's* impressive," Izzy said.

"This ass is bloody amazing!" Yasmin grinned.

"Damn right it is," I said. "God, I love this body."

I set my shot on the table, sitting down on the floor on my knees before Andrea's ass, rubbing her from there to the back of her knees, back to her ass again. Andrea squeaked when I kissed her ass cheeks, brushing my lips against the light pink handprints I left behind from earlier. When I turned my head to my left, my eyes lit up to see Yasmin's face. She was also on her knees, caressing Andrea's ass with me. Instead of using our hands, we used our tongues to tease Andrea's bottom. Even when Andrea shivered, the shot glasses remained on her ass.

"Now I'm really thirsty," I murmured to Yasmin. "Are you?"

"Yes..."

Yasmin leaned in and kissed me. When our tongues touched, I moaned. When we broke the kiss, I reached for Yasmin's glass and she reached for mine. We twined our arms together. I dipped my tongue in her brandy, and she dipped her tongue in mine. Then, together, we drank our liquor. A drop trickled from my lip to my chin. My heart raced when Yasmin caressed my cheek, licking the brandy off my chin, the tip of her tongue wiggling against my little dimple. I shivered when she sucked me there, but I shivered all the more when I saw Izzy stand, coming toward Andrea with the last two shots. She cried when Izzy sucked on her lobe, pulling her knickers down and pouring the brandy over her ass.

It rushed and trickled from her bottom, down her legs, to the back of her feet. I pounced on Andrea's snatch. I sucked her pussy lips more greedily to the flavor of the brandy, Andrea's musk, and her juices. Andrea moaned louder when my tongue slipped right into the wide and wet gap of her pussy. Spreading her labia, I shoved my tongue deeper, her pink velvet clenching around me. I heard Yasmin moan, noticing her sucking the brandy off Andrea's thighs. Andrea's pussy made clicking sounds for me as I tongue-fucked her. I heard not only Andrea, but some other soft, girlish moaning dominating hers. When I pulled out, I saw Izzy making out with Andrea. But not for long.

My mouth watered when Izzy pulled out his magnificent monster cock.

Andrea's mouth dropped. "Whoa. Now that's a *cock*."

"It's yours…" He looked down at Yasmin as he wanked himself. "And yours again, darling."

Seeing the two stand on all fours before Izzy's cock made me whip out mine. I wrapped my hand around it and wanked myself with slow thrusts as I closed my eyes, imagining Izzy saying…

"Johnny Angel. Show them how you can suck a mean cock."

I opened my eyes. Izzy's focus was only on Yasmin and Andrea. The two kissed every inch of him. Envy and arousal made me pant and gasp all at once. I wanked myself faster, my legs shaking. They took turns sucking on Izzy's cockhead like a lolly as he moaned, caressing their heads. The two cupped his balls, stroking his velvety softness with their thumbs. Gawking at the three, I rotated my hips, thrusting into the hole of my grip. I gasped as Yasmin sucked Izzy's balls and Andrea pumped her mouth on Izzy's cock. Or tried to. She was struggling, not even close to taking half his length.

"Deeper, a little deeper, Ms. Biggins," Izzy panted, caressing her cheek.

I was tempted to say, "That's how he loves it. Deep-throat. He loved fucking *my* throat," but I kept quiet, amused to see Andrea trying to take more of Izzy's cock, but her gag reflex triggered. She pulled out in a hurry and coughed. Yasmin moaned, still sucking on Izzy's sack.

"Too much, darling?" Izzy said, not sounding surprised or offended.

"You're so hung. I'm not used to a cock like yours."

"Suck on Johnny's cock like you were before. That was sexy. His cock's perfect."

My eyes widened with disbelief. His words echoed in my ear: *his cock's perfect.*

Andrea ran her tongue along my length from base to cockhead, melting me. I ran my fingers through her hair, moaning, hearing Izzy's words in my head over and over. As she pumped and sucked, my gaze was on Izzy. Our eyes met. His hand went to the back of Yasmin's head, and he pushed her down on his cock. He quivered when her lips pressed against his body. His grunting made me shiver as he banged her throat with passionate, rhythmic thrusts, his balls thudding fast against Yasmin's chin. Licking my lips, I thrust into Andrea's mouth faster. When Izzy and I looked at each other, I wondered if he was thinking about fucking my throat again? Not later. *Now.*

Izzy pulled out, his cock dripping with saliva. He sat on the couch, wrapping his hand around his monster, giving it a shake.

"Fuck…" I cried out.

Izzy lifted Yasmin's dress, revealing her dark, petite ass. He pulled her knickers to the side, and then I groaned at her cunt. Stuffed with Izzy's cock. Already stretched out. And he wasn't all the way in yet. Izzy spread her ass cheeks, thrusting slowly. I moaned at how Izzy's cock tugged the rim of her cunt every time he pulled back. When Yasmin cried *faster*, Izzy drilled into her, driving Yasmin and me crazy. I didn't bother wiping the drool from my mouth at Izzy pounding that pussy, making it juicy, her cunt scent perfuming the air. Harder and faster, I fucked Andrea's frothed mouth.

"Izzy, Izzy…" Yasmin groaned. "I want Jonathan in my ass while you're inside me!"

I blinked, thinking I only imagined she said that.

Izzy spread her ass cheeks wider. "You heard her, Johnny…" Izzy moaned, stretching her wider, thrusting to the hilt.

I didn't think they really meant it until Andrea pulled off, my cock sloppy with her spit. I froze, still in disbelief as Andrea grabbed a lube bottle, drizzling the lube on my cock and spreading it around.

"Fuck my ass, John, *please*…" Yasmin cried desperately.

I gulped hard, my hands shaking when I drew toward Yasmin, my eye on a most beautiful, puckered, dark little asshole. I rubbed my cockhead against it. My cock twitched at how warm and soft it was. Izzy kept Yasmin's ass cheeks spread for me as I popped my cockhead in deep. My base pressed against her rim, and I let out a shout when I felt Izzy's cock inside her, too, our swiveling, thrusting, and grinding in perfect symmetry.

"Oh God!" I felt a tongue in my asshole. "Andrea, you filthy bitch!"

Slapping my hand behind her head, I pushed her into my ass as she rimmed, keeping her there. I fucked Yasmin's tight little ass deeper, cringing from the mind-blowing pleasure of Izzy's cock rubbing against mine as he hammered into Yasmin. Izzy, Yasmin, and I moaned harder and louder together. Andrea's moan vibrated against my asshole. Izzy silenced Yasmin's cry by kissing her, yet I could still hear her scream even with his tongue in her mouth. I panted, feeling and watching Yasmin's ass widening rounder as I pumped faster, harder. I whimpered, pulling out from Yasmin's ass quick, pushing Andrea's head away from my ass. I turned around in a hurry, facing Andrea, wanking my cock fast.

"Drink me, baby!" I squeaked.

On her knees, Andrea opened her mouth wide, sticking out her tongue. I squeaked harder, wanking faster as I came inside her mouth. Andrea sucked on my cock, drinking more of me. I heard Izzy's grunting and groaning, skin slapping maddeningly against moist skin. My knees weakened at Andrea sucking me dry, but also at how the party guests were fucking harder, no doubt, because of us. When I had no more jizz to give to Andrea, she pulled off. I kissed her, my heart beating fast. Yasmin sprawled on the couch, the top of her dress down, running her hands through Izzy's bob as he licked his come off her tits, lapping every drop of himself. When they kissed, they swapped his load back and forth. After they swallowed, Izzy wrapped his hands around Yasmin's breast, making it bulge. He sucked the breast whole with loud and wet suckling sounds, the two moaning. He sucked on Yasmin's other breast.

"Christ…" I said as I tucked my wet, limp cock in my pants, not bothering to zip myself.

Yasmin squealed when Izzy let her dark little nip escape from his mouth. He then scooped Yasmin into his arms and on his lap, his arms around her belly. Andrea and I returned to the couch, sitting next to each other as before, panting. Izzy placed his arm over my shoulder, caressing it as he looked at me.

Andrea and Yasmin smiled at Izzy and me.

"What?" I asked. "Why are you smiling at us like that?"

Yasmin looked at Izzy, caressing his hair. "I want to watch you and Johnny kiss."

I raised my brow, trying to not look or sound too excited. "Pardon?"

"Now *that* would be a bloody turn-on!" Andrea declared.

I looked at Izzy, eager to see what he'd say.

He looked at only Andrea and Yasmin, thrusting his tongue against his cheek. "You know what would turn *me* on right now, ladies?" he slurred. "You two. Sixty-nine. Eat each other out like mad bull dykes while Johnny and I watch."

The two grinned and obeyed him. I was waiting for Izzy to kiss me while they were busy eating pussy. Andrea and Yasmin came, but our kiss didn't.

On the couch, we leaned back, sharing the rest of the blunt that we'd smoked earlier at the Hammersmith Odeon as we watched the nymphomaniacs in play. It was a lot of tongue-in-pussy action, but I needed a kiss. Just *one* kiss. I desperately hoped it would happen, even if it was only for entertaining two models. Izzy refused to let them have it. In my head, I didn't bother asking why, and I didn't let my disappointment tear me apart. There and then, I came to the most disheartening conclusion. Everything that had happened between Izzy, Andrea, Yasmin, and me was only an all-or-nothing foursome she-bang.

The sun blasted through the window, waking me before my alarm set off. The birds chirped as I rubbed my eyes. I looked at the clock; it was half past eight in the morning. A long, hot shower revived my sore body. After brushing my teeth, I got dressed in lounging pants and a loose-fitted shirt and stepped out of my suite to the hallway. The whole floor of the luxury hotel had been reserved exclusively for Izzy and his touring crew. Quietly, I crept ten doors down from my room to Izzy's. I knocked on his door three times, stopped, knocked three more times. Izzy answered the door in his pink pajamas.

"Morning, sunshine. Did I wake you?"

"I've been up." He opened the door wider to let me in. "Yasmin left a while ago."

The aroma of vanilla candles, freshly brewed coffee, lipstick, perfume, and sex washed over me as we went to the living room. The suite was spotless, unlike times when he'd make a mess of the place— curtains ripped down, couch pillows strewn everywhere, panties hanging by the chandeliers, on the kitchen countertops, and on the bathroom floor, and empty lube bottles, liquor bottles, and dirty plates and glasses scattered from the living room to the bedroom.

"What a night you two had. I can smell the evidence."

We sat on the couch. "I couldn't stop making love to her," he said. "I even made love to her in my sleep." He shivered and looked at me with a glorious smile. "Oh, Johnny, she's my dream."

"She was fun. I wasn't expecting her to be so...what's the word?"

"Freaky."

I bit my lower lip, nodding.

"Ms. Andrea Biggins was, too. Very cute. She had the hots for you."

"You think so?" I said with a sarcastic giggle. "She's a sweetie."

Izzy smirked. "Johnny, I got something to tell you, but don't tell anyone, okay?" He sat on his knees on the couch, his hands on his lap. "Last night, I asked Yasmin to be my girlfriend."

My eye twitched. "When was this?"

"Before we went to the party, after our date."

"And what did she say?"

"She turned me down."

My eyes widened. "You're kidding me. But you two were perfect."

"I know. We had a connection. Our date was so romantic. We made each other laugh. We couldn't stop smiling. Dammit, Johnny. We had *it*. There was that spark."

"So, what's her deal, then?"

He sighed. "She said she couldn't take the pressure of being my girlfriend. It would be way too complicated and far too stressful for her. So..." He shrugged. "There goes that."

"I'm sorry, captain."

"Don't be, because I'm not. I would've been very surprised if she said yes, actually. It's one thing to go on a date with a rock star and make love, but to be a rock star's girlfriend? It's bloody hard to find someone who can handle everything it entails."

"You two would've been the world's hottest and most beautiful couple."

He smirked. "We're still friends. It's for the best."

"I'm glad I got to meet her. She's sweet, intelligent, so bloody gorgeous, and...I can't get over how fucking hardcore she was, the way she begged and took all that DP we gave her."

"Yup. Ms. Ahmed's a kinky one."

"And *funny*. The way she was egging us on to snog." I chuckled and stopped. Izzy wasn't laughing and looked unamused. "W-what did you think of that?" I asked nonchalantly.

He snorted and shrugged. "It was annoying."

I blinked, burned by his blunt statement.

"I hate when people use bisexuality as a tease," he snarled. "I know that's *in* these days, but frankly, it got on my bloody nerves before it was a thing. Still does. Can't stand that bollocks."

"I know what you mean, Iz. I'm not one for fag-hags either, but Yasmin and Andrea were horny, that's all. You know how girls are about guys snogging. They're no different."

"I've *never* kissed a bloke on demand because people want to get off on it."

"The girls snogged on demand when you told them to. And we got off on it."

"Good, because you seemed uncomfortable. That was why I put them on the spot. That, and..." Izzy looked at me, flashing me a naughty smirk. "Because I wanted them to."

I was tempted to say, "I wasn't uncomfortable, Iz. All I wanted was your kiss." I said nothing.

"Anyway, shouldn't you be with family by now?" Izzy asked me, and I knew that there was a tinge of sadness in his voice, and in his eyes, that wasn't clearly shown on his face.

I touched Izzy's hand, stroking it. It was then that I saw the sorrows on his face, flashing before my eyes—and I knew exactly why. "I had to see you first, Iz, like I always do on this day."

He grimaced, his lips trembling. "You didn't have to, Johnny." His voice sounded weak.

I held his hands as his eyes welled. "Nothing in this world right now comes first before you."

Izzy looked down and burst out crying. I quickly scooped him into my arms, my eyes filling with tears as he balled himself up into my lap. "It's okay, Iz. It's okay to still mourn."

Izzy shook in my embrace. I rocked him, my lips trembling as he wailed his guts out.

"I miss my darling, baby girl," Izzy's voice cracked. "And my mummy." He choked on his tears, letting out a weak scream. I held him closer, caressing his hair as my tears rolled down my face. "I told myself that I wouldn't break down like this again. That this year, I'd change..."

I shook my head, looking down at him. "You may be grown, Izzy, but..." I paused, searching for my words. "You were so young when you lost your mother. You were just a kid. And Delilah..." I closed my eyes, nuzzling my cheek on top of his head. "How do you get over the loss of a baby?"

"You don't."

His intense pain and loss tore him down, and that open wound took me down with him. We held each other tighter as I rocked him slowly in our embrace. Together, we cried. I didn't care what time it was or how much of it passed by.

Izzy's tears were drier, but fresh still, when he looked up at me. I saw not a man, not a woman, and not a rock star, but a lost boy, a broken son and father, in his aching, melancholy eyes.

"It's so bloody hard to believe, John," he whimpered, shaking his head. "Today would've been Delilah's sixth birthday. *Six years old.* And she still would've been my precious little baby."

I held him closer to my body, caressing his hair and back as I let him weep on my shoulder. His tears soaked through my shirt to my skin.

"I'm sorry!" Izzy choked out. "I'm so bloody sorry you always see me like this on Delilah's birthday." He sniffled and sighed. "I thought the years would've made me stronger by now."

"Do you need me to come with you to the graveyard?"

Izzy shook his head. "I want to visit Delilah alone this year. And I'll be visiting Mum."

"I'll be worrying, you know."

"You better not. Have fun with your family. Later today, I'll have fun with mine."

I knew exactly what family he was referring to. I was the one of few who did. "When was the last time you've visited Ms. Lady Bunny, Candy, and Alexis Glasscock?"

"Last holiday. Christmas. It has been so bloody long. I haven't even called them. I'm a bad son."

"They wouldn't want you any other way."

Izzy wiped a tear from his eye, smiled and nodded.

I put my hand to Izzy's face, as if I were about to caress his cheek, but instead I tickled his armpits. In the blink of his eyes, he let out the most boyish squeal and laugh. I laughed, too, as he kicked his feet against my legs like a little kid. I didn't stop, and I wouldn't let him go no matter how much he kicked. His laughing intensified as I tickled him so hard we rolled off the couch, falling to the floor where I finally stopped. I breathed and sighed deeply as I wrapped my arms around him, his chuckle more girlish than boyish. His hair tickled my nose, making me laugh a little, as he laid his cheek against my chest.

"Oh, Johnny," he said, sounding more happy than sad. "Every year, you do this for me."

"No matter what, Izzy, I'll *always* be here for you on Delilah's birthday."

"I don't mean just that." He looked up at me, his face lush with hope.

"What do you mean, then?"

"Ever since I told you, you've had this way of picking me up when I'm down like this. Especially today."

I smiled. "How can I not?"

He sighed weak and blissfully. "You're the only person outside my family I trust to know about my daughter. And let me tell you, it's hard to keep myself together, but you make me feel better. You make me laugh even when all I'll do today is cry."

"Hey, you don't call me Johnny Angel for nothing." I winked.

He winked back. "One of my favorite songs. And my favorite person."

I caressed his shoulder as I blushed. "Lucky song. And lucky me."

Looking out the window from my childhood bedroom, my baby nephew, Zachary, and I smiled at Central London's finest—the West End. From our view from inside the top floor of the Maxwell mansion, Leicester Square, Trafalgar Square, Piccadilly Circus, and Covent Garden were lively before our eyes. I kissed the top of Zach's thick, short blond hair as I held him up.

"Oh my God, you're so heavy, Zach!" I playfully grimaced, pretending that he weighed a ton. "Yikes." I crouched down. "I got to put you down for a sec, or else I'll break my back!"

He chuckled, looking up at me when I held his hand.

"Hey, guess what, Zachy?"

"Wha, Uncle John?" he said slowly with a grin.

Crouching down on my knees, I held his hands and beamed. "Later today, after we have brunch with Grandma, Grandpa, and your mummy, guess where we are going?"

"Where?" he asked, his big blue eyes lighting up.

"Hamleys, your favorite toy store in the *entire* world."

He squealed and jumped. I swooped him into my arms, holding him up high. "Just me and you, kiddo." He spread his arms. "Ready, set, take off!" I made sound-effect noises as we pretended he was a flying plane. He squealed as I raised him up and down, tossing him in the air, catching him in my arms. He giggled when I kissed his button nose.

"Knock, knock."

I looked over my shoulder, knowing that voice.

"Mama!" Zach squealed and made a spit bubble at her.

"How's my baby lovey dovey bear?" Emma kissed his fat cheeks, caressing his hair.

"I'm good!" I snickered. "Thanks for asking."

Emma laughed, glaring at me, teasing. "Silly."

"Zach's excited that we're going to Hamleys later, just him and me."

"Mom and Dad took him there yesterday. He has enough toys."

"Well, he's going again, and I'm buying him more. Isn't that right, Zach?"

He nodded quickly. "Yahhs!"

Emma and I chuckled. "Brunch is ready," Emma said to me as she took Zachary from my arms into hers.

Emma and I talked and laughed as we left my room and took the elevator downstairs to the ground floor. In the dining room, the chandeliers sparkled from the sun shining through the windows. Our family piano man, Ludwig, was playing our favorites: Chopin, Mozart, and Beethoven. I didn't realize how hungry I was until I saw the long stretch of table with a week's worth of food on it. My stomach grumbled. I'd loved all this food since I was a kid.

"My word, Jonathan, on your third helping already?" Nolan said as he set a plate of food before me. "Haven't been eating well on tour?" He poured the cucumber water into my glass.

I grinned at him, and at my mother and father sitting across from me. "Izzy can vouch for me. I eat like a pig on tour." I took a bite from my poached salmon and fried egg. "Yesterday was so busy I forgot to sit down and eat proper. At Izzy's after-party, I got to meet Yasmin Ahmed."

"How was she?" my mother asked.

"Even prettier in person. Such a classy lady. And she loves Maxwell Diamonds, she told me."

"I always liked her," my father said to my mother, sounding thrilled to hear that.

"You always got stories to tell," Emma said as she was feeding Zachary a piece of salmon.

"With Izzy, it's never a dull moment. The more I know the man, the more I…well, the more I can't stop bringing him into almost every one of our conversations." I laughed at myself.

My mother smiled. "He's practically family."

"Yes!" I said, more excitedly than I intended. "Me, him, and his entourage are even closer now."

"Rub it in, why don't you?" Emma teased.

My father chuckled. "Leo's jealous, too, I heard."

"Him? Jealous of *me*? Is that why he's not here? Did he at least call to say he couldn't make it?"

Nobody responded. My mother gave me a look. "You know your brother."

"Unfortunately." Silence passed between us as we dined quietly. I dabbed my lips with a napkin. "Now I'm stuffed." I patted my stomach. "But I'll be burning plenty off when I take Zach shopping."

He clapped his hands. "Can we go *now*?" Everyone chuckled.

"Soon." I winked at him and looked at everyone. "We spoil this boy to death."

"It's like spoiling you all over again," my father said. "And you turned out all right."

I nodded and smirked, thinking about Izzy and how our upbringing and childhoods were two opposite worlds apart. I looked at my family and smiled warmly as I said, "I'm very lucky."

Everyone smiled back at me. Dessert was served. Ludwig continued playing the piano. The music was so beautiful, I was choked up. I was more than lucky. I was blessed.

My bed sheets were as crisp and cool as the fall season, my pillows as warm and inviting as spring. Everything in my Camden Square condo was as I'd left it. It seemed like centuries ago since I was here. The peace. The quiet. Knowing where everything was and that it belonged to only me. It was home. And yet, it was lonely. Something was missing.

Or someone.

I sat at the edge of my bed, looking to the right side of my room. The wall was covered with concert and movie posters of Delilah Starr. To the left side were posters of Izzy when he was only the recording artist and not the megasuperstar. *Nobody* predicted that he'd one day be a prince. I caressed the edges of the posters. I looked at the ticket stubs taped underneath them, reading the dates and places: November 5, 8, and 10, 1967, in Scotland. August 25, 26, and 27, 1968, in Wales.

June 5, 9, and 10, 1969, in our England. I shook my head in wonder. It seemed like only yesterday I saw Izzy in concert for the first time. And even then, I knew. I wished. I sighed, returning to my bed and lying down.

Wondering...

Where was Izzy now? Was he paying respects to his mother and daughter? What was he doing now? Was he at Soho with his three adopted mums, having a most fabulous time at their luxurious brothel? More than a brothel, but his home. If he was at his Hampstead Village home, was he possibly, maybe thinking of me? I smirked, knowing he was.

But only as a friend.

Everyone knew Izzy and I were as close to brothers as if we were blood. But only Emma knew my truth. She always knew. And hell, as much as we disgusted each other, I couldn't put it past Leo that he saw right through me, too. He knew.

I was *in love* with Izzy Rich.

CHAPTER FOUR

Sitting at the front row of the South Bank studio with the band, Izzy's assistants, and some members of his management team, I watched as the cameramen zoomed in on Russell Harty. The audience silenced themselves as the cameraman counted, "We're on in five, four, three, two…"

"Last time Izzy Rich was on the programme, he was a woman, the glittering, beautiful, tragic male-to-female starlet, Delilah Starr," Russell said to the camera. "Man or woman, Izzy has made a name for himself in *both* genders. He's here today to talk with us about his new hit record and hit tour. Let's welcome back the Prince of Glam Rock, Izzy Rich."

Russell stood as I and the audience clapped. Izzy walked on the set, dazzling from head to toe. After shaking Russell's hand, Izzy sat in the interviewee chair.

"It's so good to be with *you* again, Russell," Izzy teased, crossing his legs.

Russell caressed his chin, studying Izzy. "As usual, you're ultra-glamorous."

"Oh, these old jewels?" Izzy batted his lashes.

The audience roared when Izzy showed off his ruby earrings and ruby-studded collar. Russell squirmed, sitting back, keeping a straight face. "Do you ever wear *ordinary* clothes? Like jeans, sneakers, and a T-shirt instead of the glossy clothes you're wearing now?"

Izzy's mouth dropped. "What I'm wearing now is my equivalent!"

The audience laughed. I snickered, nodding.

"How do you feel about people who are threatened by how you express yourself?"

"Because of what I wear, or because of what I do?"

"Both."

Izzy lifted his chin. "Grateful. I used to be a nobody. Now everyone has something to say about me, how I dress, what I do, what I say. I find it all…" Izzy smiled. "Terminally stimulating."

"Does that explain why you're very *loud* in the way you express yourself? Is it for attention?"

"Attention can't escape me." He chuckled.

"Are you surprised your new album has created as much of a rumpus as *Rich Girl*?"

"Very much so."

"*Rich Girl* gave you that meteoric rise to fame and catapulted you to the stratosphere."

"It changed my life and my career in every sense of the meaning of change."

"And the film won you a BAFTA for Best Actor for your performance as Delilah Starr."

"I'm still coming to grips with that, honestly."

"Why's that?"

"I'm not a trained actor. And though I've always admired the art form, I never thought I'd be *in* a movie, let alone one based off my album. And to win a BAFTA? Fucking surreal."

"It was a deserved win, as well as the others you earned for the *Rich Girl* tour, documentary, and costumes. Was it a lot of pressure for you to reinvent yourself with this album?"

"Well, after being Delilah Starr for a full two years of my life and my career, I said to myself wouldn't it be lovely to show the world both my genders? This album shows how I've evolved from the woman I was then to the man I am now."

"Was it hard to break free from the Delilah Starr character, to transition back to Izzy?"

"Not hard for me, but hard for the fans, and even my entourage. They had to start calling me Izzy again and seeing a man instead of a woman. It's bloody hard saying good-bye to Delilah. But she shows up in how I dress, look, and act. I'm her, which is why my fans haven't let go of her yet."

"Maybe it's also because of your hair?"

"I think it's also my voice, how sometimes Delilah is still there."

"I still find it remarkable how you can turn her voice on and off instantly."

"My voice is a sponge, my face is a canvas, and the art is me. I've always collected the voices, faces, and accents of women. There are many women inside me. So many characters."

I knew that to be true more than anyone.

"So on this new album, you aren't being a character. You're yourself."

"Right."

"How did you come up with the album's title, *Iz Ze Rich?*"

"It's a wordplay on my name."

"When one says it fast, it sounds like a question. Is he rich?"

"Right-eee-o!" Izzy beamed. "That's the question."

"And what's the answer? Is Izzy Rich rich?"

Izzy seemed humble as he replied, "I'm comfortable."

"More comfortable than when you were that Brixton misfit you told me about years ago?"

He grimaced. "Those were the dark ages. Back then, fame was a dream. Now it's my reality. And frankly, I'm surprised it's still happening, and that people aren't sick of me by now."

Russell studied Izzy again. "You've got the killer instinct. That I've always sensed about you."

"Not only is it instinctual," he growled playfully, "it's in my genetic code."

"But what I always found interesting about you is that you seem like a mystery, I suppose."

"How do you mean?" Izzy reached out for the glass of water on the table, sipping it.

"We don't know much about your past other than that you were raised in the Brixton slums."

"Hearing the name again brings me back there. Such a terrible, dangerous place to live."

"You've told us that, and that your mother passed on when you were eight, and that you dropped out of school at seventeen. We don't know anything about what happened to you after that."

Izzy set his glass on the table, smacking his lips. "I like some aspects of my life to be private."

"But how does a star like you get privacy?"

"I don't. Like, I can't ever walk into a grocery store and buy bread, milk, chocolates, and brandy. I mean, I can try, have tried, but for obvious reasons, I can't do that anymore, so I have to have assistants do that and run my errands for me, but—" He shrugged. "No complaints. I cherish what small doses of privacy I do get, though."

"Your love life isn't private."

Izzy laughed. "What love life?"

I cringed as Russell said, "Is it true that you and Somalian supermodel Yasmin Ahmed are—"

"Stop right there, you naughty man..." Izzy glared, shaking a finger at him. "I know *exactly* where you're going with this. I see that you still have a thing for rumor, Russell."

Russell gave Izzy a smug look. "A picture surfaced today of you two. Have you seen it?"

"No."

"It's you and her, cheek-to-cheek, looking like more than mates, if you know what I mean."

Izzy leaned back in his seat, knitting his brow. "I don't know what you mean."

"Well, you're known for dating supermodels—"

"And many other talented people," he snapped. "We attract each other like bees to pollen. It isn't *always* romantic, if you know what I mean by that." He winked.

Russell smirked, clearing his throat. "Can't you blame people for wanting to see you *romantically* involved with Yasmin?"

"Because we're famous and beautiful?" he asked, sounding amused.

"That's the appeal. A bachelor like you with a bachelorette like her."

"More like the fantasy, you mean."

"If you want to put it that way—"

"Yasmin Ahmed is a good friend," Izzy said, a strict tone to his voice.

Russell looked at his clipboard, and then at Izzy. "That's all that you have to say about that?"

"Russell, if you don't mind me asking, what's it with this fascination about my love life?"

Russell paused, a few seconds of awkward silence between them. "I think the world's obsessed because they can't help but wonder who will have Izzy Rich's heart?"

Izzy licked his teeth. "Ah..."

"Who was the last woman that has had it?"

He smiled warmly. "My mum. I'm a mama's boy. Always will be."

"If she were in this studio, what would she say right now?"

He looked up, and then smiled cheekily at Russell. "She'd say that my skirt is too short."

I grinned and everyone clapped.

"Have you ever thought about writing an autobiography?" Russell asked when everyone was silent.

Izzy's eyes widened. "Never crossed my mind."

"What was the last book you read?"

Izzy uncrossed his legs, kicking back in his seat. "It was...*The Ramayana.*" He grabbed his water, taking a long sip from it. He cleared his throat, putting the glass back down. "That was ages ago. I don't have time to read a book, let alone write one. I read fan letters, though."

"I can imagine you get a lot of fan mail."

"Oh, you have no idea."

"What are they like? Dangerous? Interesting?"

"Hot. A major turn-on. Very sexually indulgent. Some are so naughty, I've had them framed."

"What are some of the framed ones?"

"Most of the framed ones are from this Chinese-German girl who lives in America."

"Have you ever responded back to her?"

"I don't have time to respond to fan letters." Izzy looked at the camera. "Sorry."

"What makes hers memorable?"

I looked at Izzy, eager, curious to know. "She's sweet. Only eighteen, but writes very poetically, has a mature soul, old soul as they say. Her letters stand out in my mind and are worth framing because they aren't kinky at all."

"What does she write about in her letters if they aren't naughty?"

"I'm not at liberty to tell you or anyone else that."

Not even me, I thought.

"Only my eyes reads these letters. It's strictly private, only between me and my riches."

Russell nodded and looked down at his board. "You have a surprise for us."

Izzy looked at the camera, breaking the fourth wall. "A new single is coming, and it's my favorite. 'Dirty Dancer.'"

The audience applauded wildly.

"Now *that* song is provocative, isn't it?" Russell asked.

Izzy looked at him. "The ladies especially get off on it." A few yelped Izzy's name.

"Is it true this song is the reason why for this tour you only have of-aged audiences?"

"I wouldn't say it's because of this song, but 'Dirty Dancer' has a lot to do with it. The fans have to show ID at the booth to prove they're eighteen or over or else they can't buy a ticket."

"Whose idea was it for you to pick a woman from the audience?"

"Nobody's idea. It happened. One night at the concert in Earl's Court, I picked someone on a whim, and did my dancing and kissing thing. The fans loved it so much, my manager wanted it to be a fixture for this leg of the tour. It's good fun."

"I've listened to 'Dirty Dancer' many times and wondered if the song is about any one person?"

I gulped lightly, looking at Izzy. He blinked, and nodded slowly.

"About whom?"

Izzy's face suddenly grew somber. "Nobody that anyone here knows," he said quickly. "I want to keep it that way, for *her* privacy, you see." Izzy's trademark smile lit up his face again. "But I'll tell you what, Russell. If I ever write a book about my life, maybe I'll call it *All That Glitters*."

"I want an autographed copy." Russell looked at the camera, announcing a commercial break.

In what felt like a blink of an eye, we were all onstage, ready to perform. When we were back on air, we did like how we always rehearsed it, except this time, Izzy picked a woman that looked to be in her sixties. The audience howled as he danced around her, caressing her cheek and hair instead of her bosom or her ass. When Izzy kissed her forehead, she swooned. The song ended with him giving her a hug and a peck on the cheek. As soon as we were off air, amidst the organized chaos, someone from management told us we had to hustle to the airport with only four hours tops to be there. Izzy jumped excitedly like a kid.

"Here we go with the go, go, go!" he declared. "Paris, here we come!"

❖

I didn't realize how exhausted I was until after takeoff on the private jet. After drinking only half a glass of wine, I was knocked out.

The whirring sound of the plane put me into a deeper slumber, until I heard myself smacking my lips, my lids fluttering to Izzy's snorting.

When I breathed, I growled. "*Izzy!*" I snorted out the grapes that he'd stuffed in my nostrils.

Izzy covered his mouth to muffle himself from laughing.

I rolled my eyes. "You're so mature. Get some sleep!"

"I'm too restless. And bored."

I yawned. "Egg on somebody else."

"Everyone's asleep. Now, you're up, so..." He patted my head. "You're the lucky winner."

I closed my eyes, snuggling into my blanket. "Wake me up again when we've made it to Paris."

"Speaking of Paris," he murmured into my ear. "Tonight's going to be a blast."

I opened my eyes, raising my brow. "Yeah? What's the plan?"

"Supper in the Eiffel Tower, you and me. We'll have it all to ourselves."

"Bloody fantastic."

"I knew you'd love it." He winked, diving his hand into his bowl of fruit.

I closed my eyes, wrinkling my nose at the smell of banana. Izzy tried to poke the head of it into my mouth.

"Now what are you doing?"

"Open up, Johnny Angel," Izzy murmured with a coquettish voice.

"Open *your* mouth," I ordered.

He paused, seeming to be thinking. "Okay!"

I grabbed the banana and unpeeled it, setting the peel on my lap. Izzy looked at me playfully as I pushed the first inch of the banana into his mouth. I thought he was simply going to eat it, but he pushed the banana's whole seven inches down his throat without gagging or batting an eyelid. He pressed his lips together, and then slowly pushed his head up to reveal the entire fruit intact. I watched him deep-throat the banana again. It was incredibly hot. My cock twitched. I was more than impressed, but surprised that he was as much a pro at deep-throating as I was. Even if it was only a banana. I smirked when he pulled up his mouth to the head, biting into it, chewing slowly.

I clapped softly, looking around to be sure that I wasn't waking anyone. "That deserved a standing ovation," I murmured.

"Damn right it does! Give it to me, baby."

There it was. That voice. The same one that I heard at the Hammersmith Odeon. Something new about it. It was so sweet it gave my ear a cavity, and it sounded nasal, lush with sass, attitude, and tenderness. When he licked the banana, I wanted to lick that voice. And him.

"I'm too tired to get up." I snickered. "Sorry."

He ate the rest of the banana, slapping my cheek with the peel. I took it from him and returned the favor, then I tossed it across the aisle. "Izzy, seriously, man. You *need* your sleep. If you don't sleep now, you won't sleep later. And you're going to regret it. I know you."

He leaned his head on my shoulder, nuzzling his cheek against me. "You win."

I snorted, watching him close his eyes. "About bloody—"

Izzy dozed off just like that. Sleeping like a baby. I was his pillow. I smiled, about to close my eyes. Instead, I laid my blanket over him. A wince graced his face.

"Sleep tight, my captain..." I mouthed, closing my eyes and dozing off, too.

❖

Being back in Paris was as much home to me as London. It was, after all, the city that helped make Maxwell Diamonds an international brand, so I knew it like family. While Izzy was at his photo shoots and press junkets, I visited the Eiffel Tower, Les Invalides, the Louvre, and L'arc de Triomphe. With not too much time to spare, I made one last stop to the Champs-Élysées for Ladurée's double-decker macaroons and canelé de Bordeaux. The aromas of the luxury pastries, the music, and the upscale vintage atmosphere warmed me like the pastries on my plate. The chatter and noise of the bakery house was just as inviting, oozing decadence and comfort.

Looking down at the magazine I had next to my plate, I moaned with orgasmic delight at my first bite into the canelé's firm caramelized crust and vanilla and rum-flavored custard center. Izzy had the front cover of the magazine, which was about his performance at Le Trianon tomorrow night. I looked up, about to turn the page, and then I stopped. An oval-faced woman with voluptuous honey-blond hair walked in. She had thick, glossy pink lips, big blue eyes, and toned arms.

Her dark red dress perfectly embraced her curvaceous figure, that big ass, huge tits, tiny waist. That body. That face. Those eyes. It was too familiar. When she spoke, my face grew pale. She wasn't a stranger. Her voice. I *knew* that voice. My lips trembled. I stared down at the magazine again, looking up again when I heard her laugh. Something about it was different—a little too high. But everything about her was too similar to the woman I loved.

And that man she was with. I checked him out, not because he was much of a looker, but because I had to see if he was the bastard that had my woman. I sipped my coffee slowly, gulping thickly. Was he the one? He was too handsome. And he looked younger. He and the woman laughed, talking to each other in French rapidly. Not friends. They were lovers. I bit into my canelé, its richness no longer a pleasure but a distraction from them. I couldn't shake off the feeling. I knew them. I knew the way she caressed the back of her lover's neck. That was my love. And I knew the way the man squeezed her bottom. That was me, with her. When the two kissed, it wasn't how *we* kissed, but how she and the bastard kissed. Slowly. Passionately. Rubbing it in that they had each other. The couple looked over the pastries, hand in hand. I quickly ate the rest of mine, dabbing my mouth with a napkin, my heart beating fast. I got up, sat back down, stood back up.

I walked toward them with firm, heavy strides, but up closer, I felt like such a fool. The *femme* couldn't be her. That face wasn't the same as my ex-girlfriend's. As I stood before them, the two looked at me strangely, raising their brows.

I looked at the woman, my voice as dry as my French. "Odette? *C'est toi?*"

"*Je suis Geneviève.*"

I blanked out. Blinking. Standing there. Embarrassed. More than lost. I was gutted.

"Monsieur?" the man asked, sounding concerned. "*Tu es bien?*"

My heart sunk again. He was not Guy Foucher.

I nearly tripped on my feet, not looking back, as I ran out of Ladurée.

❖

Knock, knock, knock. Silence. *Knock, knock, knock.*

I opened the door to find Izzy in a stunning sheer violet blouse, sheer pink tie, shimmery violet pants, and a matching-colored sequined jacket. He was breathtaking. And yet, not even he could repair the wreck that I was. With a burning fag dangling from my mouth, I blew the smoke away from his face.

Izzy's eyes widened. "Shit." He looked me down and up. "You look like shit."

"I match how I feel."

"What's wrong?" he asked softly after he closed the door. "Johnny?" he asked tenderly as I sauntered toward the living room.

I flopped on the couch, polishing off the fag. I blew the smoke in a rush, snubbing the fag in the ashtray, sighing. Izzy sat next to me. I couldn't look at him, not with tears in my eyes. I turned my head aside as he touched my shoulder, speaking softer, more tenderly.

"What happened?"

I sobbed, my lips trembling and caving into my pain. He gasped, wrapping his arms around me. He held me close, caressing my hair and massaging my scalp as I mumbled, "I thought I saw Odette today."

"Fuck. Was it her?" he asked, sounding worried.

I shook my head. "It wasn't. I know the odds of us bumping into each other is impossible, but…" I shivered. "Odette. She's still inside me!"

Izzy stroked my back as I wailed. He was silent, rocking me, then he said, "It's my fault. If I hadn't mentioned her at the Hammersmith—"

"That would've made no difference," I sniffled. "Izzy, I lied to you." I couldn't say it. I could only *feel* it. I hadn't moved on from Odette or the pain. I cried on Izzy's shoulder harder. "She looked *just* like her. It was a bloody mind fuck."

"Life really is stranger than fiction," he whispered.

I separated my face from his shoulder, wiping the water from my eyes, cheeks, and chin.

"Look at you." Izzy touched my cheek. "A pretty mess."

"And you wouldn't know what to do without me." I smirked and embraced him tightly again, my body shaking. "Fuck," I growled. "Here I go again. The pain, Izzy. It's confusing. I can't explain these feelings, why I don't have regrets. Falling in love with her. Paying for her GRS. But why did I let her leave me for him right after the surgeries, without a fight?"

"Was she worth fighting for?"

I looked at Izzy, deep in his eyes. "I wanted her to be my wife, Iz. I bought a ring. I was ready."

I choked up after he said, "You still love her."

"I love no one, anymore."

"Bollocks." He wiped away a tear rolling down my cheek. "Johnny, it's *okay* to still love her."

"But did she love me? The more I look back at that whole year, the more I see a lie. I wasn't her lover. I was more of a sugar daddy to her than a boyfriend."

"I doubt that, because trust me, I know sugar daddies and—"

"You do?"

He shut his mouth. His shock matched my surprise. A strange silence divided us even in our closeness.

Izzy cocked his chin up. "Many people in this world are cruel. Evil. Heartless. Even the ones we love can be bastards. Johnny, it was *her* loss."

I grimaced. "That's what everybody bloody says, but what about *my* loss, dammit!"

"Don't think about the loss. Think about the gain."

Well, I'd never been told that before. I didn't have to think about it. "My dream career. And an extraordinary new life. With you."

"That's right." He draped his arm over my shoulder, and I did the same. "Fuck all, man. I chose *you*, John, because you were the one. And I got...well...I *have* the best. It is you."

I smiled a little.

"You can smile bigger than that, Cheshire Cat."

"For you, Queen of Hearts."

Izzy stared at me longingly. Then he licked my front teeth and thrust his tongue into my nostril.

I wiped my nose. "God, you're so bloody *weird*!"

"My Johnny's back! Feeling better?"

"You're the best, captain."

"So are you, especially at massaging feet." He kicked off his pumps. "They need your TLC." He wiggled his toes, lying back and stretching his legs over my lap.

The smile on my face grew as I held his silky-soft right foot, massaging his sole deep.

Izzy moaned, cracking his toes. "That feels really good."

I held his left foot in my other hand, massaging both feet deeper. "We've been so busy that I haven't had time to ask you about your holiday."

He closed his eyes, rubbing his temples. "Visiting Mum and Delilah still kills me."

"I wish I was there."

He looked down at me, eyes glimmering. "You were, in spirit, anyway." He sighed happily. "My mums cheered me up. Some of the girls were there."

"Do anything fun?"

"We hung out at the brothel. I cooked a gorgeous supper for them. Rest of the night, we got stoned senseless and reminisced about the good ol' days. Sometimes I miss sex work."

"You prostituting to all those rich women. What a life." I snickered. "I'd miss it, too."

Izzy gulped, looking at me. "Jonathan, you weren't the only one that lied," he said somberly.

"About what?"

"I never prostituted to women."

My mouth dropped, my brows knitted. "What?"

"I prostituted to rich men."

I stopped massaging his feet. A long, awkward silence passed between us as I registered what he said. I wasn't sure what to think or how to feel. I was only more confused the more I processed it.

"Why didn't you tell me this from the start?" I said.

"I needed time. I wasn't so much lying as…I wanted to be sure you'd understand."

I nodded, scratching my head. "So, you prostituted to men."

"As a transvestite prostitute."

I blinked. Did I hear him right?

"Her name was Lana."

I snorted. "Now *that* you're making up."

When he wasn't laughing, I froze.

"Bloody hell, Iz…really?"

He nodded.

"Wait. Let me get this straight. These men knew you were a man, but…a woman?"

"They paid for Lana. She was any woman they wanted. They got it from the wig on my head, the colored contacts on my eyes, the size of my breasts, the clothes I wore, and my voice." Izzy's face turned roguish. "Name an accent, Johnny. I'll show you what I mean."

"Hmm. German."

Izzy cleared his throat. "As you wish, sir," he said in a low feminine pitch, mimicking a thick German accent.

My mouth dropped. "Bloody hell."

"Name another one."

"Russian."

Izzy cleared his throat again. "A gun in your mouth for your pleasure?" he impersonated a dead-on Russian accent. "*Beg for it*, cock-pig."

My eyes widened at the accent as well as the bitch-domme character.

"Name one more."

"French."

His French accent was *flawless* when he chirped, "My fist in your arse? Coming right up."

I blinked, at a loss for words.

Izzy bit his lower lip. "What do you think?"

"I'm blown away, Iz. You're a man of many voices, but I didn't know that you could do this."

"At the brothel, I was called the human mockingbird."

"How do you do it?"

"It's a natural gift, but took *a lot* of practice to perfect the voices. They *had* to be spot-on. The pitch, tone, and accent had to be flawless, or else Peggy, I mean, Lady Bunny would've taken it out on my cheque. At the time, every quid mattered. I made sure I didn't fuck it up."

I held Izzy's feet again, massaging him slowly. Too many questions swirled in my mind.

"Did you?"

Izzy held up one finger.

"That's it? That's not too bad."

"But it was enough! I learned my lesson. I *never* did again."

I looked at him. "How much were you worth?"

"A simple hand job cost fifty pounds. A blowjob, one hundred pounds. Me fucking them in the arse, two hundred pounds. Them fucking my arse, five hundred pounds. A fisting—"

"Whoa, hold on." I stopped massaging his feet, shaking my head. "How rich were these guys?"

"Loaded. In more ways than one."

I gulped thickly at his statement. "Did they really pay you that much for all that?"

His eyes darkened as did his deviant smile. "And more. Two-hour roleplaying sessions would cost in the thousand pounds range. Many clients paid even more for me to be their escort. They got their money's worth," he declared proudly. "That was for bloody sure."

"How old were these people?"

"Damn, Johnny. You're full of questions!" He chuckled. "Is this turning you on?"

Oh, he had no idea, but I didn't dare admit that or let my cock show it.

"Sorry. I'm awfully curious. Shocked. When I thought I knew everything about you…"

"It's only between me and you, Johnny. Lady Bunny has spent millions to ensure none of my clients from back then would let this out. So far, none have. I only trust you to know this."

"I'll never tell a soul, captain."

"These men were old enough to be my fathers or uncles."

"Bachelors?"

He snorted. "Oh, hardly. Most of them were married. And straight. They loved me, and I loved them. Lana loved all her sugar daddies. They treated her like a real queen, Johnny."

I quietly kept massaging his feet, my cock throbbing. "Those lucky bastards. If I were one of them—" I shut my mouth hastily.

He looked at me with a teasing smile. "What then?"

I blushed. "Never mind."

"I'd be your woman."

My heart raced when he said that. What I'd give for Izzy to be *my* woman. "I'd love that, Izzy."

He smirked, the expression on his face blank and unsure.

"Pretend I didn't say that."

"I'll be your woman," Izzy said, sounding as if doing that was nothing. "But just for one day."

It took me a few seconds to register that he meant it, that what he was saying was real.

"Why?"

"For fun. For old time's sake, to relive those golden years."

"How much do you want me to pay you?"

Izzy snorted. "Zilch." He sat on his knees. "So, what do you want? A bimbo? A bitch? A princess? A dominatrix? Name any woman, Johnny, and I'll be the best you've ever seen."

I scoffed at his tone. It sounded like a transaction. "That's Lana talking, isn't it?"

"Of course."

"I don't want Lana. Don't be Lana."

Izzy looked so confused. "Then who do you want me to be?"

"I *don't* want Lana. And not Delilah Starr either."

Izzy scratched his head. "Can't give me a teeny-tiny idea of the type of woman you'd want?"

"I want to meet a perfect stranger."

"All right. I'll do my best."

"*Wait.* I have one request. It's this voice that you've used lately."

"What are you bloody talking about?"

"C'mon, you know. The one that you used at the Hammersmith Odeon. And on the plane today."

"Hmm, I'm not so sure which one you mean. Describe it."

I did. Izzy snapped his finger.

"Is this the one?" he chirped.

"That's it!" I beamed. "That's the one."

"Why do you love it so much?" he asked in his voice.

"It sounds so wet."

"Wet?" Izzy said in that warm, breathy, beautiful voice that I now knew so well.

I nodded, biting my lip, unafraid to speak my mind. "It makes *me* wet, Izzy."

With a purr from that perfect, sweet, nasal voice, he declared, "My name is Holly."

❖

Izzy and I were two kids in a candy store, spending *hours* boutique-hopping and shopping at the Galeries Lafayette. And we were far from done; at least, that was what Izzy was saying by how he was still pointing at all the jewelry, frocks, furs, paintings, and furnishings that caught his eye. The managers of the store gathered their staff together to jot down everything he wanted so they could ship it all *par avion* to London the next day. Meanwhile, Izzy and I were still browsing, marveling. I was spent and starving by the time we made it to the *femme* department.

"*Quelle heure est-il?*" he asked one of the managers in broken French. It was eight o'clock, and our supper at the Eiffel Tower was two hours away.

Izzy whispered in the manager's ear. I only heard one word: *perruques.*

"*Venez avec moi.*"

As I was about to follow them, Izzy slapped his hand to my chest. "You. Stay."

I laughed with my hands to my hips. "Why?"

"Because I said so! Go on." He shooed. "Turn around and don't you dare look back."

I stuffed my hands in my pockets, obeying him. "Don't take too long, okay? I'm starving."

"*À bientôt...*" I heard him say as I walked over to the jewelry section. The staff had their keys in hand, removing the pieces from their cases for me to try on. I wore and loved so many rings, necklaces, and earrings. The staff wrapped them up for me as I browsed more. I looked at my watch and saw it was already eight thirty. I looked over my shoulder when I heard the clicking of heels coming toward me. I turned around. It was Izzy.

"About fucking time. Had fun wig shopping?"

"Yes, sir. Loads of fun."

"How many did you buy?"

"One."

"That's it? I don't think I've ever seen you buy *one* of anything!"

He laughed with me. "First time for everything."

"So, what does it look like?"

He glared at me playfully. "You *are* hungry. You and your silly questions."

"You had me waiting, and you won't even bloody tell me what it looks like?"

"Not only do you ask stupid questions when you're hungry, but you get so bloody whiny!"

"Well...yeah, all right. That's true."

"I guess the party's over. We'll go back to the hotel and get ready for supper."

"Good, or else we'll be here forever!"

"And that would be a bad thing?"

I waited anxiously outside Izzy's suite. I couldn't stop tapping my feet, shaking out my hands, and looking up at the ceiling. The anticipation! I stopped in front of the mirror in the hallway, admiring my new rings and earrings, my pink and white suit and tie, and my dolled-up face, modest with eyeliner, some mascara, and light pink lipstick. I jumped, facing Izzy's door.

My eyes lit up only for the excitement to crash in a heartbeat.

"What's with the frown, sad clown?" he snorted. "Were you expecting somebody else?"

I shook my head and smiled.

"What do you think, Johnny Angel?" He twirled, showing off his ensemble. He stopped, sounding concerned as he asked, "Am I underdressed? Overdressed?"

"You look…" I eyed him from head to toe. "Oh, what does it matter? You're Izzy Rich."

"Yeah, yeah, I know, but it's the Eiffel Tower. You've dined there before. I haven't."

"You're beautiful as always, Izzy. You can never do wrong."

When Izzy wore shades over his eyes, I did, too. His bodyguards went in the elevator with us down to the lobby. Tidal waves of flashing lights went off when we left the building. I looked down to avoid them while Izzy stopped for a few seconds to wave and blow kisses at the fans as the feisty paparazzi were begging for his attention. When we were inside the limo, Izzy and I removed our shades at the same time, chatting until we made it to our destination. The first floor of the Eiffel Tower was like home again, except it was only Izzy and me. The mellow moonlight entered from all directions through the glass walls. That and the ethereal gold lighting made the setting more spectacular. Looking up, down, or side to side, the entire city was illuminated around us, the stars in the sapphire night sparkling as bright.

"What a view!" Izzy marveled, sitting across from me. "Looks like champagne diamonds in a sea of darkness outside. Gorgeous. Now I see what I've been missing out on." He looked at me.

I smiled. "I hope it's everything that you've ever imagined."

"I never imagined that I'd be up here. If I did, this would be it."

I looked over the menu as he looked at his. "Know what to order yet?"

"I don't understand half of what's on here."

"What are you in the mood for?"

"What's your favorite?"

"The venison stew is to die for. It's rich and filling."

"I'll have that, then."

When the waiter arrived, I ordered the venison stew for Izzy, and the *coq au vin* for me. After he left, Izzy and I chatted, until he squirmed in his seat. "I need a wee pee break."

"I'll alert the bloody media," I said as he left his seat.

Minutes after Izzy left, the wine was served. I sipped my merlot, savoring its decadent earthy and fruity tones as I looked out the window, admiring the City of Lights. The jazz music playing complemented its splendor. The more I watched and listened, the more I had a nagging feeling that Izzy was taking far too long. I sipped more wine and stopped mid-swallow. A woman came toward me, and boy, wasn't she a beauty.

Long, thick, luminous dark brown hair framed her face, and her side bangs gave her character. Even her walk declared she was something special. Her denim pants and dark green blouse hugged her big, round breasts, cinched waist, and round ass. That face froze my gaze. It wasn't my imagination. The entire world stopped because of her, at least in my reality. Her thin, round granny glasses were totally geeky. I loved that.

When she appeared before me, I could've sworn she saw my immediate crush. I rose from my seat slowly. It almost broke my heart to break the news.

"Mademoiselle, I'm afraid that you aren't supposed to be here at this hour. It's a private supper."

"Oh? My apologies, Mr. Maxwell," she said.

That voice. It was *not* a stranger.

"Holy shit!" I blurted, covering my mouth to hide my trembling lips.

"I'm such a dummy." She shielded her eyes bashfully.

"Wait!"

She looked over her shoulder.

"Your name, mademoiselle?"

She turned around, smiling. "Holly."

"Please..." I pulled back the chair. "Join me. I've been expecting you all day."

"What about your guest?" she asked.

"*You* are my guest." I took her hand and pecked it.

Holly blushed. "Are you sure that he or she won't mind?"

"I have a feeling that my friend won't be back for supper. Besides," I looked into her eyes, "a man would be a dummy to turn away a stunning jewel like you, *belle mademoiselle*."

Holly giggled, snorting awkwardly. Fucking adorable. I kissed her hand again.

"You sure know how to make a girl blush, don't cha, Mr. Maxwell?" she said as she sat.

"And you must stop traffic the same way you practically stopped my heart."

She bit her lower lip, looking so shy. I studied her face. Her foundation was light and her contouring flawless. The soft black eye shadow, sleek cat-eye styling, arched brows, and carefully dotted beauty mole on her right cheek summoned the glow of her skin, as wonderful as her toothy, red-lipped smile.

"God, look at me. I'm foolishly staring at you. Where are my manners?" She chuckled as I took her hand. "I'm sorry, love. You're a vision of beauty, Holly. Truly you are."

She tickled my dimpled chin with her finger, sticking out her tongue a little. "*Merci*, handsome."

I blushed and looked down coyly. When I looked up, the waiters arrived with our food. My nervousness almost got the best of me when I had the swift realization that they could suss out who Holly really was. I was about to say something, but said nothing. No questions were asked.

I raised my brow, sitting back in my chair.

"Is everything all right?" she said softly.

"Everything's perfect." I held up my glass. "*Bon appétit, cherie.*" We toasted.

I couldn't help but watch Holly eat her first bite of the stew. Her eyes lit up.

"I knew you'd like it."

She ate another spoonful. "Mmm! This stew is rich and tender."

"Like you?" I snickered, taking a bite into my *coq au vin*.

"Tender, yes, but rich, eh." She shrugged. "I wish."

"What do you do for a living?" I sipped my wine.

"Oh, you'll probably scoff. Everyone else does. I'm a songwriter. And I sing."

I beamed. "How lovely."

"You don't think it's a useless profession?"

"The world can't ever have enough songs and singers."

"I'm a stubborn one, though. I have more songs than I know what to do with." She dabbed her mouth with a napkin. "Being an army brat as a kid, living here, there, everywhere—Australia, America, Canada, Asia—I had a lot to sing about. I've seen and done so much. And here I am, babbling. What about you, Mr. Maxwell?"

"Please, love. Call me Johnny."

Seductively, she asked me "Where are you from?"

"Can't you tell by my accent?"

"You're from…Australia?"

My mouth dropped. "Oh, dear, I'm downright offended!"

She giggled and sipped some wine. "I'm busting your chops. You're British."

I nodded proudly. "And you're…um, I'm afraid I can't tell from your voice, darling."

"I'm a hodgepodge of all sorts of accents and places."

"No wonder you're special."

She bit her lower lip. "So, what's it that you do?"

"I'm in the same useless profession as you are."

"You sing?"

"Heavens, no! I'm a drummer. I work for Izzy Rich."

"That's an odd name."

"Never heard of him?"

"Nope!"

I snorted, trying to keep a straight face. "You're alone, my dear. Everyone knows him."

"He's that big a deal?"

"I'd say. He's the hottest glam rock superstar in the world."

She shrugged. "I'm not a fan of rock and roll."

I shook my head and tsked. "You're lucky that you're cute." I winked. "I can't trust anyone who doesn't love rock and roll."

"I'm more of a fan of folk music. I'd say my songs are that."

"Recorded anything?"

"No label wants me." She pouted. "It's a dog-eat-dog world."

"No kidding. It took Izzy a long time to land a major record label." I blinked and shook my head. "Enough about him. What else is holding you back from sharing your music to the world?"

"On top of my stubbornness is my obsession with books. My head's too much in them."

I asked what she liked to read, and I could've sworn that we practically had the same brain as we glowed about Oscar Wilde, Arthur Rimbaud, Victor Hugo, Charles Dickens, Rudyard Kipling, Mary Shelley, the Brontës, Jane Austen, James Baldwin, Langston Hughes, and Henry Fielding. I ordered us *crème brûlée*. We spoon fed each other, and it tasted like the heaven in Holly's laughter and personality.

When the waiters removed our plates, "Body and Soul" played.

"That's one of my favorite songs," we said at the same time.

I took her hand. "*Danse avec moi, mademoiselle?*"

"I don't know what you said, but it sounds romantic."

"Say *oui*."

Even such a simple word was music through Holly's lips. I squeezed her hand, and she squeezed mine back as I took her to the center of the restaurant.

"I have a confession to make, though," Holly whispered.

"What's that, my dear?" I whispered back, putting my hand around her waist.

"I can't dance."

I tried not to laugh. "I'm sure you'll be a natural."

She rested her head on my shoulder as I took the lead and we slow danced. She wasn't kidding. She was stiff, but I thought it charming. When the band played some upbeat jazz music, we returned to our table. We played footsies, the way I hadn't done since I was sixteen. We talked more about art and music until the lights of the Eiffel Tower flickered wildly.

She stroked my dimple. "Why the long face, good-looking?"

"Our time here is up. I'm going to miss you."

"Am I going somewhere?"

"I hope not."

"Johnny, we're in *Paris*. Let's bask in the moonlight, at the Parc du Champ!"

I nearly choked on my wine as I drank the last drop. "Absolutely not!"

"Why not?"

"It's not a wise thing to do."

"C'mon. Let's live dangerously." She left her seat. "Please, pretty please?"

"But we'd have to bring them." I looked at Izzy's bodyguards.

She stuck her tongue out at them, then looked at me. "Let's ditch them."

I stood, facing her, whispering into her ear. "You're crazy. You know that?" She gave me the saddest puppy dog eyes I ever did see. "That face." I pinched her cheek. "Damn. Who could say no to you?"

"Not you." She winked. "Now it's your turn. Say *oui*."

"Fine. You win, princess."

As excited as she was, I was a ball of nerves. Until I looked around. I couldn't believe it. Nobody noticed. Nobody cared. Nobody knew.

"You see? Paris is harmless. Paris makes me want to sing!" She jumped. "And dance!"

"Don't you dare!" I wrapped my arms around her fast when it looked as if she were about to do that.

She wiggled her tush. "Why not?"

"You can't dance, remember?"

We chuckled. I let her go. She faced me. I wasn't shocked that she laced our fingers together as one hand. I was surprised that with many people around us, she didn't break us apart. She and I walked hand in hand from the Eiffel Tower to the Parc du Champ, our laughter, chatter, smiling, and flirting endless. Time, like the people of Paris, was drifting away, leaving us be. And together, we were free.

The hotel still swarmed with fans and paparazzi. Never had I ever felt so nervous to see them. I wasn't sure what to do or say when I looked at Holly.

Holly let go of my hand.

"What the bloody hell are you doing?" I tried not to shout, but I wanted to when she walked ahead. I caught up with her and grabbed her wrist in time before she even dared to cross the street. "Holly, I'm serious. Do *not* go there alone."

She looked to her right and her left. "Catch me if you can!"

I didn't even blink, and she was off and away. "Dammit!" I growled. I looked both ways, running across the street when the coast was clear. My jaw dropped. Holly was waiting for me beside the entrance in front of everyone. Not a single person knew! When I made it to her, I kept it cool. I held her hand, squeezing it. This time, not letting go.

She squeezed my hand as someone shouted, "Hey, are you Izzy Rich's assistant?"

"Who?" Holly batted her lashes. "Moi?"

"Not you. Him. You, sir." The man pointed at me.

"I'm Izzy's drummer."

Nobody took my picture, and clearly, nobody cared. "Do you know if Izzy will be stepping out again?" someone asked.

"Most likely not," I said loudly. "He's—"

A few people chuckled. I wondered why. I looked at Holly, trying to keep a straight face. She stuck out her tongue, crossed her eyes, and used her middle finger to push back her nose, making a piggy face at the paparazzi. They looked at her with appalled glares instead of cameras.

She stopped and behaved as I said to everyone, "Izzy needs his beauty sleep. Sorry."

We turned our backs to them, hearing sighs of disappointment as I opened the door for her. I looked around, in awe. Nobody in the hotel knew either. Even in the elevator, nobody did a double take. With Holly's hand still in mine, I could feel butterflies dancing not only in my belly, but down my spine as we exited the elevator and walked down the hallway toward my suite. When we made it, I let go of Holly's hand.

"Aren't you going to let me in?"

"My room?" I asked bashfully.

"If you don't mind…"

I gulped thickly. "Not at all."

My heart raced as Holly caressed my hair and cheek. She was about to do that to my chin as well, until Tim stepped out of his room. My heart was beating so fast that if it beat any quicker, I'd have a heart attack. Even though Holly was across from me, I could practically hear hers, too. Tim waved at me. Holly waved at him daintily but only for a second. She turned her head to the side, facing her back to him.

Tim checked out her ass. He looked at me and mouthed, "Damn. You always get the hot ones."

Pearls of sweat formed on my forehead as I smiled nervously and mouthed back, "I know."

"See ya tomorrow morning at rehearsals," Tim said, waving good night.

"Bright and early…"

Not moving, breathing very slowly, I stayed where I was. Holly and I were still apart as Tim walked by us, headed for the elevator. As soon as he was gone, Holly hurried toward me.

She held my hands as hers shook like a leaf. "Bloody hell, not even *he* sussed me out!"

I raised my brow. That wasn't her voice. It was Izzy's.

Holly cleared her throat, speaking in her voice. "Who was that guy?" she asked, sounding dumb.

"One of my band mates," I said as I removed my key from my pocket, opening the door.

Holly looked up at the chandeliers. "You weren't kidding. Izzy *is* a big deal. This room is proof of that!"

"He makes so much possible." I looked down coyly, then at her again. "Holly…" I fondled her cheek. "Tonight was the loveliest surprise I ever got in my life by far. Thank you, darling."

When she closed her eyes her smile became so enchanted, I wondered where was she going to?

She opened her eyes. "I have one more surprise for you. Close your eyes."

I obeyed, hearing myself breathe. She walked away from me, was silent for a moment, then came back. Holly kissed me, our lips together in harmony, linked like a major to a minor key, as if that was destiny. Holly tasted my temperature, breathing through my mouth, her tongue teasing mine as mine was hers. Our tongues explored, meshed together, crying for so much tenderness that I had broken the kiss faster than I meant to. I panted and gulped, touching my lips as if they'd been bitten instead of kissed. Holly stood panting, too. Her glasses sat on the table. Her lipstick was rubbed off, her lips a light red hue instead of dark. Instead of pinching myself, I licked my lips. She really actually *kissed* me! I tasted only Holly.

I breathed slowly, staring at those lips. That face, those eyes. I saw more than a woman. I saw—

I cupped Holly's face as I crashed my lips to hers. Her moan was so high that it didn't touch heaven, it *was* heaven. I wrapped my arms around Holly, and she whimpered my name helplessly when I squeezed her plump bottom through the denim, squeezing the small of her smooth, supple back. My knees weakened when she stroked the back of my neck. Moaning louder, I cradled her face in my hands, kissing her deeper, reborn by one kiss. What I thought I'd never have was real, and it was mine. Even if it was, at the end of the night, an illusion. I didn't bloody care. Fuck all.

All I cared about was Holly. And *she* was mine.

CHAPTER FIVE

The reflection of my goofy smile in the bathroom mirror brought me back to Holly. I never knew I could feel like this still. Sixteen. All I dreamt about was our kiss. I rubbed my sore chin. The dimple was dark pink from her licking and sucking on it so much, but that was nothing. I had a massive hickey on the side of my neck, fresh and warm. I blushed at the memory of the hungry, vacuum-like suction of her sucking, her nibbling. The hickey was more than what it was. It was a stamp, the truth. Our kiss was real.

Unlike Holly herself.

When she left, I could've, I should've cried. But all I could do was smile, even in my sleep. Dreaming about her. How could I not? I wanted more, needed her more. I missed her hand in mine. Holding on to each other tightly, finding it hard to let go because Holly was *my* woman, fearless and free. And I was her man, brave and optimistic.

I smacked my own head. "Holly isn't real!"

I leaned toward the mirror, patting my hickey, thinking about the time. I stepped out of the bathroom, looking at the clock on the bedroom dresser. It was seven in the morning.

"Fuck! I got to conceal this quick before—"

Knock, knock, knock. Silence. *Knock, knock, knock.*

"Bloody hell. As always, perfect timing."

Izzy knocked on the door again. Louder.

"Coming, Iz!" I shouted, running to the front door.

When I opened it, he rushed right in, closing the door. "Oh, c'mon. Still in your pajamas?"

"I was going to get dressed until you knocked."

"What the bloody hell have you been doing, anyway? Wanking?"

"I was distracted. Thinking about someone."

He smiled naughtily. "Oh really?"

"Iz, last night was very interesting. Wonderful, even. I wasn't expecting any of it. Thank you. And, by the way, you looked amazing in denim."

Izzy blinked with a conniving laugh. "Are you stoned already? *Me* in denim?"

My mouth dropped a little but I closed it, smirking.

"When have you *ever* seen me wear jeans, Johnny?"

"Well, never. Until yesterday."

He snorted. "Wow. Whatever it's that you smoked this morning, I don't bloody want it."

"Okay, Izzy, *enough*. We're done roleplaying."

He raised his brow. "You *are* stoned."

I rolled my eyes and groaned. "Never mind, Iz. Forget it."

"This bitch. What made her so special?"

I smiled warmly. "She was *beautiful*. As are many women, but she was extraordinary."

"Got her name?"

"Her name is, I mean, *was* Holly." I looked down, then at Izzy. "She was something."

"Why are you talking about her in the past tense?" he asked, sounding clueless.

I sighed, not out of dreaming but mourning. "Last night was a one-night affair. She's not coming back."

"A one-night stand, you mean?"

"We didn't have sex. We only kissed."

"Didn't get naked, at least?"

"We were clothed the whole time."

"Were you all right? Was she all right?"

"We were more than all right. We kissed for *hours*. It was so bloody sexy, as fantastic as fucking. The only time we took a break was when she sucked on my chin and neck."

"Ah, that explains that ridiculous hickey there."

I blushed. "I know. It's a shiner."

"A blind man could see this thing. Your chin's a little red, too."

"And sore, but—" I beamed. "Iz. She was my dream." He faced me closer, touching my hickey as I said, "Holly was unforgettable in every way."

He pouted. "Aw. It's too bad that I couldn't meet her."

"Yeah," I said dryly. "What a shame."

"She must've been one phenomenal kisser." He pinched my hickey. "To create this thing."

"Oh, she—" I paused, struck with one sinister idea to throw Izzy off. "Honestly, Iz—" I shrugged and scoffed. "She was just all right."

The look on Izzy's face was priceless. He raised his brow. "Just all right?"

"Yup."

"That's it?" he asked, sounding baffled. "Seriously? Just all right?"

"Why are you so bloody offended? It wasn't as if *you* kissed me."

Izzy blinked. "I know, but I'm not understanding how if somebody is 'unforgettable in every way' you could sum up their kiss as just all right. I'd think she'd be one of the best kissers you ever had, if not *the* best." He cocked his chin up, seeming anxious to hear my answer.

Licking my lips, I was reminded again of Holly, of how she *was* unforgettable. "The truth is that she is..." I gulped, "I mean, *was* the best kisser I've ever had, Iz."

Izzy's eyes lit up. "Well, obviously. So, why isn't she coming back?"

I was going to say, "You tell me." But I couldn't. "A girl like that only comes once in a lifetime," I said. "That's why."

Izzy stood there, speechless. I waited for him to say something. He had nothing.

"I need a quickie shower. Can you do me a favor and put a spoon in the freezer for this hickey?"

"Sure."

I was about to go back to the bedroom, but I stopped when Izzy said, "I'm sorry, Johnny."

I turned around. "About what?"

"Sorry that she's gone."

I shrugged as he got the spoon from the kitchen. "There will be plenty of others. None like her, though. She and I will always have the Eiffel Tower, I guess."

Izzy closed the freezer. "At least that's something, right?"

"Better than nothing." I watched him go back to the living room, cross his legs on the couch, and turn on the TV. "So, what were you doing last night while I was out with her?" I asked.

Izzy raised the volume. "What did you say?" he shouted above the *Tom and Jerry* cartoon.

I looked down with a stifled laugh, shaking my head and saying nothing. I quickly showered, shaved, and got dressed for the rehearsal and sound check. I used the frozen spoon to lower the temperature of my hickey, its dark reddish blue hue slowly, softly dimming. With added flesh-tone makeup, it was hardly noticeable. Right in the nick of time. We rushed to Le Trianon. The nonstop hustle from rehearsals to the show distracted me from Holly until the concert was over. When I returned to my suite, after I showered and got dressed in a new frock, I stood in front of the mirror staring at a piece of heaven. And a peace from hell. The hickey. It had nothing to hide, now that it was free.

"God. I miss her," I murmured at my reflection. Holly was inside me. Under my skin. In my brain. In my heart. I could taste her kiss, her breath, feel her kissing and breathing through me.

I smacked my head again, harder, and then hurried for Izzy's after-party.

I collapsed on the bed, looking up at the ceiling, my body oh so bloody sore. As always, the ache was a pleasure. The after-party was as hedonistic as the thousands of other after-parties I'd gone to. Izzy wasn't there, of course. I was about to close my eyes for a second. A timid *knock, knock* disturbed me. I sat up, stretching my arms after I got off the bed.

I walked around and over many packed suitcases to get to the door. When I opened it, I jumped as if I was seeing a ghost. Was I hallucinating? Impossible. The drugs wore off hours ago. I blinked at the sight of the denim pants, the brown leather belt, the denim jacket, and a white and orange striped T-shirt. "Johnny?" she chirped. "Woo-hoo!" She waved her hand in front of me.

I blinked, realizing I had been hypnotized. "H-holly. Y-you came back."

She smiled bashfully, batting her lashes. "May I come in?"

I opened the door wider to let her in. With a wink she entered with a swish. When I closed the door, I pressed my back to it, looking her over, gulping lightly, at a loss for thought and words.

"Are you okay?" Holly asked softly. "Did I come at a wrong time?"

I stepped away from the door, approaching her slowly. "Holly—" I stopped, crossing my arms and glaring at her. "Frankly, my dear, I don't like playing games."

"Who's playing games?" Holly said, sounding hurt by my no-nonsense tone. "That's not me either."

"What's going on, *Izzy*?" I was waiting for an answer. "Well?" I asked with more conviction, uncrossing my arms.

"Johnny. Why are you calling me Izzy?"

I grimaced. "I bloody know, I want to fucking know!" I shouted. "Why are *you* here?"

"Are you drunk?" she asked, sounding seriously concerned for my health.

"*Yes*." I strode toward her fast, tearing up. "Over you, over last night." I touched her shoulders, holding them tightly as I said to her, "All bloody day, girl, I tried to get over you, to forget you, but dammit! Holly—" My lips trembled. "I can't get you out of my fucking mind."

Holly's face softened, and she gulped when I let her go. She held my hands as she pressed her lips against my knuckles, brushing them lightly and looking deeply into my eyes. "I couldn't leave you, Johnny," she murmured. "I don't want to leave you. I can't. I won't."

I kissed her, tears rolling down my cheeks. Our tongues pounced, our moans swallowed each other. I pressed my palms to her cheeks and the passion of our kiss brought us to our knees. Holly broke our kiss with a gasp. I stood up, I swooped her in my arms and cradled her, grinning as she laughed. Holly wiped the tears from my cheeks as I stared at her dreamily. She giggled as she tickled my hickey and my chin.

"See the damage you did?" I chuckled with her. "I tried to hide it, and *everyone* still noticed."

The naughty minx stuck her tongue out, smiling. "I had to leave my mark on you."

I kissed her forehead. "And now, it's *my* turn!"

As I carried her to the bedroom, I moaned. Holly sucked my ear the entire journey, making me melt. She thrust her tongue in my earlobe, her arms behind my head. When I laid her on the bed, my body was jelly, but my cock was hard. She wrapped her legs around me as I kissed her madly, on top of her, touching her body all over as we moaned. When I needed to breathe, I brushed my lips over her chin. Holly rolled on her stomach with a coy smile, pushing her tush upward and spreading her legs.

I bit my lower lip, stroking that plump ass through her jeans. "Naughty girl."

She winked. "You don't know me. I'm a good girl."

"Good girl my arse." I spanked her.

Holly yelped. "Ooh! May I have another, sir?"

I was struck by her submission, her want, her need. It was me.

"Please, daddy."

My cock twitched. She was mine.

"I want you. I need you. I adore you."

And I was hers.

"I want you, I need you, I adore you," she repeated, as I ordered her to do every time I spanked her bum. I gave her so many spanks, I wasn't counting. She wailed the words weakly, passionately.

"Had enough, baby girl?" I slapped my palm on her ass again.

She moaned and looked over her shoulder as she adjusted her glasses. Mascara tears dripped down her cheeks. "Daddy, I want more," she whimpered. "Of you. I...I love you."

The three words were more than a song. It was a symphony. I removed her belt. "You love me? We only met yesterday."

She bit her lower lip. "Isn't life so funny? It's like I have known you for years."

"You know what else is funny?" I tossed her belt aside, removing her sneakers.

"What?" she asked, sounding so adorable and innocent as I tugged her jeans down.

"I always knew love at first sight was bollocks. Until I met you."

She blushed as I pulled her jeans lower. Oh, those bubble cheeks! They jiggled naturally through her sheer pink panties with her subtlest movement. I looked up at her, kissing each round and thick rump cheek, rolling her panties down, exposing her bottom. Her fair skin was warm, a blushing, light tulip pink. Her balls were hidden in her sockets, and her cock was taped back toward her asshole. I caressed her there, exploring her impressive tuck and then slowly, carefully removing the tape from her hairless skin.

She sighed when her balls escaped, and her cock was free for me to kiss. She whipped her head back in an explosive moan when I wedged my nose between her ass cheeks, spreading them and licking her crack. She silenced herself with a pillow as I penetrated her asshole with my tongue. She arched her back, groaning as I pushed and wiggled deeper. She backed her ass into me, my nails digging into her skin as she wailed, riding my tongue. I smacked her ass, spreading her cheeks wider, sucking harder on such a sweet, clean asshole.

Holly squirmed and moaned until she made herself breathless. Her hole was thickly wet with my saliva when I stopped for air. Holly's glasses fell off when she looked over her shoulder at me. I blew her a kiss, sliding my forefinger into her tiny hole. We both gasped. She was so tight, so hot, throbbing around me. Her warmth coursed around my finger as I pushed it in until my knuckle reached her rim. Holly moaned my name as I explored the depths of her with a circular motion. Her hole was a sweetheart, opening for me. I licked the opening as I explored her prostate. I tickled and rubbed that nub.

Her cock hardened. She was dripping as I licked, pumped my finger, and teased her P-spot in unison. From her balls to her shaft and cockhead, I licked in firm, loving strokes, tasting her nectar. She moaned louder, expressing her need, wanting and adoring me more. My lips quivered when I pulled my finger out gently, licking her tiny gap and the crack of her ass. I kissed and licked her ear. She squeaked, she moaned.

When I heard her desperately whimper, "Make love to me, daddy," I didn't have to disbelieve. Not anymore. She rolled on her back, and we were face-to-face. Her eyes spoke more volumes than any words. I kissed her ear and licked it. She melted as she reached for my zipper. She unzipped me faster than I could blink, making me gasp and smile.

"I want you more than anything."

"Take me, baby," I panted.

Together, we pulled my pants down and tossed them across the room. I sat on my knees, not expecting my darling to have her mouth on my cock, sucking so hard and bobbing so fast, only stopping because her lips reached the base of it. I moaned and writhed, my cock pulsating. Looking down at her, she looked up at me, my cock in her mouth, her tongue dancing along my length. I groaned when her mouth sucked and pulled, letting me go for something new to begin.

I wrapped my hand around my throbbing cock and sighed in awe. Holly removed her pants. I touched her wrist when she was about to roll down her knickers. I only gave her a look, and she knew. I pulled her panties to the side, shaking my cock. My arms behind my back, my hands to the bed, I spread my legs. She straddled me, her ass above my cock and her chest pressed against mine, our noses touching. Our lips trembled, our tongues touched, we gasped at the same time when she sat down on my cockhead and it popped into her asshole. I kissed her ardently, my arms tight around her. I clawed the back of her T-shirt with trembling fingers as I felt my cock sinking deeper into her.

She slowly bobbed her ass until her cheeks met my pubic hair. We moaned, we groaned, she combed my hair with her fingers as she bounced on my length and girth. I swiveled my hips and thrust into her. Her little hole tightened around me, and then loosened. I sucked her tongue so hard she couldn't groan. I quickened my hip thrusts, my balls thudding loudly and our warm, moist skin slapping. I let go of her tongue and dug my fingers into her ass cheeks as I hammered her widened depths. She wrapped her legs around my waist. I held her tighter, feeling her legs shake as we rode each other, my cock so deep in her ass that it hurt.

"*I love you*, Johnny!" she wailed.

My voice ached as I cried, "I love you more!"

I wanted to come. I needed to come. But I adored Holly too much to let go too soon.

My thrusting slowed as did hers. Our lips locked was blessed eternity. Our long, glorious lovemaking was everlasting. Like yesterday. Except better, now that tonight was here.

❖

From Paris, the *Iz Ze Rich?* tour blazed through Germany to Munich, Hamburg, Berlin, Düsseldorf, Frankfurt, and Ludwigshafen. From there was Helsinki, Finland; Stockholm and Gothenburg, Sweden; Oslo, Norway; Copenhagen, Denmark; Brussels, Belgium; and Rotterdam, Netherlands. So many countries, cities, and concerts, and every night, after every show, Holly and I went sightseeing and returned to the hotel to make love. Oh, so much love to make, never such a thing as too much. After, we'd snuggle in bed or on the couch, splurging on sweets while binge-watching 1920s Hollywood movies, having a blast until the dawn.

And then I'd wake up the next morning. Alone. Until the night, which was ours again.

The next stop of the tour was Zaragoza, Spain. We went straight to the Estadio La Romareda to rehearse a few tweaks Izzy had made in the set list, and then we performed "Dirty Dancer" on a few radio and TV programmes. When we finally got a moment's rest, I showered and ordered room service, admiring the gorgeous panoramic view of the Zaragoza province as I ate. Afterward, I had enough time to bask in the hot tub. As I was about to get changed into my trunks, I heard Izzy's knock.

When Izzy walked in, he was sporting a tank top, trunks, and rhinestone-studded shades.

"What a funny coincidence," I told him when he said he wanted us to relax at the hot tub.

"And later tonight, are you up for a new adventure?" he asked.

"With who?"

"Me! Who else?"

I ignored his question. "Where's this new adventure?"

"In Madrid. There's this recording studio that I've wanted to visit."

"Plotting a new album already?" I said, excitedly.

"Sorry to burst your bubble, but no. I'm thinking way ahead of time. For the future."

"What time are we and the gang going?"

"It's only you, Johnny. I asked them already. They're too tired."

I chuckled. "Lazy motherfuckers."

"Hey, they aren't young spring chicken like you, Baby John."

"The geezers," I joked. "What time are we going?"

"Midnight."

"I can't wait."

"Then *hurry* and get your ass in a pair of trunks already!"

"Okay, captain!" I laughed, turning around. I jumped when Izzy spanked my ass.

I turned around and spanked his ass back. For a split second, I thought I heard Holly in his yelp.

The recording studio was worth the hour-and-fifteen-minute ride from Zaragoza to Madrid. Located in the Centro district of the city, it had the essence of home. Inside, there were couches, retro furniture, and colorful murals, like our suites, except it had consoles, recorders, microphones, monitors, speakers, keyboards, and a drum set.

"What do you think so far?" Izzy asked, standing at the center of the studio.

"It's gorgeous, like Spain itself."

He pointed at the stairs. "Let's check out the attic. I'll meet you up there. I need to powder my nose."

"Save some for me?" I said with a wink.

"Of course." He winked back.

I turned my back to him and went upstairs to a dimly lit lounging space with more vintage furniture, Spanish paintings, and a bar overlooking a most splendid view of Madrid. I admired it for a bit and then sat on the couch and waited for Izzy.

I looked up and around, hearing music. Downstairs, a romantic guitar played a simple, charming melody. I followed the beautiful sound, creeping down stairs. I smiled at the most transcendent, soulful voice singing:

"If love can write its own love song, it would be a ballad—a ballad of me and you, babe."

My jaw dropped, and my heart skipped a beat. Holly stood in the center of the room, her hair tied in a bouncy ponytail, her side bangs thick and long. She wore a long-sleeved plaid white and pink shirt and a denim suspenders skirt, the straps lined down her breasts. Her nude-toned stockings shined, accentuating the natural glow of her long, gorgeous legs. Her flat no-heeled red shoes matched the color of her lips. As she was singing, strumming on her guitar, I quietly stared at her in awe, the butterflies in my stomach dancing, listening. The song. The lyrics. My eyes grew misty, warmed like my heart. Holly stopped, looking over her shoulder when she must've heard me sniffle.

"Daddy!" she squealed, lifting the guitar over her head and placing it on the couch.

Too moved to speak, I grinned, opening my arms to her. She ran and jumped into them so fast, she knocked the wind out of me, wrapping her legs around me so tight that I couldn't have dropped her. My hands to her ass, I held her up higher.

"Surprise!"

"Yes, it is!" I chuckled. "You don't show up at this time, darling."

She pecked my cheeks, my forehead, and lastly, my lips. I rocked her side to side, as our snogging was the substitute to making love. When our lips parted, she stood on her feet.

"What was my baby love singing?" I said as I stroked her back.

"A song for you. For us. It's a new one I wrote. 'The Ballad of Johnny and Holly.'"

"May I hear it from the beginning?"

She nodded and gave me a smooch. As she played "The Ballad of Johnny and Holly" on her guitar and sang *a capella*, I cried. I covered my face, sniffling when Holly was finished. I cried on, as if she was still singing.

"Aw, daddy," I heard her say. "I didn't mean to make you cry."

I wiped the tears from my eyes. "Oh, Izzy..." I blinked and cursed myself. "Holly!" I said in a panic, clearing my throat. She smiled. "You and your surprises. You've done so much for me. I feel like I'm not doing enough for you. What can I possibly give to a girl who has everything? Beauty. Brains. A heart that glitters."

"I have everything. In *you*, baby. I'm so in love with you, I had to write this song."

I brushed my lips against her cheek and ear. "It's the sweetest song I've ever heard."

"Perform with me, daddy?" she asked with such hope, a prayer needing the answer.

With the melody of "The Ballad of Johnny and Holly" in my brain, after I kissed her, I went to the drum set, picked up the sticks, and mimicked the harmony in the snares, cymbals, and chimes, adding my unique touch to it. With her voice and my drumming, we had it. Our song was the love child of our heart and our brain. The third and last take was the perfect charm.

After we wrapped our session, I swooped Holly in my arms and we kissed as I carried her upstairs. I deepened our kiss, sitting on the couch. In the heat of our passion, I meant to rub my palm against her hair, but I hit a hard plastic scalp. We both gasped. Opening my eyes in alarm, I saw a tiny glimpse of fox-red tresses peeking from underneath Holly's hair. She looked down and adjusted her wig so quickly that I blinked, and it was back on. Instead of apologizing, I kissed her. We kissed until our lips were sore.

She shivered when I licked her ear and murmured, "Lubricate your cock. Be generous." Her tuck was undone from her overexcitement. Holly moaned as I kissed her neck, sliding my hand up her skirt. I removed the duct tape and tossed it aside. There it was. That monster hard-on, my beauty. I squeezed it through her panties, slowly wanking her as I slipped the straps of her suspenders off her shoulders.

I kissed Holly's chin and watched her remove her shoes and wiggle out of the suspenders. She wore only her stockings and shirt. I stared at her crotch. The center of her knickers was wet. I gulped at her cock twitching. She blew me a kiss and turned her back to me. I looked away as I unbuttoned my shirt, removing my top, shoes, boxers, and pants. As I watched her lubricate, I shuddered to think that this was it. The first time that she'd be inside me.

Her cock naturally bobbed as she swayed toward me.

"That's my girl," I murmured. Her cock was glistening with lube. I rolled myself over on my belly, my heart racing when I felt

Holly's chest against my back. Holly ran her fingers through my hair, sweeping the back of my neck with her lips. I moaned as she nibbled my flesh, sucking my skin into her mouth as her slippery, hard-as-stone cock wedged between my ass cheeks, teasing me. My lips trembled from the wait. I spread my ass cheeks, my fingers deep in my flesh. My asshole tightened when Holly's cockhead circled around it. My hole relaxed as I felt that push, and then this pressure, my love's penetration. Even with all that lube, it was still a stubborn fit. We gasped sharply as she gently tried. After a few pushes, my hole relaxed more, and she popped her cockhead inside me.

I groaned. The rush of pain, as amazing as the stretched-out sensation. Intense, and she was only in by the cockhead. I closed my eyes tight, the pleasure rushing to my brain like the blood to my cock as Holly moaned, pushing into me with a slow, steady thrust.

"Oh my God!" I wailed when I reached to her cock to measure how much was in. She was almost there, every inch of her monster. I groaned harder when Holly rubbed my ass. She grabbed my love handles, pulling me toward her without needing to make that last thrust. I heard her wail, her cock deep inside my hole, throbbing and pulsing with the ache. But it wasn't *her* wail.

It was Izzy's. Deep. Daring. Sensual.

He pulled his cock back, thrust it back in slow. "Oh, Johnny. You feel wonderful." As he pumped his cock, loosening me, he quivered. "Nothing compares to you, baby." That time, it was Holly's voice. High. Shy. Humble.

My ass bucked back, for the pleasure was too overwhelming. The lube eased the pain of that beyond stretched-out feeling, such sweet agony. I groaned helplessly, my breath shaking. I let go, my fingers digging into the sofa as I yowled at Holly's cock pumping, this time less gentle, but still careful. Slow. Not sacrificing the passion, fueling it. My legs shook, as did my hands, lips, and voice as Holly spread my ass cheeks.

Groaning louder, I backed my ass up, pushing it forward and back to the motion of Holly's thrusts. She moaned achingly. The pain was *her* pleasure, not only mine. As I rode her, bobbing slow to accommodate her massive gift, I felt my asshole dilating wider. The faster, the wider. I rode her so fast, her cock slipped out of me with a cork-like pop. With a gasp, she spread my cheeks, I groaned to Holly's tongue inside my gape spitting a thick wad into it. She tapped her cockhead fast against my throbbing hole. She shoved her cock back in, the pleasure and pain elevating. Her balls thudded against my warm skin. I could feel the blushing. The couch was rocking and moving. With tears sliding down my cheeks, I opened my mouth. Holly's tongue went in against mine as she wrapped her hands around my ankles, holding them tightly as she plowed me faster, harder, without me needing to say it.

"May I come inside you, daddy?" she begged.

But it wasn't Holly.

It was Izzy. And hearing that voice made me explode.

He asked again, his voice back to Holly's as I wanked my hot load free. Riding her cock harder, pounding her instead of her pounding me, I grunted as we snogged. Holly hollered when I growled, "Come for me, baby," after I was spent, my cock limp. She slammed her cock into me so hard that we shouted at the same time. Whimpering, she stalled her thrusting. I groaned, panting, my lips trembling. Her come filled my gape. Tiny, wet-sounding thrusts prolonged her pleasure, prolonging mine, as we kissed as if it were for the very first time.

CHAPTER SIX

Holly and I were on the couch downstairs, swaying our heads and sipping merlot. We were listening to "The Ballad of Johnny and Holly." After we set our glasses on the table, we kissed, fighting to suck the wine off each other's tongues.

"Oh, Holly," I said. "When we aren't making love, it's like we are children."

"That's why I want to have children. So I can stay childish forever."

I nodded with a smile.

"Do you want children?" she asked, doe-eyed, sounding eager to know.

"I used to want nothing to do with them until my nephew was born."

"He changed your mind?"

"He sure did. Now, I can see myself having a kid. Maybe two. But only when I'm married."

"Would you want to raise a family even with a man?"

I didn't have to think about it. "He'd have to be my husband. Symbolically, anyway."

"Don't believe in having children out of wedlock?"

"It's not right. I may be the most unholy and less conservative in my family, but children should have a mommy and daddy, or daddies or mommies, who are ridiculously in love."

"I used to not care." Holly swirled the wine in her glass. "But I want things to be right. Perfect." She sipped the rest of her merlot, setting her glass back on the table. "I want to be a wife to a good man. I want to be the mum of three precious children. No! I want four."

"That's a lot of babies."

Izzy's voice somberly said, "I don't want to dream anymore. I want nothing more from life. Only an armful of healthy, pretty babies." He cleared his throat, and Holly was back. "I want the big happy family I never had. When I do marry, I want to stay married."

I held her hand and kissed it. "You'd be one fantastic wife and mother."

"And you'd be a most amazing husband and daddy. You're one of the best lovers I've ever had."

I paused, sipping the last of my wine. "You're the only lover who hasn't fucked me over."

Holly looked at me, only sympathy in her gaze.

"Sorry for the mood kill, baby girl. It's the wine. Want some more, darling?"

"No thank you, daddy. Two glasses are more than—" She looked at the tape deck. Our song had stopped playing. She pouted and scooted off the couch. "I should get going."

I leaned back as I watched her walk over to the cassette player and remove the tape. I stood up, and she gave the tape to me.

"Promise to keep it safe?" she said with a gentle urgency. "Please."

I looked at the cassette, and then at her.

"I don't want anyone to hear or know about this song. It's *our* secret, Johnny."

Our song wasn't the only secret. We were a secret, too. I looked down, wondering how long she and I were going to last. "Our song is safe with me. I promise."

She held my hands, her chest to mine, our lips near. "Good night, daddy." She brushed her lips against mine. "I love you."

"I love you." I closed my eyes, waiting for a kiss. I opened my eyes.

Holly was gone.

The cassette in my hand, I stared at this promise. I went back to the couch to get my jacket, slipping the tape into the pocket. I sat down and polished off the rest of the bottle. When it was empty, I tossed it in the trash, readying to sit back on the couch until I heard a rustling upstairs, that familiar knocking of heels. When I went up, I saw Izzy sitting on the couch, prepping and lining the cocaine on the table with a razor.

"About bloody time you made it! What took you so long?"

"Blame Holly," I said as I sat beside him. "She made a surprise visit."

He carefully rolled a piece of paper as he asked, "How's your ass?"

"What's it to you?"

He looked at me, concern in his gaze. "I'm serious, Johnny. How does it feel?"

By the tone of his voice, I knew he wasn't playing or acting. "Fucked." I bit my lower lip. "Sore," I said as he licked the side of the rolled paper. "It's as if I'm still being buggered. Feels bloody fantastic."

"Holly shagged you the way a good girl should."

I smirked. "How do you know that?" I asked as he snorted his line.

"It reeks of sex in here." He snorted loudly, tapping his nose. He blinked and handed me the paper. "I can almost taste the fuck you gave to her. That's how sweet it is."

I dropped my eyes down, snorting my line. I sighed from the astonishing rush. "We didn't only make love. We also made—" I wrinkled my nose to make it seem like I was distracted by that, and nothing else.

"Made what?"

"Nothing."

Izzy chuckled. I could already tell that he was high. "Bollocks."

"I can't tell you. It's a secret."

He winked, draping his arm over my shoulder and leaning his head against mine. With my arm over his shoulder, we swayed our bodies. Soft and beautifully, Izzy was humming...the song.

For the first time, I skipped the after-show party.

Instead, I packed my bags for our flight back to London tomorrow. After packing, all I did was lie in my bed. Instead of drinking, I was thinking. Of Holly. And Izzy. As I looked at the cassette for what felt like the millionth time, the song's lyrics took over my mind for what felt like the billionth time. Not only the words, but how they were crooned, love's essence. But was it Izzy? Or Holly? Was the song true? Or only part of the game? Did it matter? Did the song mean anything? Or was it only an act like the way we'd been acting all this time? When was the game going to end, how much longer could the act hold? After rubbing my temples, there it was.

Those timid three knocks.

I sat up, quickly slipping the cassette back in the suitcase with my jewelry and furs collection. I ran to the door and opened it to see a most stunning Holly, my heavenly darling in a pair of shiny fuchsia stilettos with a matching-colored vintage-style slip that accentuated her shape from top to bottom, flaunting her nude legs and arms in their statuesque glory. She posed with her back to me as she looked over her shoulder. She flashed her megawatt smile, her wonderful brown eyes oozing sensuality through her nerdy glasses. When she wiggled her tush teasingly at me, I wrapped my arms around her from behind. She moaned when I kissed her shoulder and kicked the door closed.

"Oh my God," she moaned deeper. "My daddy missed me."

I let go of her neck, moaning as I groped her breasts. "Fuck yes."

I turned her around and kissed her ardently, squeezing her bottom. I sucked her tongue hard, and she mewed, running her fingers through my hair. In the heat of her sucking my tongue, bobbing her lips with hunger and desire, I ran my fingers through her hair.

"Shit!" I shouted in anger and embarrassment. I turned my back to her quick in the split-second that I saw Holly's wig on the floor. "Not again," I mumbled to myself. "Sorry, baby."

I heard a laugh. It wasn't Holly's.

It was Izzy's.

I raised my brow, turning around. The wig was still on the floor. I looked at it, then at Izzy, who smiled at me. Who had to think fast first? What to do, what to say to each other? I almost went on bended knee to pick up the wig, but then who would be the one to place it on whose head?

I froze, trembling at the awkward silences. "I ruined the night, Iz." I shook my head. "Holly."

"John…" said Holly's voice. I gulped at how strange it was to hear her voice and see her face without the wig. "I'm tired of playing this game, this make-believe. Aren't you?"

It wasn't Holly speaking. It was Izzy. Serious. Not playing a game. Far from make-believing.

My voice trembled. "It has been a whole lot of fun."

Izzy's eyes glimmered. "More than that. Mind-blowing. Being Holly, being able to walk amongst ordinary people without the fame getting between us. Being able to live."

"I've loved every second of every night that it has lasted."

"And without disturbances and distractions. It's been a wonderful world."

"Especially with Holly in it," I said. "Izzy, I'm in love with Holly."

"Are you in love with *me*, John?" Izzy's lips trembled, and mine did, too. "And not like a brother." The ache in his voice mirrored mine. "Do you *love* me like I love you, Jonathan?"

My jaw dropped. I held back my tears as Izzy removed the glasses from his face, tossing them on top of the wig. My hand over my skip-beating heart, I breathed slowly as he rubbed off his lipstick with the back of his hand, smudging his left cheek. He licked his finger, erasing the beauty mole from his cheek. He kicked off his heels, wiggling out of the slip, exposing his bra. He unlatched it. The fake breasts dropped to the floor, and he flung the bra aside. After he rolled down his little fuchsia panties, he carefully peeled off the tape, unraveling the tuck. His cock and balls were free. He came closer to me, vulnerable and naked. And mine. He stood before me, his brown eyes piercing my heart. I couldn't blink, I froze, watching him looking up at the ceiling, carefully and slowly removing the contact lenses from his eyes. He flicked them off his fingers, blinked and rubbed his eyes once.

He held my hands. "Do you love who you see?"

The tears poured from my eyes as I held his hands tightly. "Damn you, Izzy Rich," I squeaked. "God." I sniffled. "I can't bloody believe this. Bastard. It wasn't Holly that I loved. It was *you*."

We held each other's hands tighter. He brushed his lips against my cheek, murmuring against my skin. "I *love* being your woman, but I want to love you as a man. *Your* man. Your boyfriend."

I bawled. "You have no bloody idea how long I've wanted to hear you say that. And how much bloody longer that I've dreamt of saying these three words to *you*. Izzy Rich, *I love you*."

Izzy cried. "I fell in love with you since the day—"

I cupped his face in my palms, kissing him madly to hush him up. I didn't want to know. All that mattered was *this* kiss. Our kiss, made of *us*. I wanted nothing else of the world. I had him, and he had me. Our love was *one*. I cradled Izzy in my arms as he sucked my bottom lip into his mouth. I cocked my head up, my bottom lip escaping from his grasp. We kissed harder, deeper, louder, heavily, the heat between us rising. Falling on my knees, I held him closer, our kiss heavier. In my kiss, I was what I was all this time: his master, prince, daddy, and lover. In his kiss, Izzy was what he always was to me: my submissive, princess, baby-girl, and my lover.

More than that, Izzy was a man. And *he* was mine.

❖

Straight from the airport, I only had a few hours at home before we'd have to be at the hotel. I had a speedy lunch, phoned a few close friends, and unpacked. I hardly had any time to organize where I wanted things. The one and only possession that mattered was that cassette. In the last moment I had, I stored it with my collection of Izzy's vinyl records, singles, and VHS recordings of concerts and TV appearances. Then I rushed out, with a cabbie waiting for me.

From inside, I saw a throng of fans and paparazzi outside the hotel.

When I got out of the car, one of Izzy's bodyguards guided me to a back entryway. The lobby was so *packed* that I could even hear the commotion from the elevator. At the top floor, the hallway was crowded with Izzy's entourage.

I approached the guys, smiling and waving. "Where's Izzy?" I asked them.

"In his room with the boss man," Larry responded.

We hadn't seen William James in ages.

"That means something's up," Tim said, sounding as excited as how I felt.

"Don't ask Izzy about it," Benson said. "He won't tell me!"

"He must have told you, Baby John," Phil said. Everyone looked at me as if I had the answer.

"I know nothing!"

And that was the truth. Everyone's adrenaline pumped. Even something about the air reeked of it as we all waited. *Everybody* turned their heads the second Izzy opened the door, looking otherworldly in his glittering pink and black suit and tie, fedora, pink feather boa, and pink pumps, his glossy pink lips, gold eye shadow, and heavy mascara an enigmatic perfection. William stood beside him, looking sharp in his suit and tie, his blond hair touching his shoulders. Standing next to William was Izzy's publicist, Cheryl, also in a sharp suit and tie, sporting an afro puff ponytail. Something was happening, and like everybody else, I desperately wanted to know!

I tried to ask Izzy when we were crammed into the elevator.

"No, Johnny. I promised Big Man I wouldn't tell a soul!" Izzy laughed, looking down at him.

"He's kept it a secret this long," William said to me with a chuckle. "Don't encourage him!"

The moment we were at the lobby, Izzy's security surrounded him as we were taken to the conference room. Izzy and William were ushered to a private entry while his entourage and I followed Cheryl's lead.

The room was crowded with reporters, their cameras and microphones ready. We sat at the front row.

The center stage had a table lined with little microphones and two glasses of water, and in the background were the *Iz Ze Rich?* tour posters and the album's glam cover art. The lights dimmed and everyone hushed. Cheryl took the stage, introducing herself as the lead press officer for Trident Studios and for Izzy. She only gave a vague hint that the conference was about Izzy's tour. I sat at the edge of my seat as did the rest of the guys, my mouth sore from grinning. William appeared from the wings. A few cameras went off when he stood before the podium, thanking everyone for making it.

"Today's main event is, obviously, about Izzy. Everything about the man is a spectacular, but *this* is special. Izzy has been waiting two years for this. Finally, it's going to happen for him. For this tour, we've been traveling all over Europe, with still many more European dates. But there's *one* country that Izzy Rich has dreamt of touring, and that place will be the United States of America." The applause was overwhelmingly loud, but nobody's clap and whistle was louder than mine.

"So without further ado, here's the man of the hour to talk more about it, Mr. Izzy Rich."

William sat in his chair as Izzy appeared from the wings. Cameras flashed in a frenzy as he sat down at the table next to William. Cheryl returned to the podium, announcing the question-and-answer period. "But *only* about the tour, ladies and gentlemen," Cheryl said firmly.

"I'm all ears, everyone!" Izzy purred into the microphone. "Please keep in mind, I only have *two* ears, but I'll try and answer as many questions as I can as if I have ten of them, okay?"

Everyone chuckled. Cheryl pointed at a female reporter.

"How do you feel about this exciting news, Izzy?"

"Scared, believe it or not."

"Why is that?"

"Because I never thought I'd ever make it there."

"Why didn't you tour America during *Rich Girl*?"

"William and I didn't expect *Rich Girl* to be the cultural phenomenon it fast became. When it charted in America, we really, really wanted to go there then, but the touring schedule at the time was booked with—" He looked at William. "What's the number again?" he asked him.

"Over one hundred and ninety European shows."

My eyes lit up with Izzy's. "Wow. One loses count after a while. Even *this* tour is booked, but America can't wait anymore. Neither can I."

"Will the set list be any different in America?"

"Come to one of the American shows, and you'll see," he said cheekily with a wink. "I will say this to my entourage out there." He looked at me, then at everyone else. "Expect that lovely twelve-hour-a-day rehearsal that we bloody love so much. It will come back in full force."

I crossed my legs, nodding excitedly.

"What are you anticipating the most for the American leg of the tour?" somebody asked.

"*Everything.*" Izzy smiled naughtily. "America has had more than enough British Invasions. I can only hope they'll welcome a glitter Brit like me as openly as the other rock and rollers."

"How many cities will you be touring at?" another reporter asked.

Izzy raised six fingers, naming Cleveland, Memphis, Boston, Chicago, Seattle, and Los Angeles.

"And at each city, we'll be performing for three nights in relatively intimate venues."

Another reporter asked, "Are tickets already on sale in America?"

"Not anymore. In fifteen minutes, *all* eighteen shows were sold out."

Cameras flashed, following a few standing ovations. After Izzy answered a few more questions, Cheryl announced that rehearsals for the American leg were going to start in a few hours.

The last reporter asked, "Do you see this leg of the tour as life changing?"

"It already is. I'll be sharing my dream with people who are the world to me. That's what dreaming is about, isn't it? Not only for me, but for us. Their lives will change, too, with me."

My heart raced when he looked at me. Only me. He had such warmth in his gaze as Cheryl closed the conference, the cameras flashing wildly for the last time. Izzy stood, bowed, and tipped his fedora, blowing kisses. He blew one at me. Even with a kiss like that, I felt it.

His love.

❖

"Are we there yet?" Izzy asked.

I snickered, looking at him from the corner of my eye. He was blindfolded and strapped in his seat belt. I tried to keep a straight face, fighting hard not to laugh.

"Izzy, we just got out of the bloody driveway!"

"Can't you give me a hint? Please? Pretty please?"

"That would ruin the surprise," I said, keeping my eyes on the road.

"I'll shut up, then."

"*Finally.*"

The five minutes flew by as we were headed nearer to our destination.

"Are we there yet?"

I said nothing.

"Are we there yet?"

I still said nothing as I drove into the lot.

"Are we there yet?"

I parked and wrapped my hands around his neck lightly, giving him a playful growl. "Don't make me choke you."

He opened his mouth in a gasp as I squeezed him, dipping my tongue in his mouth. As I deepened our kiss, I squeezed him a notch harder, and then I let go, tickling his collarbone with my lips. When I stopped to kiss his nose, he stroked my hair.

"Stay where you are."

I got out of the car and ran over to Izzy. I opened the door and unlocked his seat belt, taking his hand as I helped him out the car slowly. Izzy sniffed the air, turning his head to the right and the left. He felt around with his free hand, exploring. "What's the surprise?"

"Will you behave?"

I didn't believe him when he nodded, but I squeezed his hand and whispered, "It's not a song. What can I possibly give to the man who has everything? I have no bloody idea, but I hope you'll love it, baby."

Izzy smiled warmly as I walked us to the door. "Whatever it is, it's very quiet."

"Won't be for long."

Little Richard's "Tutti Frutti" was in the air. Izzy looked up at the ceiling, grinning and bobbing his head. He belted the song out, rolling his shoulders and his neck. I let go of his hand as he shook and shimmied.

"That was great, Iz," I said when the song stopped. "But is that how you behaved back when you could go grocery shopping?"

"Only after I'd steal the fags and liquor." He laughed, then stopped. "Wait. What?"

I untied his blindfold.

"Holy shit!" He jumped, covering his mouth. He looked at me with the most adorable, priceless look of shock. He looked at the store and the shoppers. "How in the bloody hell did you—"

"My friend is the CEO of this grocery store. I know this isn't the best timing for you to shop for groceries, but better now than never again, right?"

"John, I haven't been able to shop in a grocery store like a normal person for..." He counted on his fingers. "*Six* years."

"Then grab a cart and let's get to shopping."

Izzy embraced me. "Thank you, daddy," he whispered in my ear.

I gasped, tapping his shoulder when he was squeezing too hard. "I said grab a cart, not kill me!"

At the same time, we dashed to the carts. Elvis Presley's "Jailhouse Rock" blasted loudly as we pushed the carts like normal, and then we sped forward down the canned food aisle. I jumped my feet on the edge, riding it. Izzy lifted his legs up high in the air, his chest over the cart, gripping the sides with his hands. He sang the song, mimicking Elvis's voice.

"Watch out!" shouted someone in the aisle as Izzy flew toward him.

Izzy stopped his cart. "Rick?" he yowled in surprise and laughter. Rick was dressed as a stocker.

"Wait a bloody minute..." Izzy looked around. The customers, stockers, and cashiers were all his bodyguards and assistants, a few members of his touring management team, his publicists, booking agent, and spokesperson. "You guys!" Everyone laughed with him. Izzy looked at me, pointing at me. "*You!*"

I stuffed my pockets with my hands, smiling bashfully. "This isn't quite the real thing."

He mouthed, "I love you." When he turned around, his cart was missing. "Hey, where did it go?"

I shrugged. "I don't fucking know. Get another one."

As he ran past me, Otis Redding's "Try A Little Tenderness" played overhead. Rick and a few of the other "stockers" helped me gather a bunch of cans, treating them as bowling pins. I hurriedly ran into the fresh produce aisle, grabbed some melons, and dashed back to the aisle.

Izzy had a new cart filled with groceries already. "What are you jokers up to now?" Izzy laughed at the stacked cans.

I rolled the melon to him. "Catch!"

He picked it up, and we laughed giddily as I took my shot and knocked a few down. Izzy got the remaining three.

I whistled and clapped. Izzy turned around, stamping his heels. "Now where's my cart!"

"If you can't keep track of your cart, you shouldn't shop!" I hollered. Everyone laughed.

"All of you are so mean to me! I haven't grocery shopped in six years, and this is what I get?"

"That's not all you're getting," I said. When nobody was looking, I winked at him, my tongue to my cheek. Izzy licked his lips, winking back at me.

As the American pop, soul, and Motown music played, we spent the next two hours singing and dancing, flying plates across the aisle, and playing bumper cars with our carts.

"Damn, Johnny," Izzy said. "You went all out with this. You planned everything down to the music."

"That's not all, captain." I whispered into his ear, "Close your eyes."

He obeyed, grinning, snorting a little. "Something's up, I can feel it," he said as everyone gathered around, shaking up whipped cream canisters and bottles of strawberry and chocolate syrup. Cheryl handed me a camera.

"Open your eyes now!"

Izzy opened his eyes but snapped them shut again as everyone poured the syrups and whipped cream over his head. I snapped pictures of him bawling with laughter and holding his belly.

"You all got me!" he cried.

"It's what you get for all the pranks you did on tour," Cheryl said.

"This was John's idea!" Rick outed me.

I put my hands up. "Guilty."

He glared and pointed at me. "You're gonna get it."

"Bring it on!" I dared. "For now, we got you. And we're so proud of you, Iz."

As we gave him a group hug, all I could do was think about Izzy and me. Nothing in the world mattered. Not six in the morning when our Great American Adventure would finally happen, our British Invasion. All that mattered was our love. And how starting *now*, we'd only just begun.

CHAPTER SEVEN

Looking out the window of the private jet, I almost couldn't believe we made it. At last, we were in America, in Cleveland, Ohio. More unbelievable than that was the sea of young men and women, hundreds of them, wearing feather boas, makeup, sequins, and glitter, holding Izzy's posters, LP covers, and T-shirts, screaming only one name.

I looked at Izzy. He was dressed in a sequined zebra-print pink and black jump suit with batwing sleeves, matching platforms, disco ball earrings, and sparkly eye shadow. His mascara and glittery lips looked as black and sweet as licorice. "Look at *that, Iz*. It's like we never left home!"

He bashfully smiled. The fans were so loud outside the plane, it was difficult to hear anyone speaking. Plus, there was as much mayhem inside as outside. We all scurried for our purses and bags while Izzy's personal camera crew got their handheld cameras ready. With my luggage in hand, I stood nearby Rick. William James, Cheryl, and the cameramen gathered around Izzy in front of me.

"Is everybody ready for this one giant leap?" Izzy shouted triumphantly to everyone and at the cameras that were over his shoulders. "Not just for me, but a giant step for *us*?"

I howled, everyone howled, stamping our feet fast and excitedly to Izzy's frenzied stamping.

He stopped, snapping his fingers rhythmically as he said, "Here we go in three…two…one…"

He pointed at the door, lifting his head up high. When that door opened, the world moved. My body shook not from the fatigue or from the jetlag but with the sensational electricity in the air. The screeching and delirious crying of the fans moved me. They shouted Izzy's name at the top of their lungs. His ensemble, jewelry, and makeup sparkled even brighter in the flashes from hundreds of cameras.

Izzy struck a pose mid-step on the stairs, waving at his American riches. My ears popped as the crowd screeched even louder when Izzy jumped off the last two steps of the stairs. He lifted his arms in the air, spinning slowly. The audience lost it. I never saw anything like this back home. Women held on to each other so they wouldn't faint, and men collapsed on their knees. Izzy raised his arms up higher, ass shimmying, hips jerking, pelvis thrusting.

The fans went bonkers at the words on the wings of the sleeves: *I Love You America, The Beautiful.* I looked in awe at the mayhem, at those mascara-teared faces, at all those signs and banners sending messages of love to Izzy.

The conference room was just as crazy. As if the room wasn't already hot, it was hotter from the filming equipment and cameras. If I was blinded by all those flashing lights, I couldn't even imagine how blinded Izzy was when he stood before the crowd. William James, Izzy's bodyguards, and Cheryl stood by him, near the podium. The audience were noisy even when Cheryl announced Izzy would take some questions but didn't have time for many.

"Welcome to Ohio, Izzy!" said the first reporter. "We're honored to be the first state to have you."

"Thank you, Ohio." Izzy bowed. "I'm enjoying being inside you already. You're so hot." He smiled slyly as everyone chuckled and snapped their cameras. Many reporters fought to be seen, shouting and raising their arms higher.

"What are you looking forward to seeing the most in Cleveland?"

"I don't know where to start. Too much I want to see, but so little time! Damn my busy life."

It was bloody hilarious, seeing these professionally dressed, conservative male reporters with their hair slicked back acting like fangirls, looking ridiculously happy.

"What is it like being the King of Glam?"

Izzy looked confused. "Who's that?"

"*You,* Mr. Rich."

He touched his chest. "Is that what I'm called in the States?"

"Why does that surprise you?"

"Back home, I'm called the Prince of Glam Rock. I'm truly honored. I don't feel worthy enough."

"You have a very impressionable fan base here," said a reporter loudly above the noise. "Bisexuality has been on the rise here because of you, Mr. Rich, more in men than women."

I snickered at that. Even the look on Izzy's face matched my skepticism. "Now I don't have that kind of power. Don't be ridiculous."

"Are you bisexual?"

Cheryl looked as if she were about to say something, but Izzy interrupted. "Yes. I am bisexual."

My jaw nearly dropped.

"I buy a lot of S. E. X."

"Next question please," Cheryl snapped, pointing at another reporter.

"Why do you think you're such a cult figure here?"

"I have no clue," Izzy said, sounding serious. "What I know for sure is that my fans are inspiring, beautifully genderfluid, liberated sexually, and I love them so much for it. They made me who I am, not the other way around."

"Can you sing and perform something for us?"

"Absolutely not, sorry!" he said. "I have to save this voice for the talk shows today. Plus, I can't perform without The Diamonds behind me." Izzy cleared his throat. "Oh dear. Does anyone have a cigarette? I'm gagging for a drag."

I covered my mouth, trying not to laugh. The reporters threw so many smokes at them, Izzy's bodyguards weren't sure what to do at first. Then they began collecting the fags and stuffing them in their pockets for Izzy.

"Does anyone have dollars to spare, too?" Izzy asked, clearly joking. "All I have are pounds. No, no!" He shook his head as bills were waved at him. "I could never. I was a beggar once—" William whispered something in his ear. Izzy looked at the audience. "But not anymore. Thanks to all of you for making me a rich man. Thank you so much, Cleveland. Cheerio!"

Cheryl announced that Izzy had to go. Izzy spread his arms to show off the words on his sleeves, and the reporters whistled and cheered. As he stepped down from the stage, we pushed our way through the crowd to get to him. The moment we were out of that conference room, we were mobbed again by fans, paparazzi, and media. Getting out of the airport was a mad journey of screaming and shouting and more arms and hands trying to touch Izzy. When we could finally see a limo, we ran for it. I tripped on my heels, practically chucking myself inside the car with the band and entourage. Izzy sat next to me, the two of us slamming our backs against the velvet seat, panting and sweating.

"This country's as mad as I am!" Izzy howled. "Bloody hell. What's going on?"

"Bloody understatement of the century," Tim said. The fans surrounded the car, their screaming faces pressed to the windows.

Benson's eyes widened. "Holy shit."

"Fuck." I jumped and looked up when I heard thuds coming from the ceiling. I looked out the window, seeing dangling legs instead of faces. The car couldn't move. We were stuck.

"Americans are out of their fucking mind!" Izzy laughed.

We tried to stop him from rolling the sunroof window back, but we couldn't. Everyone covered their ears. The car felt topsy-turvy, and he had no choice but to sit back down and close the window as fast as possible. "I fucking *love* America!" Izzy shouted. "Woo! This is madness!"

"And this is only day *one*," I said.

Looking out the window still, he pouted. "I want to hug, kiss, and lick them all." He looked at us. "I'm sorry, boys. At this rate, we'll never get to the hotel."

"Will we ever be able to sleep or eat ever again?" Tim laughed.

"Or make love?" I said slyly.

Izzy winked at me. "*Nothing* in the world can stop us from making love!"

Everyone except for Larry shouted, "That's right!"

I knew by the way he looked at me he meant us. My princess. When the limo finally got out of the parking lot and on the road, I finally saw blue skies as clear as the bubbly in our glasses.

Knock, knock, knock. Silence. I knocked three more times, looking to my right and to my left.

Except for Izzy's bodyguards and a few room service people, nobody was around. They minded their own business as I stuffed my hands in my pockets, acting casual as I waited for Izzy to answer the door.

When he opened it, I looked to my left and my right one more time, and I pushed him back inside the suite, slamming the door shut and locking it.

He pounced on me like a bitch in heat, wrapping his legs around my waist as I held him up by his bottom, my fingers clawing the shiny silver vinyl. I crushed my lips against his hotly, our tongues colliding in the sweetest, warmest, lust-and-love filled embrace. He moaned in my mouth as I gripped his ass and slapped him, clawing my free hand along his back.

"Fuck me," he groaned. "*Fuck me*, daddy!" he panted. "I *need* your love. I need *you.*"

I let go of him as I sucked his bottom lip, tugging it and letting it go. The second his bare feet touched the floor, I grabbed the collar of his Delilah Starr mini tank top and yanked his body close to me. My cock hardened through my leather pants when our crotches met. I could feel his cock throbbing against me as I swooped him into our kiss. I let go of his shirt long enough to take it off him. He tore open my blouse so roughly that the buttons popped off. He gasped my name, fondling my naked abs and arms as I stroked his chest.

He yelped loudly when I twisted his nipples with my thumb and forefinger. I spanked his ass and scooped him into my arms again. We were breathless, not giving a bloody fuck for the air. We were our own oxygen, breathing through each other. I kissed him so hard I made my mouth sore. My arms were getting weak, and I let Izzy drop to his knees on the floor. He panted, looking up at me. I bit my lower lip, my hands on my waist and my fingers along my belt. I shivered as he rubbed his cock-sucking lips against my cockhead, planted a firm kiss there, and then up and down every inch of my hard-on.

"You want me bad, don't you, baby bitch?" I said.

"Yes!"

"Your pretty ass needs to be fucked?" I asked him sweetly as I removed my belt.

He nodded his head quickly, whimpering, kissing my hard-on all over.

My cock twitched beneath his lips. "Miss King of Glam, you made America explode today." I unbuttoned my pants slowly as I shivered. "Now it's my turn to explode inside you."

I yanked down my fly. I gasped and grinned as Izzy brushed his tongue against my bush. He crushed his nose against me, sniffing my musk.

I grabbed a palm full of his hair and yanked his head back. "You have to *work* first," I growled. "Now *I'm* king, and you're going to fuck *me* first. Fuck me so hard that you'll forget your name." I pushed his head back and smacked his cheek. He gasped as I barked, "Lube that cock extra, slut, unlike the one time when you were skimping. Made me sore for days, you fucking brat. This time, I won't be nice with your punishment. This time, you'll get what you deserve."

He yelped as I cracked my belt against his knee. Glaring at him, I snapped, "You better take off those pants."

Izzy yanked them off. I licked my lips, my mouth watering at his monster. Deep down, I wanted to fall on my knees before him, but I'd be damned if I'd surrender before him. Izzy groaned. His cock throbbed when I squeezed him. "Take off my pants!"

He removed my platforms and pulled my pants down to my knees. After he tossed them aside, I snapped my fingers and growled. "Hurry up, bitch!"

When he turned around, I cracked the belt against his ass. I laughed at the bright red splotch that blossomed like a rose right before me. He scurried to the suitcase of lube bottles. I dropped the belt on the floor, watching him as I wanked my throbbing cock slowly. He snapped the lube bottle open, about to pour the lube over his cock. But the phone rang. He hurried to answer it, the lube still in his hand.

With closed eyes, I wanked myself a little bit faster, tuning out his conversation. When I opened my eyes, I smiled weakly. How sexy was *that*, seeing Izzy drizzling the lube over his cock as he was speaking on the phone. He looked at me naughtily while stroking his cock. It was glossy and slick, but not ready yet. When I let go of my cock, I made it twitch and bob. Izzy stared at it as he wanked slowly, using his shoulder to press the phone to his ear. He looked up at the ceiling.

"Really?" He laughed with disbelief. "Are you serious?" He looked at me as he said into the phone, "Three thousand fans and one hundred reporters were waiting for me at the airport. Nobody in the crowd got hurt, did they?" Izzy asked, concerned. "Because you know how I don't like hearing that. Makes me feel so bloody guilty."

I slowed my wanking as he said, "Whew, thank God nobody got hurt this time. That's a bloody miracle when you think about it, really, considering how many people were there today."

I closed my eyes again. When I opened them, Izzy hung up. He jumped up and down and ran toward me, embracing me tight. "Oh my God!"

I squeezed him harder. "What's the news, baby?"

"Cheryl told me that the TV ratings from the talk show rounds today were groundbreaking, in the *millions*. She hasn't told me the exact number yet, but I can bet you she knows already."

"Being a bloody tease, as usual."

"She'll get back to me about it soon. She'd better."

I looked at his cock, and then glared at him. "You aren't done, are you?"

Izzy gulped. "No, sir."

"What the bloody hell are you waiting for?" I snapped. "That cock's not going to lube itself."

He tipped the lube bottle sideways.

"Now that's what I call generous." I licked my lips and moaned, nodding approvingly. His cock was dripping with lube. I pinched his cheek, and then I kissed him deeply, my tongue dominating his. The two of us wrapped our hands around his cock, wanking it together, gasping in unison when it throbbed. Our tongues gyrated wildly as we squeezed the monster, making it wild instead of tame. We gasped louder as one.

I cursed when the phone rang again. He let go of his cock, but I didn't. "Go on," I dared him. "Answer the damn phone." I squeezed him with an iron grip, tugging him.

His face contorted with pain and pleasure as he leaned back and reached for the ringing telephone anyway. He answered it, and I squeezed him harder. I looked him in the eyes, smiling evilly at the way he squirmed, trying to make his voice sound normal, but it was slightly high in pitch when he was talking on the phone. His legs were shaky, his cock more eager, ready and mine in my grasp. Izzy bucked slowly and rhythmically into my slick and lubey palms as he listened on the phone. I slapped his cock, harder. He bit his lower lip, grimacing. I turned around, spreading my ass cheeks and showing him my desperate asshole.

"Fuck!"

I looked over my shoulder, about to rub my asshole against the head of his cock.

"Are you serious?" Izzy said, sounding more shocked. He backed away and sat on the couch. I turned around and faced him. He grabbed the remote, turning on the TV.

"The name on everybody's lips today is British glam rock superstar Izzy Rich, who has kicked off his British Invasion today in Cleveland, Ohio, where he'll perform at the Music Hall tomorrow."

Trying not to be put out, I sat next to him. They showed a clip of when we got off the plane. Izzy grinned as he watched and listened to the phone at the same time. When he hung up, he beamed at me, wiggling his tush so excitedly I thought he'd fall off the couch.

"What did Cheryl say?"

"Take a wild guess of how many millions of people watched your boyfriend on TV today."

"Thirty million?"

"Nope."

"Forty million?"

"Not even close."

"Good Lord. How many cared?"

"Seventy-three million people!" We squealed together.

"Now that's trippy. I'm so bloody proud of you!" I kissed his nose. "I love you." I kissed his cheeks and chin. "So much." I kissed his chest, smooching down to his navel. He moaned when I sucked his belly button, circling my tongue around it. "I'm so lucky." I brushed my lips to his pubic hair, wrapping my hand around his cock and wanking it. "Fuck me!"

The phone rang again.

I groaned. "Dammit!"

Excitement and worry was on his face and in his voice all at once. "Daddy, I promise. This will be the last call I'll answer. After that, no more. At least not until after I fuck you."

"It better be," I mumbled as he reached for the phone.

I crossed my arms but smiled as I watched the clip from one of the talk shows today. It was Delilah Starr singing "Rich Girl." Leaning back, I spread my legs, my cock still hard as the reporter commented, "Izzy's startling performances as his drag alter-ego, Delilah Starr, isn't the only thing sweeping the nation. Everything about Izzy from his clothes, makeup, and ambiguous sexual orientation has everyone mesmerized." I stroked my pubes, smirking over that "I buy S.E.X." moment. In the back of my mind, I couldn't help but wonder what would happen if he confessed the truth, without a sense of humor, to not only America, but the world. I looked at Izzy. He wasn't paying attention to the TV anymore. He was busy on the phone. "The nation can't stop guessing who and what Izzy Rich is. A man? Woman? Alien? Robot? Who *is* Izzy Rich? Who is the real man behind all that glitters?"

I looked at him again. He held up a finger. I stroked that cock.

"Bloody hell, William." Izzy shook his head. "Can things get any weirder?"

I quivered, unable to wait any longer. I stood in front of Izzy, spreading my ass cheeks wider. I looked over my shoulder to see Izzy's reaction to my rubbing my asshole against his cockhead. He bit his lip hard, clearly trying to hold back a groan as I gently pushed my ass down on it. I struggled not to shout as my asshole widened and tightened around him. I slapped my hands to his shaking knees, my fingers deep in his skin as I was about to grind and bounce.

Izzy carefully pushed my ass up. His cockhead slipped out from me, my asshole throbbing. "One more second," he mouthed, continuing to talk on the phone.

I sat back down on the couch, trying to not sulk. When he hung up the phone, he looked at me, howled, and straddled me so quick that I gasped by surprise. "Christ. So much is happening right now. Baby, I can just scream!"

I smacked his ass. "Fuck my arse so hard that you *will* scream."

He bounced on me. "But, daddy, oh, there's more news, and it's fantastic!"

My eyes lit up. I waited for him to tell me, but he didn't. "Well? What is it?"

"I can't tell anybody right now."

"Then why are you mentioning it to me? Devil."

He smiled naughtily but said nothing.

"Please tell me? It's the least you can do for leaving me hanging."

He thought about it. "This is the big one, Johnny Angel. I mean, a really big secret, so you can't tell anyone. William told me that Bernie is already getting concert bookings at venues like…"

I was at the edge of my seat, waiting for it. "C'mon. Spit it out!"

"That's all I'm gonna say," Izzy said, so smug. "You're lucky I told you that much."

"Fair enough." I stuck out my tongue. "But really? More concerts? We just got here."

"I know! Isn't that bloody incredible?"

It hit me. "We're going to be in the States longer than scheduled?"

He nodded slowly with a huge grin on his face.

"Which states? Which venues?" I asked excitedly. "C'mon, baby, tell me everything!"

He sealed his lips tighter, mumbling, "Sorry, daddy. I can't."

"You told me nothing!" I laughed. "For Christ's sake, you're such a fucking tease tonight."

"It's not only the world that I got to keep on its toes." I spanked his ass so hard that he yelped.

"Fuck me!"

He wrapped his arms around my waist, nuzzling his cheek against my hair. "Baby..." He caressed my chin as he cooed sweetly "If it's all right, can it wait? So much is happening that my head is dizzy from the natural high."

"Like that has stopped us from love making before?"

"This is different, daddy. We are in *America*. Let's cuddle and snog, bask in the glory of today."

I raised my brow and touched his forehead. "This isn't you."

He pouted. "I'm sorry."

I sighed. "No, I am. I'm being selfish and petty. Today's yours, not mine."

"Bollocks. It's not always about me. You count, too, baby. Things right now are crazy."

"Like this." I looked at his cock, my lips quivering. "Cuddling and snogging all night long is fine, but..." I shivered. "God, my ass needs that cock so fucking badly, sweetheart."

His baby blues were as sad as a pup.

I rolled my eyes. "Don't give me that. I should be making *you* feel guilty, brat."

"You still love me?"

"No."

His face turned slightly pale, then glowed when I said, "I'm *in love* with you." He grinned when I held him and whispered to his ear "Only you could make me love you more, Izzy Rich."

After he whispered *I love you the most*, I pressed my lips to his as I caressed his warm, supple back. As we kissed, my need, my want, and my desire, my selfishness, my pettiness, and my greed all vanished. Our cocks may have been soft, but it didn't matter. Our kiss was hard and heavy, loaded with love. We spooned on the couch. Like song, we were simple that night. Simply, madly in love. We fell asleep, our legs over each other's thighs.

❖

My eyes fluttered, and I shouted. I opened my eyes from the pain and pleasure of Izzy's cock in my ass. I groaned, my voice shaking as he spread my ass cheeks and pressed hard against my asshole with one last thrust. He pinned my knees to my shoulders, swiveling and thrusting his hips as he pumped. His mad love split my ass in two. My hole throbbed as he thrust inside me deeper and deeper. I let him in all the way, to that hilt. My head spun. The pain made me shoot my load on the headboard. My eyes rolled as Izzy roared, bouncing my ass on his massiveness. He drilled into me with a growl, his balls thudding fast and hard against my flesh.

I smacked his cheek. "What's your name?" I growled as he rocked the bed. "Huh?" I smacked him harder when he whimpered. "Can't speak? Can't think? What's your name, bitch?"

He shook his head, squeaked, and I moaned at his stupidity, such relentless fucking. "I love you!" he cried, and I could feel his body about ready to collapse on top of me.

"Fill me up, baby," I panted. *"Fill me up."*

He slammed into me so hard we yowled. We whimpered together as I felt his load filling me up. I didn't realize how much he came until he pulled out. I gasped. I was like a cave. My fingers marveled, fingering my big round hole. I dipped two fingers inside myself deeper, and then four, paddling them in a pool of his seed. I pulled my fingers out and rolled myself over on my stomach, catching my breath as he passed out on his back, panting. I looked at him, smiling warmly as he asked, "Does that make up for yesterday?"

I wiped the sweat from my forehead. "Best wakeup fuck yet, princess."

"Really, daddy?" he asked with a cute smile, sounding surprised and flattered.

I nodded, sighing. "You almost made me forget who you were yesterday."

"Was I somebody else?" He chuckled.

I breathed and sighed. "It was the first time you ever put business before our pleasure." I looked at the time. "Good. Only four in the morning." I grinned.

The day was still ours, before it began. I wrapped my arms around him and spooned him from behind. I could feel him melting in my embrace as I squeezed him and licked behind his neck, my tongue inching to his ear. He moaned when I sucked his lobe while whispering, "You know what my dream day would be, baby?"

"What's that?" he murmured.

"You and me. In bed all day, being lazy. No work. Nobody, nothing standing in our way."

He faced me, our cocks touching as we held on to each other. "Breakfast in bed."

"Soaking in a bathtub, drowning in bubbles."

"Giving each other pedicures and manicures. Painting each other's nails."

"Taking our damn time to do it, for a change."

"No rush. No hurry."

I nodded. "Making love. As long as we want. All day, if we wanted to."

"One day…" he promised.

As we kissed, I didn't think about the sound checks, rehearsals, and performances in store for us. Or the many photo shoots and interviews Izzy had to do on top of that. All that mattered was us in bed together. Our long kiss, as sweet as our dream day, was such a bliss. He seemed intent on letting the phone ring, but I had to breathe. "You should answer that, baby."

He sucked on my chin as the phone rang. I chuckled, rubbing my sore, throbbing asshole as I gently pushed him off. He sat up and answered the phone. I closed my eyes, but they popped open again when I heard my love say, "I have an A-American hit?"

The news! And that stutter. The first I ever heard from him! "A n-number one single? *Here?* On the USA charts?" I had to cover my mouth as my heart raced at his words.

I sat on my knees slowly as he said, "*Rich Girl* is number two? *Rich Girl* and *Iz Ze Rich* are on the charts, too?"

He looked as if he were about to faint. After he hung up the phone, he was so still, very wide awake, but his eyes had tears in them.

I touched his shoulder. "Izzy?" He looked at me, his smile weak, lips trembling. Then he broke down and cried. I wrapped my arms around him, his skin still warm and sweaty from our hot lovemaking.

"'Dirty Dancer' shot to the number one spot on the charts overnight." He bawled, holding me tighter, his body shaking as he panted. "I can't believe this. 'Rich Girl,' the single, is number two. The album is number one, and *Iz Ze Rich* is number two. Here. In the States. Bloody hell!"

"That's *history*. Baby, not many Brit rockers make it this far in their whole career, and you did it after only one day." I shook my head and cried. "You did it!"

Tears trickled down his face. "John, I used to be poor." He grimaced. "I was nobody's child. I had nothing but a stolen guitar. I was homeless. I was a prostitute for four bloody years. Now—"

"You are king, my love." I cupped his face in my hands. "You hear me? You are king!"

He whimpered, the tears, such pretty little pearls, still rolling. "Why me?"

"Because America loves you, sweetheart. No, more than that, baby. The world loves you!"

His lips quivered. "If this is love, why am I crying like this, daddy?"

I rocked him, tears rolling down my face, too. "It's simple, sweetheart. Because this love is real."

"Izzy Mania has landed at LaGuardia Airport..." said the newscaster on the radio as the limousine was taking us from LaGuardia to the Plaza Hotel. "An estimated four thousand fans and one hundred reporters were in attendance this afternoon..." As we were listening, Izzy sucked on his cigarette with a timid smile while I and the entourage were drinking. I looked out the window. As usual, we were being chased. "Tonight, he will be performing the first of three sold-out Carnegie Hall shows. His critically acclaimed tour has been praised in *Rolling Stone* as 'mesmerizing a masterpiece as it is theatrically moving by a superstar who is the sex embodiment, striking as a man, heartbreaking as a woman.' In the *New York Times*—"

"If I listen to this any longer, my ego will explode," Izzy said, blowing smoke opposite from me. "We've been in America for two months, and I still feel like this is a mind fuck."

"It's like we're still dreaming," Tim said.

"I don't want to leave here!" I stomped my feet. "America has been too much fun."

"Especially the women," Phil said. "A tease sometimes without the payoff, though, but still fun."

"They haven't with me." Izzy chuckled. "With me, they have no limits."

"Nobody would," Larry said.

I smiled. We looked out the window together, Izzy and me. "I still don't understand what drives these people nuts for me," he said. He chuckled as we watched them run faster. "Look at them go." He cracked open the window, shaking his fag while daintily waving at them. We covered our ears. Izzy closed the window quick and giggled, sucking more of his cigarette.

"Look at you being the tease," Benson said. "Such an American woman."

"That I am," Izzy chirped in a feminine Manhattan accent.

"Bloody hell, that was quick," Tim said. "You've picked up the accents here already."

"It's as easy as Sunday morning," Izzy mimicked a Southern belle accent.

I pouted. "Oh, Sunday."

That was when we'd be flying back home.

"William, do we *have* to go?" Like some naughty, spoiled boy, he clung to William.

"You want to stay for the cheeseburgers and milkshakes," William snorted.

"Hell, yeah! And for the American girls." Izzy draped his arm over my shoulder.

Finally, we were at the Plaza Hotel. As usual, the gang, Izzy's film crew and photographers, William, and the rest exited the car first. We got no reaction from the fans until Izzy got out, and that was when the madness started. His bodyguards had to quickly guide him inside the Plaza for a short lunch, then off we went to Carnegie Hall for the four-hour-long sound check. Before I knew it, the main event arrived. Delilah Starr stood before us backstage, not Izzy Rich.

"It's time, darlings," Delilah cooed. "I have a feeling that this might be the show of our lives."

I could feel it, too. I wasn't sure if it was Carnegie Hall or what, but I could feel something. She pointed at me, the rest of the gang, and the backstage crew. She jumped excitedly in her diamond-studded heels when someone from management gave us the green light that it was time. She gave us her version of Izzy's *I love you* sign, blowing a simple kiss to each of us. In unison, the five of us blew her kisses back.

We stood in the wings, listening to the audience scream as the projector screen appeared over the stage. It played a scene from the

Rich Girl film. Sean Edwards, played by Izzy, is begging for the voodoo witch doctor, Doctor Zane, to transform him into the woman he was meant to be.

"But I don't have any money, sir. I'm just a poor London boy," Sean declared to Doctor Zane.

The audience howled like mad when Sean begged, "I'll do anything to be a rich girl. It's what I *am*. Can't you see it, Doctor?" Sean grabbed a hand full of his blond hair and pulled it, his lips shaking. He gritted his teeth. "You know what." He stared at Doctor Zane. "I don't care what people see anymore. I know who I am. And I want to be her. But you're the only one who can help me. Please, please, transform me into a rich girl."

I looked over my shoulder at Dee. She embraced herself as she looked down at her pumps. Her eyes were closed and her lips moved. Was she praying to the hell below? She then looked up and prayed to heaven above as Doctor Zane showed Sean a tiny sapphire bottle.

"What's that?"

"Your destiny."

The audience roared as the doctor said, "With this potion, you'll not only be a rich girl, but this will take you away into a world called Fame. Drink this, and Fame is yours." As Sean was about to swipe the bottle from the doctor, the doctor sneered. "Nuh-uh. There's a catch."

I got chills as Doctor Zane said, "You'll be a rich girl for ten days, *unless* you find true love."

"Will my love be a he, or a she?"

"*He* will be everything. One kiss, and you'll be his rich girl forever."

"How much money do I need to steal?"

"This can't be bought with money. Only with your soul."

The audience howled and screamed as Sean said, "I didn't know I had one."

"Yours is the purest. Give it to me, and you'll be *rich*. You'll be *famous*. And you'll be *adored*."

"Why?" Sean asked. "For what?"

"You'll be the sparkling diamond of the movie screens and magazines. Everybody will know who you are. They'll know where you're going, what you're doing, who you're seeing, and what you're wearing. Drink this, you will be a *star*."

Sean asked, "Wait! But is it safe?"

"If and when you fall in love, the potion turns to poison. Who cares if you die? You'll be a rich girl in the afterlife. Die in fame, it's only good-bye. Maybe only a kiss will save you."

"I won't die." Sean stood tall, facing the doctor without fear. "I will live, I'll give, and I'll love."

"And your soul will be mine." The doctor's mischievous laugh sounded like the devil.

"Take it!" Sean dared Lucifer. "Take me."

The smoke from the dry ice crept along the stage when the band and I took to our instruments. I could only see the glittering sparkle of my platforms through the clouds. I knew the scene playing above me so well, I could see it with closed eyes. Sean drank the potion. He broke out in a bloodcurdling scream, body convulsing. He collapsed to the floor, and he screamed, not like that poor London boy, but as a broken lady. The audience howled when the lights came up full on The Diamonds, and we played the *Rich Girl* theme. The applause swelled when I tapped my drums and sounded the chimes. As we performed, the lights dimmed again.

The stage darkened completely. And then a single light shone on the broken lady in the flesh.

Delilah was lying on her side, sparkling. The audience broke down when she rose from the ground, the dry ice smoke surrounding her as she touched her face, stroking her cheek inquisitively. She looked down at her breasts in shock, stroking her waist, hips, and ass in bewilderment as she spun slo-mo. She looked up, down, over her shoulder, creeping as if she were floating along the stage in pantomime. She stared at the fans in wonderment. She turned to the band. She stared, swaying to our melody. When she turned, she explored the stand with her caress, gazing at the microphone. She fell to her knees, holding herself. She looked up, touched her head. When she caressed the headdress, she focused again on her shoes. When Delilah reached to the stand of the mic, the audience rejoiced when she started to rise.

"Am I born again?" she crooned. She stood tall and regal. "In this new life, will I ever be the same?" Her hand around the microphone stand, she belted, "Hello, world! In Fame, what's my name?"

The audience screamed, "Delilah Starr!"

"What is this new world I'm in?" She absorbed the audience, singing achingly. "Is it whimsical? Fantastical? Intergalactic at all? Or is it me?" She pointed at herself. "Or is it you?" She pointed at the audience, and they howled as she crooned, "Or is it *us* that dreams are made of?"

I played with mad decadence as did the rest of the gang, our music twisted and free.

"I believe in…who? Me? Delilah Starr!" She spread her arms like wings, spinning. When she stopped, her diamonds sparkled and her furs swayed. "I'm all I can feel. And all I can see." She looked at the diamonds and furs on her body, reveling in them. "Ooh! Are these real?" The fans roared as she touched them. "I'm a rich girl. Can I really have all that money can buy?" She stroked them again and looked down at her sparkling shoes, touching her head. She let out a sultry coo. "All these diamonds. And these furs. Oh, how I love them! Because now I know they're real." Her high note soared. "And so am I!"

Delilah belted the rest of "Rich Girl," her pipes as chilling as ever. The audience seemed to know every move, spin, twirl, and pantomime that she'd make. At the next to last song, she sat on her knees at the edge of the center stage. "I love him!" she sang, looking at the fans in the front row, then the ones in the cheap seats. "The poison's not inside me." She balled her fist to her heart. "It is my man. My poison. Mikaal. His kiss. Is it really made of this? Immortal. Exquisite, beautiful, how wonderful, sweet, as he. He's inside me. Under my skin, in my heart within. Can you taste it, feel it, *love*, my love?"

The audience howled when she reached her hand out to a man in the front row. The light shone on someone, but not a man. It was a woman. Her hair was bright auburn, lioness-like, long and thick, her bangs shiny with hairspray and glitter. Glitter also sparkled on the lids of her slanted eyes, her cheeks, and her pouty red-lipped mouth. I stared as I drummed, watching Delilah caress her hair. Delilah stepped back as I and the band struck up the melody of Delilah's swan song. We could still hear the audience's shrill agony as we carried Delilah away to the wings. Delilah rose from the dead, sitting cross-legged, as we were still carrying her on the stretcher. She raised her arms.

"Bravo, everyone!" howled not Delilah's voice, but Izzy's. "You were bloody fantastic!"

We set the stretcher down. Izzy immediately scooted off and everyone in his entourage and the backstage crew applauded. He hugged the guys as fast as he could, embracing and rocking me last of all. I laughed as he jumped up and down, whispering something into my ear. I couldn't hear him.

"What?" I shouted. All I heard was "That girl."

He let me go. After the usual routine, Izzy sipped a glass of wine and dashed to the dressing room to get changed. This time, I couldn't join him, for time was tighter than it had ever been.

After management gave us the green light, we returned to the Carnegie Hall stage. I narrowed my eyes at the Asian woman Delilah caressed. The light wasn't on her, and yet, there she was. Though she was indeed a screamer, she seemed shy in comparison to the other rock and rollers around her. She wasn't a mover, jumper, bouncer, or shaker. She didn't dance at all as the "Dirty Dancer" melody played. The raw power of Izzy's riff was a monster. As he made it roar, he descended from the wings, wearing an outrageous star-patterned glittery gold and crème leotard. The gaudy gold bangles in his ears and on his wrists were dazzling, as was the matching gold collar around his neck and his gold knee-high six-inch pumps. The smoke surrounded him as he wiggled his ass and danced side to side to the rhythm. As he boogied, his guitar was an animal needing release.

"Carnegie Hall!" Izzy howled. "You're giving me life tonight!"

I drummed lighter when he stopped playing his guitar.

"But this stage is kind of...lonely."

The audience knew full well what was coming next.

"The world knows that I *love* to dance. But I want to dance with somebody on *this* stage tonight. Is it..." He pointed randomly at faces. "You, honey? You, love? How about you, sweetie? Or is it..." He pointed at someone. "*You.*" The light focused on the Asian girl. Her eyes were big and wondrous when the bodyguards helped her onstage. There, she stood, frozen. As I tapped my snares and toms, I got a good look at her. Definitely the classic soft-butch. Denim was her thing: denim jacket, denim jeans. Her unflattering and hideous striped purple and white shirt embraced hardly a bust. No tits. But that ass! What an ass, thick and juicy. I almost skipped a beat, but caught myself quick, drumming on the toms, tempo on point, relieved I didn't throw anyone off. I tapped my foot on the beater, controlling the mellow, sexual groove as Izzy sashayed to the Plain Jane. He took her hand and stroked it as he drew his lips to her ear. I looked out to them, my drumming intact still. Not only was she surprised, she had stage fright. She didn't answer the questions. That was a first. My gaze froze on Izzy, watching to see how he'd react.

He whipped his hair sideways and looked over his shoulder,

flashing us a loud, menacing smirk. I shrugged, and I noticed the gang raising their brows. The girl was still frozen and mute.

Izzy gyrated his hips when we played louder. He faced her, rolling his shoulders and shimmying that chest and ass as he danced around her, crooning and shouting "Dirty Dancer" with such fiery sensuality, his guitar imitating that soul. The girl didn't move, as if she was paralyzed—not only by Izzy, but by the stage, the audience, the lights, and the smoke. I head banged, drumming on the snares, toms, and cymbals simultaneously, shaking my head, and looking at that odd girl. Izzy seemed to thrive on her fear, making love to it with his voice, guitar, and dancing, more masculine and feminine, a superhuman. Not once did he touch the girl. Not once did she touch him. And yet, the distance between them was somehow like sex. Sex without touching.

"Man or woman..." Izzy sang, not shouting, but crooning angelically as if it were a love song. "Be the man and the woman that you see, baby, outside and within the dirty dancer inside of me." He touched the girl's face. The only part of her that moved was her lips, shaking. "Or you can just..." Izzy's guitar was silent. I and the band stopped. "May I have this kiss?" Izzy purred.

I raised my brow. That was the first time he asked a girl a question aloud during this song. The audience screamed. The girl paused. Everyone was waiting. And still, nothing.

"Do something already, man!" somebody in the crowd shouted.

I tapped my foot near my pedal, impatient myself, as the time was ticking.

Izzy held her hand, stroking it. "May I kiss you here?" he asked coyly.

The audience screamed when she nodded.

They screamed louder when he kissed her hand. My mouth dropped when she slowly backed away, not needing any of Izzy's bodyguards to drag her away. That *never* happened!

The audience booed, but Izzy nipped that in the bud by strumming on his guitar the dirty dancing melody. Something was different about it. It was romantic, even sweet, as Rick led the girl back to her seat. "How I wish that you'd kiss me..." Izzy crooned, looking in her direction. He looked down at his pumps. "Kiss me till our lips hurt, love, till we can't dance dirty anymore."

I drummed faster and smirked. Izzy's leotard showed that he was well-endowed. He faced us and placed the guitar between his legs to hide his boner. He faced the audience again and mimed a wank job as he played one wild, killer chord. He licked the head stock and then lifted his guitar in the air. The fans squealed. The lights darkened. From time to time, as the show went on, I'd look to the front row. From afar, that girl was shy, but she was curious. We were dripping with sweat, practically limping to center stage.

I stood next to Izzy, my arm draped over his shoulder and his over mine as he, Benson, Phil, Tim, Larry, and I bowed to the standing ovation. The audience's screaming hurt my ears, but I could have sworn that she made the loudest noise. What a scream. Did it somehow imitate her? Not too loud. Not too shrill. A balance. Modest. Strange. Like her. From where I stood, I could really see her close. I smirked at that baby-woman face. She had such a boyish smile, tiny dimples, and big doll-like dark almond-colored brown eyes. Her makeup wasn't on point. Her eyeshadow was sloppily applied, her mascara uneven, eyeliner not on the smooth and narrow. The concert couldn't be blamed. I looked at Izzy. My heart strangely jumped. He blew *her* a kiss. He took my hand. He squeezed it, and my heart was full, as we made a final bow. Izzy stood alone, center stage, panting. "Carnegie Hall!" he roared. My heart jumped again. For a split second, it fell right out of my chest. My stomach twisted in knots. I could've sworn Izzy's gaze was on only her again. When we left the stage, I could still hear the screams in my ear. But only *one* made me deaf. Hers.

CHAPTER EIGHT

The fans were putting Plaza Hotel security and Izzy's own to work again. The band and I could hear them as we were relaxed on the couch. I was next to Benson and Larry, taking a bite of my New York–style pizza. The two kicked back their beers as Phil and Tim sat across from us, eating pizza and chugging beer, too. We looked at Izzy. He stood in front of the opened window, strumming on his acoustic guitar, jerking his hips, shaking his ass, and singing. "I love New York City like I love my baby!" he shouted and crooned. The people screamed as he belted, "And how she loves me, too. New York City, when it's time for good-bye, I'll be so blue, because I'll miss you. Woo-hoo! New York City. Even now, how you make me want to cry!"

I bobbed my head to Izzy's folksy melody, drumming on my knees, mimicking the bluesy hook. Benson clapped first, Tim, Larry, and Phil followed my beat. The five of us stomped our feet to our rhythm. Izzy whipped his hair and looked over his shoulder, strumming louder.

"That's my boys!" he howled, beaming like a proud mama-papa. "The riches are digging it!" Izzy looked out the window. "What do you think of my new song, ladies and gentlemen?" I covered my ears at the noise, grimacing. He looked at us. "If that's not a 'we love it,' I don't know what is!"

"When did you write that song, boss?" Larry asked.

Izzy turned his back to the window. "I didn't. Came from above to my head through these lips."

"Sounds like you should record it as an A-side," Phil said.

"Or maybe perform it for the show tomorrow," said Tim.

"Nah." Izzy scoffed. "I'm only having a laugh with the fans. Ooh! Johnny, toss me a pillow."

"Sure thing, captain."

"Get one from the bedroom."

I got off the couch and went to *our* bedroom. Our lovemaking—the aroma of sweat, come, and ass—and the scent from our anise cigars lingered in the air. I reached for the nearest pillow on the bed. It was still warm and wet with Izzy's saliva. It smelled like his hair, of coconut oil and hairspray. With a smile, I nuzzled my nose against the pillow. With closed eyes, I squeezed it as I thought about making love to Izzy before the guys got here. Not even the fans woke me up from such a beautiful then-reality.

"Baby John!" I heard Benson shout. "What's taking so long, man?"

"The fans are waiting for *you*!" Izzy called. "Come out, come out, we know where you are!"

I tossed the pillow, grabbed the other one that was dry and unsoiled, and rushed out the room.

"About time, Baby John," Tim said, laughing as Izzy handed everyone a marker.

"What were you doing?" Larry asked.

"Sorry, had to stop at the mirror and check myself out." I tossed the pillow at Izzy.

After he caught the pillow, he tossed a marker at me.

"We better sign this quick, boys," Izzy said as the fans screamed louder.

He placed the pillow on the table and signed his name first at the center of it. I signed my name above his, and the gang signed theirs around his signature. Izzy cradled the pillow in his arms as he said "They're going to go *nuts*." He skipped to the window. He stuck his head out, the fans went delirious. When he tossed out the pillow, even more so. "More, more, more!" they hollered.

"You got it!" Izzy howled, and he strummed on his guitar, breaking out into song.

As I was about to bob my head and drum again, I heard a knock at the door. Izzy was so much on a roll that he couldn't hear it, and I didn't dare interrupt his groove. I checked through the peep hole. It was Rick.

He looked sweaty and exhausted. "The kids are out of control tonight. Those girls. *Crazy.*"

"You poor, poor thing."

"I've had to kick out hundreds of them! And they keep multiplying! The boys are as bad."

I chuckled. "Need me to get Izzy for you?"

"Can you?"

I looked over my shoulder, and then I turned to Rick again. "Um, I'm curious, man. I know you can't keep track of all the faces, but by any chance are any of those groupies that—"

"The Asian lass from the concert tonight?"

"How did you guess that?"

"Izzy has asked all night since we got back here."

I raised my brow. "Really?"

"Why do you ask?"

"I'm nosy. Fuck!" I shouted and jumped when I heard Izzy, speaking in a butch-like Manhattan accent, say "Nosy about what, Baby John?"

"God, I hate it when you surprise me like that!" I slapped his shoulder. "Wanker."

Izzy chuckled, draping his arm over my shoulder as he purred, "What's up, Ricky? Nobody is hurting themselves or anybody else, are they?"

"There's been some hair pulling and bruising."

"No harm in rough playing," he said jokingly and suggestively. He winked at me.

I winked back as Rick said, "Could you make an appearance to keep things under control?"

"Ooh, afraid not." Izzy tsked and shook his head. "It's boys' night."

"You're breaking a lot of hearts tonight, boss." Rick snickered.

"Sometimes one has got to be cruel to be kind. I'm making up for it by giving an impromptu performance from the suite. Speaking of that, we better get back to it, Johnny!"

After we said good-bye to Rick, we raced back to the living room, sitting with the guys. Izzy leaned back on the couch, stretching his legs out as he strummed out a smooth melody. "I love New York City like I love women," he crooned beautifully. "How I want to kiss her, touch her, hug her, and squeeze her..." I swayed my head, about to smile, until he sang, "Like the baby-faced lady with auburn hair, wild and long, as beautiful as her brown eyes are big and her glitter's strong." I had to smile when he looked at me. I drummed my knees lightly as he sang, "I love New York City like I love to dance for her as I sing my dirty ditty." I tapped my foot to his guitar as he leaned his head on me. "If only I knew her name like how I know this great city!"

"Dammit, Iz!" I growled and grimaced. "Did you have to *shout* that in my ear?"

He laughed. "What's the matter? You didn't seem into it like you were the last time."

"The song's fine," I bluffed. "I'm sluggish now. Ate my weight in pizza and booze."

"Like a true American, huh?" Izzy raised his beer bottle.

"Except we're doing it the English way!" Benson howled, hoisting his glass.

Everyone else did, too, ready to toast. "Going to join us?" Izzy asked me.

"No more booze for me." I covered my mouth to belch. "I'm done."

"This isn't the Baby John that we know," Tim said. "C'mon. Drink up!"

I gave Tim a naughty look. "You all are bad influences." I grabbed a bottle, raising it.

"And how easy you cave to the temptation," Larry teased.

I stuck my tongue out at him, and then looked at Izzy.

"Cheers to the best band in the world," Izzy said proudly. I and the gang hollered for ourselves. "Cheers to our hard work, slaving away for this amazing tour. Cheers to our next two Carnegie Hall shows. Cheers to the future MSG shows. Cheers to America. Cheers to all the men and women of this lovely country who're rocking our world every day. Cheers to our beloved family who miss us terribly as much as we miss them. Cheers to England. Cheers to our Queen, and—" He knocked back his beer and slammed the bottle on the table. "That's all!"

I sipped my beer instead of chugging like the guys were.

Phil belched. "I really miss the kid. I only phoned him once since I got here."

"I haven't phoned home at all," I said, putting my glass down. "How could any of us, really?"

"We hardly have time for breakfast sometimes," Tim said. "Let alone making phone calls."

Benson agreed. "Separation makes the heart fonder. We'll have a lot of stories to tell."

"And Lord knows that I have a lot of pictures and souvenirs for the wife and kids," Larry said.

"I talked to the mums last night," Izzy said, stroking his guitar strings without making music from them. "It's funny. They told me glam rock artists are popping out of nowhere all over London, and they're trying to imitate what I've been doing."

"Now that will be interesting to come back home to," I said. "But, remember, you are king."

"Speaking of that, they also told me that the British press have borrowed America's nickname for me. The hounds are calling me the King of Glam now." We all laughed. "I won't believe that until I see it! Believe it or not, I kind of miss them, too." Izzy strummed his guitar lightly. "And home, how I miss home. But in a way, this country's my home, too. I'll miss her." I smiled as I watched Izzy playing the same melody as before. He sang, "And the women. My riches. My dears. How I love them. They make me sleep easy at night, you know what I mean. They wash away my insecurities, my doubts, and my fears. And the boys, the most beautiful I've ever seen. Their smiles carry the light of the world. And their love is full in their handsome tears."

He stopped. The audience outside roared.

"My word, was I singing that loud?"

"Not nearly as loud as when you were singing about that Asian lass," Tim said.

"Hell, if I could sing, I would shout," Phil said. "She's cute."

"And all shades of awkward, all kinds of bloody sexy." Izzy smiled slyly. "I don't know why, boys, but there's something about her. I can't get her out of my mind tonight."

I looked at him. "Why?" I snapped. "I mean," I spoke calmly, "she didn't *do* anything."

"That's what made her so sexy!" Izzy giggled and blushed. "Her nothing was something."

"She's a looker," Larry said like a giddy schoolboy. "Adorable face. Nice body. If I wasn't married…"

I raised my brow. "Larry? Is that you?"

"Hey, just because I'm married doesn't mean that I don't fantasize." I was shocked to even hear that. "Oddly, she's the opposite of you, boss."

Benson nodded. "She did have this masculine energy about her."

"And not only physically," Izzy said. "She has this boyish charm, I suppose."

I snorted. "I don't know about that. And didn't any of you see her makeup? It was dodgy."

Izzy snickered. "Okay, so she needs to work on that. But…" Izzy looked at me. "She's hot. She makes Plain Jane hotter than hot. Did you boys see my hard-on?"

"Who could miss that!" Benson said. "I almost shouted 'down, boy.'"

"I was afraid that you'd get arrested." Larry laughed. "You got balls. I mean—oh, bugger."

"Better keep that *Titanic* steady at the last MSG show or else you will get arrested," Tim said.

"Oh, I'll be extra careful. This time couldn't be helped."

Though Izzy didn't actually mention her again, he did in my head. And wouldn't stop talking about her. She made him glow. His smile shined. Even the way he sang and played his guitar again oozed a devotion to the nameless girl. Or maybe it was the high from all the reefers Izzy, the guys, and I smoked together kicking in and fucking us up, making me believe Izzy was different when he wasn't. Maybe it was me. We were legless, rolling on the floor. It was boys' night, and nothing else in the world mattered but Benson, Phil, Tim, Larry, me, and Izzy. And nobody else mattered. Not the fans, not the groupies, not the press, not the country, or the world.

Not even the girl.

❖

The hot needles of water rained over my head as Izzy leaned back and moaned at me massaging his scalp—and to my cock twitching inside his hot, tight ass. I kneaded my fingers deeper into his skin at the same time that I thrust deeper inside him. The shampoo lathered into a thick, fluffy, frothy cloud of bubbles, framing his smiling face. I stopped lathering his head up and slapped my hands on his ass, sinking my fingers into his flesh as I swiveled my hips and shoved my cock inside him harder. We wailed. He whimpered my name, wrapping his legs tighter around my waist as he bounced his bottom nice and slow on my cock, tightening his asshole around me. I gasped and growled, clawing my fingers along his smooth, wet back as I pushed him toward me.

The water washed the bubbles out of his hair until the fox-red suds were gone. I bucked my hips swiftly, and we slapped hard and loud against each other, the water pouring over us. He sucked on my tongue and bobbed his mouth on me as I slammed his ass down on me, wrapping my arms tight around him. Slowly, I picked him up by his ass, my cock still in it. As the shower cleansed our bodies, Izzy groaned and wrapped his arms around my neck. My balls thudded against his skin. The temperature of the air in the shower was hotter, and not because the water was steamy.

"I'm going to come, baby!" I panted, my hips out of control as I pounded him faster.

He sucked on my chin. "Kiss me!" he shouted.

I blinked at how achingly he cried for me to kiss him. It sounded so much like the way he sang "kiss me" to that girl at not only that first Carnegie Hall show, but at the second and the third.

"Make my lips hurt!" he wailed, bouncing on my cock desperately.

Even the way he said that brought me to all those shows. And to that girl. Nothing changed. She was still the same. But he wasn't. Every time, his dancing, singing, and guitar playing was different. More raw, passionate, and soulful. Needy. Burning. Yearning. For her. And as hard as he tried to hide it, the beast was back every time.

"Oh, *John*. Ooh, daddy!"

I blinked and realized I had stalled and was just standing there, letting him be in control. My legs shook as I growled. "Yeah, baby. Want daddy to come? Make me come."

I kissed him hard, and we both moaned and groaned. He pounded my cock with his ass in an animalistic fervor, his desire setting me free. I howled when my come filled my baby, filling him up deep as he bounced his ass on me, sounding wet and sloppy, his asshole loose and open. I nipped at his bottom lip, sucking it hard.

"Too hard, daddy, too hard!"

I let go of his lip and licked it, the steam raising the air temperature. My cock softened and slipped out of him as he turned off the faucet. When he stood on his feet and stepped out of the tub, I smacked his bottom, and he let out a surprised giggle. I scooped him in my arms when he must have least expected it. He reached for the towels and placed them on his stomach as I carried him back to the bedroom. The morning news played on the TV as I laid him on the bed, kissing him madly before I topped him. I shivered when he smacked my ass and wedged his thumb between my cheeks, stroking my hole. I lay on my back and spread my legs. In a blink of my eyes, he'd put his head between them.

"Cock whore!" I giggled as he wiggled his tongue on my cock from base to head. "I fucked your arse three bloody times already today, you greedy—" I moaned. Izzy penetrated my ass with his tongue. My legs shook, and I was melting. I closed my eyes, smiling as he spread my ass cheeks and sucked on my asshole. He squeezed my balls gently in the palm of his hand.

"Fans have been here at Madison Square Garden since eight this morning, waiting for tonight's first of three sold-out shows for the remarkable *Iz Ze Rich* tour," said the TV reporter.

I opened my eyes and sat up, caressing the back of Izzy's wet hair, gasping as he sucked my balls. My heart flipped in my chest when the reporter spoke to a familiar face in the long queue. Those eyes. That face. That hair. That body, donning a Delilah Starr tee, leather pants, and a leather jacket. Inside, I was bugging! I massaged Izzy's scalp, managing to somehow stay still.

"What's your name?" asked the reporter to her.

"Roxanne Foster Shengyi," she said in a soft-spoken, thick Chinese accent.

"Hmm?" Izzy raised his head, releasing my balls from his mouth. He wiped his mouth and looked over his shoulder at the TV screen. I was tempted to swipe the remote and change the bloody channel, but I was frozen in the moment as if time stopped because of…Roxanne.

"What's it about Izzy that brings you here today, Roxanne?"

"Everything!" She beamed, the dimples in her cheek prominent. "He's a revelation!"

Izzy slowly got on his knees, sitting, staring at the TV.

"Will tonight be your first time seeing him in concert?"

"Oh, no! I've gone to six of his shows so far, and I'll be seeing all three of his Madison Square Garden concerts."

The reporter looked as surprised as I felt. "Which show would you say was his best?"

"*All of them!* Each one, the best."

"Bloody hell, that woman gets around—"

"Shh!" Izzy cut me off, grabbing the remote and turning up the volume.

"Izzy is incredible," she gushed. "I'm obsessed with him, obviously. I'm in love!"

That glow on her face overshadowed all the fans around her. I looked at Izzy, my eye twitching at how I could feel and see that very same glow on his face.

"It was nice talking with you, Roxanne Foster."

"Roxanne Shengyi," she corrected him. He turned his face to the camera, stepping back to talk to another fan in the queue.

"That name." Izzy looked at me. Never had I seen him so bewildered. "I know that name!"

I snorted. "So do I. Everyone knows. She said it on TV."

"No, no—" He sounded more hyper. "Johnny, this is some *freaky* shit!"

"What are you talking about, baby?"

He took a deep breath. "You won't believe me if I tell you."

"Just tell me."

"Remember that fan girl I mentioned to Russell?"

"That feels like ages ago. Yeah, kind of."

"That girl's name is Roxanne Foster Shengyi."

"And?"

"She has to be the same Roxanne that we just saw on TV!"

I laughed. "Don't be a nutter. There are a lot of Roxanne Foster Shengyis in the world."

Izzy shook his head. "Yes, a nutter I am. I know I'm talking crazy, but I believe. I mean, baby, the name. Sure, a lot of girls named Roxanne have written to me, but not with that middle and last name. And she looks like she's eighteen, obviously has to be if she's attending my shows. Even the way she talked to that reporter sounded like one of her letters!"

"How so?"

"Her maturity. That sweetness. That shyness. It points directly to her."

I tried to keep a straight face to his goofy one, but I couldn't help myself.

"It's not that funny!"

I held my belly. "You are crazy. Baby, the bloody odds of that girl being the same one that sent you the fan letters is slim to zero. Coincidences like that don't happen in real life."

"In my life, anything can happen."

Well, I couldn't argue with him about that.

"Somehow, some way, I need to meet her before Sunday." He rubbed his chin and snapped his fingers. "Tonight, I'm going to have Rick bring her onstage again. When she leaves, he'll give her a VIP pass for a private meet-and-greet at the hotel right after the concert's over."

This time, I couldn't laugh. My throat dried. Not even a swallow could revive it.

"What do you think?" he asked me eagerly.

"That's so last minute," I said flatly. "And if she has turned down your advances onstage, what makes you think that she wouldn't turn down this opportunity?"

"She won't," he said affirmatively, as if she had no other choice. Neither did I. "She's going to be in for the surprise of her life tonight. I'm going to call Rick, let William know, phone the guys, have my assistants talk with the hotel staff so they can make arrangements."

"Not wasting any time, are you?"

"You're right. Why am I talking about this?" In a hurry, he crawled over me to get to the phone, grabbing it so quickly he almost dropped it. He caught it, rolling on his back beside me as he phoned. I looked up at the ceiling, my temples starting to throb lightly as he went on and on about his plan to everyone. When he finally hung up the phone, my hair and body were dry, and I had my powder, mascara, lipstick, eyeliner, and eye shadow on.

"It's official!" Izzy jumped on the bed. "It's going to happen!"

I looked up at his soft massive cock flopping up and down, his balls swinging as he jumped. "How old are you?" I smacked his thigh. "Stop jumping on the bed. And finish eating my arse."

"No, no, baby. We don't have much time!"

He jumped off the bed, landing on his feet and running to the bathroom. When I met him there, he already had his makeup ready. As he was applying it, I dried and styled his famous bob, running a dollop of coconut oil through his hair to give it a hairspray shimmer. We could only kiss by touching tongues. We hurried to get dressed, for it was almost time for the talk and radio shows, sound checks, and main event. I was more than ready, but what I wasn't anticipating was the future. I already wished time was on my side and that the meet-and-greet was over.

❖

Izzy swayed his hips to Duke Ellington. As Benson, Phil, Tim, Larry, and I were taking it easy on the couch, Izzy explored the lounge. He nodded approvingly at the candles lit all around and the trays of finger food on the table. He stopped at the bar, chatting to the male bartenders flirting with him. The guys were talking, but I was hardly listening. My stomach was twisted into knots, and not because I was starving. My mouth was parched, and not because I smoked too much or needed a drink. Well, maybe one. Or two. Hell, I was close to requesting a bottle. Instead, I lit up a fag. I blew the smoke from my mouth when Izzy sat beside me, crossing his legs, our hips touching. Izzy clapped his hands and rubbed them fast. "She should be here any minute now."

Larry chuckled. "Look at you beaming like some schoolboy."

"You're acting as if you never met the girl before," Benson said.

"That was the stage. This is different. This is like meeting an old friend."

I rolled my eyes, looking at Phil. "This joker still thinks she's the letter writer."

He laughed. "I don't know, Baby John. She could be."

"She is, I'm telling you, boys! I feel it. I know she's the one."

"We know." Smoke escaped through my nose as I inhaled. "You won't shut up about it."

"I don't blame you, boss," Larry said, grinning.

"And you are as bad, you perv." I glared at him. "I'm telling Nancy!"

"Ha! Go ahead! Hell, I think even she'd check Roxanne out. She's gorgeous."

Izzy growled with a sly smile. "She has this *je ne sais quoi*."

"She turns you on, we know."

Izzy bit his lower lip, blushing. "You all want to know why?" We all looked at him, me undoubtedly most curious. "She plays hard to get. You know how rare that is?"

"As rare as virgins, I can imagine," Phil remarked.

"Damn right it is. The girl's so bloody unusual. She stands out. I like that. And I want her. I can't stand the wait. And soon…" He looked at the door. "She'll be here any minute."

I looked at the door, too. I imagined Rick walking through that door to announce that a groupie turned down Izzy Rich for once. My thumb and forefinger shook when I saw the way Izzy's eyes lit up as Rick opened the door. The guys stood, but I put my fag out in the ashtray before I finally stood. I smirked coldly at the sight of Roxanne jumping and squealing. When Izzy stood before her, she froze, looking up at him in awe as if it were the first time she ever stood before the holy glam rock revelation in the flesh. Roxanne looked even more boyish than usual, dyke-like in her bell bottom jeans, glittering golden belt, buttoned-up flannel, and gold tie. But that makeup was still terrible.

Izzy pecked her hand. "I'm so glad that you came, darling."

She covered her face, shaking her head. "This is surreal."

"You can say that again." Izzy held her hand, chuckling. "You know who I am, and I know who you are. Those five blokes over there are more than my band, but my best mates."

She beamed. "You are Benson." She pointed at him, and got all the other guy's names and person right. She looked at me and said with a smile, "And you are Jonathan Maxwell."

I forced myself to smile and shake her hand. "Nice to meet you."

Roxanne let go of my hand.

Izzy caressed her wrist. "Sit, love. Be comfortable."

Roxanne sat next to me where Izzy had been, and he sat next to her. "Sorry I'm so starstruck," Roxanne said, more soft-spoken.

"I bet you are wondering, what the bloody hell am I doing here right now?"

"You read my mind!"

"I'm afraid you didn't win the lottery, but there is a reason why I brought you here."

"Which *is* winning the lottery!"

Everybody laughed except for me.

"Feels that way for me, too. I told the guys about my intuition. They think I'm loony."

"Why's that?"

"Let's say I'm clairvoyant." He cocked his chin up with a sweet, menacing look. "I know you, or at least I think I do."

"Don't scare the poor girl, Iz," I remarked.

"How could Izzy scare anyone?" Roxanne said.

"You'd be surprised." He winked. "Your parents don't favor me or my music."

"That's correct."

"I make them squirm. Typical, since that's what I do, scare the parents and elders."

"You make them recoil in horror," she said as she chuckled.

"My music is devil's music, and I'm his spawn because I'm a glorified queer, yes?"

She didn't at all look as amused as the guys were. I blinked, raising my brow as Izzy said, "Your mother is Chinese. Your father is German."

Roxanne still wasn't shocked. But I was starting to understand. I gulped nervously. He was asking about things she'd told him in those damn letters.

"You and your little brother were born and raised in Beijing, China, until you turned ten."

Roxanne beamed wider, nodding. "Since we moved from China, I've lived all over the States."

"Here, there, and everywhere, like a true army brat," Izzy purred.

I trembled at Izzy's chuckle. It was almost Holly.

"Okay, you already know, don't you?" he asked Roxanne.

"You got my letters!" She shouted so loudly that I jumped.

"*See!*" Izzy pointed at us. "I told you all! And I told *you* first!" Izzy pointed at me, smirking naughtily, and then he looked at her, glowing as he gushed, "I knew it was you, Ms. Shengyi."

I blinked. "Unbelievable," I said dryly.

"You pronounced my name right! Most don't even bother."

"So I heard when Jonathan and I saw you on TV this morning."

"Oh my God, you saw that?" she asked, sounding so embarrassed, looking at only him.

"I wanted to tear that reporter off, so bloody rude, and you were so sweet."

"I'm used to it."

"That doesn't make it okay, love. Your name is as gorgeous as you are," he purred, taking her hand and stroked it with his thumb. "I know that in Mandarin, your name means business. *Sheng* means birth, life, growth. And *yi* means idea, wish, and desire."

Roxanne's lips trembled as she swooned. "You know my language."

"Only because of you, my dear." He pecked her hand again.

"This really is bloody weird," Larry said.

"You can fucking say that again," I mumbled.

"What?" Izzy asked, looking at me.

"I didn't say anything."

Izzy looked at everyone. "Still think I'm mad, boys?"

"Yes!" everyone said. Tim added, "Trust me, Roxanne. He *is* the Mad Hatter."

"That's funny." She batted her lashes. "All I see is the Queen of Hearts."

As everyone was cackling like hyenas, I raised my hand at the bartenders.

"Perfect timing, Johnny!" Izzy waved at them. "What would you like to drink, my dear?" he asked Roxanne. "You can have any cocktail you like. Any other poison you'd like, it's yours."

"Oh, thank you, but I don't drink or…take anything. I'm as clean as a whistle."

I ordered a whiskey sour. Everyone ordered their drinks. Roxanne requested a Shirley Temple.

Izzy crossed his legs. "I told Russell Harty that."

"Who's he?" she asked.

"Oh, I forget, he's unheard of in the States. He's the leader of the BBC's arts programme. Of all shows in Britain, I've been interviewed on his the most." Izzy carried on about that interview.

"He was all creepy about it," I teased, looking at him, not her. "He *framed* the letters."

"Just yours." Izzy beamed at her as the bartenders brought our drinks. "Anybody have questions for Roxanne?" Izzy asked.

"If you don't mind me asking, how in the world were you able to see so many of Izzy's shows?" Larry asked, beaming at her as foolishly as Izzy and everybody else was.

"You are eighteen, right?" I stirred my beverage, looking down at the swirling ice. "The average girl your age usually struggles to afford one ticket to Izzy's shows. And you've been at six."

"Nine," Izzy corrected me. Something about his face told me I was rude. Not only that, but stupid. "Silly boy. Can't you count?"

I ignored his condescending tone and smiled at her, no matter that it was fake. "Sorry," I bluffed. "I'm awfully curious, that's all."

"Um…" She set her glass down, sitting quietly during a long, awkward pause in the conversation.

"Is everything all right, my dear?" Izzy asked.

"Just so you all know…um…my parents have no idea I've been away seeing you in concert. They think I've been spending a week away with friends."

Izzy swallowed his drink hard, and he grinned as if he was intrigued. "Really?"

She blushed. "It's not like me, but…Izzy." Roxanne looked at only him, her eyes welling. She fanned herself. "Your music. Delilah. *You.* You've set me free."

I turned my head away so nobody could notice me rolling my eyes as I sipped my drink.

"I found my calling because of you."

"And what's that, sweetie?"

"Singing and dancing."

Of bloody course, I said in my head.

"To answer John's question, I got the money for your shows by"—her smile was as cheeky as Izzy's for a split second—"I became a stripper for a whole month."

I coughed and choked on my drink, pounding my chest.

"Get out!" Izzy shouted as Benson patted my back, asking if I was okay. I nodded as Izzy said, "*You?* Sweet and innocent you, pole danced just for me?"

"As soon as news broke about you touring America, I had to do it."

"You must have been fantastic," Izzy purred, his voice drenched in sensuality and intrigue.

I cleared my throat, gulping thickly as Roxanne spoke modestly. "Yes, I was popular."

"Did you enjoy it?" Izzy asked, the light in his eyes a little too bright.

"It was fun, but sex work isn't my calling. Dancing and singing's where my heart is." She picked up her bag, opening it as she said, "I bought *Rich Girl* on its release day here. A week later, I recorded a demo. I sang five songs from it." She took the tape out.

I thrust my tongue in my cheek, grinning. I was waiting for Izzy to reject the tape. We'd laugh about it later, and Izzy and I would talk shit about her tackiness. I sat at the edge of my seat, but Izzy actually took the tape.

"I'm so looking forward to hearing it, truly," he said. I couldn't believe it! "You were fifteen when you recorded this?"

"I've taken voice lessons since, though. I've been singing at the church choir this past year, so my voice is far better now than it is on this. But I hope that you'll enjoy it, Izzy."

"I'm sure I will, Roxanne." He slipped the tape in his jacket, holding her hand and rubbing it in circles. "I must say, love, you're more fascinating in person than you are on paper. And frankly, I'm surprised you're innocent but with a right touch of naughty."

"There's always a touch of the devil behind an angelic face," she said in that same soft-spoken, sweet voice.

I blinked, shaking my head as I ordered myself a scotch.

"Ah, fellas, she knows me well already!" Izzy winked and burst out in an obnoxious giggle.

I fake laughed. "I'll admit, I'm surprised, too, Roxanne. You're a bit of a rebel."

"That's nothing. Look at this."

She got off the couch, stepped back, and unbuttoned her blouse. I was the only one not drooling like a bumbling schoolboy as she removed it. She had a red tank top on, showing off the ink on her right shoulder.

"Bloody hell." Izzy got up from his seat, looking at her tattoo closer. We all did.

It was a true work of art. One half of Izzy's face was the Hollywood glamour of Delilah Starr, the rendering of the makeup done perfectly. The other half was Izzy.

"My word. This is unreal. Delicious. Don't you want to touch it and lick it, boys?"

"You can if you like," Roxanne said, her voice far from shy, but still not sexual.

I sat as Izzy caressed the lips of the face with his finger. When he licked the tat with a slow tongue stroke, she shivered. "What do you think, Johnny?" Izzy asked.

"Nice." I looked at the table. My scotch was already watered down from the ice melting. As everyone sat back down and Roxanne buttoned up her shirt, I chugged the drink as if it were punch.

"How are you going to explain that to your parents?" Izzy snickered. "Naughty girl."

She chuckled. "Wear long-sleeved shirts around them for now on?"

"What about the TV?" I said, clearing my throat, and then speaking with a normal tone. "I imagine they or their friends or coworkers or your relatives saw you."

She shrugged. "They hardly watch TV. If they find out from someone, well…" She grimaced a little, her face lighting up at Izzy. "They'll see how much I love you." She blinked and cried.

He hugged her quickly, rocking her as he cooed, "I love you, too."

"My world is better with you in it," she cried, sniffling. "You've made being bad, good."

He rested his chin on her shoulder as he held her closer. I chugged the last of my drink and requested another. Izzy had the bartenders whip Roxanne up another Shirley Temple, and then we all went to the table, munching on the foods and chatting. After I polished off my drink and plate, we lounged on the couch. I requested another drink.

"Ready, John?" Izzy asked me.

"For what?" I slurred, blinking. Izzy cradled his guitar. "Where did that come from?"

The guys laughed, Izzy chuckled, and Roxanne smiled at me.

"Where were you when Roxanne asked if I could perform a song for her? I mentioned the song we performed yesterday to the fans, you know, the New York one. Then I told Rick to get my guitar from upstairs. Now..." He drummed on it lightly, petting the strings. "I got it."

"Wait. You said yes?"

Izzy nodded slowly. "Why wouldn't I? Tonight's all about you, darling."

I smiled goofily, only to frown when I realized he was talking to Roxanne.

"The way you drummed yesterday, Johnny, repeat that. And the way you clapped your hands, boys. Do it exactly as you did it. Okay?"

I started drumming on my knees, forcing a smile on my face.

"Not yet, John. Damn." He snorted. "I haven't even started the bloody chord yet."

Everyone laughed. I laughed more loudly, to snap myself out of my tipsy stupor. We stopped when Izzy strummed his guitar. Roxanne couldn't contain herself when he sang. He looked at Roxanne, singing, "...how she loves me, too. New York City, how...John. John? Hello!"

I sat up straight and struck up the groove and the beat on my knees, nodding to the rhythm.

Izzy shook his head. He stopped. "Jonathan, what the hell?"

I laughed, not caring that Izzy and the guys were looking at me as if I lost it. Or that I had.

"Your voice threw me off," I said. "That wasn't how you sounded yesterday either."

"That's because Roxxy is here. Mind if I call you Roxxy?"

"You kidding me? You're Izzy Rich! You can call me anything!"

I couldn't stand watching the two of them giggling together. "Go on," I said. "Play it again, Izzy."

"Get it right this time."

He strummed his guitar. His voice sounded even more magical, more moving. I could see on Roxanne's face that she was as much in love with his voice as I was in love with him.

"There you go, Johnny," Izzy ad-libbed, nodding approvingly as I drummed my knees.

The guys clapped their hands, and we were in synchronicity with each other.

"I love New York City like I love women!" Izzy howled, batting his lashes at Roxanne. "How I want to kiss her, touch her, hug her, and squeeze her like...*you*, Roxanne Shengyi. Oh! How you make me want to dance now that I know your name like how I know this great city—fuck."

I lost the beat, throwing everybody off.

Izzy grimaced, glaring at me. "Just when we were on a roll, you fucked it up."

Roxanne scoffed, and I glared at her as she said, "Oh, it doesn't matter."

I bit my tongue.

"I *loved* that song. What is it called?"

Izzy blushed. "It doesn't have a name. Maybe I should call it 'New York City (I Love You).'"

"You should perform it at the show tomorrow! Can you?"

"I'm sure we can squeeze it into the set list somehow."

"Really?" Tim asked, smiling while I was stupefied. "That's what I suggested yesterday," he said to Roxanne. "But he was like, nope."

"My mind's changed," Izzy said with a smug look. "That will mean that rehearsals will be tougher, more ambitious. This song *will* work and fit into the show."

"But, Iz, that's so last minute!" I said in a rush. "If we're going to perform it outside of what we did yesterday and today, it can't be tomorrow. It needs to be spectacular, you know."

"Ah, I see what you're getting at." Izzy nodded, sounding and looking chipper. "This is why I adore this man," he said to Roxanne. That look on his face. Oh, his joy, it was my joy! Finally, the smile on my face was real. More than that. It was glowing because I was alive. "Singing it at the last MSG show would make it not only spectacular, but special. That show, by the way, Roxanne, will be recorded *live* for American TV, filmed by my good friend who filmed the *Rich Girl* documentary. And the special will air on the BBC, too." Roxanne squealed, but then covered her mouth as Izzy said, "Shh! Don't tell anyone." He winked. "It's a surprise. You're the only fan in the entire fucking universe who knows now."

"You okay, John?" Tim asked into my ear. "You're so pale."

"I'm good," I said dryly.

"I can't wait for the show!"

"Same here!" I shouted so loud, everyone looked at me. I raised my drink. "Cheers to that!"

"See why I love him?" Izzy said to Roxanne cheerfully as they all held their glasses up. "We're blood brothers."

A chill rippled down my spine to *blood brothers*. I forced a weak smile. "Cheers!"

After we clinked our drinks together, the door opened.

"Ah! Here's the man that you should really thank for everything," Izzy said to Roxanne, standing up and taking her hand. "This is *my* boss. I call him the Big Man."

To my surprise, even William was extra-delighted to see her when Izzy introduced her to him. "Here's Foxxy Roxxy! That's my nickname for her now. And yes, boss, she's the one."

"Are you okay, man?" Larry said, touching my shoulder.

"Huh?"

"You look so out of it."

"What are we doing being rude? Let's join them."

I shook out my wrists, pulling myself together as we joined Izzy, Roxanne, and William.

"I'm afraid our happy hour is up, Roxanne," Izzy said solemnly. "But I brought my camera crew. We can take some pictures so you can remember this day forever." Roxanne grinned, speechless. "Gather around, everyone," Izzy declared when his crew arrived.

I sauntered over, hurrying to stand next to Izzy to his left. At his right stood Roxanne.

"Smile!" William said from behind the cameramen. "John, c'mon. Smile!"

"My Cheshire Cat's not smiling?" Izzy said in shock.

When he looked at me, I smiled so wide that it almost hurt. Because it was real. And my heart melted when Izzy called me his Cheshire Cat. We took one serious photo with Roxanne, as if we were taking a promotional photo. The last few shots, we all made goofy faces at the cameras.

"Now, a few of only Roxanne and me," Izzy said.

Benson, Phil, Tim, and Larry all scooted away, but I stood frozen between them.

When everyone was staring at me, I backed away, not saying a word about my zoning out. And nobody else did, either. I couldn't force myself to smile when Roxanne wrapped her arms around Izzy's waist. When she looked up at him, my heart grew numb and fell to my toes when Izzy looked down at her lovingly, as did she at him. When the photo was snapped, I blinked, and not because the lights were glowing before my eyes. It was them.

After another photo was taken, Izzy smiled warmly and pecked Roxanne's hand. She smiled goofily. When the two hugged, I covered my sneer as if I were yawning. As Izzy smooched her fingertips, dotting her skin with his glittery pink smooches up to her wrist, Roxanne giggled bashfully. I glared.

"Izzy!" I called to him with a slight hint of daddy-dom in my voice. "It's time for us to go," I said in my normal voice, but with that dominant *look* in my eye that only he knew.

My submissive darling looked at me. How I wanted nothing else more than to say to Roxanne, "Sod off!" when we shook hands and said good-bye. When she *finally* left, heaven rose from the ashes of hell. When Izzy and I returned to our suite, we made music in the key of sex, so beautiful, strong, and powerful that it almost made me forget the meet-and-greet and Roxanne. Yet in the back of my mind, as Izzy was making love to me, something far less sweet left a bitter taste in my mind. Was it possible that his reason for snogging me this way, so out of control, breathless and wild, was because his Foxxy Roxxy was in the back of his mind? Was her kiss still his forbidden fruit? Did it mean more than ours? Or was it me, again? What was to blame this time?

It was the booze and the Hard Rock.

Izzy and I sat side by side on the couch in our platforms, sparkly frocks, jewelry, and feather boas, watching a news report about the long queue to Madison Square Garden.

"Tonight is the *last* show to end what has been called a career-changing move for the King of Glam. Since touring here, his legend, culture, and mythos has skyrocketed to the top of the charts, and has touched the hearts of men, women, and celebrities alike."

"They're sure hyping this up." I popped my collar. "I'm almost nervous."

"I'm horny." Izzy waggled his brows, holding one end of his boa and tickling my cheek with it.

I laughed and bit it, growling at him playfully as I tugged the boa.

"More torture, please, daddy?" He pulled the boa, and I spat it out. "Please?" he begged.

I slapped his face with my boa. "End this show with a bang, and you'll get it. And I'll bang you, too."

"Goodie!" He bounced on my lap, raising his leg as he stroked my hair. "I love you, daddy."

I stroked his thigh through his space cadet costume. "I'm so lucky."

He turned off the TV, got off my lap, and we stood up. "Ready for the last concert of our American life, daddy?"

"Yes," I said. "Because"—*I'll never have to see Roxanne ever again*—"I love you, Izzy."

"I'm the luckiest man in the world."

He quickly kissed my lips, held my hand, and we said *I love you* at the same time. The second the door opened, he dropped my hand. Every step he took was history being made. No matter where we looked, up, down, or side to side, hundreds of cameras were filming Delilah Starr and Izzy Rich. How cool and composed Izzy was, wearing a spectacular red, white, and blue leotard with a long flowing Union Jack cape. "Madison Square Garden!" he howled. The venue roared. "New York. This song is for *you*." I drummed the beat of "New York City (I Love You)." The audience reacted as if it was one of Izzy's biggest hits. Izzy was nearly on his knees. "...to kiss her, touch, hug, squeeze her..."

The band and I were jamming, and then Izzy stopped playing. We looked at each other, confused. What to do? I shrugged at the guys, drumming as they carried on for a bit.

"Hold up." Izzy raised his hand, and we stopped. Izzy looked ahead at the front row, stretching his arm out to Roxanne as the light shone on her.

I tapped my foot on the floor as Izzy's bodyguards brought her on the stage. As she stood there, grinning, Izzy cooed, "There's the lady. My lady." My body was shaking, and not because of the adrenaline. The audience screamed as he purred, "How I love to dance for *you*, Roxanne." He spun on his heels, facing the band. I picked up my sticks immediately when he gave us the thumbs up. By the way he was dancing, I swiftly struck up the beat to Benson playing the chord for "Dirty Dancer."

Roxanne removed her jacket and flung it to the side, sporting a short-sleeved tank top. The audience screamed. Izzy danced as if he had expected her to toss her jacket away. Either that, or he was too engrossed to care. Roxanne surprised me even more by dancing around *Izzy* as he belted the tune with uninhibited sexuality. The tension welled up not in his crotch, but in that divine voice. Roxanne backed up to Izzy, shaking her ass. He ad-libbed, "Damn."

I licked my lips, and not because of the salty sweat pearl I tasted in my mouth. Roxanne's plump ass, round and luscious, jiggled as she stamped her sequined boots, in synch with the band as if it were a part of her. When she turned around, she and Izzy were face-to-face. They danced in unison, their every roll, shake, and shimmy in perfect, breathtaking symmetry. I looked at the guys, and they looked at me, nodding with satisfaction as I smirked and jammed harder.

Izzy leaned back, gyrating his hips. "Now this is what I call a dirty dancer, ladies and gentlemen. Miss Roxanne Foster Shengyi, or, as I call her, Foxxy Roxxy!"

I shook my head as I didn't bang, but *pounded* the drums in fury. And not because of the music.

"Dirty dancer..." Izzy crooned. "We're only dancing..." He looked deep into her eyes as he wailed, "But how your body *talks* to me, oh, how it moves, sugar, how it..." Roxanne turned her back to him again, shaking her ass. He choked out, "Hot damn!" Izzy was about to pat that ass. Roxanne faced him with a naughty smile, rolling her shoulders. "The way you dance that pole lady..." Izzy shivered. "How it makes me whole, how it steals my soul!"

My eyes widened when Roxanne leaned toward Izzy's microphone. "All I want to do is make a baby!" she sang with a most electrifying growl, and then they belted, "With *you*. All I want to do is make love to you, like you want me to..." Izzy stamped his pumps maddeningly, ripping a killer riff from his guitar. He jumped in the air and landed on his knees, looking up at Roxanne as he sang, "You turn me on! How you turn me on, my dirty dancer." Roxanne sang softly, "Take me. I'm yours..."

I hid my growl at their obvious chemistry behind my drums. They were my savior. Izzy rocked harder on his guitar, his legs spread, his groin thrusting against the back of his instrument as he strummed. Roxanne whipped her wild child hair, shaking that fat rump. Izzy got on his heels. The two danced. He let her dance alone, the spotlight shining on her. And then they danced as one.

"Be the man and the woman that you see outside and within the dirty dancer inside of me!" he sang more passionately than ever before.

Roxanne growled at a breathless pace "Or you can just—" She stopped, and then Izzy dropped his microphone. I stopped my drumming. The band stopped playing. It happened too quickly. Was I dreaming? Had I really gone hysterical?

Izzy cupped Roxanne's face in his hands, and he kissed her hotly. I panted, but not the same way as everybody else. The screams were hard, loud, and aching, like my heart. This wasn't a dream. This was a nightmare. And it was here to stay.

"Five," I said, more pearls of sweat dripping down my face. "Four. Three. Two."

At *one*, Izzy held Roxanne closer, their snogging deepened. I counted backward.

Rick held Roxanne's jacket for her until Izzy leapt toward them. My heart dropped as Izzy kissed her, fondling her cheek. I looked at the guys, and they looked at me. I sat there lost until someone from management shouted, "Play!" I blinked, and we went back to performing "Dirty Dancer." Izzy tore himself away from Roxanne, his lipstick smeared. He panted into the microphone. "Woo!" he howled as I drummed harder, louder. "That kiss was so good even my band felt the *heat*. Could you?" He touched his lips. "How my lips hurt." He strummed his guitar. "How my heart is breaking, my body aching for Roxanne." The fan's howled at her name. "Our kiss. It's made of this."

Without any more deviation from the set list, the gang and I played all the songs exactly as rehearsed.

"Since I was a poor London boy…" Izzy said shakily into the mic, mascara dripping. "…I dreamt of this. The American Dream. America, *thank you*." He bowed and curtsied. "I came to this country as a prince, but because of you I'll be going home as a king." Izzy bowed and curtsied again as they played "God Save the Queen." Backstage, Izzy was surrounded, struggling to keep himself together, bawling. When I finally had him, he hugged me. We cried together, saying, "We did it," repeatedly. When he let go, he mouthed, "I love you" so fast one could've missed it. But how could I? Not I. "I love you!" I wanted to scream. My heart raced. I looked around, surrounded by so many people that loved me. But where had my lover gone?

❖

Knock, knock, knock. Silence. *Knock, knock, knock.*
Nothing.

I knocked on Izzy's door again, waiting. "Where the bloody hell is he?" I whispered, knocking on the door one more time.

I looked down at my platforms, and then at the door, rubbing my arms as if they were cold. Fresh off the stage, I was still hot and sweaty. I could still hear the fans screaming as that kiss played over and over in my mind. Turning my head to my right and then to my left, I pondered if I should knock on somebody else's door and ask if they'd seen Izzy. Instead, I went back to my room and locked it. After taking a long shower, I went to the living room with a towel wrapped around my waist, expecting Izzy to be there. He wasn't. When I sat down on the couch, I raked my fingers through my wet hair, sitting there wondering where could he possibly be at half past one in the morning.

I sighed, grabbing the phone, setting it on my lap. I thought I should call somebody in the entourage to ask them if they knew where he was. I was about to dial any of their numbers by random. I picked up the phone quick and it rang a few times.

"Oh, John?" Emma said, sounding groggy but overjoyed to hear my voice. "You haven't called since you've been in America."

"You know me. Always the bad baby brother."

"You must have seen and done so much. Behaving yourself?"

"Trying." I smirked. "America is something."

"I bet you don't want to leave."

"You kidding me?" I choked out.

"I was only egging you on, John. Are you that homesick?"

My lips trembled. I covered my eyes, rubbing them, and then my temples. "Um, New York City and its skyscrapers. They're so claustrophobic. I miss London."

She pffted. "It can't be that. I know you, John. You are rubbing your temples right now."

I snorted, keeping my hand by my side. "No, I'm not."

"Sure you aren't." She snickered.

"All right, all right, you sussed me out. Um…"

"There you go umming. Now you're worrying me. What's wrong?"

"Emma…" My lips trembled. "I've been holding on to something the past few months now, and I haven't told anyone, so if I tell you about it, you can't tell anyone, okay?"

"Did you finally ask Izzy out?" She laughed. "Wishful thinking, I know."

I gulped thickly. This time, out of fear from uncertainty. And the unknown. I cleared my throat. "Yeah…"

"Yeah about what?" Emma asked, sounding excited, confused, and freaked out at once. "That you asked Izzy out, or that it's wishful thinking?"

I bit my lower lip to stop it from shaking. "Oh, bugger." I fake-yawned. "I'm bloody exhausted. I should get going to bed, long flight tomorrow. Tell everyone about the *Izzy Rich in Madison Square Garden* BBC special. It airs next Saturday. And guess what? I have a day off that day."

"John! You wicked boy! You can't keep me on hold like that. What were you going to say?"

"That was it." My hands shook. "The BBC special. And that I'm visiting that day. Surprise!"

"Oh, that's great, John! I'll have Nolan tell everyone straight away. I can't wait."

"Me too, sis. I love you." I hung up, feeling guilty. I always told Emma *everything*. Until now.

"It's nobody's business, anyway," I said to myself. "We are in love. We don't need the whole bloody world knowing about us." I blinked, realizing for the first time that Izzy and I never talked about whether or not we'd ever tell the entourage, our family, and closest friends. For that matter, we never talked about what would happen if the world knew, either. Feeling a headache coming on, I went back to the bedroom. I took an aspirin and crashed on the bed, turned on the TV, and watched a replay of Izzy on *The Tonight Show Starring Johnny Carson*. After it was over, I watched a few more late-night talk shows until half past three. I closed my eyes and didn't realize I was dozing off until I felt something warm and wet in my ear.

"Izzy?" I moaned softly.

When I opened my eyes, my baby was there.

"Hey, sleepyhead daddy." He licked me from my chin to my cheek, giving me a kiss there.

I grimaced. "Where the bloody hell were you?" I snapped when I sat up. "You had me worried!"

He twisted his mouth as if he sucked on a lemon. "Somebody's a grumpy daddy."

"Answer my question, brat! Where were you?"

"I was caught up in the media, fans, and paparazzi, then I was swamped with business stuff with William and Bernie. Then..." He smiled with a peculiar softness, a startling innocence. "I picked up Roxanne, and we hung out at my suite."

"What?" I shouted. "Why didn't you let me know you were going to be with her?"

He shrugged. "It wasn't planned. Spur of the moment."

"Oh, bollocks, Izzy! I'm supposed to believe *that?* You probably want me to believe that what happened on stage tonight was some fucking random rubbish, too."

"Whoa, baby. Why are you so ticked off?"

"I'm not ticked off!"

"Baby, what happened, it was random. We were bewitched." He smirked naughtily.

"Well, it looked like you two had a ball."

"Didn't everyone? Didn't you?"

"The kiss lasted too long."

"What did you think about everything else? Her dancing. Her singing."

"That kiss." I glared. "It lasted for *ten* seconds, Izzy. What was that about?"

"She's a really good kisser." He blushed. "Such a talented tongue, such warm, soft lips."

"Was she a good shag, too?"

Izzy's coy, boyish smile disappeared. "We didn't fuck."

"Now I know you're bluffing! Yes, I'm a bit pissed off that you were with Roxanne behind my back, but whatever. The cat's out of the bag. You can tell me, how good was the fuck?"

"John," he said dryly. "Roxanne is Catholic."

"So?"

"Devout. She's a virgin. She only believes in making love after wedlock."

I let out a laugh but Izzy wasn't laughing. I looked into his eyes and mouthed *wow.* "You're dead serious."

He nodded slowly. "I was kissing her, almost took off her knickers, and then she told me."

I grimaced for him. "Oh, dear. I bet that turned you off."

"It turned me on! But...her body, her rules. I kept my cock in my pants and respected her virginity and chastity. I didn't have her explain anything. All we did from there is kiss."

"And drink Shirley Temples afterward?" I said condescendingly.

"What's with the attitude?"

"Can't take a joke?"

"Don't like Roxanne?"

I kept my mouth shut, glaring at him.

"Roxanne's a very nice girl. What do you have against her?"

"*Nothing.*"

"Oh c'mon, there's something—"

"I don't understand her. I mean, she's okay with stripping, getting ink, and lying to her parents about seeing a rock star they see as the Antichrist, but she won't make love?"

"She's confusing, but not confused."

I smirked.

"And baby, she's got talent. And she's *smart*. Whether what she did was calculated or not, it was brilliant. She's a star, daddy."

"Yeah? Well..." I smacked his face five times. He gasped after each loud smack of my palm against his cheek. "That's for throwing me and the guys off onstage!" I spat. "That was so bloody cruel of you, you know that? You had any bloody idea how fucking lost and confused we were?"

He shivered and rubbed his cheek, and then he smiled at me, snickering. "Wasn't that fun?"

"We were *live*."

"Live spelled backward is evil."

"Roxanne's an opportunist!" I hissed. "What balls she has, doing absolutely nothing onstage all this time, pretending that she was oh so bloody shy and pissed scared, until now, suddenly, on live national television, she turns into some gyrating sexpot, and she had the gall to sing, too?"

Izzy was about to say something, but I barked, "She used you, Izzy. Can't you fucking see that?"

"Damn." He grimaced. "You don't like Roxanne at all, do you? Bloody hell. She's just a fan."

"She's a kid, Izzy."

"And what am I? A cradle robber?"

"Might as well be."

Izzy's face softened. "Daddy, what's with that long face?"

"It's obvious that you like her, Iz. As more than a fan."

"How do you mean?"

"The way you kissed her, that's not how you kiss a fan. You never kissed any fan like that."

"What's up with you and this kiss obsession? All right, so it lasted far longer than normal. That's only because she *is* a great kisser. But I also did it on purpose. For the show."

"You kissed her like the way you kiss me!" I shouted so hotly that it left me cold, and I shivered. I held back my tears, wiping my eyes quick. "Show or not," I said gently. "That's what I felt."

"That was the adrenaline," Izzy said calmly. "We got carried away, all right? I'm sorry."

I turned my back to him, holding on to my pillow.

"Don't be mad. Please."

I looked over my shoulder at him, saying nothing.

Izzy studied my face, and smirked. "Ah. I know what it is. You are jealous."

"Me? Jealous? Of a kid?" I shook my head. "I'm not jealous. I'm afraid of losing you."

"To a girl," he scoffed.

"To a girl. To a boy. Doesn't matter! The thought of me losing you to *anyone*—"

"I love you!" He crushed his lips against mine, and then looked at me. "You are my daddy." He kissed my cheek. "My boyfriend." He kissed my nose. "My king." He kissed my neck. "Lover." He licked me and rubbed his nose against mine. "My everything, Johnny Angel." He whispered, "I'm sorry. I've been a very bad boy. I should be punished with torture. Tickle torture!"

I snorted, shaking my head. "After all that you did tonight? No way. Asshole."

"But you promised!" he whined. "I ended the show with a bang. Now you have to tickle and bang me to hell! Please," he begged. "I'm the sorriest asshole ever, I swear. I need you."

I rolled my eyes, looking at that pathetic face and his sorry tears. "Spoiled brat. Get the boa."

He rolled out of the bed, prancing over to a feather boa on the floor. When he returned to bed, I pounced on him, lifted his arms up against the headboard, and tied his wrists together with the boa. I did it so tightly, he gasped. He couldn't free himself.

"Who's your daddy?" I looked down at him, tickling his chin with a feather.

"You are!" Izzy cried. His cock sprung, tenting against his glittery pants.

He writhed and squealed as I tickled his smooth, hairless pits with my fingers. He laughed so loudly I covered his mouth, not with my hand, but my lips. Our tongues meshed, and we moaned like our first kiss as man and woman, man and man. Nothing was wrong. Everything was right. The tickle torture was as orgasmic as our sex, beautiful as our love. Him and me, drunk, no, madly in love. Nobody changed our world. Not even Roxanne Foster Shengyi.

Chapter Nine

When our jet took off from John F. Kennedy Airport, so did my mind. I was finally free. The weight of the world lifted off me without any drugs or alcohol. While Izzy was gazing out the window at New York City and her skyscrapers, all I could do was smile. At last, no more burdens. After the plane landed without turbulence, Izzy, the entourage, and I toasted to the American leg of the tour and to the next leg to come.

While knocking back a few glasses and smoking a joint, we reminisced about what we'd miss and not miss about America. I sure as hell wouldn't miss Roxanne, but I no longer had to worry. I thought about Izzy and me, all our moments bringing us closer together. They played back in my mind when I closed my eyes, smiling from memory to memory, until music stirred me. I turned my head to look at Izzy. He had headphones on, and a tender smile graced his face. His eyes were misty.

"What are you listening to?" I asked him.

He removed his headphones, putting them on me. A voice so beautiful, powerful, and nuanced sang: "Am I born again? In this new life, will I ever be the same?"

It wasn't only my ears, but my heart the singer touched. She reached striking vocal heights, exuding the paranoia, worry, and awakening of Delilah Starr as well as the liberation that went with it. The singer was far from being Delilah or Izzy, but she was close.

Izzy lifted up a headphone and said, "What do you think?"

I rubbed the corner of my eye. "That voice's heavenly."

"And as clean as a whistle."

That simple phrase drained my face. I slowly removed the headphones.

"Roxanne was fifteen here, Johnny. Fifteen and so emotional." He looked at me. "I can feel the promise even in the slight weaknesses of her voice. I didn't think she'd sound this good."

I smirked and gulped thickly.

"Like you, I'm blown away."

"I wouldn't say I was blown away."

"You said her voice was heavenly. And you got teary eyed. If that's not blown away—"

"Bollocks. I wasn't teary-eyed." I snorted. "Why would I? All I heard was one verse."

"Listen to *all of it*, Johnny. I've listened to her demo about five times already today."

"Since when?"

"While you were sleeping like a baby," he whispered into my ear.

"So that was the noise that woke me up."

"C'mon, Johnny. Listen to the whole thing with me?"

"I heard enough."

"In one verse?"

"I need a nap to catch up on the sleep I didn't get last night."

When I felt his pout coming on, I said, "Look, I'm sure the rest of the demo is"—I almost shuddered to admit it, and even as I confessed, I felt that chill down my spine—"exquisite."

Izzy cocked his chin with a sly, proud grin. "It is. More than that. It's perfect."

I took a deep breath and closed my eyes with a nod. "Let me sleep."

"Oh, c'mon, please, Johnny? You know you want to hear more of it."

I opened my eyes and growled, "Stop it!" as I batted his hands away when he tried to put the headphones over my ears again. "Let me sleep on this goddamn plane for a change, okay!"

"All right, fine," he huffed. "I'll force somebody else to listen with me."

"Go do that."

Though I was smiling playfully as I said that, I was trembling, haunted by her voice. My eyes were misty when I closed them. How could it be? It was *Roxanne*. Only fifteen. How was it that she could swell my ears and my heart with emotion? How could a voice so young be so rich? She had the gift. Who needed a poison when her voice was inside me? Instead of free, I was caged again. I opened my eyes, turning my head.

Izzy wasn't there.

I peeked down the aisle and saw Izzy and William James sitting beside each other, listening to the demo together. William nodded his head with that serious chin rub and approving smile. Izzy got up from the seat, and I overheard him say, "I'll want it back, Big Man." I closed my eyes quick when I sensed Izzy sitting next to me. "Yes! I knew he'd love it!" I heard him say quietly, joyously.

"Hmm?" I asked, pretending he woke me up.

"You know what's funny, Johnny?"

I opened one eye, looking at him.

"We've only left America for a few hours, and I already miss her."

"America?" I asked with a quiet desperation that wanted nothing more but to scream *You better not mean Roxanne.*

"Who else would I mean? Naturally, I miss England more," he said with a smile. I smiled, too.

When we landed at Heathrow Airport, the adrenaline was in my veins. The screaming, cheering, shouting, and bawling was just like America but it was more, because it was home. We were greeted by thousands of *Welcome Home Izzy!* banners and *We Love You, King of Glam!* signs. I stood a distance from him and watched as he took that giant leap off the steps back on the soil of our native country, decked out in a dazzling Union Jack body suit. His batwing sleeves said, *England, My Love, My Home.* The riches and the media were madder as Izzy bowed to the ground, kissing it, and then blowing kisses at the riches. With each step Izzy took, I raised my head above a sea of people and cameras to keep a steady eye on the man who was now king. The harder I tried, the more I got swallowed, but I never let Izzy out of my sight. I'd never let go, like the fame, the fans, and the hounds.

❖

"Back from his tour of America is the newly crowned glam king."

I clapped with the audience as Izzy graced the stage decked out in a jaw-dropping leopard print dress with glittery hearts for black spots. Didn't Izzy ever look so bloody glam, the finest. Izzy curtsied, blew kisses, and wiggled his ass as he walked to Russell and shook his hand.

"Hello, hello again, Russell," Izzy purred at him after he sat. "How I bloody missed you."

"You still have your British accent. You've been away for so long, thought you'd lose it."

"Are you sure about that?" Izzy chirped, being that Southern belle. "Because you never know." He changed his accent into an East Coast one. "I might be a whole other person now."

Russell smirked, and I couldn't tell if his nod was approving or condescending. "I'm now realizing, you're always wearing a form-fitting skirt or a slinky dress on my show. Why?"

He batted his lashes and winked. "Down, boy."

Russell squirmed as Izzy crossed his legs, flashing a thigh. That got some applause from the audience. Russell cleared his throat after we calmed down. "I see America hasn't changed you at all."

"It has, actually, in many ways."

"Career-wise, it has created a new dimension for it. You are now a glam *king*."

Izzy looked down coyly. "Yes sir, I am."

"Why are you modest?" Russell said in a serious, curious tone.

"You see, since I was a kid, I only dreamed of touring America, never would've thought that it would actually happen. And to have top-charting albums, selling out concerts there?" He shook his head. "I thought I was going to be chalked up in the States as just a cult sensation."

"And instead, you became simply a sensation."

Izzy nodded with that same bashful smile.

"And this was your first time going to America?"

"For me and for most of my crew. It was like journeying into the great unknown. We were like kids in Disneyland. Hell, we were kids when we went to Disneyland."

I beamed at that whimsical memory.

"Is it true you met Elvis?"

Izzy nodded anxiously. "And many more of my rock and roller American idols who inspired me since childhood. Meeting Elvis was the most humbling, of course."

"Would you two ever record a single or something?"

Izzy rolled his eyes and snickered. "You and your fantasies again, Russell. We have no business relationship. The King and I are just friends."

"What did you love the most about America?"

"My American fans! Not to knock my fans here and elsewhere, but the Americans are different."

"How so?"

"They're crazy! And so bloody horny."

Russell squirmed again. "What did you like the least about America?"

"No offense to America, but their tea is bloody awful." He grimaced and stuck out his tongue a little. "And the country is too big. Each state felt like its own country. It was overwhelming."

"You experienced a lot of culture shock?"

"Oh, yeah. Like the Bible Belt and some American accents and phrases I couldn't understand, still don't. And the way everyone treated me, not bad, but like I wasn't human at all."

"Even people here are still trying to suss out *what* you are, Izzy," Russell said jokingly. "In America, when did it hit you that your fame was changing?"

"When we were landing in New York City, it truly registered that my career wasn't going to be the same anymore. I was looking out of the window, seeing all those skyscrapers, and I imagined that it was this giant squid or gargantuan monkey pulling us down because this is *America*, you know, and *New York City*, where anything can happen."

"All your concerts captivated people, but that last Madison Square Garden one was special."

"So I've heard." He smiled naughtily.

I crossed my legs and rested my chin on my balled fist, gazing hard at Izzy.

"It aired last night on the BBC, and I was told before you got here that it had ten million viewers, which makes it the most-watched TV special this year, and one of the most-watched programmes on the BBC at number two, with the *Rich Girl* documentary being number one still."

Izzy stood, and bowed and curtsied to the howling audience. "I love you," he said to us. "My fans amaze me," Izzy said to Russell after he sat back down. "I envy them."

"That's strange. I can imagine they envy *you*."

"They get to enjoy my work more than I can. Their love for it is my love."

"You seem more relaxed."

"That's because I feel like I've truly made it, you know? Like I've accomplished the impossible. Nothing to prove anymore. Such amazing things have happened in America, on and off stage."

"Especially at Madison Square Garden."

Russell mentioned Roxanne. I didn't dare swallow in fear of choking on the lump in my throat. Even my own family and some of my relatives couldn't stop talking about Roxanne. As painful as it was, I pretended I was swept away. To be fake was more than kind.

"You called her Foxxy Roxxy, but her real name is Roxanne Foster."

"Roxanne Foster *Shengyi*."

"Shengyi?" Russell said, stumbling on the pronunciation.

Izzy repeated her last name correctly. "She's Chinese-German. She has only lived in America for eight years but is fluent in English as well as Mandarin and German." I kept my head up, holding on and holding still, as Izzy went on about how Roxanne was the fan girl that he mentioned during an interview ages ago. I looked behind me, at so many surprised faces.

"How did you meet her in person?" Russell asked, sounding shocked.

I could almost hear a pin drop as Izzy told Russell. Now the whole United Kingdom knew.

"I *had* to keep meeting her, up to the very last show."

"Did you two rehearse the dance at Madison Square Garden?"

"That would've been impossible. I know it's hard to believe, but it was random."

"And the kiss?"

"Random, too."

"It's now the most talked about dance and kiss in the British press."

"Oh, really?" He giggled. "Wow, I didn't know that. Since I've been home, I've been too busy preparing for the next leg of the tour to notice what's being said about that, or about me."

"Roxanne's dancing and singing had some great reviews."

I read some. I shuddered, admitting to myself the critics were right.

"Roxanne is talented. Nobody can deny that. She has that *it* factor."

"Will we possibly see more of her?"

Izzy smirked. "No bloody idea. I'm one busy man! This week has been grueling with rehearsals for the next leg of the tour that I'm calling The Homecoming. I'll be touring my roots in the UK, Scotland, and Wales."

As Izzy finished up the interview, the entourage was quietly escorted to the backstage area, surrounded by the South Bank stage people and tech crew. Instead of hearing Izzy, all I heard was the fans outside the building. At the instant the audience clapped, Izzy dashed toward us, and we all ran down the hallway to the exit. Our limousine was waiting amidst hundreds of screaming fans. They pushed through to get to Izzy, trying their hardest to reach the window or climb on top of the moving car. Once the coast was clear, we were Brighton bound.

❖

I could still hear the screaming fans at Guild Hall from last night as I was sleeping. Two weeks into the Homecoming leg of the tour, and the ride was still a roller coaster, a nonstop trip that had a beginning, but whose ending was not in sight. I opened my eyes a little when I heard a silky, professional voice. I smiled warmly, holding, spooning Izzy closer as he spoke softly over the phone, as if being careful not to wake me completely.

"I'll be over there in a few minutes, Big Man," he whispered and hung up.

I kept my eyes shut on purpose. I felt him turn over so he could lie on his back. I put my head on his bare chest, nuzzling his hard nipple with my cheek as I wrapped my arms around his waist. I melted as he brushed my forehead with his soft lips. He kissed, and then I felt him trying to separate my arms from his waist, trying to break us apart.

"Oh, bugger," he said when I squeezed him harder. "I didn't mean to wake you, daddy."

I yawned, embracing him closer. He giggled.

"What's so bloody funny?"

"Ever since we've been back home from America, you've been so bloody clingy."

"Got a problem with that, brat?" I hissed in his ear and gave his lobe a lick.

"It is fucking adorable."

He gasped when I nipped at his ear and tugged. He gasped louder when I kissed him. I shivered as he brushed the small of my back with his fingers. I deepened our kiss, Izzy whimpered and sucked the tip of my tongue.

He panted, letting go. "Daddy, I got to get dressed."

I looked at the time. It was half past eight. "You don't have any plans yet."

"I'm having breakfast with Big Man."

"For business or for fun?"

"For fun. It has been a while since him and I spent time together mucking about, alone."

"Why so early?" I kissed his left nipple. "And why the hurry?"

After I circled my tongue around his right nipple, I kissed him all the way down to his abdomen. Just when I was about to cup his sack in the palm of my hand and rub my nose along the shaft of his soft monster, Izzy chuckled, pulling the covers away.

"Daddy, you know how William is. He's the morning person. If it were up to me, I'd rather us meet for dinner, but he's so bloody hell-bent on us meeting for breakfast instead."

"What about mine? I *need* my protein shake." I opened my mouth wide. My tongue only touched the tip of his cockhead, and he grabbed my hair and pulled my face upward.

He purred against my dimpled chin and gave it a needy lick and a tiny suck. "Daddy, just because Big Man and I are meeting for fun isn't an excuse for me to be late."

"I know, I know." I kissed his nose. "Get sexy."

I spanked his ass when he got off the bed. He turned around and pecked me on the lips. I stayed underneath the covers, bundling myself as I watched Izzy sway to the walk-in closet. I licked my lips and rubbed my soft cock to Izzy's ass, how gorgeous it was with my little hickey and belt whipping marks on his flesh. I turned myself over on my back, spreading my legs and closing my eyes to Izzy sweetly singing "Johnny Angel" as he was getting dressed in his swishy tangerine orange pants and pink and gold blouse. His voice brought tears to my closed eyes, because now those words were true. I beamed as Izzy kissed my eyelids, and I opened my eyes to a face so gorgeous it made me teary-eyed, too. I stroked his hoop earring.

"Get some more sleep, daddy. We got a *long* day ahead."

I wanted to suck the pink gloss off his mouth, but I let him go, unwrapping my arms from his waist. "Have fun, princess."

"I love you."

When he left his suite, I got so chilled not even blankets could warm me. I realized why when my stomach growled. The orgies worked up an appetite for something besides the hedonistic. In the outside world of lovely Southampton, the sky was cloudy and dreary, unlike my memories of last night's smashing concert and a most wonderful evening with my boyfriend. Life couldn't be any better, especially now that I was going to one of my favorite posh restaurants, a ten-minute walk from the hotel. The cozy atmosphere sucked me in. I was hankering for their famous skirt steak and eggs.

"Welcome back, Mr. Maxwell," chirped Charlotte, the waitress.

"Hello again, love." I scanned the restaurant, looking for a table near a window so I could people watch. My eyes lit up when I saw Izzy and William sitting in a secluded corner. I smiled but noticed William was dressed in his pinstripe suit, his sharpest formal wear.

Charlotte must have noticed my staring at them. "Are you joining them for their business meeting?"

"Business meeting?"

"That was what Mr. Rich told me."

I scratched my head. "Are you sure that was what he said?"

"It's what he told me. Would you like to be seated with them?"

"Oh, no. I don't want to disturb them. I'd like to be seated near them, though."

I followed Charlotte as she led me to the seat that I requested. William and Izzy were so immersed in conversation that William didn't see me, and with Izzy's back to my table, he couldn't see me, but I could clearly see and hear them from where I was sitting.

"The usual?" Charlotte asked.

"Yes," I said quietly. "And the espresso."

I looked up, seeing Izzy taking a bite of his fried egg and William sipping his coffee after he munched on his bacon. I shielded my eyes with the menu as I overheard the two speaking.

"If I wanted a video babe to dance the way I tell her, there's no point. I'd be the vixen myself!" Izzy said as William laughed. "In all seriousness, it's not about getting a girl who looks the part. She has to *be* the part, you know what I mean? Dancing can't be something that she does. It has to be something that she *is*. I have to feel it in her every move." I stared. "She has to turn me on. Literally, William. She has to give me a relentless boner when she dances. I've been keeping in touch with the one woman so far who has done that from the start."

I looked down at my table quick as William spoke.

"Yes, I agree, Izzy. She has to turn everyone on for the video to work. 'Dirty Dancer' is doing well on the UK charts, but I want it to be at the top where it belongs. A daring video will take it there."

"Exactly! I can feel it in my bones, Big Man. But I can't do it alone. I need her."

"How soon can you reach Roxanne?"

I was too stunned to thank Charlotte when she served my food. I took a slow sip of my espresso.

"At five, which will make it noon in America. If she says yes, I'll fly her here in two weeks. We can start filming and put her to work straight away."

"What if she says no?"

"I'll have auditions in London next week."

I knocked back my espresso and slammed it down on the saucer. My hands trembled, not from the caffeine kick, but from trying to register everything that I heard. The steak and eggs I ordered was hard to swallow. Only one bite, and I couldn't have another.

"I hope she'll say yes," William said eagerly.

"Trust me," Izzy said cockily. "She will."

Quieter than ever, I forced myself to eat as they ate. They talked about gardening, William's children, the cartoons they both loved, and some politics. My mind was heavy, my soul burdened with a secret. Theirs. Izzy's bluff. The worst. It caved in on me. The instant I finished eating, I left the table, paid my bill, and dashed back to the hotel. When I closed the door of my suite, I panted, flustered as I slammed my back against the door. I shook my head, telling myself *It's no big deal. It's no big deal. It's no big deal! Don't cry. Fight. Don't...*

"Dammit!" I shouted, grabbing a fist full of my hair as I choked out a good cry. I pressed my back harder against the door as I thought about Izzy's lie and Roxanne. The harder I fought, the slower I crumpled to the floor, sitting with my head against the wall, fists balled. I only stopped crying as I told myself he loved me. *He loves me.*

As tempted as I was to get stoned on joints, ditzy on ecstasy, or tripped out on LSD, I didn't dare—not with the sound checks and the concert on the horizon. Instead, I had my fifth fag in my mouth. I coughed, but that was only because my throat was so hoarse from all my crying. My fingers shook as I smoked and looked at the time. It was half past five. I wiped the corner of my eye when it welled again. What the hell was my baby doing? Who had he been with this whole time? His meeting with William was nine bloody hours ago. I slumped back on the couch, my hands shaking more as I wondered, was it best to take the easy way out? Drink something. Take something. Do something, other than cry. Here I go again. Crying again, wondering how long Izzy had been keeping in touch with Roxanne. Had he been keeping in touch with her since we've been home? How did he make the time?

My heart jumped when I heard those *six* rhythmic knocks. "Already?" I wiped at my eyes, looked at the time. Impossible! But was this a good thing?

I snubbed my fag in the ashtray crowded high with butts. I emptied it in the trash can, then dashed to the bathroom sink. I splashed my face with cold water and scrubbed away my tears. After drying myself, I stepped back, breathed, and sighed.

"That was the longest breakfast ever," I said after I let Izzy in. "Had a great time?"

"Jolly fun, not talking business for a change. Sorry it took so long. I had some other plans."

I cocked my chin up. "What were they?"

Izzy jumped as if he needed to pee, as if he wanted to scream.

"What did she say?" I asked desperately, with every fiber of my being.

Izzy stopped jumping and raised his eyebrow.

I blinked, thinking fast. "Cheryl. I'm assuming you were with Cheryl."

"I wasn't."

My hands shook. Almost got caught! To distract him, I sat on the couch and patted my lap. He straddled me, arching his back. I pinched his ass. "What's the news? I know the drill."

"'Dirty Dancer' will have a music video, and I'll be *directing* it!"

"Really? Fuck. That's wonderful! My baby, a director?"

"There's more."

"Auditions?" I asked excitedly with bated breath. All I wanted to hear was yes. Only yes.

I gulped as he said, "I already have my video vixen."

"Somebody famous? Yasmin? Andrea?"

"Neither. She's not famous now, but if the timing and cards are played right, she will be."

"Who is she?" I asked, wishing, telling myself that it wasn't who I knew it was.

"Roxanne," he said nervously.

I looked at the time. "Wait. But it's only after five. How did you get her to say yes so fast?"

Izzy looked at me funny. *Fuck.* "What do you mean? I talked to her over three hours ago."

My eyes widened. "What? You did? Why for that long?"

"Her fucking parents." He rolled his eyes. "I was talking to them more than her. That was fun."

"What were they like?"

"As tight as your arse, but all pain and no pleasure."

I snorted. "What did you and her mummy and daddy talk about?"

"I couldn't get a word in," he said. I never heard him sound and look so agitated. "With their talking down to me and lecturing me with their religious dogma. Bloody exhausting! I had to take a nap after the call."

"Aw. My poor baby."

"I wasn't asking for much. All I wanted was their fucking permission to bring Roxanne here with their blessing. Instead, they ripped my ear off, and flatly refused to give Roxanne to me. They even threatened me." He flashed a sinister smile. "Until my money talked, baby."

"Wait. Are you telling me that you *bought* Roxanne, basically?"

Izzy's face grew long, and he grimaced. "Oh, daddy, c'mon. Don't put it that way."

"But it's the truth, isn't it?"

"So what if it is? She's a hot commodity. Or will be."

"How much did you pay her folks?"

He smiled slyly. "Not much. Five thousand pounds."

"No wonder they agreed."

"I gave them a price, and that shut them up." He snapped his fingers. "Just like that, they gave in and gave her to me. Money talks, daddy." He sneered. "Money *always* does."

"I'd know. I was born into it." I smirked. "Does Roxanne know?"

"Why does she need to?"

I shrugged. "Just to know."

"Even if I told her, she would have been too excited to care. I had to cover my ears! When she calmed down, we talked some, and then we hung up so she could start packing."

"Packing already? Two weeks in advance before the filming?"

He blinked. "How did you know that we'd be filming in two weeks?"

"Wild guess," I said.

"Ah, well, you guessed right, daddy. But she'll be here next week."

"Why?" I asked sternly. "I mean, what for?" I asked innocently.

"She's never been to the UK before, so why not make a holiday out of the rest of The Homecoming for her? She's most excited to see London before we start filming the video. I want you to be a part of that fun, daddy. You and me, giving her a tour. Would you like that?"

I only said yes, for him.

He raised his arms and squealed, his eyes lit up and his voice so hyper as he said, "Daddy, I have so many ideas for this video. I wish we could start now. And I'm so excited for Roxanne."

My forced smile ached. "Lucky her. She'll meet London under the wing of the most famous glam rock superstar. Isn't that something? That's every fan's dream come true."

"And with the best drummer that a glam rock superstar could have. Don't forget that."

"We will have a blast!"

Izzy grinned, and his eyes teared up.

I looked deeply into his baby blues. "Why so emotional, princess?"

"I'm thrilled that you're as happy for her as I am." He wrapped his arms around me. "And grateful." He squeezed me and whimpered. "I thought you'd kill me, daddy. I really did."

"I'm more than happy." I gulped hard, my breath shaky as I lied. "I'm at the top of the world."

CHAPTER TEN

My body shook, curled fetus-style underneath the bed sheets, detoxing, refusing to give in. With closed eyes, I felt around for Izzy to my left then turned myself over and felt for him to my right.

I wobbled out his name. "Baby."

I turned myself over on my belly and flopped my head into his pillow, pressing my nose in deep. It smelled of his distinct, faint aroma of coconut, hairspray, mint, nicotine, and his favorite sweet, tart cherry licorice. I could hear him. His breathing. Him humming an ethereal melody in his sleep. Exciting. Inviting. Everywhere. The warmth of the world on top of a silk pillow, soaked in his essence. The aroma, the sound of him, was alive, so present that I was drifting to him. If only he was here to take me away.

When I opened my eyes, I took a deep breath, breathing my lover in. When I sighed, I was outside myself, outside my body. I continued to shake, and not because the room was cold. I rubbed my temples and shook my head. My body dependency on Izzy was a poison. He was *inside* me, not only when we'd make love, but even while he was away. Where was he? What a daft question to ask myself. I already knew. My stomach flipped without me needing to think about her or say her name. Staring at the ceiling, I stopped.

"Not today, God," I whispered. "Not today." Today was the beginning of the end.

The last spellbinding show of the Homecoming Leg was finished. As was Roxanne's week-long holiday in Scotland and Wales. We'd made it to London last night. Day after today, the filming of "Dirty Dancer" was going to begin. But next week, Roxanne would be *gone*. No more of her tagging along as the ass-kissing fan girl enjoying the free ride without the pressures. No more seeing her front row at the concerts.

At least it wasn't torture. Izzy didn't bring her onstage at all. She got to see what the world had been seeing all this time, Izzy dancing, bumping, grinding, and kissing oh so many girls. Roxanne was never behind the scenes, nowhere near the mania. She'd already be in the limo. Instead of having hedonistic after-show parties, Izzy closed down the bowling alleys, cinemas, and bookstores. All for Ms. Clean As A Fucking Whistle. And everything would be clean until our world would take hold. In our suites. In our beds. The restless beast was relentless again!

Until the morning, and I'd wake up alone. No warm body beside me. No kisses to melt me. No baby to hold closer to me. I was wide awake, but being alive was a whole other story. Confronting the morning was now a daily struggle, a drowning. But still, I survived. When I sauntered to the living room, the sunlight streamed through the windows, but where was my sunshine? Even in this room, I could smell that wonderful man. The love we made on the couch, floor, tables, and against the wall. Our post-sex Earl Grey tea and anise cigars. I could even hear his desperate moaning, his kooky giggling, and his hound of love, howling for more of me. What was heaven was now hell. The loneliness, emptiness, a frost. I breathed it in and breathed it out, telling myself again *Not today, God. Not today.*

No more worrying. No more sulking. No more numbing myself with paranoid thoughts. I was not a loser. I was the Cheshire Cat, and the grin on my face proved I was fucking *happy*, dammit. I stepped out into the hallway. Through the walls I heard voices from television, snoring, and fucking. I pressed my ear casually to Izzy's door. It was peculiarly quiet. I went five doors down to Roxanne's, but I wasn't hearing fucking there either. Only the TV. Whose door to knock up first? *Go ahead. Knock on the bitch's door.* After two firm knocks, Roxanne opened it.

"Looks like someone is already rearing to go, bright and early."

"Today feels like Christmas!" she said in a voice less soft spoken, bursting with charisma.

"There's something different about you this morning."

She looked like a living China doll. She was almost goddess-like. Her makeup was polished. The powder on her face was smooth, the contouring, perfect. Her cat-eye was on-point. Her lids were shimmery in gold, fuchsia, and blue. Even her eyebrows were manicured, trimmed, and arched. Her dark pink lips had a startling, smoldering, glam richness. The womanly side of her popped like the colors, a startling contrast to her glam boy jeans, pin stripe flannel, and pink tie.

"Your makeup looks very nice."

She beamed. "All Izzy's work."

I smirked. "Of course."

"He taught me so many makeup techniques this morning. And how to trim my brows."

"You are learning from the master."

"It's insane how much he knows, as if he really were a woman in another life."

"Or more like in this life." I looked over my shoulder when I heard a door opening and closing. Nobody was there. I raised my brow and turned to Roxanne, forcing a smile. "Ready for today?"

She laughed. "I was *dreaming* about it!"

"What are you looking forward to seeing the most?"

"Lots. Buckingham Palace, Westminster, St. Paul's Cathedral, Big Ben, Kensington Palace—"

"And that's not even scratching the surface. Izzy and I have a whole lot more to show you."

I looked over my shoulder when a door opened and closed again. It was William James.

"Morning, boss."

"Good morning, Mr. James!" Roxanne chirped and waved at him excitedly.

He said hello to me and wished Roxanne a good time in London. "I want to hear all about your London adventure at our meeting," he said to Roxanne.

It truly hit me then that the music video was really happening tomorrow. Or, technically, tonight. Izzy told me yesterday that she, he, and filming crew were going to join William for supper to talk about Izzy's vision. If only I knew what that vision could be.

"Yes, sir, I sure will," she responded.

After I smiled and waved at the Big Man, I looked down at my watch. "I should get more dolled up before we get going." I couldn't believe I had to ask *her*. "Do you know where Izzy went?"

"Back to his room, I think. He told me he'll call me to your room when he's ready."

"Jolly good. I'll see you in—" A phone started ringing in her room. "That must be him!" She closed the door on me.

I hurried back to my room. I sighed deeply and quivered, breathing in a new scent of gardenias. I sniffed the air again, wrinkling my nose. Then, I didn't dare breathe, and couldn't even blink when suddenly, I heard a graveled voice belting out "Singing in the Rain" from the bedroom. Cautiously, I opened the door.

"Holy shit!" I choked out.

What I saw was so unbelievable that I gawked and stared instead of calling security. On the bed sprawled a wrinkled, long-nosed old woman dressed in a hideous blue and white floral print dress. She wore so many chunky pearl necklaces that I couldn't see her neck. The only striking thing she had going was her long legs, but even that asset was ruined by off-white thick-heeled shoes. She looked up at me, her eyes as big as saucers. She stopped singing and shrieked in horror. I jumped back when she stood on her knees, arms up, her fists balled and ready for action. "Who the fuck are ye?" she shouted. "Intruder!"

I didn't dare submit to my fear. "*Me?*" I roared. "You are in *my* room, madame, and if you don't *leave* right this second, I'm calling security! Sod it." I rushed to the phone, and as I did, she asked, "Can you let me get undressed first before I'm in handcuffs?"

"Oh my God!" I blinked at her fake saggy tits. "*Iz?* Is that really you?"

"Right-eee-o, daddio," he said, trying to sound seductive in that gravelly voice.

"My baby's here behind this face?" I gawked, shocked.

"Yes, daddy!" he said in his normal voice. "Damn. You can't see me? My disguise is that good?"

I nodded. He giggled obnoxiously as he leaned back on the bed and spread his legs. As he kicked from his laughter, he exposed his granny knickers and his most flawless tuck job yet. I laughed so hard that my sides ached. I climbed on the bed, lying beside him.

"You loon." I gently dabbed his wrinkles, jumping my hand back. "Shit. It feels real."

"These, too." He groped his breasts and pushed them up. "Feel them."

I snorted. "I've never felt up a granny before."

"Shirley Kate Bush is the name, dear," said that gravelly voice. "But call me Old Shirley."

I covered my mouth, laughing so hard that I snorted.

Old Shirley glared at me. "You have a problem with my voice, chap?"

"You sound like a chronic smoker! Why not go for something less intimidating?"

"For Roxanne, you mean? I don't want to scare the poor girl."

I stopped laughing. "Yeah. Don't want that."

"How about this one?" He cleared his throat and changed the character. He sounded like the Wicked Witch from the West. "Is that better, my pretty?"

"That scares *me*." I shook my head. "Think about our Majesty."

Izzy cleared his throat. "Is this a voice suited for a lady Majesty?"

I smiled warmly to that soft, proper voice. "Gorgeous. It would make the Queen proud."

Old Shirley clapped and beamed like a proud mum and granny all at once. She faced me, lying on her side as she smiled warmly at me. I blushed, looking deep into her eyes. I brushed my finger along the tip of her life-like prosthetic nose and pecked it.

She looked down coyly. "Do you have a girlfriend?"

"No ma'am. I have a boyfriend," I declared proudly.

She gasped. "A *boyfriend?* You're a homosexual?"

"I'm bisexual." I waggled my brows. "And so is my boyfriend."

"You and your boyfriend like men *and* women?"

"That's what bisexuality *is*, Ms. Bush. The equal sexual and romantic attraction to the sexes."

She grimaced. "Disgusting! Hogwash! You can't possibly swing both ways!"

"Oh, love, it is possible," I purred into her ear. "Us bisexuals, we are *alive*." I looked deep into her eyes. "We exist. We are real, and we are proud. Let me tell you, there's a whole lot of swinging. Every single night, my man and I make love. To each other. To men and women— models, actors, actresses, groupies, and hookers. The fuckery all night long can make your head spin. It's a wonderful world that my boyfriend and I made."

"How does your family feel about that?" she asked condescendingly.

"About me being bi?" I smirked. "I came out to them at eighteen. They were worried, afraid, because after all, I am a Maxwell. Everything we are represents a brand. When I started introducing boyfriends to them, they came around because they saw I had good taste. With the exception of my brother and a few other relatives, most Maxwell family are perfectly fine with it."

She snorted. "Boyfriends, eh?"

"Lots. Posh. Sophisticated. Debonair. And I've had plenty of socialite girlfriends, too."

She wrinkled her nose in disgust. "Selfish! That's what you are. That's what you and your boyfriend are! Perverse, greedy faggots who think they can have their cake and eat it, too!"

"Yaas!" I slyly grinned. "I dare you to tell me twice."

She glared. "You know what you really are? You are a freak."

"Why you foul-mouthed prude! I should wash your mouth out with soap!"

"Better yet—" She patted my cheek. "Handsome boy. Wash my mouth out with your come."

"Then open that mouth, Old Shirley, because I got plenty!"

She squealed, kicking her legs wildly until I sat on them. She gasped when I straddled her, and she ground my crotch against hers as I grabbed her bosom. My eyes lit up. "Wow. Iz, I mean, Old Shirley, your tits do feel…" I squeezed them. "Natural."

I crept my free hand up her skirt, stroking her knickers.

"You filthy man. I should call security on you!"

I pressed my lips to hers. She moaned loudly and pushed her tongue hard against mine. "Oh my God!" I gasped from the power of her tongue-sucking. I sucked her bottom lip until she groaned as loudly as I did, and I let go. She panted and blushed. I moaned when her massive dick pushed up against her knickers. "Ooh, hello, my darling."

"Tuck me back in?" asked Old Shirley. She quivered when I squeezed her.

"Why should I?" I murmured.

"Because Roxanne will be here any minute now, daddy," said Izzy.

"Dammit."

"I told the lass to be here in twenty minutes," said Old Shirley.

I got off her and snapped my finger. "On all fours."

She obeyed me so fast, my cock twitched. I lifted her dress, exposing her ass. My mouth watered at that sweet monster's head saying hello from her knickers. After I rolled them down, being careful not to disturb the girdle straps, I wrapped my hand around her meaty shaft. I gently pulled her cock back between her ass cheeks and pushed it so far up it looked like she had a tail. Instead of shoving her balls back in her sockets and slapping the tape back on, I traced my tongue around her head, opened my mouth, and suckled the huge, bulbous beauty.

"Daddy!" Izzy cackled, not Old Shirley. "I told you to *tuck* me, not *suck* me!"

I moaned, about to bob my mouth on Izzy's cock until he slapped my cheek lightly. "No, no, later, daddy, blow me later." He squirmed. "Roxanne's coming."

"And so will you, I mean, Old Shirley." As I was about to lick her tight little asshole and shove my tongue in it, Old Shirley crawled away. "Hey, where are you going, old girl?" I growled. She moaned as I wrapped my arms around her thighs and pulled her toward me so quick the tip of my nose ran into her ass crack. I licked her there, kissing that warm, velvety textured pink hole, about ready to suck and stretch it open with my tongue.

"She's here!" Izzy said to the little knock on the door. "Distract Roxanne. I won't be long."

I rolled my eyes, dropped my head between his cheeks, and groaned against his asshole. "Fine."

I gave his crack a quick lick and got off the bed, pretending I was hurrying to the living room. Once I got there, I took my time to get to the front door. Once there, I looked down at my watch and was going to let three minutes pass by, but she kept on knocking. I took a breath, sighed, and opened the door. Roxanne jumped.

She laughed. "Oh! I was almost going to knock on your chest. That was close."

"Izzy's not here yet, will be soon."

"Cheerio, dears!"

Roxanne raised her brow when Old Shirley slowly walked in with her sequined cane, rocking her hips with pep to her step. Roxanne looked at me funny as Old Shirley batted her lashes at her, and then looked at me slyly.

"Is this your girlfriend, Johnny boy?"

"No!" Roxanne and I shouted at the same time.

She chuckled. "You two could have fooled me, cute couple. I know you, Ms. Shengyi, from Izzy's Madison Square Garden show. Was all that dancing and booty shaking your idea, missy?"

"In Jesus's name, no, ma'am. I was caught in the moment."

"And so was he! I know Mr. Rich personally, you know."

"Are you his grandmother?"

I smirked at Old Shirley.

"I'm his *old* friend. He told me you are beautiful and sexy, but look at you! Sweet Lord, you're one cutie-patootie." She winked and looked Roxanne over from head to toe.

I snorted, and not because of that bewildered, turned-off look on Roxanne's face.

"And he told me that your kisses can turn anyone into a believer." I covered my mouth, holding back the urge to laugh hysterically when Old Shirley puckered her lips at Roxanne. "Kiss me, dear?" she cried desperately. "Kiss me until our lips hurt."

When Roxanne's eyes widened with wild shock, Old Shirley and I burst out laughing at the same time when Roxanne backed away. She looked at us. "What's going on? Is this a prank?"

"Not a prank," Old Shirley replied, and then Izzy said, "It's my disguise, darling."

Roxanne jumped, squealed with fright, and her face paled. "Izzy? No. Can't be!"

"Don't be afraid." He kissed her hand. "It's me."

She squinted, looking him over from head to toe. She looked into his eyes and stared at Izzy in wonderment. "It really is you!" She touched his face, at the wrinkles.

"Don't smudge it," I mumbled at her.

"You truly didn't recognize Izzy at all, love?" Old Shirley spoke.

"No, ma'am," she said with a chuckle. "I didn't see you, I mean, Izzy, at all, Ms.—"

"Her name is Shirley Kate Bush," I said.

"But you may call me granny dearest." She winked at Roxanne.

"Granny dearest?" I said.

"Out in public, you'll be my granddaughter, in case anybody asks," she said to Roxanne.

"And what does that make me? Roxanne's uncle?"

"Granny dearest," Roxanne beamed. "You have Izzy's dreamy eyes."

Old Shirley blushed, batting her lashes. "Not as beautiful as yours, my dear."

I rolled my eyes, about to cross my arms, but instead, I cleared my throat. "So are we ready for the tour or what?" I asked anxiously. I blinked when neither of them were listening to me.

"Your eyes are like your smile," Old Shirley purred. "Could they be magic?" She brushed Roxanne's cheek with her trembling finger, and then brushed her lips against her skin. Roxanne smiled, melting at her touch.

"My car's ready," I said softly but firmly to them.

Roxanne opened her eyes, blushing not at me. Only at *my* Old Shirley.

Old Shirley finally looked at me, her arthritic hand on her cane. She looked at Roxanne and said in Izzy's voice, "Ready, Foxxy Roxxy?"

"You know it!"

I forced myself to grin when I really wanted to gag. "Let the fun begin!"

❖

I wasn't surprised not one person sussed out Izzy in Old Shirley. At the heart of West End, we were surrounded by illuminated advertisements and tourists. Cars honked and cameras snapped as we strolled to the Shaftesbury Memorial Fountain. Roxanne looked up at the statue of Anteros and snapped many pictures.

"Who is that, granny dearest?" Roxanne asked. "He's gorgeous."

She looked at me. "Take it away, chap." She smacked her chops. "I've talked my mouth dry."

"And Roxanne's ear off."

"I could hear granny dearest yap all day!"

As if she hasn't already, I thought.

"Don't encourage me." Old Shirley winked at Roxanne. "Go ahead, Johnny. Tell her who he is."

"Are you familiar with Greek mythology, Roxanne?"

"Some, but not much, honestly."

"That statue up there is Anteros, the god of—"

"Excuse me, ma'am," said a freckled, redheaded teenage lad.

"Talking to me, young man?" said Old Shirley, her arthritis kicking in, her cane shaking.

"No, ma'am, sorry. I was talking to her." He looked at Roxanne with big and wondrous puppy dog eyes and the cheesiest grin, his face glowing. He was star struck. "Are you Foxxy Roxxy?"

I rolled my eyes, telling myself, "*Again?*"

"That's me," she said bashfully.

"Oh my God! This is awesome!" He jumped excitedly. "You were amazing in Izzy's show."

"Aw, why thank you. That's so sweet of you."

"Is it possible to take a picture with you?"

"Sure! But only if you let my grandmother in the picture, too."

"Oh, sure." The boy turned to me. "Would you mind taking the photo, sir?"

Here we go again. Not saying a word, I held his camera. Roxanne stood center with the lad to her right, Old Shirley to her left. I snapped one photo of the three smiling at the camera.

"One more picture?" asked the lad excitedly.

I nodded and snorted when Old Shirley dropped her cane, moved, and made a peace sign over their heads. I snapped the photo, and an older gentleman picked up Shirley's cane.

"Thank you, man," said the lad to me.

"They turned out great. Especially the last one." I handed him his camera.

I glared when Old Shirley shouted, "Thank you, sir! I can just kiss you!" She puckered up and smacked a loud smooch on his cheek, leaving behind a lip imprint. The man tipped his hat and wiped his cheek as he walked off quickly. "What the...?" the lad said, and he burst out laughing.

"Dirty Dancer" was playing from somewhere. Old Shirley wiggled her ass and swiveled her hips to the melody, even more so when my drumming kicked in.

"Your grandmother is bloody hilarious, Roxxy!"

Roxanne and the lad weren't the only ones laughing and staring. Up to ten people drew closer, and they were whistling and clapping at Old Shirley grabbing her crotch as she kept wiggling her ass and swiveling her hips. I gave her a dirty look, but she kept on dancing.

"That's my granny dearest," Roxanne said.

When Roxanne planted a smooch on Old Shirley's cheek, she stopped and blushed. "My granddaughter lights up my life!" Old Shirley declared loudly to the tourists. She kissed Roxanne's cheek. "She keeps me young! She's why I can still dance like this."

I glared darkly, and when she was about to dance, I grabbed her wrist and growled in her ear "Don't you bloody dare, Ms. Bush. Or else you might hurt your back." I squeezed *hard.* "Ow, ow!" she said, grimacing. I let go and backed away.

"Are you okay, granny dearest?" Roxanne asked, looking at me as if I had done something horrible. She rubbed Old Shirley's back as she was hunched over.

"No worries, my dear. I'm not as young as you are, love, but not too old. I won't be needing this!" She straightened her back and raised her cane, the sequins flashing.

"Don't!" I gasped when it looked as if she was going to throw it. Roxanne and I reached for her cane at the same time. We looked at each other, and let go of her cane quickly. Old Shirley laughed.

"Very funny, granny," Roxanne said with her hands on her hips.

I fake-laughed. "A riot." I held Old Shirley's wrist, tightening the grip again as I growled low and deep into her ear, "Do that again, and you'll get a mean whipping later tonight. Behave."

She gulped, and I let her wrist go.

"Now we know where you get your talent from," said the fan boy to Roxanne. "Thank you, Roxxy! And nice to meet you, madame," he said to Old Shirley as he walked away.

"My granddaughter, the celebrity! That was what, the fifth fan boy that approached you?"

"The eighth, actually," I mumbled.

"I wasn't counting," Roxanne said. "Eight, John? Really?"

"I couldn't make that up."

"How wonderful! How does that make you feel, love?"

"Like Izzy Rich, maybe?" She winked.

I laughed. Roxanne and Old Shirley looked at me. "No way. Izzy Rich puts Piccadilly to a stop completely. And there's no way in fucking—"

"Watch that language!" Old Shirley snapped. "For my granddaughter."

I coughed. "Izzy couldn't possibly stroll through London like some ordinary person. Not with everyone following his every move, stopping him every second to take pictures and sign things."

"Well, lucky for us that we aren't him," Old Shirley said, arm-in-arm with Roxanne. "Ready to see what I've been told is Izzy Rich's favorite place in all of London?"

"On to the National Gallery we go!" Roxanne squealed.

"And then, I'm afraid that will be our last stop of the tour, love," Old Shirley pouted.

"Darn. What a shame," I said sarcastically.

"Let's not waste any more time, Foxxy Roxxy."

I glared, and Roxanne covered Old Shirley's mouth quick when she accidently said her nickname in Izzy's voice. I looked around, my heart racing, but nobody heard or noticed except for me. They looked at each other, and they bust out giggling. I wasn't laughing. I glared at Old Shirley again, and she immediately stopped.

As I stood next to Old Shirley with my hand over her shaky wrist,

I noticed Roxanne still hadn't let go of Old Shirley's arm. Together, we walked a few blocks back to my car as if Old Shirley was too old to walk as fast as Roxanne and me.

"I should've been born in London!" Roxanne said as I was driving. "I *love* it here. It's everything I imagined. Piccadilly Circus reminds me of Manhattan and the Shibuya district in Tokyo."

"And there's still so much more of London that I'd want you to see," Izzy said.

"If we had all day, I'd take you to where us local posh West Enders hang out," I chimed in.

"Ooh, Trafalgar Square!" Roxanne squealed, and she whipped out her camera.

"The fountains and the lion on Nelson's Column are worth hundreds of pictures alone," Izzy said, leaning back against the seat. "When I was a kid, Roxxy, during school, I'd spend hours here, smoking, playing my guitar, making a few quid here and there to afford more fags."

I smiled warmly, and then looked up at the overhead mirror. I narrowed my eyes at Izzy. He was clinging to Roxanne, arms still locked. I glared at the road as the two chatted away as if I wasn't there. Izzy pointed at a few historical street signs and statues. After stalling a few times because of traffic, Izzy halted his train of thought, and said to Roxanne in Old Shirley's voice, "Almost there! John and I have the same taste in art from da Vinci to van Gogh," she said to Roxanne. Finally, I existed again.

If she wasn't talking about me, I would've stopped the car and tore them off for ignoring me like she had all bloody day. What was I, a photographer? A fucking chauffeur?

When we got out of the car, I walked beside Old Shirley and her cane as Roxanne held her free hand. Inside the National Gallery, we were surrounded by art, steeped in it. Where to go? Where to begin? Old Shirley lead us down the hall to the Barry Rooms. Gradually, we went to the Pennethorne, Taylor Wing, and Staircase Hall. I didn't have to look at Roxanne to know she was moved by the aesthetic majesty of the Neo-Renaissance design of the walls and ceilings. She marveled at almost every painting we saw and admired. She touched her chest as we stood before Vincent van Gogh's *Sunflowers*.

"I've always wanted to see this one in person," Roxanne said. "It's so beautiful."

I smiled at a painting ahead. "This is my favorite." It was Henri Rousseau's *Tiger in a Tropical Storm (Surprised!)*.

"Never heard of it," Roxanne said, she and Old Shirley by my side.

"It may be Rousseau's most underrated, misunderstood painting, but..." I had my eye on the tiger. A flash of lightning illuminated the frightened striped creature in the midst of the raging gale. How it made my face glow. "Since I was a kid, I was moved at first sight. Still am."

"Why's that?" Old Shirley asked me what Izzy already knew.

"It's an enigma," I said. "Is the painting capturing the tiger's story at its end or at its beginning? Does the tiger get the upper hand of the storm? Does it survive? And what is it preying on? Who is the predator? The tiger? Or is the storm the predator, the tiger its prey?"

Roxanne yawned. "Ooh! What's that painting?" She ran to the work three paintings down.

Old Shirley beamed. "That's Nicolas Poussin's *The Adoration of the Golden Calf.*"

Standing side by side, Roxanne and Old Shirley looked at *The Adoration*. While Old Shirley was showing off her knowledge of the religious work of art inspired from the Book of Exodus, Roxanne marveled at her granny dearest the way the Israelites in the painting were reveling over the golden calf. The brighter she glowed, the lower my spirit dimmed. My body drifted farther away from them. Not that I mattered, nor did they care. Never had I felt so cold in a place of warmth. And so alone for being surrounded by people. Roxanne and Old Shirley moved on to another painting, laughing, talking, and leaving me behind.

Instead of following them, I went back to *Tiger in a Tropical Storm*. The creature was a mirror, and I was staring at myself. I looked at the couple and faced the storm in the painting.

Knock, knock, knock. Silence. *Knock—*

I swung the door open and saw my Izzy in a glittering suit and tie. I grabbed his wrist and pulled him in so quick that I forgot the door. Izzy quickly slammed his back against it and locked it. He gasped when I pinned him to the door.

"About fucking time you came back from that business meeting!" I said.

He kissed me so hard that I whimpered. When I kissed him harder, he melted with me.

"How did it go, baby?" I said as I kissed his cheeks.

"Very well, daddy." He gasped when I sucked his skin right near his collarbone. He stroked my hair as he cooed, "Everything's ready. Tomorrow's showtime! Everyone's thrilled and excited."

Everyone, except for me. I kissed him eagerly and sucked on his tongue. He opened his mouth with a desperate, whimpering moan. I sucked his tongue harder, pulled away, and nuzzled his bottom lip until his red lipstick was sucked off.

"You haven't told me anything about it…"

"Nobody knows except those at that table."

"Why is this a top secret? You won't even tell me the story."

"You already know it."

"What?"

"Think about it." He winked, sucked my chin, and then kissed it. "All packed and ready, daddy?"

I backed away from him, and looked over my shoulder at all my bags. "This fucking sucks. A whole week without you, baby love, is going to be torture. Hell, it is torture already."

"I know." He held my hands and squeezed them. "When was the last time we were away from each other for this long?"

I squeezed his hands back, tears welling up in my eyes. "I can't remember."

"Don't start crying," he said.

I grabbed Izzy and held him close to me, so tightly, rocking him. "I'm going to miss you."

"I'm missing you already, daddy."

We looked at each other and rubbed noses, the water still soft and glossy in our eyes.

"Twenty-four seven with you isn't enough."

He smiled coyly. "There's nothing to get hung about, daddy. I know it's going to be tough, but we will both be busy. Apart, yes, but you'll see. The week's going to fly by."

"For you, with you being a director and all. Your first time. Nervous?"

He shook his head. "Neither is Roxanne."

I forced myself to smile. "Not surprising, I guess."

"Will you miss her? After the filming's done next Sunday, that's it. She'll be back home."

"We said our good-byes," I lied.

"Did you have fun today, daddy? Please, be honest with me."

His face was soft, warm, and desperate, his voice, sounding so…
hopeful. I gulped nervously. "Old Shirley was a hoot. I wanted to fuck
her." He giggled. "I'm this close to making you go back into that drag
so I can fuck her, you. Right here, right now. You owe me that for how
naughty you were today, almost blowing your own cover."

"That wasn't my fault!"

"*Izzy*," I growled, and his expression went from silly to serious.
"You know better. If anybody were to ever find you behind the drag,
that's it. No more fun and games. No more freedom."

He gulped hard, and nodded. "I know, but I still couldn't help it."

"Let me guess, you blame Roxanne."

"And her fan boys."

"What the bloody hell was that about? Roxanne's not famous.
That was so bloody annoying."

"That's not very nice. You don't find my fans annoying."

"That's because you are famous. You know what else I found
annoying? The fucking flirting."

"But that's what fans boys do."

"No, not them. *You!*" I hissed. "You and her being so chummy!
You were shamelessly flirting with her as an old bat, for Christ's sake!
And no, I won't watch my goddamn language!"

Izzy had his hands to his hips. "Can you at least tone down your
voice? Don't need to shout."

I took a deep breath and sighed shakily.

"Fuck," he sighed. "I thought you had a great time today. Guess I
was wrong."

I groaned. "It's not that, Izzy. It's…be honest with me. Does
Roxanne even like me?"

"She doesn't know you. She wants to, though."

"Did she tell you that?"

He stood there, frozen. "Well, no, but I think she does, can't see
why she wouldn't."

"Has she said anything about me to you since she made it to the
UK?"

"Baby, Roxanne's still starstruck by me. You know that. I'm all
she cares about."

I rolled my eyes. "No shit. Since day one of being here, she hardly
says anything to me while she kisses everyone else's ass, especially
William's. She didn't give a flying fuck about anything I said or showed
her on the tour. She was your bloody shadow. I might as well not been

there at all. I was a third fucking wheel, and even worse than that, I was providing a service to her."

Izzy's face grew long and sad. "Daddy…" He held my hands tight. "I'm sorry."

"I bet she isn't." I scowled. "She wished that it was only you two today, didn't she?"

Izzy's face grew cold. He smirked and shrugged.

I glared. "Okay, then." I nodded. "I get the picture. She feels that I was in the way."

"I didn't say she said that!"

"You didn't have to!" Izzy looked at me, wiping at his watery eyes. I took a deep breath and sighed, opening my arms. "For fuck's sake. Come here, sexy."

"I'm sorry, daddy!" He ran into my arms, and I squeezed him tight. "Now I feel so bloody awful. If I knew that this whole day would've made you feel this shitty at the end, I would've changed—"

"Stop it." I patted his bum. "I'm overreacting. It's me." I looked into his eyes. "I'm forgetting that Roxanne's still new to you, new to all this, and to London and everything. I was oblivious to the fact that she's a tourist and still one of your goofy fan girls. And the truth of the matter is"—I gulped hard—"I like Roxanne. Like a kid sister I never had."

Izzy's eyes lit up. His face glowed. "You really mean that, baby?"

"I'm putting that lightly, of course." I smirked. "It was nice having her around, but I'll admit, I bloody miss the after-sex parties on top of our private ones. What happened to those?"

He smirked. "I didn't want Roxanne exposed to all that. It was a nice change, wasn't it?"

"It was cute. Fun. It's too bad she won't be joining us for the rest of the tour. I can't believe it's almost over."

Izzy grimaced. "Don't remind me. For now, first things first. The music video."

"I wish you'd tell me something about it."

"I already did."

"No you didn't!"

"Think about it. I want everyone to be surprised when they first see it."

"Even me?"

"Especially you."

I looked into Izzy's eyes as if the secret was in them. I saw a warmth, a promise. But what was the surprise? "It better be fucking worth it." I smacked his ass. "And you better call me during the week."

"I'll try, but you know I can't promise that, daddy. You know how I am when I'm working."

"Oh, don't I know it." I spanked his ass harder. He jumped and yelped.

"Want me to get into Old Shirley before you go?"

I shook my head. "No. I want you, Izzy Rich. Only you, my love."

He moaned. "You have me."

I scooped him into my arms, holding him up. He wrapped his legs around me, running his fingers through my hair and massaging my scalp as I planted kisses on his neck. On his collarbone. On his chin. His cheeks. His nose, forehead, and ears. When we stripped each other naked and rolled on the floor, I wished we were past this week. The music video finished, Roxanne home in America *for good*, this time. Only us, my baby love and me, his daddy heart, together with the days, hours, and minutes no longer against us. Our world was ours again. But now…

I was hurt. It stung to hug Izzy and say good-bye. I wasn't going to miss or pine over Izzy's tour, his music, the fans, groupies, fame, media, and the madness that embodied a lifetime of passion, hard work, and love. Only him. My man. When I left the hotel, thinking about him grew painful. As I was driving home, I was bawling, drowning in tears. I was as dark and cloudy as the sky, with a brutal storm brewing in my heart. More than ever before, I was madly in love with a poison. It was more than rich. It was Izzy.

CHAPTER ELEVEN

It was Friday night, and the Kings Bar, the most posh and sophisticated bar in all of Camden Lock, tucked away from the tourists, exclusive for the locals, was a blast from my past. I knew almost everyone from the bartenders and socialites to the bands performing. I grinned at the smiling faces and perky tits of the door girls when I walked into the packed house. I squeezed through the crowd of snotty rich girls and snobby trust fund boys sipping their martinis and boasting while flirting and hitting on each other. I waved at the many who greeted me as I went to the stairway where I saw my childhood friend and ex-bandmate, Joseph Davis, waiting for me. His eyes lit up, as did mine. I opened my arms, and he ran into them, giving me the biggest bear hug.

"It has been forever since I've seen you, man!" he said cheerfully, his fat arms around me tight.

"I know! Fuck. Last time was when we were plotting Izzy's big surprise."

"Jesus. That was when?"

"Not sure. I've lost track of time these days."

"You're looking good, man." He whistled. "Look at those drummer arms."

I flexed, winking at him as he groped my biceps.

"And look at that *ass*," he declared as I turned around, showing off my body. He spanked me.

"You still want me, don't cha, baby?" I wiggled my tush.

"Fuck yes." He spanked my ass again. I faced him. "Typical me, right?" he said as we went to the table. "Always wanting what I can't bloody have."

"I've been there." Thinking about Izzy.

He chuckled as we sat down. "Bollocks. You always get what you want. You always wanted to work for a famous rock star, and now here you are, with the most famous of them all."

"And you always wanted to start your own business, and look at you. Your stores are everywhere in London. I'm so bloody proud of you, mate."

We looked to the waitress who served our usual tall German lagers. "Thank you, darling," Joseph said to her. "So tell me, what have you been up to on your super-rare week off from the tour?"

"Catching up on a lot of sleep. Only hell knows how much I needed it."

He sipped his drink. "Not that you need the beauty rest. You are beautiful enough."

"You flirt. Mostly boring stuff. Paying bills, meeting up with friends I haven't seen in ages, and unpacking only to pack again for the last leg of the tour."

And talking to Izzy on the phone in-between. The conversations consisted only of pleasantries and little tidbits, but how could I dare ask for anything more?

"What are you going to do with yourself after the tour ends?"

"Knowing Izzy, he probably has hundreds of songs already written for the next album. I can imagine us being in the recording studio in three months or so." I snickered.

He raised his glass. "Cheers to you, baby. And to Izzy."

"Cheers to you, sexy." We toasted.

As we drank, I looked at the TV. I set my glass down, my eyes frozen on the reporter standing outside of a gentleman's club. It was *Le Chaton Rose*, mobbed by sobbing boys, screaming girls, and feisty cameramen.

"It's pandemonium here at the Soho district," said the reporter excitedly, stepping aside so the camera could focus on Izzy. "Izzy Rich and Roxanne Foster have stepped out of the nightclub where they're filming the highly anticipated music video of Izzy's hit single, 'Dirty Dancer.'"

The camera shook as it caught a clear view of Izzy in a brilliant short, yellow silk dress embroidered with glittering blue and red Chinese characters, his face glammed like a doll. Roxanne stood beside him in a suit and tie. My throat dried up as I chugged my beer and watched them staring at each other not arm in arm, but hand in hand.

"I don't know what it is about her," said Joseph with a naughty grin. "She's hot."

I rolled my eyes. "Going straight for her?"

"Nah, man. It's not that deep. I only find her attractive, that's all. I'm not changing orientations on you. What is she like in person?"

I shrugged. "Typical teenager."

"And *lucky*. So many girls would *kill* to be in her place right now."

I lifted a panicky hand up at the waitress; the bartender was already pouring us a pair of lagers.

"Is it true those two are going out with each other?" he asked when our beers were served.

"Where have you heard that?" I asked, trying to hold back the fear creeping inside me.

"In the papers."

I looked up at the TV screen again. The two waved at their fans as they dashed to the limo. When they left, I looked at Joseph with a smirk. "The tabloids? Burn them. They are garbage. Ninety-five percent of what they write isn't true." That was a fact, but in the back of my mind, I wondered. "What *have* they been saying?" I asked.

"There have been a lot of pictures lately of the two looking like they have something going on."

"What do you mean?"

"Like yesterday, there were pictures of them shopping at Bond Street and making out while they were at lunch."

I gulped my beer so hard, it went down the wrong tube.

"You okay?" He patted my back as I coughed.

I cleared my throat. "I'm fine, I'm fine!" I said with a growl. I took a deep breath and sighed. "Big deal," I said, more to myself than to Joseph. "Trust me, they *aren't* dating. I'm sure of that."

"Okay, okay, man. Damn. I believe you."

"Besides, Roxanne's not his type anyway." I knocked back my beer and slammed the mug on the table. "For one, she's too young. Second, she has no body. Sure, she's cute, but...basic."

"You don't find her attractive at all?"

"Absolutely not."

He laughed. "You're crazy."

"You think I'm crazy? The world's gone crazy. I don't understand the hype."

"She may not have a lot in looks, but she makes up for it with her talent. And what she lacks on her chest, she has in her ass. She's thick."

I gulped and nodded slowly in shy agreement.

"You'd at least fuck her ass, wouldn't you? Because I would!"

I pinched his cheek. "You sure you aren't bisexual?"

"Fuck no!" he scoffed. "Like I said, man—not changing sides, only admiring and fantasizing."

I lifted my hand up again for another drink.

"Thirsty?"

"Not for her ass, if that's what you mean."

"You're already on a third drink when I haven't finished one."

"Well, it's a time for celebration, my friend," I slurred. "My life can't be better."

When the waitress served my drink, he raised his glass. "Cheers to the luckiest man I know."

After we toasted, I thought of only my Izzy and having him as mine alone, even if it was only over the telephone.

As tempting as it was to dash to the kiosk and snatch the first tabloid I saw, I drove home, telling myself not to trust in the rubbish. "Only trust in Izzy," I said aloud, over and over again.

My baby didn't call me. *John, don't lose yourself.* The more I talked to myself, the lonelier I felt. But I had to trust my baby. The Saturday distracted me. I went horseback riding with my pals in Hyde Park and had brunch after. Shopped for new frocks and jewelry with my girlfriends at Harrods and Fortnum & Mason, and had tea with them at their luxury West End lofts. When I made it back home, I dropped my bags and collapsed on the couch, turning on the TV. I saw Izzy and Roxanne sitting with Russell Harty on the BBC. My heart raced.

"What I find most striking about you two are that Roxanne seems to accentuate Izzy's strong femininity while Izzy brings out Roxanne's soft masculinity. How is that?"

They looked at each other, smiling. Izzy giggled. "I have no clue. It's not like we planned it." He looked at Roxanne. "What do you think, doll?"

Roxanne smiled coyly. "I'm far from being as pretty as Izzy." She nudged his shoulder, and Izzy playfully nudged her back. She giggled. "But he makes me so comfortable. I feel beautiful. I'm myself with him, unafraid to be the person that I have always been inside."

My heart was beating fast. The ache devoured me, throbbing when I touched my chest. That glow on her face, and that sparkle in Izzy's eyes were poison, killing me.

"Roxanne, what is it like to go from dancing onstage with Izzy to being in what's already the most talked about music video of the year?"

"I dream big, but this is huge," she said timidly. "Izzy pinches me all the time, and still, I'm not completely convinced that I am living *this* dream!" She yelped loud and girlishly when Izzy pinched her thigh. The two stuck their tongues out at each other as the audience clapped.

My hands together in prayer, I rested my chin at the top of my fingers as I stared and listened.

"People are still in awe of you, Roxanne, from that Madison Square Garden show."

"I'm never tired of people talking about it," Roxanne said with a hint of slyness.

"What was your first thought, Izzy, when she performed the way she did?"

"I didn't show it, but I was thinking...*wow*. Ballsy. I loved everything. I loved her."

"Was it a calculated move on your part, Roxanne?"

"I've been hearing that people think that I'm an opportunist, but they don't matter."

"And it's not true," Izzy said. "If being one smart cookie makes her an opportunist, so be it. And hell, if I were her, I'd do the same. It's all how to show off your talent at that right time and moment."

"But you seem so shy right now," Russell said gently to Roxanne. "And yet onstage, you are—"

"A character," Roxanne said sternly. "Not that I'm acting or being fake, but like, here I am this shy, quiet tomboy. This is me. In the music video, I'm vivacious. Please," she pleaded, "don't take that on-screen persona and twist it. I'm still a devout Catholic. Although I'm very sexual in the video, I'm still a virgin and plan on keeping it that way until marriage."

"Shit..." I growled when the audience roared and clapped. "Fuck!"

"You're Catholic?" Russell asked, sounding surprised. "And a virgin?"

"You heard her right, Russell. Don't need to clean out those ears."

Roxanne chuckled as Izzy fluttered the tip of his boa around her ear. "You're such a big kid!"

"You love it!"

I wanted to turn the damn thing off, but I couldn't! I watched them join hands as one, fingers laced. I aimed the remote at the TV, punched down the power button, and slammed the remote to the floor, dropping my forehead down into my sweaty palms.

"This can't be real," I cried, shaking my head and pulling my hair. "This can't be real!"

I kept telling myself that over and over as I wiped at my face and sat on the couch, looking up at the ceiling as I replayed what I saw of the interview in my mind. I didn't dare cry. How much more tears could I shed? And what for when I could do something much better.

My reefer stash waited for me in the kitchen. I returned to the living room and smoked so much of it that I could stroke the clouds in the air. It was all I breathed, the only taste in my mouth, that aroma of skunk, my throat scratchy. My mind was dizzy, but better. When I looked out the window, I blinked in disbelief that it was night. Far too early for Izzy to call. When I thought about him not calling me last night, I began to cry. My eyes were bloodshot and my nose, dark pink from blowing so much snot into tissues. I was as pale as a fucking ghost.

I snubbed out the last joint I'd rolled in the ashtray. Breathe, John. *Breathe.* I jumped when the phone rang and nearly knocked over the base when I ripped it off its hook.

"Izzy!"

"I love you," he sang. "Ooh, how I love you so much! How I miss you, my love."

"You have no bloody idea how much I miss you!" I sniffled. "Why didn't you call last night?"

"Oh baby, I'm so sorry. I was so tired. I could have slept for a whole day if it weren't for today."

I gulped hard. "I saw the interview. Why didn't you tell me about that?"

"It was a last-minute booking. If Bernie had let me know sooner, I would have told you straight away."

I smirked and sighed with relief. "I know you would've, princess."

"I'm so happy you got to see it. What did you think?"

"It was...great...um, so, is the music video done yet?"

"*Yes!* And it's everything that I envisioned it to be. William *loves* it. I hope you will, too."

"I'm sure I will, baby. When will I see it?"

"Well, I was going to invite the crew over tomorrow. That's still going to happen, but I want you to be the first to enjoy it with me."

My eyes lit up, and then I grimaced. "But wait. Isn't Roxanne still here?"

"Her parents wanted her back home tonight. They got their wish."

I held back from screaming, laughing, and crying. How my bottom lip trembled. But I could hear the disappointment in Izzy's voice. How could I rejoice? "That's it, then. Roxanne's gone for good?"

"Yeah...I'll miss her."

"Sounds like you two had a great time filming."

"Oh, we sure did. On the set. Off the set. We had a blast."

I breathed, thinking about those pictures I didn't see but now knew about. I gulped hard, my breath shaking and my head throbbing as I thought about whether or not to confront him on it.

"John? Are you there?"

Should I ask him about the pictures? Their shopping? Their kiss? The two holding hands on TV? I even went as far as thinking about what else the two had done together, not publicly, but privately. I couldn't even imagine, couldn't dare.

"Hello?"

I rubbed my eyes. "What was it like for you being back at *Le Chaton Rose*?"

"A trip to the best of times and worse of times."

"Were you okay, baby?" I asked him gently.

"Yes. And then, no. At home yesterday, I broke down and cried. I had to talk to Peggy."

I sniffled, but this time, it was for him. A pang of guilt tore my gut, knowing that was probably the reason my baby didn't call yesterday. "I wish I could have been there for you, love."

"Me too."

"Was the video about Vivian?"

He was quick to say no.

"Does she even know yet that the song is about her?"

"She knows, but she still won't talk to me. Peggy has tried to get through to her, but..." He sighed. "What more can we do? How much more can I give to show her that I still care?"

"Oh, baby," I said with a grimace. "I'm so sorry."

"Hurts like hell, but with you coming over soon, I'll be in heaven in no time."

"When?" I asked impatiently.

"Come over to my place in a few hours?"

"I wish it were now! I need you."

"You will have me very soon! Come here hungry. I'm cooking tonight."

"Aw, sweetheart." I blushed. "I bloody miss your cooking!"

"And I bought you lots of stuff from Bond Street."

I was broken. I sobbed.

"Whoa, Johnny Angel. Bloody hell. Why are you crying? You don't even know what I got you!"

I looked up at the ceiling and groaned. "I'm so bloody sorry, baby!"

"About what?" he asked, sounding confused.

I wiped at my eyes. "Um...sorry for being so damn emotional."

"I love you, and I can't wait to spoil you tonight."

I looked at the time. "God, why can't time speed up?"

"You're telling me. I need your love, our love. I haven't made love to anyone since we parted."

For a split second, in my mind that anyone became a someone. Roxanne. "You, a whole week without sex? Are you serious?"

"I did it intentionally, so making love to you will be like the first time."

"I love you!" I said desperately. "I can't possibly love you more, and yet, I do!"

"Daddy, making love to you tonight is going to be beautiful."

I closed my eyes, and goose bumps rose on my skin.

"After a week of not making love, not even masturbating...ooh, daddy."

I heard his want, his need, his lust and love for me. "I haven't made love to anyone either." I petted my groin and shivered.

"Been that busy?"

"With friends, family, bills, unpacking, packing, and constantly dreaming of you."

"I've been working like a dog, but you are my dream, Jonathan. Without you, I'm dreamless."

I sniffled, and more tears tumbled down.

"Now, I better go so you can get ready for me, and I for you."

I looked at my collection of Izzy's music. I glowed, my eyes and my thoughts on only one cassette amongst them. "I'll be listening to my most favorite song in the world."

❖

"Ooh, God," I growled and grunted. "Izzy…" I gripped Izzy's hands hard, his wrists and ankles strapped to the chair.

Sweat dripped down the small of my naked back as I spread my ass cheeks, fucking myself with my princess's hard, throbbing cock. Izzy groaned and cried, writhing in his bonds. He was my piece of furniture, and how much I loved him, no matter what he was. He and the chair rocked as I swiveled my hips harder and faster, my ass bobbing up and down every inch of him. We both groaned and yelped each time the base of his cock and his balls met with my cheeks.

My heart pounded against his when our chests met. I panted and leaned back, wanking myself in lightning speed as I rode my lover's cock faster, wailing to that pained, stretched-out sensation that my ass adored. As desperately as Izzy tried to thrust his hips and pound my gape, he couldn't. When he whimpered my name, I spread my ass cheeks wider as I pulled up, his cock escaping from my ass with that cork-like sound.

I spread my legs wider as I cupped his face in my hands and kissed him passionately. I let one hand free. I shaped my hand into a duck bill, and gently, I was inside myself, bouncing my ass slowly on my balled hand. I groaned into Izzy's mouth as my anus tightened around my wrist, and I punched my loose hole. Scooting my fist to the right made space for my baby's cock. Izzy shouted. I groaned and drooled when I felt not only him, but my fist, inside me, together. My hole throbbed more than ever. The pressure. The pleasure. The stretching. It was everything and more! I slowly gyrated my ass in a circular motion and bounced in unison. We shouted and cried at the intensity. When it started to overpower me, making my legs shake and my eyes tear, I pulled my fist out. My hands on his knees, I slammed myself down on Izzy's cock.

"*I fucking love you!*" I groaned.

I fucked myself so roughly that Izzy's body shook as we pushed the chair back. When he moaned achingly, I knew he was coming. I sucked hard on his tongue as his load warmed and filled my ass. I gasped and wailed when my thick, hot load flew from my cock over his sweaty chest. I leaned my chest forward against his, smiling weakly. When my asshole loosened and tightened around him, milking him, his cock twitched inside me.

Izzy panted, his eyes on me. "This is what happens when we don't make love for a week."

I panted, wiping the sweat from my eyes. "We fuck like rabbits."

He smiled weakly as he nodded. I licked his cheek and gyrated rhythmically, my asshole holding his soft cock before it slipped out of me on its own. I wrapped my hand around his limp dick with a firm grip. He sharply gasped.

"Oh, daddy, please," he said. "Break."

"You, needing a break from sex? Do your tongue, fingers, fist, and ass need a break, too?"

"Yes! I mean, no! But daddy, what about the—?"

"What about the music video?" I rubbed his nipples.

"I'm starting to think that you're using our lovemaking to distract us from watching it."

"That's not true!"

"I was *joking*!" He giggled. "One week away from me, and you lost your sense of humor."

"I love you."

"I love you, too, but…"

"Okay, okay, fine, you win. Music video. Now."

He wiggled his fingers and toes. "I can't feel my legs or hands."

"Oh, shit!" I pushed myself off, standing beside him. "My poor baby!" I quickly untied the rope from his ankles and wrists. He sighed with relief when he stood and shook out his wrists. He wiggled his ass and danced on his feet to bring his ankles to life again.

I spanked his ass. "Hurry and pop the film, or else I'll pop my cock into your ass first!"

"Yes, sir!" He looked at me from over his shoulder. "Hmm… choices."

I winked, caressing my limp cock as he made his choice.

He rushed to the shelf with his shiny BAFTA award at the top. I climbed on the bed and lay back with my arms behind my head, smiling warmly at the candles lit around the room and the vases of white, red, and yellow roses. I placed my right arm on my stomach, smiling down at the diamond-studded watch that he'd bought me. As I admired its sparkle, I thought about his gorgeous three-course meal and the other gifts that he bestowed on me. I was more than a man. My queen made me feel like a fucking king. I wiggled my toes, soft from the pedicure, and admired my painted nails, done by my love, of course. I closed my eyes, and then opened them when I felt Izzy lying beside me. I looked at him. He had the remote in his hand.

"Ready?" he asked me daringly. Something about his eyes oozed sex.

"Yes." I kissed him, forcing my tongue in his mouth.

He laughed and moved away. "Don't start until *after* the video."

"Fine."

He kissed my nose and snuggled beside me cozily.

"Wait!" I shouted when he was about to press play.

"What now?" he asked, sounding slightly irritated.

I lifted up the bed sheets. "Let's get under the covers."

"What's the bloody matter with you?" He wiped the sweat from his brow. "As if it's not already hot in here. From all the sex we've been having, it's so humid we can roast Satan on a spit."

"Under the covers, *now*, bitch."

In a hurry, he went underneath the covers with me. "Ready now, daddy?" he asked eagerly.

I nodded. At least this fake smile wasn't as painful as some of the others. But it was still an illusion.

When Izzy pressed play, I looked at the screen, my arms still crossed.

"Dirty Dancer" played as Roxanne bent over to tie her shiny black shoes, wearing a plaid skirt and white blouse. Her skirt swished as she swayed to the music. I blinked at the little peek-a-boo glimpse of her midnight blue schoolgirl panties. The camera focused on Roxanne standing before a mirror, putting her rosary beads and golden necklace with the Holy Cross around her neck, petting the emblem with a naughty little smile.

When "Dirty Dancer" played louder, she swung her arms behind her back and snapped her fingers to the beat, rolling her neck and shoulders, whipping her hair side to side. She backed away and stood at the center of what looked to be her bedroom. She faced the camera, dancing her shoulders and swinging her hips to the hypnotic beat of the piano and drums, exuding raw passion. She turned around, spinning, wiggling that ass, her body in the groove and rhythm. I breathed slowly when Roxanne faced the camera, her eyes smoldering with lust. She crept her hand down to the crotch of her Catholic school skirt, but she was interrupted by a knock on the door. She stopped dancing.

"Are you listening to Izzy Rich *again*?" an angry man called.

"So what if I am?" Roxanne sassed, crossing her arms.

I uncrossed mine.

"Don't talk to your father that way!" a riled-up woman roared.

"We told you that Izzy Rich's music is the devil's music," shouted the man. "And you are forbidden from listening to it."

Roxanne covered her ears and closed her eyes, looking about ready to scream. Her parents bickering faded when she looked at the TV and uncovered her ears.

"The rumors are true, riches!" said a female reporter. "Izzy Rich will be touring in America! You have three months until tickets are on sale, so save those pennies, because Izzy Rich is coming!"

Roxanne smiled teasingly at the TV. She quickly turned it off when the door swung open, and dashing in was a petite Asian woman and a tall, slender blond-hair, blue-eyed man. They glared at a nervous-eyed and tight-lipped Roxanne, their nostrils flaring.

"Turn that music off!" her father roared.

"And hand us that record!" demanded her mother.

Roxanne grabbed the *Iz Ze Rich* vinyl sleeve from the wall, holding it close to her as she glared at them. "Mom, Dad, this is my life," she protested. "My music. And you know what? Izzy is my man." My stomach sank at not only what she last said, but *how* she said it— like she was me. She closed her eyes, and "Dirty Dancer" played again.

When she opened her eyes, Roxanne stood in front of *Le Chaton Rose*, looking up at the dingy neon pink sign that flashed its name. A long flowing red jacket showed nothing more than the six-inch heeled red stripper shoes on her feet. How they glistened when she walked inside the club. The men stared at her, following her moves as she crept to the stage. She stood there, her eyes big and curious as she looked up at the pink neon stage lights above her head. She gulped and looked behind her at the pole that was shining, waiting for her.

I looked at Izzy as he said, "This is the money shot."

My eyes widened when Roxanne removed her jacket and flung it to the side. That skimpy red dress showed off a...*body*. Those legs. Those arms. No bust, but good God, what an ass! The men howled as she struck a pose, spinning on her heels, and stopped to face the pole, her back to them. Roxanne's thick, round, confident bubble tush jiggled before their eyes. So. Goddamn. *Beautiful*. I gulped harder, and I couldn't blink. She only bent over, and my cock stirred from its sleep. Strange jolts of pleasure tore me up inside, making my dick throb as she turned to face the screaming men waving their money at her.

Those rosary beads and crosses around her neck swung to her shimmying flat chest. I gulped when Izzy wrapped his hand around my hard-on. I should've closed my eyes, but I was burning in this glorious hell of sweet heaven. Roxanne danced with more than lust, she danced with *power*. In her ass jiggle, chest shimmy, pelvic thrust, and groin grab, she was taking me to her newfound sexual freedom, her liberation awakened, escaped. When she whipped that wild auburn mane, her knees on the floor with her legs open, my cock twitched in Izzy's firm grasp. When he let go, he hid himself underneath the covers. I blinked and gasped when Roxanne stood and leapt toward the pole like a lady panther, spinning with her legs spread-eagled. I gasped as Izzy sucked and bobbed on my cock. I gyrated my hips as if I had no control of my pulsating body. With a groan, I made love to my Izzy's mouth.

I squeaked, and a manic voice inside my head screamed *"STOP!"* but there was no stopping now. I swiveled my hips in time to Izzy's desperate, pained moaning. He sucked me off with fervor as Roxanne made love to the stripper pole. I bit my lower lip so hard that it hurt, my eyes wide and stuck on the devil, Roxanne Foster Shengyi. I shook my head, panting heavily. The lights dimmed, and Roxanne stopped dancing. I touched my chest with shock and awe to a snow of glitter falling down like moon dust from the sky. Izzy strutted on the stage as if it were a catwalk. His glossy virgin white six-inch pumps, skimpy white halter dress, red lips, light mascara, and sparkly white eye shadow was eerily innocent compared to Roxanne.

The two stood beside each other, bumping their hips together and striking a pose, driving the boys off the wall when they bent over and shook their asses in sweet, hot unison. The two held hands and leapt toward the pole together. I slapped my hand to my mouth so I didn't scream as Izzy sucked and bobbed on me harder while he and Roxanne were pole dancing together. They spun like a carousel, their legs split, high above their heads. I gritted my teeth, panting fast and hard as I balled my fists and slammed them to the bed.

"Oh my God!" I choked out, my whole body trembling as Izzy sucked the come out of my dick.

Izzy still sucked me like a vacuum, prolonging my pleasure—and my pain, agony, and defeat. Sweat dripped down my face as I panted wildly at Izzy and Roxanne dirty dancing together, at one with their booties shaking, hips swaying, and heads rolling, reveling. They stopped with their backs against the pole and each other. They gyrated their asses against the pole as they walked, and then they spun on their heels away from the pole and faced each other. With a growl, I slapped my hand behind Izzy's head and held him down on my dick. He sucked so hard, I thrust my hips in a maddened rage, his nose pressed hard against my body.

The voice inside my head screamed out of my mouth. *"Stop!"*

I let him go and slammed my head against my pillow, my body shaking. Izzy let my cock slip out of his mouth as I glared at the screen, at Izzy clutching Roxanne's rosary beads. With a sinister smile, he used the rosary beads to pull her closer. With that jerk, Roxanne and Izzy locked lips, one hand cupped to her ass, the other cupped to her breast. I sighed at the same time the video jumped to Roxanne rolling over on her back on the bed, panting, her eye lids fluttering as if she'd just had an orgasm. For all I knew, maybe she actually did.

She looked at the camera with a most striking, unbelievably naughty gaze as she embraced the vinyl record, pressing it to her chest and stroked it with a wink. The video faded to black.

Izzy freed himself from the blankets, taking a deep breath of fresh air. I looked at him, bewildered, my lips trembling as did my sigh. Izzy wiped the sweat from his face. "Hell. You look ashamed, baby. Didn't you like the video?"

Though it wasn't on anymore, I replayed it in my mind. My stomach felt a little sick, and my brain was dazed and confused, but my heart and my groin…The waves of pleasure drowned me like the most perfect storm, and I didn't want to live. I wanted to *be free*. I looked at Izzy, smiling weakly as he smoothed back my wet hair.

"You got yourself a money maker," I said. "The video's fantastic."

Izzy grinned with such pride. "That's precisely what I wanted to hear, baby!" He looked down at my groin and waggled his brows. "And on top of that, I also got what I really wanted to see."

As he crushed his lips to mine and our tongues were dirty dancing, how badly I wanted to scream and bawl. But instead, I was letting go, free in only Izzy's kiss.

❖

"The number one single has a hit music video that Europe and the USA can't get enough of," declared the Top of the Pops host. "You know it—it's 'Dirty Dancer,' and it stars the dirty dancing lady whose name is still on everybody's lips weeks since Madison Square Garden, Roxanne Foster, or as Izzy and his fans call her, Foxxy Roxxy."

The *raw* power of lust and love didn't only emanate off Izzy as he was standing before the microphone in his sparkly red platforms, sheer black stockings, vinyl black and white checkered skirt, and short sleeved red vinyl jacket with dramatic puffy sleeves. Izzy's teenage riches smiled and cheered from all directions around us, as we were performing in the round.

"Izzy's back on the Top of the Pops, and here he is now to perform that hit song, 'Dirty Dancer.'"

"Woo!" Izzy howled when our smashing performance was done. He jumped, bowing and blowing kisses to his riches. I shook out my wrists and rubbed the goose bumps on my bare arms as the host approached Izzy.

"Wow. That was incredible and exciting," Reggie said. "How does it feel to have a number one hit song all across Europe and in the USA, and to have a critically acclaimed music video for it?"

"It's like being on acid," Izzy said, breathless. "Except more pure and natural."

"Does Roxxy know how well the video is doing?"

I smirked as Izzy said sweet and boyishly to Reggie's mic, "Oh yes, she absolutely does."

It took every ounce of strength in me to not roll my eyes as the audience went crazy, screaming.

"And in fact..." Izzy took the microphone from Reggie. I looked at the guys, and then at Izzy.

"For the last leg of the tour starting tomorrow, Ms. Foxxy Roxxy will be joining me on tour for the Dirty Dancer portion of the set list. In fact, she's on the plane right now!"

My heart dropped, and my face paled. I got cramps in my stomach. The room was spinning, but I could still see Larry, Tim, Phil, and Benson clapping and grinning. Did they already know?

My blood boiled, my dark, cold, and trembling gaze on Izzy. My legs shook, my temples throbbed, and my breathing was heavy. Izzy didn't look at me once. We were off the air. I stood, slouching, my hand on my belly.

"John?" asked Tim as I ran past him to the wings.

I collapsed on my knees at the first trash can I saw and dunked my head into it, vomiting.

"Sir, are you okay?" asked some members of the backstage crew.

I saw the guys heading toward me, concern on their faces.

My voice wobbled. "I'm okay..."

One of Izzy's assistants handed me a towel. "Need water, John?"

"Yes, please." I nodded and spat out the last sour taste of bile and vomit. After I wiped at my mouth, I knocked back the water. Three quick gulps, and I was halfway finished with the bottle. I stood, doubled over for a second, then I straightened my back with my chest out and took a deep, heavy breath as the guys came up to me.

"Jesus, John," said Tim, rubbing my back. "What happened?"

I rubbed my head as if it was hung over. "Did you guys know about Roxanne joining the tour?"

Benson and Phil nodded as Tim and Larry said yes.

"When?" I asked hoarsely, squeezing the bottle as I forced down the last sips.

"William told us this morning at breakfast. You weren't there."

And neither was Izzy. We were too busy snuggling, snogging, and making love. "Why didn't you guys tell me?" I asked weakly as I tossed the bottle into the trash.

"We figured Izzy did," Phil said. "He tells you everything."

"Hell, we figured that you knew before even William did," said Larry.

"That's right." I forced myself to chuckle. "I knew a long time ago."

Benson scratched his head. "Why are you shocked, then?"

"Because we didn't talk about it together as brothers. Like we always do. You know." I wiped at my eyes and gulped hard when Izzy rushed toward us with a menacing smile.

He howled, stamping his platforms and shaking that ass. "I love my boys! That was *great!*"

I looked down at my platforms, stuffing my pants pockets with my hands. When I glared at him, my lips were tight, my gaze cold. He glowed with his toothy grin, his eyes lit up as if he really were on acid.

"Who's ready for Roxxy?" he asked us excitedly. "She'll be here after ten in the evening."

I said nothing as the guys were saying how ecstatic they were to hear she was coming.

"John?" Izzy softly said to me.

"What?" I snapped and glared at him.

He smiled nervously. "I heard you upchucked. Not cute. That's not you. You okay?"

"I'm fine, captain. *Perfect.*"

❖

Knock, knock, knock. Those three raps were slow, timid. *Knock, knock, knock.* Those three were sharper and more confident, tinged with fear.

"May I come in?" Izzy asked nervously when I swung the door open.

I said nothing. I stepped aside. He closed the door, locked it, and whimpered "Daddy…"

When he tried to kiss me, I turned aside, my arms crossed and my nostrils flaring.

His voice shook. "Baby, you have every right to be ticked off. I can explain."

When I turned back to glare at him, he gulped. "Why didn't you fucking tell me?" I growled.

Izzy took a deep breath and looked me deep in the eyes, his baby blues lost and helpless. "I was scared that if I told you earlier, you would have been furious."

"So waiting until we got on *live* television was a better idea? How bloody considerate of you!"

"I was daft." He grimaced. "I wasn't thinking as straight as I thought."

"And oh! Not only that, but everyone bloody knew except for me! You have any fucking idea how bloody embarrassed I was? The guys thought that I knew even before William knew!" I talked so fast, hard, and loud that I took a deep breath and had to storm off to the couch. When I sat, Izzy carefully came toward me.

"Baby, do you have an issue with her touring with us? Is that what this is about?"

"No! My issue is *you*," I huffed. "That was a rotten thing you did."

Izzy grabbed the top of his hair as he cried, "God, baby, I said I was sorry!"

"Whatever." I crossed my arms. "Whose stupid idea was it to bring her on tour anyway?"

"Mine. But William's, too. Baby—" He sat next to me and took both my hands in his. "Only *two* months." He looked at me dolefully as he kissed my hands all over. "Twenty-four shows. That's it. The end."

I yanked my hands away from him when he was about to kiss them again.

"The only reason why she's touring with us, baby, is because of

'Dirty Dancer's' success. It's my fastest charting single to date. And the video is turning on my fans so much, it only makes sense to bring her on tour with us. Why are you taking it personal, daddy? It's business."

"The video was soft core porn." I glared at him. "You used her virginity as bait."

"What?" he laughed. "Baby, that's *her* business. I don't give a bloody damn that she's a virgin and religious."

"But the media does. Practically the goddamn world—"

"So it's *my* fault that people are fascinated by her being a virgin Catholic schoolgirl?"

"You said it."

"*She* was the one who put that out there. Not me. I had nothing to do with that."

I glared at him, unsure of what to believe.

"I thought you'd be happy for me. And for Roxanne. I guess I was wrong. Again."

I sighed. "Maybe I am overreacting. Again."

He kissed my fingers, his eyes so doleful and sweet. "I fucked up."

"No shit."

"But be honest, aren't you happy for me?"

"What a bloody stupid question. I'm ridiculously proud of you."

"So why can't you be happy for *her*?"

"I *am* happy, dammit!" I snapped. "But this bombshell. Christ, Izzy!"

"What do I have to do to show you how sorry I am?"

I cupped his face and growled against his lips. "Don't ever do that again. Promise?"

"I promise." He murmured so softly it almost sounded like a song. And I believed it as if the words had a soul. "But there's one thing that I have to know, John."

"What's that?" I gulped at the urgency of his voice.

"Do you like Roxanne or not?"

"Why do you ask?"

"Since the video, I can't tell if you like her more or less."

He couldn't be more wrong about that. I haven't changed. The only difference was...the bitch, that she-devil, oh how she turned me on. The video didn't even have to play in my mind anymore to get me off. I could close my eyes and see Roxanne dancing. That incredible, phenomenal ass seduced me and made me so hard. As much as I'd deny my hot lust, the boners, wet dreams, and soiled boxers were the true hell of it.

I cocked my chin up. "She's all right…"

"But?"

I gulped at the way he stared at me as if he could read my soul. "She loves you, Izzy."

Izzy let out a laugh. "What?"

"It's a feeling. And I can't shake off this vibe that she's your girl."

"Why?"

"In the music video, she said you were her man. She said it like she meant it."

"Good, because I taught her that. So the audience would *believe* her."

I sighed.

"Oh my God, Johnny—"

I shook my head. "I'm telling you, I knew. I always knew. She wants my baby."

"Every man and woman wants me." He whispered into my ear, "There is only *one* person in this whole wide world that has me. Who is that man, baby? Who is my man?"

I shed a tear as I whimpered with pride, "*Me*."

"Don't *ever* forget that," he snapped in a firm, dominant tone that frightened me.

When I looked at him, something about his gaze was dark, authoritative. The chills took me over, dancing down my spine and making me quiver.

"I won't, captain. I mean…princess."

"You will promise me one thing," he growled, his voice strict. "Be nice to Roxanne."

That voice. It was more than ruling. It sounded like a threat. I gulped harder at how puny and powerless I felt, the submissive awakening inside in me.

"I will," I said dryly, giving in to his strange, dark force.

"You better, Jonathan."

He said my full first name and looked hard at me, as if he was the devil. No longer *my* devil. In the blinking of my eyes, Izzy softened his gaze and his submissive voice returned with a vengeance.

"Remember. Two months. Twenty-four shows. She will only perform on 'Dirty Dancer.'"

"What about all those girls that expect to be picked from the audience? They'll feel cheated."

He shrugged. "I know it will break hearts, but you've got to be cruel to be kind sometimes."

"Don't you think it's a little too cruel?"

"My fans *love* Roxanne. Girls want to be her, and boys want to fuck her."

My cock throbbed to the way he said that, so sexual and sure.

"Why should I deny them what they want?" Izzy said excitedly. "They want my Foxxy Roxxy."

"*Your* Foxxy Roxxy?"

"Oh, you know what I mean, daddy. She's everyone's dirty dancing sweetheart."

"How much did you pay her parents this time?"

"Double."

"I hope you'll get your money's worth, captain."

"Aren't I already?" He winked. I gasped and grinned when he straddled me and gyrated his groin against mine, swaying his hips. He stroked my chin as he purred, "Daddy, I'm so bloody rich that if I could buy myself, I can!"

I snorted and something inside me snapped. I laughed madly.

"That's what I love to hear!" Izzy laughed madly with me. He stopped, got off me, held my hands, and pulled me away from the couch. "Your happiness." He cupped my ass, squeezing my cheeks. "All I want is that, my love."

"You are my world, Izzy," I said desperately. "You are everything to me."

"You fucking belong to me," Izzy said with a startling growl that made me gulp, shiver, and my cock pulse at the same time in one loud, confusing rush. "You're my man. You're mine."

My tears returned and poured down my face as Izzy kissed me so hard and passionately that my lips hurt. When he picked me up and cradled me in his arms, I had not a care as to where he was taking me. His hot kisses took me away. To heaven. His heaven. The most glorious hell. And I was burning, melting in the deep.

CHAPTER TWELVE

The adrenaline felt like thunder in my body, buzzing right through me as if I were still on the stage. The frenzy was already starting. When they pushed the crowd back and Rick opened the exit door, not even the dark lenses of my shades could blur those hundreds of hot flashing lights, and I could hardly hear anything but the fans and the paparazzi. Everyone rushed to the limo. Inside, I grabbed two bottles of cider from the bar, twisted off the cap from one of the bottles, and chugged.

"Damn, you aren't wasting time, baby John," Larry said.

"Bottoms up." I winked at him.

As the guys were choosing their poison, I sipped more slowly and looked out the window. Izzy stepped out in his sequined mermaid skirt, midriff top, pumps, and tiara. Roxanne stood beside him in a more understated ensemble of a suit, tie, and fedora. They were hand in hand, but they separated to sign autographs. I belched and chugged the last of the cider. After I tossed the bottle in the trash, I popped open the other.

"Whoa." I jumped when the driver started the limo. "Why are we moving already?"

I looked behind the back window and saw another limo behind us. As the car steered farther away, I caught a glimpse of Izzy and Roxanne dashing to that one. I glared and scowled, turning back to face the gang. I knocked back the rest of my bottle and grabbed another from the bar. By the time we made it to the hotel, I was so drunk I needed to lean on Benson as we sauntered to the elevator. In the suite, I crashed in bed, lying on my back and smoking reefer until I mustered up the strength to get dressed for the after-party. Feeling high and oh so fine in my tight sequined pants and matching jacket, I picked up the phone and called Izzy. No answer. I slammed the phone on its hook after I called him for the tenth time. Still, no response. And it was nearing closer to three o' clock in the morning. I lay on the bed in a fetal position, still in my party frocks.

I didn't realize I was dozing off until I flipped myself over on my back fast, and shouted "Fuck!"

Izzy jumped, too, sitting on his knees. "Hey, daddy," he said calmly. "It's just me."

I turned myself over on my side, facing away from him with crossed arms.

"Had fun at the party?" he said into my ear, his hand on my bottom. "I heard that it was delicious, the orgies outrageous." He squeezed me. "And you were the ringleader, weren't cha?"

"I didn't go," I said flatly.

"Why not?"

"You stood me up."

I smacked his hand off my ass and turned over on my back, glaring at him.

"Shit. What did I do?"

"It's what you *didn't* do. You didn't answer any of my calls."

"I was busy."

"With Roxanne, right?"

"Not only with her…"

"Bollocks. I barely saw you all fucking day, and whenever I did, she was your shadow." I sat up against the headboard. "And why were you two in a separate goddamn limo?"

He rolled over, lying on his back. "I don't have time for this."

"Of course you don't, because you only have time for *her*!" I snapped.

"Jesus, John. We're only into day one of this leg of the tour, and you're mad."

Well, I couldn't argue with him about that. I was mad crazy. Mad jealous. And mad horny.

"Is this how you're going to act for the next twenty-four shows?" Izzy asked as if he were challenging me. "Whining and pining over me because Roxanne is taking time out of my day."

"*Our* day, *our* time together!"

He smirked. "We're together *now*. Instead of arguing, why not kiss me, daddy?"

"And have her sloppy seconds?"

He rolled his eyes.

"Don't roll your fucking eyes at me!"

He looked at me, pouting. "Sorry, sir."

"You better be sorry. Leaving me here alone all day. What were you two doing?"

"Nothing too exciting. We hung out at her suite, had supper, and watched some TV."

"And?"

"Made out, of course…"

"And?" I glared. "Did she jump your bone? Go down on you? Eat out your arse? Peg you?"

"Ha! I wish! I only sucked her cute little titties."

A sudden pang of jealousy and pleasure rushed from my brain straight to my groin. "What? How did you get her to let you do that?"

He licked his lips, his eyes oozing lust. "It's not the first time I sucked on them. How else do you think I got Roxanne to be so sexy in the music video? That was my bad influence."

I gulped as my cock twitched in my pants. "How naughty."

"Oh, no, Ms. Shengyi is the naughty one. The day before we started filming at *Le Chaton Rose*, she was very self-conscious. Wearing that dress for her triggered so much insecurity because it made her look even more flat-chested. As she was telling me about it, she opened her blouse like this." Izzy ripped open his top. "And she did this." He shimmied. "And she said, 'Look at them, Izzy! They're so little!'"

My cock suddenly hardened, tenting in my pants. Izzy smirked at it, then at me. "Then w-what happened?"

He laid his hand on top of my hard-on. "I told her, they are *beautiful*." He crept his finger along the length of my cock as he purred, "And then she said…" He leaned toward me and whispered in Roxanne's voice, "Izzy, I want you to touch them. Suck on them. Please. Make me beautiful."

I gasped when Izzy yanked down my zipper.

"So I did," he said in his normal voice. He licked my ear, teasing my sensitive lobe. "I touched them." He caressed my nipple while pulling my cock out from my pants, and he quivered as he wanked me slowly. "And I sucked her tit whole. I sucked until it turned pink."

I snapped my eyes shut and groaned, thrusting my cock into the hole of his tight grip. Izzy giggled and squeezed harder as he said, "And she had her very first orgasm."

"Shit." I licked my lips as Izzy wanked me faster. "That's so bloody sexy. Lucky bitch."

"That I am."

I opened my eyes and panted, looking down at him. "Trombone me the way I like it, baby."

He yanked down my pants and tossed them aside. I pressed my legs together and raised them over my head, my cock aimed at my mouth. With a groan, Izzy spread my cheeks, and I shouted as his tongue split my ass open, his hand gripped around my cock, wanking me at the same time.

"Ooh, daddy, how your ass gapes so big and wide for me!"

"Say that again," I moaned. "But in that voice you used before."

Izzy's wanking stalled. With his face between my legs, he looked down at me and grinned. "You're a sick fuck." He cleared his throat and said in Roxanne's voice, "And I love you."

I panted heavily, closing my eyes and groaning with an ache that made me a prisoner, a slave to Roxanne. I clawed the sheets and grabbed hold of the fabric as Izzy pushed his tongue deeper inside me, thrusting and spinning into my ass hard and fast as he wanked me with fervor.

"Yes, yes…" growled Izzy in Roxanne's voice. "*That's it*, daddy."

"Fuck!" I snapped, my eyes rolling. My hot, thick come splattered on top of my nose, but Izzy didn't stop. He ate out my ass and wanked as I opened my mouth wide, and my come flew right in. Tears welled up in my closed eyes as Izzy kept on going.

"How I love you!" Izzy cooed, the timid Chinese accent still on point. "Jonathan. My Johnny…"

"Stop!" I gasped, come sliding down my throat.

Izzy fell to one side as my legs collapsed on the bed flat. I looked up at the ceiling, swallowing my jizz as my dizzy mind raced with my heart. Izzy's lips met mine, and he sucked on my tongue hungrily, taking the flavor of me from my mouth until I couldn't taste me anymore. The harder Izzy kissed me, the harder I kissed him back, out of our love but also out of my loathing for that bitch.

I pushed him off me and pinned him on his back, wanting, needing his cock in my ass. I rode him with hate for the lust eating me alive and swallowing me whole. Like Izzy. Sucking Roxanne's breasts whole. With that image in my mind, I fucked Izzy to *my* hell until he begged for mercy, whimpering as he came. I held him close to me, our wet bodies reeking of sweat, come, musk, and heat. With my arms wrapped around him, we kissed and slept until the dawn rose. I woke up to the clap of thunder, of rain drops sounding like needles shooting into glass.

"Baby?" I murmured.

Still on my back, still wet from our love, I turned my head to my right and to my left. My princess wasn't there. It was only eight in the morning. I looked to my drawer. No note about his early departure. I checked the bathroom and the walk-in closet. Nothing. I dashed to the living room. Izzy wasn't there. Or in the kitchen. I even looked out of the windows up at the sky as if he'd fall from heaven into my arms. My hair was soaked, and I didn't care. I sat at the edge of my bed and phoned him. I was taken straight to the elevator music. I hung it up slowly, gently. I lay on my side and held back my tears. I closed my eyes, shook my head, and the tears pooled. He not only left me. My baby *abandoned* me.

❖

For six concerts in a row, nothing changed. Everything was the same.

Lonely mornings. Empty afternoons. I only saw him at the sound checks, rehearsals, and concerts. They took a separate limo. Him being a no-show at the after-parties. Him returning to my suite at the crack of dawn only to leave my side around four hours later. Our time together shorter, yet sweet. I didn't bitch or whine to him anymore. Not even to myself. What kind of fool was I?

The twelfth concert began and ended so fast.

Before I'd shower and apply my makeup in the morning, I'd check the tabloids and watch the news to see Roxanne and Izzy hand in hand, smiling, and openly making out for the cameras in Germany, Italy, Switzerland, or Luxembourg. They smiled and waved at the paparazzi as if they were their chums. In France and Austria, pictures were taken of them shopping. Izzy didn't present any new gifts to me.

The headlines gave them a new name: *The King and Princess of Glam.*

It wasn't only a title.

Every single night, I could see it, feel its power in their dirty dancing and in their kiss before, during, and after the show. It was as hot as my lust, madness, anger, and jealousy. But it made me feel cold, leaving my body shaking in its frost each and every morning when I'd wake up, the sheets still warm and wet with Izzy's scent. It was my natural high.

Though high, I never felt so low. And cheap.

Like all the other days, on the morning of concert eighteen, my body was shaking, yearning for my fix of Izzy. After I showered and dressed, I left my suite. At the same time, Tim appeared. "Oh, hey, baby John! I was going to knock on your door," he said.

"What for?" I smirked.

"Boys' night is now boys' morning today."

"What?"

"Didn't get the memo?"

I shook my head, rubbed my nose, and snorted as we drew to the elevator.

"Are you all right, John?" he asked when we stepped inside.

"Why do you ask?"

"You're so quiet these days. You look strung out. And have you been eating well?"

I snorted again, still feeling the burn from the cocaine. "I've changed that much?"

"You don't seem like yourself."

"It's the tour." I scratched the back of my head. "It's taking its toll on me, I guess."

"It sure has been more grueling."

"It's not the workload," I said, looking into his eyes. "Random question."

"Shoot."

"Do you think Roxanne and Izzy are going steady?"

He shrugged. "A lot of us have been wondering, but who knows?"

"Am I the only one who finds Roxanne annoying?" I asked him with a sigh. "She's always around Izzy all the bloody time. It's no fucking wonder people are suspicious about those two being…lovers."

"That's Izzy, though, isn't it? You never know with him."

The elevator door opened. I kept my mouth shut as we walked past the business men and women and staff members of the hotel and into the hotel's restaurant where the guys and Izzy waited.

"Speaking of the devils!" Izzy beamed, an empty seat across from him. I sat there, smirking at him as Tim sat next to me.

"Wouldn't you believe it, boys? Today's our first boys' morning. And I'm *starving*."

I cleared my throat, thinking about last night. I tickle-tortured him and fucked him so hard, it was no wonder he was glowing.

"So, before we order…" He clapped his hands and rubbed them fast. "Business talk."

I looked at him, not as my boyfriend, but as my boss.

"Starting tonight and here on out, your solos will have to be cut short. No more thirty seconds. Too fucking long. Only ten seconds between each of you."

I looked at him and glared. "Why?"

"'Dirty Dancer' is going to be extended to eight minutes."

"What kind of fucking bullshit is that?" I choked aloud, spit flying from my mouth.

"Whoa," I heard Larry say. Everyone else's eyes widened. My hands shook as I breathed heavily, staring at Izzy. His stare. His gaze. If it had been any colder, hell would have frozen over.

"Does anybody else have a problem with my decision?" he growled.

I could see the nervousness in everyone's eyes. They shook their heads. Except for me. I held my gaze on Izzy, my arms crossed. That stare. That gaze. I gulped hard. Now I was frozen, burned. Nobody, not even me, dared moved as Izzy removed himself from his seat.

"Elevator. *Now*," he said firmly into my ear.

I removed myself from the table as Izzy said to everyone that we'd be back in a few minutes. Neither of us said a word to each other as we went to the elevator. My stomach was churning from the tension. Even the way he jabbed at the elevator button put me on edge, the hairs on the back of my neck rising. When we were in, he slammed the button to stop the elevator.

"What the bloody fuck is your goddamn problem?" he growled, his eyes dark, menacing. "You've *never* spoken out of line like that with me. In front of the guys? What's your deal?"

"What did Roxanne do to get this special treatment all of a sudden? Suck your dick?"

He flashed a smug look at me. My face paled, and I almost wanted to throw up.

"She did? She sucked your dick?"

"Ding, ding, ding!"

"What? I was only kidding..."

"I'm not. And she sure wasn't."

I blinked, the picture too hard to imagine. Roxanne? Going down on *my* man? "When did this happen?"

"Last night. In my dressing room. She sucked off Ms. Starr."

"That's not fair. I don't even get to suck her off. And I *begged*."

He shrugged. "She didn't have to. The girl's learning about the business. It's not who you know, but who you *blow* that gets you a... *head*." When he chuckled deeply, I glared, my right hand shaking. "Roxanne didn't need to suck me off. I was going to give her more show time anyway."

"Was she any good?"

"Oh, you'd love to know, wouldn't you? So you can wank off to her like a teenaged twat!"

I smacked his cheek hard and loud with a grunt.

Izzy gasped from pure shock. It was in his eyes, too. I was going to say I was sorry, but Izzy grabbed me by the collar of my shirt and hissed, "You hit me? You hit me."

"S-shit," I stuttered.

"What we do in bed is one thing, Mr. Maxwell. But outside of that is another."

"Y-yes sir, c-captain."

"Do that again, and I'll cut your drum solo altogether."

"You wouldn't."

I gagged when he grabbed my throat and squeezed it hard. "Try me." He pushed me back, slamming me against the elevator door. I breathed slowly as I touched my pulsating neck. He panted and shivered, his glare darker than ever. "Have any more issues that you want to address? Because now's your only chance."

I wiped away the sweat that budded on my forehead. "With her new solo, does that mean that she gets paid more, too?"

"Since when has that been your business?"

"Answer my question," I said gently. "Please."

He cocked his chin up and stood there for a second. "Her salary is less than The Diamonds."

"You are bluffing. I know you, dammit. You had to think about it."

"If you have a problem with it, talk it over with William. He takes care of payroll. Now, we better get out of here, or else the boys will be suspicious."

I blocked the door still. "Have you told any of them about us? Have you told anyone?"

He dropped his eyes down and then looked at me coldly. "That's nobody's business."

"How about Roxanne? Does she know?"

"Bloody hell. What shit have you been on lately?"

"God, Izzy, fucking *tell me* the *truth*!"

"Why of all bloody people does she need to know?"

"Izzy, we need to talk about this. When are we going to let the entourage know?"

"Why do you suddenly give a damn? What happened to that posh and uppity rich boy that was protective over his family background and love life? Oh!" He snapped his finger. "I know. I know *exactly* why. It's because you are dating *me*."

"Are you bloody kidding me?" I shouted. "You aren't my blasted trophy wife!"

"But you'd love to show me off like one, wouldn't you?"

"I didn't say that I wanted the world to know. I don't give a bloody fuck about the damn world!"

"I do!" he barked, his nostrils flaring, his eyes livid as he roared. "The world may be mine, Jonathan Maxwell, but that doesn't mean that I have the power to change it. The entire fucking world finds out about us, that's it! They will tear our world apart. They will *burn* it, you hear me?" he said so loudly that spit flew from his mouth. "The world will destroy our love."

"That may be true, but what about you and Roxanne?"

"What about us?"

"You two can hold hands and make out publicly."

Izzy stood there, frozen.

"And the world accepts you two as you are. On and off the stage."

"That's the way of the world, John. You know that."

I looked down, then at him. "It's too bad I am a man. If I was a woman, we could be out in the open as the lovers we are instead of being lovers after dark, hiding behind closed doors."

"It's a bloody shame. A crime." He grimaced. "It is what it is. I can't control everything."

"So what's it then? Are you and Roxanne lovers, too?"

He smirked. "You believe that?"

The words "I'm starting to…" came out of me as crystal, clear, and sharp as an icicle.

"That's precisely what Cheryl wants the world to believe. It's PR, baby." He winked.

I breathed heavily, looking him over. "Why?"

"For the record, the singles sales are still soaring at the top of the charts." He rubbed his thumb and forefinger together. "And it's making us a whole lot of money, baby. We are drowned in it."

"How could I forget? Roxanne's your cash cow."

"What did you call her?" he cracked.

I raised my hands up. "Hey. It was a joke, baby. Can't take one now?"

He shook his hands out. "I'm starving. This stops. Right now."

"Baby. I love you. I'm sorry. For everything."

He smirked and pressed his chest against mine. He stroked my cheek. "I know it's been hard keeping us a secret for so long."

I grimaced. "It almost makes me wish that you could be Holly again. We had it all then."

"And we can have it all again, baby." He sucked my bottom lip and let go. "Just not now."

"Can we at least show everyone that we are…whatever we are?"

He stroked my chin and murmured "What do you have in mind?"

"Us holding hands."

"Tomorrow is group breakfast," he purred. "Everyone will be there, daddy. And Roxanne, too. We will walk in together, holding hands. Would that make you happy, my love, my dear?"

"Yes."

He brushed my lips with his. "We should have done it sooner."

"I can't stand the secrets anymore."

"Meet me at my door at seven tomorrow morning."

I cupped his face in my hands and snogged him. He sucked on my tongue and then pulled away. I wiped at my eyes. "How do I look?"

"You're a pretty mess."

"And I'd be nothing without you, Izzy Rich."

He licked my cleft. I stepped aside for him to press the elevator button. When we returned to the restaurant, we assured the gang everything was fine. More than that. *Perfect.*

❖

Knock, knock, knock. I shook out my wrists and knocked three more times. I checked my watch. It was seven on the dot. I looked to the door as I heard steps. When the door swung open, I blinked, unable to believe my eyes. Standing before me was Izzy in his pumps, swishy pants, and frilly blouse and Roxanne in boots, jeans, and a T-shirt. "Oh, hiya, morning, John!" Roxanne chirped and smiled.

I shook my head in disbelief as I looked at their clasped hands. Izzy squeezed her hand as he looked at me. That mischievous little smirk did it. I felt the blood draining from my face.

"Are you okay, John?" Roxanne asked.

I stumbled back as if Izzy had pushed me off a cliff. And he really had, standing there with that smug face. Saying nothing. Doing nothing. His hand still in her hand. I dashed down the hallway as the tears blurred my vision. The walls were caving in on me and the hallway was spinning as I rushed to the door of my suite, shakily turning the knob. When I realized that I needed my key, the shaking worsened. After I slid the key in and turned the knob, I pushed open the door and stumbled into my room.

I collapsed to the floor, crashing on my knees. The truth, at last, was out. I wasn't Izzy's boyfriend anymore. I was his dirty little secret. I was hidden, forbidden. Because I was a man. To the world, only Izzy's drummer. To Izzy's world, only his closest friend. A blood brother. Fuck all. And sod the world. To see Roxanne and Izzy holding hands meant everything. And yet, it meant nothing. What were they? My pain boiled into pure anger. I'd wanted to believe him yesterday. I believed *nothing* now. It wasn't my fault! Only his. I had no other choice. One way or another, my baby be damned, I was going to suss out the truth of his and Roxanne's alleged love affair once and for all.

CHAPTER THIRTEEN

Hundreds of people were there, and I knew every face. The entourage family. Famous supermodels, actresses, actors, songwriters, dancers, film directors, and artists signed by Trident Studios. The men were dressed in conservative suits and ties that clashed beautifully with their gaudy makeup, jewelry, furs, feather boas, sequins, and glitter. Most of the women wore their hair as long as their dresses, their furs and boas, longer. Everybody was dancing. I stood below a disco ball spinning above my head as I looked at everyone, struck by the realization that in this crowd of hundreds, I was alone, feeding my misery with vodka. I knocked back my shot and slammed it on the table, reached for another, and polished it off. I grimaced, shaking my head to the spine tingling rush. I gritted my teeth as I sauntered to a corner, crossed my arms, looked out at the party, and pondered, *why the fuck am I here?*

I winced and scowled at the sudden applause, claps, and whistles that drowned out the music. From afar, I could see them. The King Queen herself as himself stepped gracefully down the stairs. On top of his bob sparkled a replica of Queen Victoria's crown. His dress was a perfect throwback to the imperial majesty of Queen Victoria's Robe of State. He mirrored the shiny red velvet, gold, and white in his makeup. Those red velvet lips, gold eye shadow, and powdery white face popped, nearly blinding me.

Roxanne was glammed out in a beaded evening dress, glittery golden tie, and gold collar. Her makeup as flawless as Izzy's, she was neither a king nor queen. Just the bitch. I snatched another vodka stinger, squinting at the two raising their arms up, hand in hand. Everyone cheered as if they were heroes that saved the world, but they'd ended mine. I was caught in a traffic jam of handshakes, group hugs, fist bumps, and brotherly and sisterly embraces. No matter where I looked or where I turned, the spaces were only tighter. Izzy posed nearly every step, showing off his long train of a robe and his long-heeled pumps as he had his arm around Roxanne. I licked my lips, not because of the liquor that I could still taste on them, but because of her. I turned my fingers into fists, leaning my back against the wall as I closed my eyes.

The she-devil was my poison.

I opened my eyes, breathing heavily as my hands shook over my face. From concert eighteen to concert twenty-two, I was a wreck, constantly crying. And here they were, the tears fierce again. Only three more concerts, and…what then?

My stomach cramped and sweat beaded over my forehead. I was having the shakes. Was it from taking too much dope, weed, crack, and ecstasy over the course of the weeks? Alone. In my room. Talking to myself and feeling old, lonelier. Watching TV by myself. Drinking by myself until it was time to punch in to work. After the show, wanking off into another woman's mouth, fucking another cunt, another ass, sucking another dick until I was bored. Returning to the suite, reefer lulling me to sleep. And then, the following day, like yesterday, repeated, like all the days. I scratched and rubbed my arms, looking up. Roxanne was coming toward me.

"Bloody hell," I mouthed to myself, realizing I had been sitting on the floor. I stood up quick, slicked back my hair, and cocked my chin up when Roxanne smiled and waved.

"What are you doing all by yourself, John?"

I rubbed my eyes, knowing how bloodshot they were. "Needed some space."

"Enjoying the party?"

"It's great," I said flatly, not bothering to smile. "Congrats. For 'Dirty Dancer.' You did it."

"Oh, shucks. It wasn't me. Izzy did everything."

"But *you*, God, you made it extra sexy, darling," I slurred. "So fucking sexy."

Roxanne cocked an eye at me. I wasn't sure if she was embarrassed or disgusted by my most sincere compliment. I only laughed a little because I sounded so bloody pathetic. Who cared?

"Let's make a toast?" I said.

"Are you sure you need another drink?"

"What makes you think I had any at all?" I asked hoarsely.

"A hunch," she said with biting sarcasm.

"C'mon, have a drink with me?"

"I don't drink. Remember?"

I snapped my finger. "Oh, yeah!" I smacked my palm to my head. "Silly me! How about we toast with your Shirley Temples then? You like those!" I said in a loud, condescending tone.

"And you don't, evidently." She glared at me. "What's your problem, John?"

"Pardon?" I hissed.

"*Everybody* in this room likes me, except you. What have I ever done to you?"

I wanted to scream. My lips shaking, I bit my tongue, kept my mouth shut, and glared at her darkly.

"Now I know for sure what I thought all along. You hate me."

"Let me guess. Izzy told you."

She shook her head. "Nope. You've made it obvious from the beginning."

"Well, you are wrong."

"Oh, am I?" she said daringly. Her eyes reeked of temptation and lust.

It couldn't have been my imagination.

"I like you, actually." I eyed her from head to toe. "Izzy was right about you."

"What do you mean?" she asked, her eyes lighting up, seeming so eager to know.

"You are a hot commodity. He said it, knew it, and here you are. One hot commodity."

"A hot commodity?" she said, sounding shocked, her voice tinged with hurt.

"That's right, baby!" I snapped. "A product. Bait. His money-maker."

She shook her head, glared at me, and sneered. "Bullshit."

I gasped. "W-what? Did I hear Ms. Clean as a Whistle *curse*?"

"Izzy *loves* me," she said with a conviction that pierced into my heart. I gulped thickly as she smiled warmly and said, "He'd never think of me that way."

The sweat on my forehead dripped down my face. "Oh, he loves you all right, sweetheart!" I bellowed. "He loves you for your big ass! That's what you are to him, Roxanne. And that's what you are to the damn world! A hot piece of *virgin* ass." Roxanne turned her back to me, so I raised my voice louder. "Oh! And there's something else that Izzy told me. Your mummy and daddy are making money off your ass, too."

She stopped, turned around, and hissed "What?"

"Izzy *paid* them tons of money!" I didn't care people were staring at me in horror. "He paid them off and they sold you out like a bloody prostitute!"

It happened too quickly. In a split second, Roxanne's eyes bulged in rage, then she hit me. I touched my warm flesh as I watched her storm off.

"The bitch slapped me?" I growled.

"Hey, Jonathan!" somebody called. "What was that about, man?"

"Sod off!" I shouted at nobody and pushed my way through the crowd.

Ahead, I saw a baby grand piano with Izzy on top of it.

"Helloo, my darlings, my princess and princesses!" Izzy said coquettishly into the microphone. And everyone, and I mean *everyone*, including me, stopped to stare at the Queen-King of the world. "Isn't the world a perfect place tonight?" he howled. And everyone howled with him. "I would like to make a toast to—" He flashed that trademark smile. "Why, to me, of course!"

Everyone laughed except me. I inched closer and froze when I saw Roxanne standing closest to the piano. Izzy chuckled boyishly. "In all seriousness, I must thank William James for throwing this gorgeous party, and Trident Studios for believing in the album and in the song's promise as a single. Very few know this, but it's my most personal one yet."

I rubbed my arms from this sudden chill. Izzy looked at Roxanne. It should have been me.

His voice was tender and soft as he continued. "But everyone knows that the *Iz Ze Rich* album is my most personal album to date. Those who have touched me have made the album what it is. One of those people being my boys, The Diamonds."

Everyone clapped and cheered when Izzy commanded everyone to give us a hand, but when he should have been looking at us, he was gazing at Roxanne, smiling brighter than ever.

"And of course, of all people in this room, I want to thank Miss Roxanne Foster Shengyi."

That gigantic smile of hers burned me like hell fire.

"When I first met you, Roxanne, I knew you were a star. More than that, I knew in my heart of hearts that we would take over the world. With this single, we did that, didn't we, my love?"

I shuffled my feet against the floor and growled when Roxanne nodded quickly. Everyone clapped and cheered like we were at the concert. What was wrong with my eyes? All I could see was Izzy's trophy. His prized possession.

I sauntered closer, my jealousy radiating all over me, more powerful than adrenaline, than any drug. My toes curled in my platforms as the anger raged through me, hotter than hell. When I was near her, I stretched my hand out to tap her shoulder.

"What do you want, asshole?"

"You."

With a grunt, I grabbed her by her waist and jerked her to me, forcing her chest against mine as I groped the hot commodity's biggest ass-et.

"What are you doing?" she said as she tried to tear my hands off her.

"Ooh, feisty!" I said. "I like that in a woman." I forced her closer to me.

"Stop it! Get off me!" Roxanne screamed, squirming and writhing in my clutches.

I pressed my lips against hers, and the squeal that came out of her was pure panic as I tried to open her mouth with my brutal tongue. "Open your mouth for me, baby," I muffled against her lips so warm, plump, and tender. And then, I felt a stab of pain and tasted copper in my mouth. "*Fuck*! You bit me." She panted and stepped back. "You stupid little bitch!" Suddenly, I heard something tumbling down.

The Queen Victoria crown rolled over to my feet. With hot raging eyes, Izzy grabbed me by the collar of my shirt, threw me to the ground, and kicked me in the side. I flipped myself on my back. Like a tiger, Izzy pounced on me with a growl that gave me the shudders. I snapped my eyes shut when he smacked my face so hard I saw stars even with my eyes closed. I smacked him back, not once. Twice. And then I felt strong arms pulling me away from Izzy.

"Get of me!" I roared, writhing in the clutches of whoever was trying to keep me from him.

Rick held Izzy back.

"Where's Roxanne?" Izzy shouted. "Roxanne!"

"Let me go, man. Please…" I was speaking to myself, not to Tim. He gently and slowly let me go as I looked down. "The show is over."

I was free. But did I want to be free?

I fled upstairs. I felt like I was drowning. The pungent, bitter taste of blood in my mouth was more overpowering with each passing second.

I blinked, the tears poured as I rushed to the bathroom. Standing and trembling before the mirror, I jumped at my own reflection. My eyes were more bloodshot than I thought. Everyone was right. I was too thin, my face too cheek-boney, and not for any beautiful reason. And pale, oh so ghastly pale, goth. Not even the glam could disguise it. I stuck out my tongue and winced. Roxanne had pierced the flesh all right. Instead of rinsing the two red holes, I frowned and trembled, sobbing. I fell on the floor. My fingers turned into tight fists again. I punched the ground and screamed as if I really were in hell. Even breathing was hell. Rocking in the fetal position, I bawled until I had no more strength. I stopped when I heard steps clopping toward the door. Or more like running. Even from behind closed doors, I knew who it was.

My body shook from the cool air that Izzy let in. Though my eyes burned with tears, I looked up not only at Izzy, but his pure rage. A true demon.

"What the fuck were you doing out there?" he bellowed. "How fucking dare you! *Why?*"

I smirked defiantly. "I did what I had to do."

"You lost your bloody mind!"

"You were right! Her lips *are* luscious. Oh, what I'd give to touch that ass again!"

The beast in his eyes intensifying, he yanked me off the floor by my shirt collar and body-slammed me against the wall with a brute force that practically knocked the wind out of me. My back throbbing, he slapped my right cheek with a blow so strong, the room spun in circles.

"Nobody kisses Roxanne but *me*, you hear me?" he roared. "If you *ever* touch her ass again—"

I writhed in his grasp, my eyes hot with my anger. "I was only putting on a show, baby love. That is all. I learned from the best, from *you*! It's all about the show, isn't it?"

"Not this time!" he barked, and let me go. "You went too far with it!"

I stood tall, glaring at him. "And you haven't?"

"Bitch." His nostrils flared. "Have you forgotten who I am?" he roared. "I am the *King* of Glam Rock! I can get away with almost anything, John, because that is what I was always meant to be! And Roxanne, she is—"

"Your virgin whore?"

"Roxanne's not my whore," he said with calm, a shake to his voice. "She's my girlfriend."

"Cut the fucking act already, Izzy!" I choked out, my breath shaky, hyper, and as dry as ashes. "Your publicity stunt worked, my princess. You don't have to use that little girl anymore!"

"I will tell you for the last time, John," Izzy spoke solemnly, his stoic gaze hanging over me like a dark cloud. "It's not a PR stunt. It never was. Roxanne is my girlfriend." I shook my head as he said, "She has been my girlfriend since after Madison Square Garden."

I could hardly breathe.

"Baby," Izzy gasped as I collapsed on my knees, screamed, and bawled.

"You fucking lied to me!" I shouted, shaking my head as Izzy fell to his knees. I wouldn't let him touch me. "You bloody *lied* to me! *Again.* You are a liar, Izzy Rich, a blasted liar, and I can't take your games anymore."

"I know baby, I know," he groaned, trying to wrap his arms around me.

"Get off me!" I kicked him away.

The tears were dripping from his eyes and down his face as he moaned. "Do that again. Beat me like the way Eric always did when I was a boy that only wanted, that only wanted to be a girl!"

"Oh, God!" I cried and grimaced. "No, Izzy. No…"

"I'm yours. Your girl. And you are my daddy. Be Eric. Do it. Beat me!"

"Stop it!" I screamed. "Have mercy on yourself, Izzy. Have mercy on me. Stop it!"

Izzy smacked at his own face multiple times. With a gasp, I grabbed his wrists and yanked them down as I looked into his bloodshot, water-soaked eyes.

"I'm not your father." I said slowly, shaking my head. "But hell." I let go of his wrists and whimpered. "I'm not your daddy. I'm not your boyfriend. I don't know what I am anymore."

"You are still *my* man!" he shouted, his eyes burning into mine.

I shook my head. "No. I am not. What am I, really? Tell me what I am, Izzy Rich. Your daddy dom? Your side piece? Your butt boy? C'mon. Tell me what I am nowadays."

Izzy's gaze was deep, and yet, empty. Alive with sadness.

"Huh? What am I to you now, Izzy?"

His silence was murder. "Answer me!"

"I love you!"

"Then why did you leave me for Roxanne?"

"Because I, because I…love her as much as I love you, Johnny! Why can't I love you and her at the same time, baby? We can be one as three—you, her, and me. Wouldn't that be marvelous? You want to have it all? We can both have it all, my love!"

"Have you lost your damned mind?"

"If we can fuck women together, why can't we date a woman together, three as one!"

"What the hell?"

"Let's get married! We practically are! You, my husband. Roxanne, my wife. I'll be Mrs. Maxwell. She'll be Mrs. Rich. She will carry our children. We will have a perfect family, a most wonderful life."

"Dammit, you can't always have everything your way, Izzy Rich!"

That bewildered look of his. Before my eyes, I saw his defeat. He wasn't a god, nor a goddess. Far, far from them. Izzy Rich was human. A mortal like me.

"You just can't!" I choked out. "It's either her or me, Izzy. Who will it be?"

He was as still as I was weak and hopeless. I gasped when he wrapped his arms around me. He held me so close, so close to him, I couldn't move. I cried wildly at his kiss. Our tongues met with heat and passion. The love. The love! I could taste it, feel it, breathe it in, and breathe it out. It never left! I took only one breath from his mouth, and I wanted to give my all to him but *no!*

I ripped my mouth away from his, gasping for air. "Her or me?" I said. "Her or me, baby."

"Don't leave me!" He rocked me, stroking my hair. "I am nothing without you. You are everything to me, my darling."

"I can't take the hurt anymore!" I sobbed. "I love you so bad, Izzy, that it hurts. It hurts! I can't handle the fucking pain anymore. You have no fucking idea how much you are *killing* me!"

"Johnny—"

"I'm quitting the band."

He paled. "What?"

I said slowly, "I quit." I weakly pushed him off me and stood up, my voice shaking as I talked down at him. "I'm quitting the band. And most of all, I'm quitting *you.*"

"You can't." He shook his head and sounded panicked. "You wouldn't dare leave me," he growled. "I own you, Jonathan Maxwell. You are under contract. Nobody quits Izzy Rich!"

I never saw such fear on his face. "I talked it over with William already today. It's official. After this last concert, that is it. I'm done."

"Johnny!" I heard him as I rushed to the door.

I was ready to open it, until Izzy yanked me away and threw himself against it.

"What are you doing?" I asked as he locked it.

Izzy took my hand, pulling me to him. Our chests crashed hard together, and he stole my breath with his desperate kiss. I felt the warmth of his breath. The depth of his tongue pushing against mine. Desperately stroking him, giving in, and letting go of the pain, the anger, the jealousy, and the hurt. Our moans were hot, but our bodies were hotter. I shook my head, and he grabbed my face, his fingers sinking into my sunken cheeks. In his eyes, I saw nothing. Not fear. Not anger. No hurt. No pain. Only a man. The man that I still loved.

He licked my ear, and I trembled when he said, "Life is shit now. But I know the cure." I gulped thickly as he whispered, "My mother's killer."

He kissed my earlobe, and I froze, barely breathing as I watched him lift his robe. Strapped against his leg by a garter was a thin case. I gulped harder, knowing exactly what was in it. He opened it, and I saw the needle. He held it up in the air, smiling at it with a goddess-joy. It wasn't only on his face. Those eyes. How they lit up as if that needle really was his mummy.

"Love," he crooned softly to it, petting the needle. "There's always time to make it, can't fake it, baby…" He quivered. "My love. There's never a wrong, or a right, when you can just take it, ooh, take me." He pulled from the case a silver spoon, ribbon, lighter, and a tiny bag filled with the poison. He dropped them to the floor, and the knee-jerk thing I did was grab the lighter.

"That's my daddy…" Izzy purred when I sparked the flame.

He tore the bag open with his teeth. I stopped the flame and stood by Izzy's side. As he was humming "Fly Me to the Moon," we were at the bathroom sink, cooking up our devil's elixir in the silver spoon, heating it with the lighter until it bubbled into a *crème brûlée* brown. With the ribbon in my hand, Izzy snatched it from me, quickly tying it around my arm until blue veins bulged underneath my skin. I licked my lips as Izzy held the needle. I sharply gasped, beaming at the instant I felt that tiny prick to my vein. "Daddy always gets the first kick," I moaned.

I blinked myself out of the rush fast enough to tie the ribbon around Izzy's arm. His veins bulged, those light blue lines fat and clear through his skin. He gasped when I pricked him. I could still hear him humming "Fly Me to the Moon" even though he wasn't anymore. We dropped to the floor, ripping each other's clothes apart like animals. As the spaceship in my brain took off a zillion miles, I kissed my girl. She howled when her cock penetrated my ass. I cried. No lube. Only pain. And I *loved* it. She broke me, split me open. It burned. My gape throbbed like my head. And I didn't care! Back and forth, back and forth we dry fucked each other, hammering into each other's asses like mad as we were blasted off to a place holier than our sex. It was the moon in heaven! My man and I were making love on it and across the universe until we came all over the stars.

CHAPTER FOURTEEN

This is it," I said to the guys. Larry pouted and patted my back. Tim, Benson, and Phil gave me a three-way hug. "I love you guys." I hugged them all, and everyone said, "We love you more, Baby John."

"Where's Izzy?" somebody from management called. "We only have a minute!"

I heard shoes clopping toward us. I looked over my shoulder and saw Roxanne in her go-go boots and shimmy dress. To everybody's surprise, Izzy wasn't with her. Where was he? I turned my back on her, tapping my platforms impatiently as everyone was waiting. By the way the fans were roaring and chanting Izzy's name louder, more anxiously than normal, time was slipping away. They were impatient, as we all were. I looked to the wings and then at the guys. We shrugged, unsure if we should take the stage and perform or just wait. Then I turned around to see Delilah Starr. Everyone else looked at one another in shock. She wasn't supposed to be in the set list until the second half of the show!

"Surprise!" she slurred, petting her furs as she batted her lashes at us.

"Delilah," someone from management said nervously. "You are early—"

"I know that!" she barked angrily. And it was Izzy's voice that yelled, "It's my show. *Mine!* If I want to fucking kick off the show this way, *my* way, sod it, I can do what I fucking want!"

I looked at the floor. Izzy flashed us his grin and then chirped in Delilah's voice, "It's show time, my darlings!"

She twirled with her arms spread out like wings. She jumped in her pumps and then leapt toward Roxanne, grabbed her, picked her up, and pecked her glittery lips.

"Diamonds, hurry, get out there! We are ten minutes behind!"

The five of us took to the stage. Shaking out the confusion in my head, I played as Delilah Starr crept the length of the stage. I sighed with relief. She sang in flawless tune, danced beautifully, and mimed with mastery. Unlike the last two shows where she was out of tune, stood more than danced, and wasn't miming. I swayed my head and drummed.

"Will I forever be trapped in this cage?" Delilah belted with such startling ferocity. How it still gave me chills when she boldly pointed her finger at the audience, and sang, "Look out, world, I'm the lady of rage! I'm coming out, coming for you on this stage! Watch out, watch out for *me*, this distinction! Trust me, trust me, I'm on the verge of my own extinction…" I winced when her voice wobbled. "Can't you see? I'm losing myself, losing my mind! Or is…" She froze and crooned slowly "Love…the hardest to find?" She stood still and her voice trembled. "Delilah…"

I kept my eye on her as the band played on. I gulped hard in worry when she paused.

"Delilah…" she squeaked after a few seconds of silence. Was she shaking?

"Delilah…" She patted her chest and wailed, "Keep me, keep me sane! Save me—or I'll lose you, fall in the sorrow, and the pain, to the devil living, taking over, inside me, again, and again…"

I gasped when she let her microphone go and had her hands over her face, sobbing as she rocked herself. I looked to the guys. We looked at each other. My heart raced, and my eyes welled at seeing Delilah already dead. I stopped drumming. The band stopped, too. The audience was chillingly quiet. Delilah cried the loudest cry I ever heard.

It wasn't Delilah. It was Izzy.

In the wings, Izzy's tour manager mouthed, "Play!" We played lightly as the light shone on Delilah. It paused on her as she pulled herself up and gazed out to the fans. They came alive again, chanting her name. Slowly, Delilah picked up the mic from the floor and raised it, pointing it at the riches. She belted the song, and her show carried on as it always was: a dark, twisted, beautiful fantasy. When we carried her off on her stretcher, she jumped off before we put her to the floor. I blinked, and already, she ran, with her bodyguards and assistants in tow. And of course, Roxanne. Damn her. Damn him. Damn them. Damned me.

I wiped the water from my eyes, trying my hardest not to break. My mascara was running. I was sweating like a pig, my foundation melting. I had no time to reapply my makeup. Izzy arrived in his dazzling Asian-inspired shiny white satin jumpsuit and high heels.

"This is what I will miss!" Izzy howled, raising his arms up. "This mad spontaneity!"

I smirked when he looked at me, as if he expected me to say something. I had nothing.

"You had us worried, boss," Benson said, rubbing his shoulder. "Were you okay out there?"

"Of course I'm okay. Why wouldn't I be?" He smiled naughtily. "Part of the show, yup yup! The rest of the show will go as we planned and rehearsed, okay, boys?" He looked at me. "Promise."

He turned his back to us when Roxanne came toward him. She jumped in his arms. He held her up, cupped to her bottom. I rolled my eyes as he drummed on her ass, the two giggling. I looked to the wings. It was time for their song again. This time, the last time. Izzy took the stage like all the stages of the world he had dominated. Not only him. Roxanne, too.

While I drummed "Dirty Dancer," I couldn't look at them any more. That kiss. It tried to break me. I could only choke. When that song, dance, and kiss were done, I watched Izzy performing his last for this tour. Izzy Rich and The Diamonds were closer and closer to the end. I trembled. The audience howled as Izzy exited the wings, strutting center stage. I gawked at his attire. That vintage fuchsia slip. The matching pumps. The makeup, every detail about it. Even the way he walked to the mic fucked my mind. My heart skipped a beat, jumped to the thought of only one woman. Izzy twirled, flaunting his arms, that ass, and those legs.

"I love you!"

That voice. It was Holly!

"My riches," Holly purred. "This is it!" Izzy declared. "I can't believe it. Can you?" he purred. "Tonight is the last show of the *Iz Ze Rich* tour. Thank you, my riches, for making it one of the best we have ever done. It won't be the last. This end is only the beginning. This tour has been a life changer." He looked offstage. "Especially because of you, Ms. Shengyi." I gulped thickly when he declared, "Baby, let's show the world who we are!"

My throat dried as Roxanne took to the stage, as dazzling as her man. I should have looked away, but I couldn't. Izzy opened his arms, and Roxanne jumped in them. He spun her around, looking up at her as she wrapped her legs around his waist. Their lips met, and the audience howled as they kissed long and passionately. Izzy set her back down. The audience howled deliriously. My face paled when Izzy went down on his bended knee.

I shook my head and grimaced when Izzy took Roxanne's hand and removed a giant diamond ring from his pocket. Sweat pearls dripped down my face and stung my eyes as he slipped the rock on her ring finger. I looked at the guys gawking, shocked. But they weren't as shocked as I was.

"Foxxy Roxxy won't be a virgin any longer," Izzy declared into the mic.

"Yes, rock and rollers, we are engaged!" Roxanne screamed. "I'll be *Mrs.* Rich!"

My whole body shook, crumbled, breaking. The two snogged. Unbelievable—the pain! My head pounding, I dropped my drumsticks on the stage and ran into the wings, holding my chest. I heard voices shouting "John?" and "Where are you going?" as I ran faster, panting, choking on my tears. All I could do was run, run, for it was my life I was fleeing from. I exited the Hammersmith Odeon as if it were burning. I was out in the open air of one chilly, foggy night. For only a moment, I wondered if anyone could hear my heart flatlining. Oh, God. The pain. Was the show going on without me? Did anyone else notice? Who really cared?

I wailed. I didn't matter. Not even to myself. Tears dripped down my face and snot dribbled on my chin. I staggered to the parking lot and found my car. Sniffling and still sobbing, I collapsed on the floor of my living room, my tears blinding me. My hands shaking, I crawled to my bedroom, desperate for the only thing that could save me. The cocaine lines on my bathroom floor, all five of them, were as thick as my weary soul. I snorted them into my nose hard, so hard, I made myself bleed. I had *nothing* to give, only hoping that by the mercy of whatever God out there, I'd crunch down and die from its excess. In my cocaine-induced stupor, I pictured what the headlines in the papers would say tomorrow. I could literally see them flashing before my eyes.

JONATHAN MAXWELL OF IZZY RICH'S BAND THE DIAMONDS FOUND DEAD AT HIS CAMDEN HOME FROM A COCAINE OVERDOSE.

In **actuality**, JONATHAN MAXWELL DIED FROM A BROKEN HEART.

CHAPTER FIFTEEN

God had mercy on me that night. But not in the manner that I hoped. I lived. To be alive was death. I couldn't eat for days. For weeks, I only lived on two hours of sleep, functioning as a zombie. To still be alive as time went on? Death was better. But I didn't need it, for the pain was worse. Why? Odette, the love of my life, fucked me over. I only got over her because of Izzy. And now...

He fucked me up. In trying to move on, he fucked me harder. How could a person who had been my world hurt me this bad? Izzy destroyed me in the cruelest fashion. I desperately hoped that drugs would erase every memory of him from my being. I wanted nothing else more in the world than to rid myself of Izzy Rich, to blur every single detail of the man that I once loved. And I now hated him because I still *loved* him. I craved a miracle. I yearned for the days when my heart and soul were my own. Invincible. Independent. Free. I missed the days when I had me. All to myself. How daft was I to think I could turn back time, that I could cut the circuits of so many memories. I tried, but no one could change time. Not even me.

How could I forget a love who gave me too much to remember?

Three months later and nothing had changed.

I yawned loud and deeply as I carried my garbage out one morning. More than a few of those bags were packed with tissues wet or stained with my long-ago tears. I opened the front door of my flat and jumped when I saw Joseph standing there.

"Holy shit!" I said. "What time is it?"

He looked me over. "You told me to come over at three. Here I am."

"Fuck. Um, hold on."

I ran down the steps, dumped the trash, and rushed back to him, draping my arm over his shoulder as I looked at him and forced a smile. "Sorry, baby. The house's still a mess."

"I'm not worried about the house. How are *you*, baby?"

"I'm fabulous!" I declared when we were inside and I had closed the door. I smiled nervously when Joseph went to the living room and stopped before a stack of tabloids on the table. He picked one up, and then another. He looked at me. "Jonathan. I'm worried about you."

"You too?" I laughed. "Why is everyone so bloody worried about me? I'm fine."

Joseph set the magazines back where they were. "This is a lot. Garbage, right?"

I gulped and said nothing.

"Johnny. Baby. You haven't been right since the tour. Frankly, you look terrible. You're too thin. Have you been eating? And have you been sleeping? I'm only asking because I love you."

I snorted from feeling small traces of cocaine still in my nose. I rubbed it. "I love you, too."

He sat on the couch and patted his lap. I sat there and closed my eyes, smiling as he wrapped his arms around me. "Johnny, you still never told me why you left Izzy."

"I don't want to talk about it."

"What are your plans for the future?"

"I'm a Maxwell, remember? These days, it's all about the diamonds."

He pushed me up so he could look at me. "What did you say? You always despised working in the family business. What's stopping you from drumming?"

"The music industry is too cutthroat. It stole my nervous system. I can't take it anymore."

He scoffed. "Bollocks. You love it too much to let it go."

All I could think about when he said that was Izzy. I rubbed my eyes and then scooted off him to sit beside him. "Let's watch TV."

"Don't you want to eat first? Get some meat back on those bones."

I shook my head and turned on the TV.

I froze when the screen showed Izzy and Roxanne hand in hand, in Russell Harty's interviewee chairs. A tear fell down my face. This was their first TV appearance in three months. God. How was it possible that Izzy was even more beautiful?

"You're looking good for thirty, Izzy. How did you two celebrate your birthday?"

"I don't *ever* celebrate my birthday," Izzy said with a stern voice, stoic face.

"Why's that?"

"It's a drag. I want to celebrate life, not aging. Every day is a birth. I haven't cared for celebrating my birthday since I was eighteen."

Russell nodded. "Are you afraid of aging?"

"Don't be silly, silly man. It has nothing to do with that."

Of all I knew about him, why he didn't like to celebrate his birthday was still a mystery. Whatever the reason, he forbade everyone in his entourage from wishing him a happy birthday. We couldn't even sing him a song.

Russell paused, looking at Izzy as if expecting another word. Izzy had nothing. "Mr. and Mrs. Rich, you two have been married for, what? Three months now?"

Roxanne smiled warmly as Izzy nodded eagerly.

"How has life been treating you two since your honeymoon?"

"It can't possibly be better," Roxanne said sweetly, blushing as she looked at Izzy.

"You two disappeared since your return to London from Hawaii."

"We wanted to be off the radar," Izzy said. "But I'm sure you've heard, we moved into the mansion of my dreams."

"I've seen the pictures," Russell said.

So did I. Izzy's mansion really was built from his dreams. Beautiful. Luxurious. Paradise.

"That's all we'll give, though. Only pictures. We haven't had any guests, parties, nobody but my wifey and I, doing normal things. Like watching TV, cooking, gardening, baking, dancing, singing, making music, and making love, as much love as we made on our honeymoon."

The audience whistled and roared as Roxanne crossed her legs. I rubbed my eyes and breathed deeply.

"Are you okay, John?"

"Shh!"

"Believe it or not, we are already planning on starting a family!" Izzy declared. Roxanne's smirk looked forced and awkward.

"He doesn't waste any time, does he?" Joseph said.

I shook my head and sniffled. "Izzy wants to be a daddy so bad."

"And we have been in the studio—" Roxanne said.

"A Mrs. Rich album is in the works," Izzy interrupted abruptly. "Coming very soon."

The audience howled. "Will you be on it, too?" Russell asked, and the audience howled louder.

I noticed Roxanne's agitated facial expression.

"I wrote all the songs on it," Izzy said, "but I won't be singing in any of them. And no duets."

"How soon will there be a new record from the King of Glam?"

"My focus is on being a daddy. My wife's career is also what matters. And her being a mummy."

Roxanne looked terrified when he said *mummy*.

When they began to kiss, I grabbed the remote and shut the TV off. "That should have been *me!*" I shouted. "I should be Mrs. Rich, dammit!"

Joseph jumped. "What?" he said. I never heard him sound so shocked. "Shit!" I dropped my head on his shoulder and bawled. Joseph held me close and fast. "John, what are you saying? You mean you two were—"

"*Husbands!*" I held on tightly as I whimpered and cried louder. I looked at him, sniffling. "Was it obvious? Did you ever see it? Did you?"

Joseph nodded. "I've always wondered and wanted to ask—"

I shook my head, grimaced, pointing at the table. "I should be on the front covers!" I pointed at the TV. "I should be the one in there! I was the one. I *am* the one. It should have been *me!*"

Joseph rocked me in his arms, holding me closer. "Honey. Why didn't you tell me?"

"I told *no one!*" I choked, my body trembling. "A secret, we were a secret for too long. It felt like years. I was eaten. I'm chewed up, spit out. I'm hurt, *hurt.* I still…I still *love* him, Joseph," I screamed.

❖

Three months more passed. My soul wasn't fine-tuned. I belonged to Izzy.

I thought about him every single day. I could finally sleep but only from crying. I kept busy working alongside my family at the Maxwell Diamonds headquarters, overseeing West End stores and preparing for the debut of a new Maxwell Diamond at Harrods. Still, I couldn't escape Izzy. No matter where I was in London, he was there. On the radio. On the TV. In the tabloids, on magazine covers. The man on top of the world. With his wife beside him. He had a new number one single from the *Iz Ze Rich* album. Mrs. Rich had a smashing hit record, cozy at number two. Two months passed. Their singles were still chart toppers. But something else was very new.

The rumors. I read them all. Izzy's controlling ways in the studio, stifling Roxanne's creativity and artistic freedom. And the fighting, the two always going at it in the limos. One photo showed that Izzy was scratched on the ear and Roxanne's cheek was caked with makeup to hide a bruise. That floored me, but the biggest mind fuck of all was the rumor she was cheating on Izzy with Rick. Where, how, when, why did it all happen? I'd never know! I thought it was a joke. I even laughed about it, until a photo surfaced in all the papers of Rick and Roxanne in public, smiling, hand in hand. And Roxanne wasn't wearing her wedding band.

On my way home from Harrods, I was listening to the radio, expecting the talking heads to still ramble about the infidelity. Strangely, nothing else was said about it, and the music carried on. After the station played Izzy's and Roxanne's singles, I stopped at the red light and heard the host announcing, "Breaking news! Glam rock star Izzy Rich has been arrested at his mansion for allegedly abusing his wife, glam starlet, Roxanne Foster."

"What?" I shouted. I was limp, my face draining to white. Was I hearing that right? Cars honked at me, but I still couldn't move, not even blink. Finally, I had to know the truth. I slammed my foot to the pedal, driving over the speed limit.

❖

I hit the floor so hard, my knees hurt. I turned on the TV. Izzy was in handcuffs, hanging his head as he was led into a cop car. Roxanne lay on the stretcher with a giant black eye and a bandaged, bleeding nose. Tears poured down my face as I gripped my hands to the side of the television, wishing I could be Alice and walk through the screen as if it were the Looking Glass.

Do something. Be somebody. Save Izzy. Help Roxanne. Anything, to get them out of this!

I balled my fist and banged the glass, screaming. "How could you, Izzy? You swore that you'd *never* be your father!"

I banged on the glass harder and collapsed on the floor, looking up at the screen as the clip showed the ambulance and cop cars driving away. I crawled to the phone, dialing the numbers I knew by heart: Tim's, Benson's, Phil's, Larry's, William's, and Cheryl's. I also phoned Izzy's assistants, agents, anyone and everyone of his world. They were my family. But every single line was busy.

❖

Izzy didn't serve jail time. He paid out a hefty fee for the domestic abuse charges. He wasn't free. Roxanne's parents sued Izzy for using their likeness in "Dirty Dancer" without their consent. They won, taking more of his money. Roxanne filed for divorce. It was pending. Not too long ago, Roxanne's fans were burning Izzy's records in the streets.

There hadn't been any news about Izzy for a couple of months since. Silence.

Stepping out into the open air from a Soho gentleman's club where I got the best blowjob money could buy, I didn't know what time it was, and I didn't care. The music from the clubs was starting to fade as I sauntered away from the night life. The streetlights were dim. I looked up at the sky, seeing that the moon behind the clouds was dimmer. With my hands stuffed in my jeans pockets, I walked farther ahead, seeing *Le Chaton Rose*.

As I walked past it, I stopped, hearing a wet, loud, suckling, pumping sound. From the corner of my eye, I saw a woman down the alley. She was on her knees, sucking off a silver fox. Going to town on him, blowing him with lightning speed. I watched them, trying to not make it so obvious that I was taken by her.

Even on her knees, I could clearly tell she was a tall woman. She may have been a prostitute, but she was beautiful. She had ratty shoulder-length brown hair. Her stockings had more holes than fabric clinging to her fair skin. I stared, this time, not caring if it was blunt. Those platforms. They were red, sequined, glittering, like her skimpy red dress. I blinked, turning away, my hand pressed to my chest. What was it about those platforms? That dress? Everything about it screamed Izzy. His glamour. His makeup. His fashion. Him. It was all coming back to me. The screaming fans. Izzy's animalistic guitar, rumbling. Izzy's dancing. His laughter. His voice, singing, changing souls and saving lives, including mine. I drummed the air, performing.

"What the fuck is wrong with me?" I stopped and touched my head. "I need sleep."

Onward I wandered through the Soho streets, drawing closer to the parking lot. The night was darker. The air was suddenly chillier, uncomfortable. I squinted when I looked ahead, and there it was—a sparkle, as wild as the wind. It was those red platform shoes and that red dress.

"Fuck!"

It was that woman! She was lying on the sidewalk, close to a gutter, alone. I ran to her, fell on my knees, and lifted her head up. Her left eye was bruised. The other eye was shut. Drool ran down her chin. Her lips were dry, quivering. Her poor, trembling body was a wreck.

I cradled her into my arms, patting her cheek. "Wake up, darling. Wake up!" I stroked her hair. It was a wig. When it fell off, I cried, "Oh my God!"

My shaking hand brushed over her fox-red hair cut in an overgrown bob, dull blond at the roots. The woman opened her good eye. It was the most precious, bluest eye I've ever known. I traced my thumb along those red-smeared lips, plump and pouty. Slowly, gently, I stroked her waist, her chest, thighs, legs, and ass through her dress. I grimaced. I knew that curvy body from top to bottom!

"My princess," I said weakly, achingly.

"J-Johnny Angel..." That voice. It was Izzy's. Weak. Pained. Shallow. "Jonathan!" he choked loudly, coughing up his own spit.

I covered his mouth, muffling his scream, as he sobbed. I looked around. Yes! The coast was still clear. Nobody would ever know. I placed the wig back on Izzy's head and scooped him into my arms, cradling him. His startled eye was half-open, widening when he murmured my name again. "Johnny. J-John..."

"Yes, baby, it's me," I said as I placed him in the backseat. "I'm taking you home."

Lying on his back, his hand to his chest, he trembled. "I'm already there."

CHAPTER SIXTEEN

Izzy groaned when I flung the door open. He breathed heavily and shakily from the cool breeze, panting with crazy eyes. I gently scooped him up in my arms again. The wig almost fell off his head, but I pressed it firmly back on him as I ran to the front door of my flat. He gurgled and groaned, and I gasped. He was so pale. His body was weaker, unable to hold on to me.

He tried to stand on his two feet.

"Oh God!" I grimaced when he collapsed. He rubbed his arms and then scratched his stockings as I hurried to grab my key and unlock the door. He lay on his side, gagged, and vomited. He regurgitated harder, bile coming up. I swung my door open, and hurriedly dragged him inside. I closed the door and locked it. When I had him inside, his voice wobbled."Help!"

"John…" he said over and over, bewildered, as if I wasn't real.

He hyperventilated. I ran to the trash can and hurried back to Izzy in the nick of time. He dropped his head the second the trash can touched the floor, vomiting fiercely. I thought he'd never stop. He groaned and screamed, sitting on the floor, hugging himself, rocking, and gasping for air. I held him and picked him up, rushing to the bedroom. I put him on my bed and rushed to get another trash can. He dunked his head in when I had it at the bedside. He vomited straight away, sounding awful. I calmly coached *let it go* as he puked over and over until nothing else came up.

I rubbed his back, and he breathed calmly, though he was shivering as I helped him to lie on his back. He shivered even more, and my bedroom was far from freezing. I pushed the bed covers over him and fluffed the pillows, nudging them behind his head. I grabbed a towel from the bathroom and ran warm water over it, fetching a thermometer, cotton balls, and a bottle of alcohol. After I placed those under the lampshade, I got a bottle of water and an ice pack out of the kitchen.

By the time I got back to him, his eyes were closed, and he was breathing slowly. He was so out of it, he didn't budge when I slid the tip of the thermometer underneath his tongue. He had a slight fever. I couldn't tell if he was dozing off or beyond strung out when I forced him to drink. He coughed up the water at first, but then drank in loud, heavy gulps. When he'd had his fill, I pressed the moist towel over his forehead and wiped away his makeup. With the alcohol and cotton ball, I dabbed around his black eye, cleaning up the dirt and blood. He smiled weakly when I stroked his cheek and lips. He opened his good eye, marveling at my face, touching my cheek and lips, too.

"Sorry!" He grabbed his wig, threw it, and sobbed. He screamed, pulling his hair. "I'm so sorry!"

I grabbed his wrists and held his hands tight, panting with him as we stared at each other. Then I wrapped my arms around him and held him hard as we cried, as if we were born, built to break.

Izzy slept for three days straight, and not a day went by where I wasn't by his side, watching over him. Nursing him. Sponge bathing him. Constantly checking his temperature. Forcing him to drink water or broth while he was knocked out cold. Watching him sleep until I'd doze off in the chair. On the third day, Frank Sinatra sang "All the Way" from my record player as Izzy was sleeping and I was getting dressed after taking a shower. I watched him, and for once, I smiled. He looked so peaceful. Innocent. I gasped when he stirred and opened his eyes, looking at me. I wasn't something to be afraid of anymore. He batted his lashes, then he flashed that famous smile. My heart raced when he sat up. He looked around.

"I'm at your place…" he said dryly, his voice masculine and vulnerable.

"How do you feel?" I said after I sat by his side on the bed. I looked at his face. The black eye hadn't cleared up yet and his bruises and cuts were still there.

He blinked. "I don't know how to feel anymore."

"That makes two of us." I touched his forehead. "Finally, that fever's gone."

He looked at the time. "How long was I asleep?"

"Three days."

"*Three* days? Why, that's a fucking coma."

"I know. I was worried." I looked at him. "I was going to call my family doctor and his nurses to come in today to do more that I can't, but you pulled through."

"Does anybody know I am here?"

I shook my head.

His face softened. "You took care of me all this time?"

I nodded. "Why wouldn't I?"

"And you kept it a secret this whole time?"

"And let the public know? That would've been cruel."

"I thought you'd sooner let me die." He covered his mouth and coughed.

"Even a man like you deserves mercy, Izzy Rich. You aren't your mistakes."

He snapped his eyes shut and shook his head. "I *fucked* up!" He said it twice. He leaned and put his head in my lap. I lifted it up and put it on my shoulder. "Why?" he asked. "Why do I do such goddamn awful things to people I love? Roxanne. I, I, I didn't mean it to go that far. Vivian. All she wanted was me. Me. And my baby. Our baby."

I rubbed the corner of my eye, rocking him as I stroked his hair, the bob now shinier and brighter from me grooming it.

"Vivian…"

"What happened to Vivian?"

"She's…" He gulped thickly. "G-g-gone. Dead."

I wrapped my arms around Izzy. "She d-d-died the week before you f-f-found me. She overdosed." He panted. "Heroin. Oh, God. Mummy. Mum! My heavenly darlings," Izzy groaned. He cried "Delilah!" three times.

He let himself cry. His pain couldn't ever be mine, but I was crying anyway. His torment was mine, as it had been for the last four years.

My shoulder was soaked with his tears when he mellowed. He sniffled, looking at me. "You," he whispered. "How could you still be here, after all I did to you?"

Something in me snapped. I wanted to choke him. Beat him. Hurt him like he'd hurt me. And Roxanne. And his baby's mother. Vivian. I was about to punch his face. He flinched, ready for it, but I couldn't.

"I *hate* you!" I cried achingly at the ceiling, and then I screamed at his face. "You were my poison, and you made me sick!" I breathed slowly, my heart racing, seeking the right words. All I could say was, "Fuck you. I *love* you."

"Can you, will you forgive me for everything?"

"*No*," I snapped down at him. "What do you think I am, Izzy? Forgive you now?"

We were frozen, quiet in time. We could almost see what silence looked like.

I took a deep breath. "I'm only a man, Izzy. I can forgive, but it's not going to happen today. It's not going to happen tomorrow. I won't even promise it will be next month." I whispered against his lips. "But with time, maybe I will forgive you completely."

"My fans. My family. My band. My world. I tore *everything* apart."

"You fucked up. You got fucked, as you deserved. And you paid your dues. Everyone's all right."

"But still…"

"Everything will be all right."

"I lost you."

I smirked. "I have a secret that only one person knows. And it's not you. I quit the band. But I never said that I signed the contract."

His face went from pale to glowing. "What? How did William let you get away with that?"

"Like you, he didn't want to let me go. He told me to cool off. When you're ready to record a new album, I'll let him know if I want to leave permanently or stay for good."

He cried. I tousled his hair. "May I please have your kiss? It has been forever."

I looked down and shook my head. "You will wait. Even for my kiss."

He nodded and batted his lashes. "Yes, sir."

I got off the bed and snapped my finger. He slowly positioned himself on all fours, staring at me with those longing, submissive eyes. "Get off the bed and stand," I snapped. He obeyed. I jumped. "Oh my goodness!" I felt my eyes light up as he stood before me, looking so adorable in my yellow silk onesie. "You are standing without falling over. Fucking finally." I clapped.

He smiled coyly and bowed.

"Can you do jumping jacks?"

"I think so."

"Do it." I snapped my finger, and he obeyed, his hair bouncing up and down.

I chuckled. "Hop on one foot."

He obeyed, balancing himself on one leg and hopping on one foot.

"Spin."

He did it. He even stood *en pointe*, spinning slowly like a ballerina.

"Impressive. Do what you're doing, but with a hand over your eye."

He obeyed, and I laughed when he almost lost balance, but caught himself, his *en pointe* intact.

"All right. Now…" I went to the vinyl record player, lifting the needle to stop Frank. "Sing."

Izzy stood on his two feet and blinked. "Which song?"

"Anything that's in your head."

"Way to put me on the spot."

"Sing," I ordered.

He gulped. "Well, hundreds of songs were in my head while I was sleeping. Here's one." His voice sounded so soft, weak, and moving as he sang, "All my life, in all my lives, I've dreamt of you. Because of you, I found my heart. Since the day I met you, I found that love is one, but more beautiful with two. Since we've been apart, I've learned love is never old. Only new."

I gulped thickly as he slowly came toward me, his voice now invincible, alive, and confident. He crooned, "Our love. We'll make it new again, my love, and start over to where it all began." I felt my face warm for the first time in what felt like years. My heart melted when he took my hand and sang, "Do you remember the simple days of you and me? Let's stand together, my love, hold hands, and go back to where we used to be. And if, by chance, this new love is better, let's remember this. Our love started with a simple—"

I pressed my hands to his cheeks, holding his face, and kissed him. It was so electrifying that we gasped and parted at the same time. We blinked at each other. Our lips met again, embraced, united. The taste and warmth of him made me tremble as our kiss deepened. I held him so close, but it was our kiss alone that made it hard for us to breathe. We caught our breath, and then, that kiss, oh! Our love was new already.

❖

Izzy's divorce was finalized on the same day the band and entourage reunited at Izzy's two-story mansion. On that very same day, after we cried, laughed, talked, and danced the night away, at dawn, we returned to our home away from home. Trident Studios.

CHAPTER SEVENTEEN

After seven months out of the public eye and two months in the studio, the King of Glam Rock was ready to rule the world again with a new hair color and a new album, with his glitter, his glamour, his fashion, his androgyny, and his rock and roll. Nine months was like nine long years, practically a lifetime for show business. And now, the tortured wait for the world was over. His fans, the media, the paparazzi, and the music industry were ready for the King to return to the throne.

And I was ready to explode.

Backstage, in the cozy lounging room of the South Bank studios, I could feel it all over. Everyone was smiling, jumpy, excited, as Izzy gathered us around.

"This is it, everyone." He rubbed his hands, looked at the ceiling, and sighed. He pressed two fingers near his glossy apple red lips. "This is it," he repeated, as if he were speaking to himself.

"Is Izzy Rich nervous?" I called him out on it. Everyone chuckled.

"Yes…" Nobody was laughing, anymore. "Frankly, everyone." He looked at everyone. "I'm scared. I'm oh so bloody scared."

We looked at him and each other. Scared. Izzy tightened his lips. They trembled. He burst out in a wicked cackle. Everyone laughed or rolled their eyes. I shook my head, chuckled, and crossed my arms.

"Gotcha, fools!" He blew us all a kiss with his head high. "Nervous? *Never*."

"It's show time soon, Mr. Rich," a stagehand told us. "One minute."

"Go, everyone, go," Izzy shooed. I turned my back to him, waiting as everyone exited the lounge. I made only one step.

"*You*. Stay," he said.

When I turned around and stood before him, we smiled and stared into each other's eyes.

"Baby," he murmured. "I wasn't kidding. I *am* scared."

He was serious. More than that, he really was afraid.

"What if the world still hasn't forgiven me?"

"Don't worry. You have *nothing* to be afraid of. Who are you?"

He smiled weakly and looked down. "Izzy Rich."

I lifted his chin. "Blow their mind, captain."

I squeezed his hand, and he squeezed mine. Somebody knocked on the door. "Ready, Mr. Rich?"

Side by side, we walked down the hall of the studio. We separated, and I sat in the front row with the guys and the entourage along with our parents. I sat in the empty seat between my mother and father. We were as excited as the audience behind us. Russell Harty stepped out from the wings and took the stage. That was when it truly hit me that this was it. Izzy Rich was back.

"Three, two, one…"

The cameras faced Russell Harty.

"I'm happy to have back on the show today a man who doesn't need an introduction," Russell declared with a serious look and tone. "He's likened to a demi-god, a messiah, a pariah, and even a tragic hero. After a hugely successful album and tour, an ill-fated marriage that ended quickly in divorce, and a nine-month hiatus from the public eye, Izzy's here with us today on his first TV appearance since then to talk about his upcoming highly anticipated new album and more. Please welcome back, ladies and gentlemen, the King of Glam Rock, Mister Izzy Rich!"

Izzy appeared from the wings with his trademarked sway and wiggle. Izzy looked out to the audience, who were delirious. He blew kisses and waved at them. Shaking hands with Russell, he sat down.

"Welcome back, Izzy," Russell said, sounding unusually cheerful.

Izzy smiled coyly. "It feels good to be back."

I covered my ears when the audience screamed.

"For being away for so long, you haven't changed or aged a bit."

"And I still have my British accent." He winked.

"And your usually outrageous fashion taste."

Izzy stood and showed off his glittery six-inched spiked gold pumps, a gold and black form-fitting, bottom-hugging zebra print skirt, and a matching jacket with devil-horn-shaped shoulder pads. He wore no shirt. His chest was bare, sparkling with body glitter. His marigold hued to-the-shoulder bobbed hair was thick and luminous. It made his androgyny pop brighter, as did those smoldering lips, dramatic black and gold eye shadow, thick and long lashes, contoured cheekbones, and his mesmerizing figure. As Izzy sat and crossed his legs, I couldn't help but grin and shiver. My cock twitched at the rushing thought of me on my knees on the bathroom floor of his mansion.

"So, the last time you were here, you were married. How have you been since the divorce?"

Izzy rubbed the side of his nose. "Most days are wonderful, then other days, not so much. I'm still taking everything in. It happened so fast. I got divorced as quickly as I got married."

"That's very true."

"Divorce is hard, but that's a given, right? I'm not the first, nor will I ever be the last man to get a divorce. The only difference between me and the average person is that mine was, for a lack of a better word, a fucking hell hole."

"And public."

"Unfortunately. And pretty messy."

I could feel his fear creeping up again by the way he looked at Russell, and then at the camera.

"There's this one rumor I always found interesting—"

Izzy smirked. "Oh no, Russell. Not again."

"Many people in the press and even some fans thought you and Roxanne only married for a publicity stunt. And I only found that funny because you two seemed very much in love. Why didn't some people buy it?"

He shrugged. "I'm a rock star. A fantasy. It's that simple, really. People love to corrupt that." Izzy leaned back and said with a serious tone, "People think that being this rock god means all I do twenty-four seven is get stoned, drunk, bugger groupies, and all that. Yes, there is plenty of that when I'm on the road, but when I'm not working, my life is galaxies away from those things. I'm family oriented. I loved being a husband. And Roxanne was a good wife. I don't think I was ever meant to be husband of the year, but I loved being a loyal husband, and I really wanted children more than anything with Roxanne. She wasn't ready to be a mother. I pressured her, loved her too much. If I could start over, I would. But I'd change the person I was, for sure."

"Do you still love Roxanne, despite all that's happened?"

With my head held high, I smiled warmly for him. And for her.

"I'll always love her. Roxanne was the first woman I've ever truly loved. I wouldn't have married her if I didn't love her like that. She always will be that first woman for me."

"What about the affair she had with your bodyguard? That hasn't tainted your love for her?"

"Ow. Hitting below the belt, are you, Russell?" He cleared his throat. "All I'll say is, I wish Roxanne and Rick luck. Hope they're well, and will always be well."

Russell looked at his clipboard, then at Izzy. "She still has a restraining order on you."

A heavy and awkward silence stalled the energy of the studio. My body tensed. I breathed slowly, chewing on my lower lip nervously for Izzy. He nodded slowly, his face composed.

"A lot of people found your mug shot and the abuse photos disturbing."

"It haunts me to this day. That whole night still tears me up as did the whole marriage. I'm aware of what the press has been saying, how my fans and her fans felt. At the end of the day, only Roxanne and I know our marriage. We were the only witnesses."

"Why did you disappear after the scandals?"

"I was…" He looked at the camera and confessed. "Scared. Not only of the death threats and lawsuits that kept piling up to my bloody chin every day, but scared of what I'd do to myself. That's why the next album is dark, slightly paranoid, angry, sad, and some might even say depressing. But there's hope for the future. For the newer person I hope to become one day."

"I have it here." Russell held the LP cover, showing it off. The audience clapped. "I was hooked from beginning to end. It's a giant leap in sound from your other records."

"Some might say it's ambitious. It's taking a new direction. There's gospel, rock and roll, blues, and Indian music. And the songs I wrote are all personal and vulnerable, basically highlighting the rise and fall of my marriage. But they're also giving tribute to the people that I love."

I smiled wide, knowing who all those people were. His mother. His baby. Vivian. His fans. His mums. His friends. And me.

"*On My Own (Not Alone)* is about love. Forgiveness. And conquering demons."

"*That* explains this outfit you are wearing."

"Right-eee-o!" he exclaimed, rolled his shoulders and whipped a sensual, naughty glare at him.

"This album is already popular, and it's not even out yet."

"We're already rehearsing for the world tour. It will begin in Asia."

The audience clapped and cheered, as did I.

"I've never gone before, so, here's to a new adventure! I especially can't wait for India."

"Exciting. There's a lot riding on this record."

"No kidding."

"While you were recording this album, with all that you went through, and even now, with this upcoming world tour, did you feel the immense pressure?"

He nodded. "I still do, but I was inspired. This session was different from the others. It was magical like the rest, but it was a reunion with my best mates, The Diamonds, and us really having a ball making this new music. And patching up old wounds, reconnecting, and creating something beautiful together. This is our baby. And finally, it will be out for the world to love."

"And you'll be debuting the album's first single here today."

"It's one of my favorites on the album."

I wiped the corner of my eye, being sure to not smudge my mascara.

"Is there a reason why you chose this one as your first single?"

He glowed, and he was definitely looking to me as he said "It's for someone very special."

I, Tim, Larry, Phil, and Benson stood when we were cued to take the stage. On my way, I stopped to blow kisses and wave at my family. I completely blew off Leo, and he ignored me, as if I was a stranger. I sat down at my drum kit, cracked my knuckles, looked at the audience and to everyone we loved. I waved and then had my drumsticks as Izzy leapt on the stage, standing near me. The cameramen faced us, lifted three fingers. And then there were none.

"Welcome back, ladies and gentlemen," said Russell earnestly into the camera. "I'm proud to introduce the one and only Izzy Rich and his backing band, The Diamonds, who are here to perform the new single from his incredible, upcoming new album, *On My Own (Not Alone)*, that will be released next week. And here they are..." He pointed at us.

The audience cheered loudly, shaking up the studio as Izzy draped the strap of his electric guitar over his shoulder. With his guitar hanging close to his chest, Izzy winked at us. He gave us that diva finger point. We gave it back to him. Izzy curled his fingers around the microphone stand, his pretty mouth drawing close to the mic's silver head.

I lifted my head up high and proud, smiling as I kicked off the song with a sweet, modest, and catchy, hypnotic beat, the tempo slow and gorgeous. The rest of The Diamonds followed, creating the dreamy groove with the piano, bass, electric guitar, and the saxophone. The most beautiful instrument of all wasn't Izzy's guitar, but his heavenly, angelic voice. His androgyny was in his throat, and he crooned loud and triumphantly from his gut.

"If love can write its own love song, it would be a ballad—a ballad of me and you, babe. We will sing it all day and all night long. It's as simple—so real for me—as beautiful as the sweet day when I first laid my eyes on you, babe. This ballad. It's the ballad of Johnny and Holly."

He sang it with the same intensity of depth, love, and emotion as he did the first time he sang it to me, which gave me chills *and* goose pimples. The power of his love for me reigned with every high note, with every howl and whispery moan from his man-woman, woman-man voice. His guitar cradled the melody, and love was bursting from Izzy with every smile and wink he made at my direction. That look was quick, but I saw it, felt it, whipped back at me in slow motion. I smiled at him as I nodded my head, tapping my drums. My heart was still broken, but I was not hurt. It was Izzy Rich, my love, who made me whole, and I was healed. The past wasn't dead yet. Izzy and I still had a whole world to rebuild, but we were prepared for the future.

More than ready. Born for it.

"Some people say that all love songs are one and the same," he belted at the edge of the stage and crooned gloriously, "That all ballads have the same message, the same theme, and the same rhyme—even some with a similar name. All of them, a goddamn sing-along!"

As I swayed my head and drummed, my eyes lit in surprise as he turned to the side and sang to me. "I choose not to believe that this song won't sell. 'The Ballad of Johnny and Holly' will prove them wrong. It will last, standing the test of time. This love song is no illusion." He swayed his hips as he belted, "Trust in me. There's no confusion. 'The Ballad of Johnny and Holly'—it's *our* love song!" He spun on his heels, striking a pose with a hair flip, his guitar howling miracles.

I looked up and beamed, seeing how my man's rock and roll was clearly putting a spell on the audience. My family. His family. Our family. And all the men and women out there. They were swaying their heads, tapping their feet. How could they not? The song was a hard spell to break.

When the song was finished, Izzy got a standing ovation.

At the same time, the band and I stood beside him. I smiled at my family, surprised to see Leo clapping. My heart flipped with astonishment. Izzy took my hand. We looked at each other. He squeezed tightly and raised our joined hands.

It was only him and me.

Then the guys, Izzy, and I held each other's hands and raised them up high, together. We bowed three times to the loud love of our fans and family. All the cameras stayed on us.

They were still rolling.

"I love you, Jonathan Maxwell," I heard Izzy whisper tenderly in my ear.

I looked at him in shock. Izzy looked at me with a sweet, cheeky grin, his face all aglow, his blue eyes the brightest star. Izzy curled his arm around my waist. I didn't think anything of that. But he moved me closer to him until we were hip-to-hip. And that quickly, he moved me even closer to him. Our eyes met. We were face-to-face. He closed his eyes.

"Izzy!" I gasped when he kissed me. I closed my eyes and whispered into his mouth, "Oh my God!" Our tongues touched, our lips meshed. Water and mascara trickled down my face as I drowned in Izzy's deep, passionate kiss. We held each other tight, for the mystery was solved. Our tongues were the victory. The bravest, strongest, the greatest love of all. We didn't stop. Not for the silence. Not for the gasps of shock. Not even for what I could have sworn was four pairs of hands clapping behind us. Not for the fans. Not for our family. Not for TV. Not for the world. I didn't count the seconds. Our kiss was more than time.

It was called a scandal. An abomination. A horror. A milestone. A history. The footage of us kissing was re-aired numerous times on the BBC, more times than the actual Russell Harty interview itself, a record. Still shots of our lip-lock were printed in a countless number of magazine covers all over the world. Ballsy. Risky. Dangerous. That was what our kiss was called by just about everyone: the media, critics, and most of all, by William and Cheryl. It wasn't at all. To Izzy and me, it was only a kiss. A simple kiss announcing our bond.

Not for show. Not for fame. Not for money.

It was only for love.

About the Author

Vanessa Clark is intersex, transgender (agender, gender non-conforming), androgynous, pansexual, and at the end of the day, a laid-back, down-to-earth person in love with life's simple pleasures—drag, art, culture, fashion, food, film, literature, music, and beauty, in all its gorgeous diversities. Many call Vanessa mysterious, and they are right. Vanessa is not an open book, but has joy in sharing part of who they are through their contemporary/historical LGBTQI erotic romance fiction. Vanessa's writing career started in high school where they gained a reputation for their short stories, having been given a couple of Gold Key awards from Scholastic, Inc. They got their start writing erotica during college. After having many short erotica stories published on Oysters&Chocolate.com, they have since had various erotic shorts published in anthologies under their initials, V.C. Their book with Bold Strokes Books, *The Man on Top of the World*, a bisexual romance that spotlights the wild, complex relationship between a David Bowie–esque glam rock superstar and his drummer, is their debut novel.

Visit author profile on:

Facebook: https://www.facebook.com/vcerotica

Twitter: @FoxxyGlamKitty

Blog: http://vceroticaglitterotica.blogspot.com/

Books Available From Bold Strokes Books

The Man on Top of the World by Vanessa Clark. Jonathan Maxwell falling in love with Izzy Rich, the world's hottest glam rock superstar, is not only unpredictable but complicated when a bold teenage fan-girl changes everything. (978-1-62639-699-9)

The Orchard of Flesh by Christian Baines. With two hotheaded men under his roof including his werewolf lover, a vampire tries to solve an increasingly lethal mystery while keeping Sydney's supernatural factions from the brink of war. (978-1-62639-649-4)

Funny Bone by Daniel W. Kelly. Sometimes sex feels so good you just gotta giggle! (978-1-62639-683-8)

The Thassos Confabulation by Sam Sommer. With the inheritance of a great deal of money, David and Chris also inherit a nondescript brown paper parcel and a strange and perplexing letter that sends David on a quest to understand its meaning. (978-1-62639-665-4)

The Photographer's Truth by Ralph Josiah Bardsley. Silicon Valley tech geek Ian Baines gets more than he bargained for on an unexpected journey of self-discovery through the lustrous nightlife of Paris. (978-1-62639-637-1)

Crimson Souls by William Holden. A scorned shadow demon brings a centuries-old vendetta to a bloody end as he assembles the last of the descendants of Harvard's Secret Court. (978-1-62639-628-9)

The Long Season by Michael Vance Gurley. When Brett Bennett enters the professional hockey world of 1926 Chicago, will he meet his match in either handsome goalie Jean-Paul or in the man who may destroy everything? (978-1-62639-655-5)

Triad Blood by 'Nathan Burgoine. Cheating tradition, Luc, Anders, and Curtis—vampire, demon, and wizard—form a bond to gain their freedom, but will surviving those they cheated be beyond their combined power? (978-1-62639-587-9)

Death Comes Darkly by David S. Pederson. Can dashing detective Heath Barrington solve the murder of an eccentric millionaire and find love with policeman Alan Keyes, who, despite his lust, harbors feelings of guilt and shame? (978-1-62639-625-8)

Men in Love: M/M Romance, edited by Jerry L. Wheeler. Love stories between men, from first blush to wedding bells and beyond. (978-1-62639-7361)

Love on the Jersey Shore by Richard Natale. Two working-class cousins help one another navigate the choppy waters of sexual chemistry and true love. (978-1-62639-550-3)

Slaves of Greenworld by David Holly. On the planet Greenworld, the amnesiac Dove must cope with intrigues, alien monsters, and a growing slave revolt, while reveling in homoerotic sexual intimacy with his own slave Raret. (978-1-62639-623-4)

Final Departure by Steve Pickens. What do you do when an unexpected body interrupts the worst day of your life? (978-1-62639-536-7)

Night Sweats by Tom Cardamone. These stories are as gripping as the hand on your throat. (978-1-62639-572-5)

Soul's Blood by Stephen Graham King. After receiving a summons from a love long past, Keene and his associates, Lexa-Blue and the sentient ship Maverick Heart, are plunged into turmoil on a planet poised for war. (978-1-62639-508-4)

Corpus Calvin by David Swatling. Cloverkist Inn may be haunted, but a ghost materializes from Jason Dekker's past, and Calvin's canine instinct kicks in to protect a young boy from mortal danger. (978-1-62639-428-5)

Brothers by Ralph Josiah Bardsley. Blood is thicker than water, but you can drown in either. Jamus Cork and Sean Malloy struggle against tradition to find love in the Irish enclave of South Boston. (978-1-62639-538-1)

CPSIA information can be obtained at www.ICGtesting.com
Printed in the USA
LVOW10s1612170816

500775LV00002B/261/P